THE WILD GOOSE CHASE

MERLIN RADICAL FICTION

edited by
John Lucas

Out of Work by John Law (Margaret Harkness) (1888)
Sandwichman by Walter Brierley (1937)
The Story of a Modern Woman by Ella Hepworth Dixon (1894)
The Wild Goose Chase Rex Warner (1937)

THE WILD GOOSE CHASE
by
REX WARNER

Introduction by
Andrew Cramp

442

LONDON
MERLIN PRESS

Published in 1990
in Great Britain
by the Merlin Press Ltd.,
10 Malden Road
London NW5 3HR
ISBN 085036 388 8 (p)
ISBN 085036 401 9 (c)
and in the United States of America
by Ivan R. Dee Inc
1332 North Halsted Street,
Chicago
Illinois 60622-2632
ISBN 0 929587 38 3
First published in 1937
by Boriswood
Introduction © 1989 by Andrew Cramp
Made and printed in Denmark
by Nørhaven Rotation
Viborg

GENERAL INTRODUCTION

The aim of *Merlin Radical Fiction* is soon stated. It is to make available for present-day readers a number of once well-known novels which have been languishing out of print, if not out of mind. Not all novels that were famous in their day deserve or need resurrecting; the ones we have chosen to re-print are important, not merely because they were once celebrated, but because they have qualities that make them durable works of fiction. We certainly do not intend to re-print novels that can be called radical only because of their "message". We understand radicalism in a more rewarding way, one that includes the means of telling as much as what is told. For example, Rex Warner's *The Wild Goose Chase* is a wonderfully inventive political and social allegory, entirely different in conception from the social realism of Walter Brierley's *Sandwichman*. Yet Brierley's method works. It is admirably suited to the grim, moving story he has to tell. Different as they are from each other, Margaret Harkness's (John Law's) *Out of Work* and Ella Hepworth Dixon's *The Story of a Modern Woman* are adroit and compelling works of fiction in their own right.

It is part of our ambition for the series to range as widely as possible, over time, style, authors. Later re-prints will be of fiction of the 1790s, at one extreme, and of the 1950s, at the other. We also hope to include novels from North America and, in translation, novels from Europe. Each book will be introduced by a writer who is an authority on the novel and its author, and the introductions will blend biographical and critical matter. It is our hope that in the coming years the Radical Fiction Series will enable new generations of readers

"To confer with who are gone.
And the dead living into counsel call."

John Lucas

INTRODUCTION

by

ANDREW CRAMP

"It has taken a risk, a leap in the dark, and has sinned."[1]

This comment about *The Wild Goose Chase* is no overstatement. There are few other novels quite like it.

The Wild Goose Chase makes frequent and inventive use of popular culture. The result is a novel of wild eclecticism. Chaplin, Lloyd, the Marx Brothers, Eisenstein and Fritz Lang are some of the identifiable cinematic influences. Literary genres pulled into the story include Boys Adventure, the Thriller, Popular Romance and open allusions to *The Waste Land* and H.G. Wells' *Time Machine*. In addition there is a sprinkling of thirties motifs such as frontiers, youth, bicycles, a regard for fresh air, and the symbolic journey. Not surprisingly, Warner occasionally has trouble holding all this together but the novel still works. It is, above everything, an allegory about conversion to Marxism, and the destruction of a pernicious Fascist dictatorship.

Little that Warner wrote during the thirties specifically indicates the nature of his political commitment. Furthermore, there is a scarcity of biographical material about this period of his life, perhaps because his subsequent rejection of Communism in the forties and fifties led him to play down his earlier left-wing sympathies. However, it can be assumed that Warner was interested in Communism whilst at Oxford in the mid-twenties, the more so because his closest friend, C. Day Lewis, was already actively involved. Yet when it came to the General Strike in 1926, Day Lewis supported the TUC as a driver whilst Warner became a blackleg, conducting a tram in Hull.

To justify this action Warner argued that the sooner the workers lost a battle they could not win, the better it would be for them in the long term. There is no doubt about Warner's sympathies, but the playful unorthodoxy of his argument here suggests political thinking which was reluctant to be constrained by rigid dogma.

After Oxford, Warner's commitment to the left became more firmly established. He worked frequently for the Communist Party[2] and in 1930 was apparently selling the *Daily Worker* on the streets of Reading.[3] His resignation from a teaching post in 1929 was hastened by a disagreement with the headmaster and if a parallel incident in C. Day Lewis' novel *Starting Point* (1937) (involving a character based on Warner) may be trusted, this disagreement was over the nature and strength of Warner's political beliefs.

In 1930, Warner took a teaching post in Egypt. He was there for three years. This break from British political activity forestalled any intention Warner had of joining the Communist Party, but it did at least grant him time to experiment with one of the most frequently debated issues amongst socialist writers of the thirties: the convergence of left-wing ideology and left-wing literature. It was during this period in Egypt that Warner wrote at least the first draft of *The Wild Goose Chase*.

It is perhaps partly as a result of this detachment from British political argument that *The Wild Goose Chase* is not a highly theoretical Marxist novel. There are, however, sections of orthodox dogma (where the hero, for example, argues against the individual and for collectivism[4]) which foreshadow views Warner later expressed in two essays that both make the case for a Popular Front. The first of these, a pamphlet entitled *We're Not Going To Do Nothing* (1936)[5], argues against Pacifism, positing "collective force" as the only means of resisting aggression. The second essay, 'Education'[6], tries to disarm prejudice against Marxism by aligning it with what Warner regards as its synonym, "common sense". These two ideas form the basis of the politics of *The Wild Goose Chase*. The hero of the novel is converted to Marxism through a series of experiences that prove it to be the only common sense ideology to support. After failing to initiate change on his own, he realises that only "the organised movement of the masses"[7] can launch a successful revolution. Warner's limited theorising in *The Wild Goose Chase* and in the two essays shows how closely aligned he was to the political position adopted by *Left Review*. But the novel's value does not depend upon any left-wing dogma. Warner puts little emphasis on theory because extended political argument is exactly what he tries to avoid. *The Wild Goose Chase* is a unique and entertaining thirties' novel because it is an attempt to find a form suitable both to convey the necessity of Marxism and revolution, and to appeal to as wide an audience as possible without depending on overtly intellectual, and hence possibly alienating, political debate.

Day Lewis said that Warner was "intolerant of intellectuals, in whom he found a clique mentality both shallow and pretentious".[8] This partly explains the emphatic use throughout *The Wild Goose Chase* of popular culture as opposed to intellectual theorising, and it is an important factor in Warner's attempt to popularise Marxism.

In the first chapter, the narrator, "a citizen of a seaside town", introduces three brothers who are about to undertake a search for the wild goose. Two are comic stereotypes. Rudolph is an upper class twit whose plans to "blaze a new trail" are quickly thwarted by the discovery that there is no petrol in his motor cycle. The slapstick comedy of the scene (it could easily be the Marx Brothers or Charlie Chaplin) is carried by Rudolph's cliché-filled speechifying. His brother, David, is an intellectual distanced from the masses by his learning:

... [David] said that the purpose for which he was setting out was one which was sure to seem difficult to many people, while others, perhaps, would be totally unable to understand it. It was none the less notable for that, however.

Alongside Rudolph and David is George, an unconventional but likeable rogue (very loosely based on Fielding's Tom Jones) who shows more concern for the Prebendary's wife than the dangerous journey he is about to undertake. It is George who becomes the hero of the novel and Warner makes use of the traditional folk tale theme of the lucky third son whose sometimes haphazard but well-intentioned actions succeed where others fail. There is a clear connection here with Auden and Isherwood's poetic drama *The Dog Beneath the Skin* (first performed in 1936) which was originally entitled, 'The Chase'.

There follows discussion about the wild goose itself. Warner makes no bones about its obvious symbolism. It stands for liberation in much the same way as wild geese do in E.M. Remarque's *The Road Back* (1931). Remarque's novel begins in the trenches during the last days of the First World War. A group of soldiers hear an unfamiliar noise above the shell fire:

> "There they are! Wild geese!"
> Again the whirr of wings straight above us: again the hoarse, throaty cry swooping down into our hearts like a hawk; the lapping pulse of their wings, the urgent cries, gusts of the rising wind all united in one passionate swift sense of freedom and life.[9]

There are many similarities between this scene and the occasional episodes in *The Wild Goose Chase* where geese appear. In both novels the birds become apocalyptic harbingers of liberation, peace and justice. Warner does not suggest a more exact political meaning than this because he wishes to avoid an over-mechanical allegorical structure. More importantly, however, Warner is reluctant to endorse a particular political system to replace the old order. The advantage of this is that he avoids criticism from opponents of Marxism, and so maximises readership support for the mass movement against the Fascist government of the town. Warner's support for

Popular Front politics is clearly evident here.

After the introductory chapters, the novel splits into two halves. The first deals with the various experiences George has on his journey, up to his first visit and subsequent escape from the town. His political conversion begins during this journey and is completed when he realises that the only way to establish a new and liberating regime is through the destruction of the town and its government.

During his journey George unwittingly travels "over the frontier", an action linked to the idea of a personal quest, but not specifically to a class 'going over', since George's brothers cross the same frontier yet pursue very different objectives. Again, Warner avoids a specific political recommendation and has George simply reach "a new country", roughly aligned with a new level of consciousness. Here, George finds a poor village and spends some time observing the oppressive control the government exercises over the lives of the agricultural workers. He also notes the weakness of their political resistance to the government. George pities their helplessness but, despite falling in love and actually seeing wild geese fly overhead, he leaves the village, having decided that his quest must take him onward, to the town.

George finally manages to enter the town and is reunited with his brother David, who has become deeply involved with the work of 'the Convent'. It quickly becomes clear that the Convent is a satire on university life: cloistered elitism and privilege maintained in the midst of deprivation. Since the Convent is regarded as the town's most outstanding cultural achievement, George is finally convinced that he is in a "rootless society, purposeless and powerful". These words echo the feelings of a generation of young British writers toward their country and at this point the town and its government become clear symbols of capitalism—degrading the workers, refusing them rights and seeking to appease them with deceitful media (the "all-you-need-news") whilst condoning the pointless aestheticism of hare-brained professors of the Convent. In a later essay about allegory, Warner wrote that Bunyan and Swift seemed to be saying, "Look carefully at these strange creatures we show you. You and your world are like this".[10] The comment is appropriate at this point in *The Wild Goose Chase*, where the satirical thrust of Warner's allegory is at its most forceful.

George narrowly escapes being murdered in the town and realises that the genuine wild goose (not the stuffed version that the town reveres) will only be discovered after the town is destroyed. With his political convictions secured and endorsed by the experiences of his journey, George returns to the village and helps form a revolutionary army. In the battle with the town which ensues, the army fights against the major forces of capitalism in the form of giant mechanical policemen and sinister priests with poison gas under their hassocks. Eventually, with the help of miners from the town (led appropriately enough by a man called Arthur), the army smashes its way through the defensive walls and defeats the government.

The Wild Goose Chase was, as *The New Statesman* review said, "a leap in the dark". Warner's use of allegory was a bold move in a decade when left-wing intellectuals were chastising detachment from the proletariat and recommending social realism. When *Left Review* began publication in October 1934, it advocated a new form of literature, to be guided by the Writers' International, which would confront the lives of the working classes and "describe things as they are". This was considered to be "a revolutionary act in itself".[11] Such pronouncements filled the early issues of the *Left Review* and Warner must have been broadly in sympathy with the periodical's political policy. He did, after all, have a pamphlet, an article, three poems and a contribution to a questionnaire about Spain all published by *Left Review*. Furthermore, his support for a Popular Front was in line with the periodical's stand and his closest friend C. Day

Lewis was a regular contributor. Yet *The Wild Goose Chase* makes no attempt to "describe things as they are". Warner's apparent disregard for the *Review*'s policy on so crucial an issue as literature and the proletariat raises a number of points pertinent to many left-wing writers of the thirties.

The most obvious explanation for Warner's decision to write a novel like *The Wild Goose Chase* is that he was being tactful. Like other middle-class Marxist writers, he knew nothing about the proletariat. In Day Lewis' *Starting Point*, an anti-intellectual, rugby-playing Oxford undergraduate clearly based on Warner works as a blackleg during the General Strike. Whilst arguing with a Communist striker, he sadly asks himself the question: "was not contact possible between them?"[12] This incident touches on a whole Oxbridge generation's incomprehension of the lives and feelings of the proletariat. For Warner, as part of that generation, social realism was out. To have attempted it would have meant an act of intellectual and imaginative dishonesty.

A further problem faced by Warner and other left-wing writers was that they lacked a theoretic basis on which to build fictions in accordance with the vague directive to "describe things as they are". What exactly was "social realism"? What was "proletarian literature"? Montagu Slater wrote that *Left Review*, for example, had: ". . .not done much in the theoretical line yet. It will have to. One of its functions is to begin to catch up on the leeway of forty years' stoppage of Marxist theory in England."[13]

More recently, Gustav Klaus has suggested that the organisational and intellectual weaknesses of the Communist Party of Great Britain contributed to this lack of direction in Marxist literary theory:

> The Communist Party, which anyway never numbered more than a few thousand members, had hardly any creative writers or literary intellectuals on whom it could count. Charles Ashleigh, Ralph Fox, T.A. Jackson, Tom Wintringham are the names that spring to

mind, but this is already a fairly comprehensive list, and they could hardly have been expected to run a cultural journal between them.[14]

Without being given more specific guidelines, the left-wing writers' set task of finding an appropriate form and content for the expression of and support for socialism was evidently a confusing one.

Warner's use of allegory might therefore be seen as an evasion of the problems associated with class division and inadequate Marxist literary theory. But this is to put the matter negatively. More positively, we can say that allegory was a traditional and secure form about which Warner already knew much. Two important influences on his writing were Swift and Bunyan. *The Wild Goose Chase* has many parallels with *Pilgrim's Progress*. Both avoid an intellectual or highly organised allegorical structure and many figures and incidents that spring up in both works are created for the sake of an immediate effect, and are not always related to the main structure of the allegory. Furthermore, both storylines include the idea that an obstacle (the town, Vanity Fair) must be passed before salvation (the wild geese, the Celestial City) can be reached. Clearly, Warner's use of the framework of *Pilgrim's Progress*, and the general effect that the work of these two earlier allegorists had on his writing, provided a solid foundation upon which *The Wild Goose Chase* could be developed. If Warner had decided to "describe things as they are", he would have had little to build upon.

There were, of course, other works of fantasy and allegory in the thirties which must have influenced Warner in varying degrees. An early example is Upward and Isherwood's 'Mortmere'—a kind of conspiratorial escape from the old order and, at the same time, an attempt to control and satirize that dying world. Upward went on to experiment further with allegory, and his short story 'Sunday' (written in 1931) certainly seems to have influenced Warner's choice of three cyclists in a seaside town as the opening scene for *The Wild Goose Chase*. Auden's *Paid On Both Sides* (1933) is a fantasy where the past is a curse, as it is in the village of Warner's novel. Auden's first collaboration with Isherwood, *The Dog Beneath the Skin* (1935), uses representatives of right-wing reactionism in the form of the clergy, the military, and the aristocracy. *The Wild Goose Chase* adopts a similar technique, using three kings representing Fascism, Science and the Church. Auden and Isherwood's subsequent dramatic collaborations, *The Ascent of F6* (1936) and *On the Frontier* (1938), are also political allegories which help to support and legitimise Warner's use of that form.

Auden and Isherwood's use of allegory and fantasy, like Warner's, was partly an attempt to develop an appropriate form for the expression of left-wing politics in literature. But *The Wild Goose Chase* stands apart as wilder, and more eclectic, than anything else written during the thirties. Warner's audacious and quite unique use of allegory as a popular form is an attempt to attract and convince as wide an audience as possible of the necessity of both "common sense" politics and dramatic social change. These elements distinguish Warner's novel from much of the other allegory and myth-making of the thirties.

In a review of Malcolm Muggeridge's *The Thirties*, George Orwell wrote: "What a decade! A riot of appalling folly that suddenly becomes a nightmare, a scenic railway ending in torture chamber."[15]

In many ways, this comment is an appropriate metaphor to describe the progression of Warner's fiction during the thirties. *The Wild Goose Chase* is an often openly comic satirical allegory of capitalist Britain which includes a Utopian vision of a new world. This is in great contrast to Warner's next novel, *The Professor*. Warner moves from an indiscriminate and anarchic use of fantasy, to simple allegory directly paralleling the contemporary world of Austria's Anschluss in 1938. *The Professor* is a dark prophecy of the very near future where liberalism is moribund and Fascism is quickly grasping power. Only the concerted efforts of a powerful Communist counter-attack holds any hope, but one of the closing scenes of the novel, where hundreds of enemy bombers block out the sky, suggests the first battle has already been lost.

Contemporary events made it impossible for Warner to continue to employ the style he had so successfully discovered for *The Wild Goose Chase*. The eclectic experiment he began in that novel was pushed aside and replaced by a bleak but necessary rational argument. The style of a Boys Own Adventure was clearly no longer appropriate.

NOTES

1 V.S. Pritchett, review of *The Wild Goose Chase*, in *The New Statesman* (September 25, 1937) p.448.

2 See an unpublished interview in a doctoral thesis: *Prose Fiction of the 1930s*. Andrew Cramp, Loughborough University (1984).

3 See introduction to section on Rex Warner in *Seven Writers of the English Left. A Bibliography of Literature and politics 1916–1980* compiled by Alan Munton and Alan Young (Garland, 1981).

4 See p.233.

5 Rex Warner, *We're Not Going to Do Nothing* (London: *Left Review*, 1936). This pamphlet was first attributed to C. Day Lewis but the British Library catalogue now accepts that it was written by Warner.

6 Rex Warner, 'Education' *The Mind In Chains*, C. Day Lewis (ed) (Muller 1937).

7 See p.233.

8 Sean Day Lewis, *C. Day Lewis. An English Literary Life* (Unwin paperbacks 1982) p.111.

9 E.M. Remarque, *The Road Back* (Putnam's 1931) p.7.

10 Rex Warner, *The Cult of Power* (John Lane the Bodley Head, 1946) p.118.

11 Montagu Slater, 'The Purpose of a Left Review', *Left Review* vol.1 no.9, 1935.

12 C. Day Lewis, *Starting Point* (Cape, 1937) p.182.

13 Montagu Slater, *op. cit.*

14 Gustav Klaus, 'Socialist Fiction in the 1930s', *The 1930s: A Challenge to Orthodoxy*, John Lucas (ed.) (The Harvester Press, 1978) p.15.
15 George Orwell, review of Malcolm Muggeridge's *The Thirties*, *New English Weekly*, 25 April 1940.

For our contention is not with the blood and the flesh, but with dominion, with authority, with the blind world rulers of this life, with the spirit of evil in things heavenly.

Ephes. vi, chap. 12.

CONTENTS

I
Far on Bicycles   15

II
The Wild Goose   28

PART I
The One Remains   37

PART II
The Many Change   231

I

FAR ON BICYCLES

I

FAR ON BICYCLES

IT seems, though it was many years ago, only yesterday that we citizens of a seaside town, standing in ranks along the esplanade, watched, cheering at the same time with all the force of our lungs, the outset of the three brothers who, with the inconsiderate fine daring of youth, were prepared, each in his own way, to go far on bicycles, distinguishing our town by an attempt which even the brothers only dimly understood and which seemed to most of us who stood spectators vociferously cheering impracticable, to some even ridiculous. Young and vigorous they looked, different one from the other, as they wheeled into the square their diverse coloured bicycles, made by the same maker at different dates, and they seemed, by the expression of their faces, already in thought upon the moorland road which was to lead them to the frontier miles away, where very few of us had ever been, and those few shook their heads with a hint of dangers to be met, saying nothing but doubting much, as the rest of us doubted, whether the brothers ever were destined to achieve the purpose which they all, though very indistinctly, had in view.

Of late the weather had been stormy, though now the sun shone and a stiff breeze blew from the sea, exacerbating the waves in the bay over which, at a great distance from the shore, far from their nesting places, sailing on enormous wings that flashed in their high turnings against the sun, long ribbons of light, or like the rims of metal discs set firm and hardened in the velocity of steep falling, were fishing the great pelagic gannets, seldom to be seen so clearly with the naked eye. Over the cliff-face, facing eastward, helter-skeltered strangely, like something supernatural, the ghostly quick shadows of the screaming gulls; there seemed, though no doubt it was only our excited nerves which made us think so, an unusual restlessness of hurry in the natural scene and, for relief and surety, we stared with new eyes at the sobriety of our town architecture, the church's straight brown spire, the cobbles in the square, and the sharp angles of the comforting exterior of attics. In window-boxes geraniums flared, and from the windows protruded the anxious heads of eager girls and vicariously enthusiastic matrons. In the square blared the brass of the town band as with pride and something tense in our expressions we stared in each others' faces, waiting for the brothers, orphans, to start.

Rudolph was the first to go. Wheeling easily with one hand (the other being raised graciously to acknowledge the cheers with which he was greeted) into the square his enormous red racing motorbicycle, he stood straight for a moment silhouetted against the sun, a fine figure of a man in his expensive motoring suit, his peaked cap covered with oilskin shading his masculine features, bright eyes, firm audacious jaw from the limits of which protruded the carefully waxed ends of a military moustache. For a second he stood still and with a superb gesture blew what appeared to be a kiss in the direction of one of the upper windows of a house overlooking the square. Some said that within there was the Mayor's daughter, others that it was only a waitress, but, however that may be, Rudolph's gesture was conspicuously gallant and did not fail to impress the onlookers. Then some of Rudolph's more intimate friends approached him and, with tears of admiration in their eyes, wrung his hand, or, stiff-lipped, hit him upon the back. 'Stout fellah!' they would say, appraisingly, and Rudolph, easily smiling, would reply: 'Thanks, old man.' At length he was prevailed upon to make a speech, though, with charming diffidence, he struggled a little as he was raised shoulder-high by the young officers of our yeomanry, who had been his constant companions. Smiling and blowing kisses to us, who cheered till we were hoarse, he at length obtained silence and, speaking bashfully at first, as though the warmth of our enthusiasm had put him out of countenance and as though he himself regarded the journey which he was about to take as some ordinary expedition, or as simply his duty, he addressed us:—

'It's awfully decent of you fellows to make such a fuss. Really it's quite unnecessary. I don't deserve it.' He smiled with great charm, and the cheering was renewed. Then with graver set features he continued: 'I can only say this, that I am doing my duty. It's going to be hard, damned hard, but I'm going to see this thing through.' He paused, and reverently we clapped our hands together. Then he smiled lightly, and went on speaking: 'After all, what were we all born for? What's life without adventure? If anything, I'm a bit sorry for you chaps who are staying behind. I can tell you it's a jolly good thing to be blazing a new trail. There's a poet johnny who says, "Beyond the west the sunset, beyond the east the dawn" or something like that. I think the josser's quite right. Anyway that's what I feel like. And now I must say good-bye. Good luck, everyone, and—oh, by the way, if anyone would care to have a photograph of me, just to remember me by, there are some on the table over there.' He pointed to a table which was just being carried out from the Town Hall by two footmen. Naturally everyone rushed immediately to the table, and in the scuffle which followed several women fainted, and a small child was severely injured. These events we were careful to conceal from Rudolph, who, no doubt, would have been distressed, and finally, when we had each received a photograph, we surrounded him again, cheering and cheering, watching him start his engine.

Once more he flashed quickly an ambient smile, then pulled his cap firmly over his forehead and, with a practised foot, motioned to start the motor bicycle. We stood, waving our hats, waiting for the engine's roar and the sight of Rudolph speeding to the moor, along the straight avenue of the esplanade. The first kick failed, and so, to Rudolph's evident annoyance, did succeeding attempts. As we stood sympathetically silent, people whispered one to another: 'Something is wrong with the engine.' Rudolph turned round with what, if we had not known him, would have seemed a startled expression on his face. 'Where's that damned garage man?' he said, and the little proprietor of the town garage, whose duty it had been to overhaul the bicycle, came forward from behind the crowd, holding in one hand a photograph of Rudolph, bowing apologetically with his bald head dipping up and down, so ridiculous that, in spite of the gravity of the occasion, some people began to laugh. Rudolph appeared relieved, and while the mechanic was bending over the bicycle, he sauntered amongst the crowd and signed his name in autograph albums. Soon the mechanic turned: 'I thought you said you would see about the petrol, sir,' he said, and Rudolph, frowning, replied: 'Nonsense.'

It appeared that the petrol tank had been quite dry. It was filled, the engine started, and with one hasty wave of the hand, while the engine roared, Rudolph was off, soon a speck at the far end of the esplanade, and we cheered while we could see his body bent over the low handlebars and the large suitcases strapped to the luggage carrier. Then, as he faded into the distance, only dust marking him, on the way to the moors, one whom we would never see again, we were silent, with a sense of climax passed, looking at each other, disappointed and relieved.

Soon, however, another jubilee. We began again to wave our hats and cheer when we saw David, the second of the brothers, coming with short steps that seemed hesitant or else premeditated from the shadow of the great gothic porch of the Town Hall, where

18

he had been entertained at breakfast by the religious and educational authorities of our town, out into the white sunlight where he paused, screening his eyes, and then turned to his friend, the Prebendary, making some remark that we could not hear but which must have been of an amusing character, since it was uttered with a slight curling of the lip and a whimsical ironic glance to the face of the Prebendary, a man renowned for his tolerant learning, who in turn smiled, though gravely, and pointed to the title of a book which he was carrying underneath his arm. David was cheered even by the yeomanry, although, not being fond of field sports, he had never been so friendly with them as his brother Rudolph had been; but now, considering the nature of his adventure, these honest fellows forgot past differences of opinion, rapturously hallooing, for was he not on the way to bring great honour to the town, besides being, as they remarked loudly to one another, a damned clever fellow who knew, as accurately as it was possible to know, what was what. In the warmth of reception they were rivalled by the members of our fire brigade who had, not long ago, been addressed by David in the Town Hall on the subject of pyrotechnics as practised in the ancient empires of Babylon and Assyria, a subject about which very little definite information is available and consequently a large field for conjecture, a field filled in a scholarly manner, as we all agreed, by David, who, with the utmost brilliance, discoursed for two hours, aided by lantern slides, which had been specially constructed by the penal labour of malefactors in our gaol, as illustrations for his theories.

All this had not been forgotten by the fire brigade vociferous with the rest; but he was given the most uproarious reception by the young people of both sexes who had recently graduated from the High School to become poets, artists, or philosophers. These, better perhaps than the rest of us, were aware of David's rare intellectual distinction which, from the first year in the High School,

19

had marked him out from the rest of the pupils and had secured for him the tender friendship of the staff with Prebendary Garlic, our acknowledged leader in educational and religious thought, at their head. He had read papers, universally admired, to our Literary and Debating Society on very various subjects including: 'Shakespeare,' 'The Arcado-Cypriot dialect in the poems of Homer,' 'The Culture of Sweet Peas,' 'Thoughts on an unknown sculptor,' 'Ipsism,' 'The novels of John Galsworthy,' 'Milton,' 'Bi-metallism,' 'Dandelion wine,' 'A scheme for a further utilization of water-power,' 'Cricket,' 'The thought of D. H. Lawrence,' and 'Towards a synthesis.' In view of these triumphs and of others including the recent publication of a volume of verse, it was not surprising that, though all applauded him, since, free and accurate thinker as he was, he had always contrived to get on fairly well with everybody, nevertheless he should be most cordially hailed by our young intellectuals, of both sexes (for he was as popular with the boys as with the girls), who on the preceding day had made a presentation to him of exquisitely bound copies of the three books which he proposed to take upon his travels.

Now Prebendary Garlic, whom we all respected, raised his hand, claiming silence, and we stood silent looking at the group at the top of the steps leading to the Town Hall. David was wearing a new lounge suit, blue, cut in the latest fashion. His hat was one specially adapted to cycling, brimless, and did not hide from us his pale ascetic features and the nobility of his expression, arch of eyebrows with consonant lines of slender side whiskers. Some of the bluffer members of our yeomanry used to say that his appearance was effeminate, but this, no doubt, was partly due to jealously, since the gentleness and charm of his person, combined with the known emancipation of his mind, made him very much sought after all over the town by people of both sexes, young and old, and indeed his appearance was not so much effeminate as indeterminate, expressing in one person the beauties of opposite things, the male and the female, youth and age, sobriety and licence. In one hand he held a printed copy of the speech he had just delivered in the Town Hall, and in the other the handlebars of his push-bicycle, which had recently been repainted blue, a fast model, with three speeds and an oil-bath, slower, no doubt, than Rudolph's vehicle, but probably more reliable, for David carried a spare tyre, two bicycle pumps and a very modern equipment for repairing punctures. This had been presented by the Bishop of the Diocese in exchange for the coupons which David had collected by his success in examinations on the books of the Old Testament.

Our Prebendary spoke words, few but well chosen, pointing out on the one hand our sorrow at losing (he hoped only for the time being) one whose life in our town had been at the same time both instructive and endearing to us all, and on the other our pride in the foretaste of those distinctions which must inevitably be awaiting him beyond the frontier. 'The day,' he concluded, 'is one meet-to-be-marked with a white stone,' and we clapped our hands together.

David spoke cheerfully and at some length. Among other things he said that the purpose for which he was setting out was one which was sure to seem difficult to many people, while others, perhaps, would be totally unable to understand it. It was none the less notable for that, however. The stars are to be reached by up-hill work, if at all, and if this is true of the material heaven, how much truer is it of the intellectual universe? But he was inclined to suspect that some of the difficulties, viewed at any rate from some aspects, had been in the past, to some extent at least, over-estimated. He thanked his friend the Prebendary, who was, he was pleased to say, still a friend in spite of some divergence of their opinions on some of the received dogmata of the Church (here the Prebendary chuckled), for a eulogy which he had, so far, done

21

little to deserve, and he was grateful to the rest of us for a reception the enthusiastic character of which had by a long way exceeded his expectations or his merits. He concluded, smiling, with a graceful and scholarly jest, which not all of us could understand, but which was loudly applauded by those who had received the benefit of our high-school education. Some friends of his, he said, had asked him (in fun, of course) to choose an epitaph, for which he sincerely hoped there would be no occasion just yet. He had liked that remark of the emperor Nero: 'Qualis artifex pereo,' but had lingered on the possibility of adding the word 'opifex', whose insertion, of course, would, besides endangering the rhythm, take away from the peculiar terseness of expression for which the sentence was famous even in a language whose genius was most aptly employed in the constricted and restricted style. But he would wish his friends to remember his predilection for those two Latin words which, as he was sure they all knew, were common in gender.

All of us were greatly impressed by the apparent light-hearted-ness of David on an occasion of such importance that in any man some trepidation might have been expected and could easily have been forgiven; but we knew the irony of his disposition which masked the confidence of one satisfied with his own powers. A roar of cheering broke out, wildly startling gulls from their rocky perches, as David mounted his bicycle, having stopped a moment to regulate the adjustment of the bell, and pedalled at a moderate pace along the esplanade. Many of the young people wept as he advanced farther into the distance; and the Prebendary with other dignitaries of the Church smiled sadly, commenting on the reckless daring of youth, in their hearts sad for the loss of their companion. After his departure printed copies of the speech which he had made after breakfast were freely distributed among the crowd.

By this time many of us, who had not yet had breakfast, were beginning to think of eggs and bacon not cooked, since our wives and maids had all come with us to the spectacle, and some of us, being perhaps somewhat indecently impatient, were a little glad that it only remained for us to give a send-off to George, the youngest of the brothers, a boy infinitely less talented than David and not so good a motor cyclist as Rudolph, but a good lad still, somewhat unambitious, whom we all wished well. He had been a favourite of the elder women, the pious, and beautiful, who were on the verge of losing their charms; and this is not mentioned to his discredit, for it is well known that such women, when not completely infatuated (as too often happens), show a rare discrimination in men, contrasting in this way with most elderly men, who are of all people the most easily deceived by young women.

George, for whom impatiently we waited, had been a frequent visitor to the houses of rich, beautiful, good women, unhappily married; and his simplicity and innocence were such that no one, however disappointed, had spoken ill of him. With the girls of the town he had been inclined to be outspoken, and so had the reputation of being rather a boor, although no one denied that he was a good-natured fellow. It was not in the least surprising that the girls preferred his brothers to him, for, though he was good at football, he had not joined the yeomanry, and though he had done quite well at the High School, he had never read a paper to the Literary Society. Mrs. Garlic, who had once been the Beauty Queen of our town before, at the age of fifteen, chaste she had become the Prebendary's bride, commended George's intelligence (and she was an intelligent woman herself); but, since the Prebendary himself had made it fairly plain that in his opinion George had not half the promise of his brothers, most of us, such was our respect for the man, had come to be of his opinion, and recently George, for want of a job, had left the town and gone to live farther along the coast, idling away his time, the Prebendary said, though we all knew that in reality he was working on a farm, playing football for the village on Saturdays, and in his spare time watching sea birds through field-glasses, for he was interested in nature.

Some of us laughed as we remarked to ourselves that George's ability as an ornithologist was perhaps his chief qualification for the extraordinary task which the brothers had undertaken, but our laughter was interrupted by the appearance of George himself, who came unceremoniously into the market place, as though it was not crowded, and, while shaking hands with a few of his friends, propped against the Town Hall his rusty bicycle with solid tyres and only one brake, once the property of his father. An offer had been made to raise a subscription for the purpose of buying him a new bicycle, but George, rather brusquely we thought, had declined it, saying that the bicycle was good enough to take him out of the town, and that afterwards he would probably leave it in a hedge and walk. We were now somewhat ashamed of his appearance. He was about the middle height, not so slender as David nor quite so sturdy as Rudolph, quite a good looking man if he had taken the trouble to dress properly and to brush his hair. As it was he looked rather like a workman in his blue blouse and corduroy trousers, and to his shoulders a piece of hay was clinging. This was removed by one of our constables. His face was honest enough, often sulky and often very cheerful; indeed, if his manners had been better, it would have been a really attractive face, since, in spite of his angular stony features, he had a very sweet smile, the sign, as Mrs. Garlic said, of a truly amiable disposition. He carried field-glasses and a small magnifying glass used in botany, and seemed now to be talking about a plant to a friend of his, a girl from the coastguard station, who stared at him with sad eyes, foretasting the want of him.

The Prebendary, when George had first entered the square, had waved his hand in a dignified though distant salute, but George had not noticed him, and the Prebendary had retired to the Town Hall. The yeomanry too, after they had half-heartedly sung 'For he's a jolly good fellow', had gone away hurriedly to breakfast, good fellows themselves, but a little annoyed by George's indifference to their singing, and indeed we had all expected that at this time he would have attempted to cut a better figure, might have raised one hand or even made a speech, instead of standing with his eyes away from us, talking to his friends. Still he was given three cheers by the fire brigade, who then departed the least bit offended, since George, when the cheering was over, had just turned to them and waved his hand, without saying a word, even without seeming particularly pleased. Some of us, wishing after all to give the lad a good send-off, began to clap our hands, shuffle with our feet, and cry 'Speech! Speech! Speech! Hooray!', but George simply smiled, shaking his head, and went on speaking to the girl from the coast-guard station. And indeed we should one and all have left the square disappointed with a kind of nullity in George, whose attitude was so different from that of either of his brothers, if Mrs. Garlic, at the last moment, when George had one foot on the pedal of his bicycle, had not surprised us all, and shocked some of us, by running out of the Town Hall, wearing even at this late hour her dressing-gown. It was observed that through a broken pane of glass in one of the lower windows of the municipal buildings her husband, the Prebendary, was watching her with a face that was uneasy, although there was also some justifiable anger in his expression, even a hint of horror, as he saw his wife, once our Beauty Queen, appear on this day of all days in public in her dressing-gown. She quickly passed through the crowd and, throwing her arms around George's neck, kissed him on the mouth while we preserved a reverent silence, some envying the young man, who returned her embrace with warmth. Mrs. Garlic then turned to the girl from the coastguard station and whispered in her ear something which no one heard, but which caused the girl to look gratefully at the elder woman, as though she had made her some pleasing offer of assistance, perhaps, or protection. This girl, who had lately begun to show an interest in botany, following George in his long walks along the coast, had been renowned while at the High School for her docility and decorum, but now, probably because the crowd were becoming impatient and felt hunger for breakfast, or perhaps because some resented the honour which Mrs. Garlic had done to George, there was some whispering from the back of the assembly and some unkind and totally undeserved criticism of this young lady's virtue. She now laid her head, mouse-like, resigned, on the sleeve of George's coat, looking up at him with her nebulous eyes. George, with a trace of exasperation in his expression, shook her by the hand and left in her keeping his vasculum for the collecting of botanical specimens, with which she went away well pleased. He then once more embraced Mrs. Garlic, who was now weeping profusely, wishing him good luck, hinting that she too when young had been on the point of going on this very journey. At the sight of this woman, still beautiful, in tears, most of us were ready ourselves to weep, but we were recalled to our right senses when her husband, the Prebendary, with a jauntiness that was strange to him, stepped from the Town Hall and, taking his wife's arm between his fingers, breezily remarked: 'There, my dear. I think that is enough.' He then touched George lightly with the handle of his umbrella, saying: 'Come on, young man, you must be off. Already you are a long way behind.'

It was then that there happened a terrible thing, one that will be long remembered in the annals of our town. George drew back his hand and drove his fist into our Prebendary's face, while we stood aghast, not conscious of our bodies or of our surroundings, staring

26

at our Prebendary who lay on the ground with blood coming out of his nose. George had taken advantage of his shocking action by jumping on his bicycle and pedalling away down the esplanade for some time unobserved; but soon, to our comfort, the Prebendary rose to his feet, demanding with his first words that the young man should be brought back to justice, although his wife, with tears in her eyes but a somewhat happier expression than she had shown before George's departure, begged him to forgive what was only intended, she felt sure, as a kind of practical joke. Her plea incensed the Prebendary yet further, but he was forced at last to acquiesce in George's escape, for it was hopeless to pursue him on foot, and as for the cycling squad organized by our Commissioner of Police, it was discovered that there was not one of the officers whose bicycle was without some disability for the road, a puncture, a broken chain, or a buckled wheel. Consequently, while the brothers at different speeds and on different vehicles advanced towards the frontier, the Prebendary was content to hold only a judicial inquiry, while we went home, commenting on the strange events which we had followed with our eyes, rather pleased that otherwise with the excursion.

II

THE WILD GOOSE

I T was, of course, evident to everyone that to chase the Wild Goose was a course of action which implied a long journey beyond the frontier, and consequently when the brothers first proposed to go in pursuit we expected to lose them, only half-hoping that perhaps one of them might in course of time revisit us; and, though we were sorry to miss them, we remembered others who in the past had gone on a similar errand and who, though no certain news of their successes had ever reached us, had been held ever since their disappearance in great honour; for in our town we are naturally disposed to honour the departed, and, although none of us, conscious of our unfitness or lack of enthusiasm, would have cared to venture life and property on so dubious a quest, we were sincerely proud of those members of our community who, spurred by an unusual ambition, were ready to go out of sight beyond the esplanade. But all the same we argued for many days about the brothers and their action, since, honourable as their purpose was and has always been held to be, we were not agreed on the motives which had impelled them to the chase, nor indeed on the precise character of its object. And to this day it is impossible for anyone to be quite sure of what they were about when they left us, and why they had resolved at the same time to attempt the same thing, if to each of them (and this too is doubtful) it was the same thing that was presented whether in imagination or memory or as the result, perhaps, of calculation.

Various stories were told, their veracity debated, and explanations put forward. Some of the more credulous amongst us said that it was George who first, while watching from the cliffs, heard or saw the Wild Goose going away from him, but this was difficult for the majority of us to believe, since there exists no record of its appearance in our locality, and, as the Prebendary pointed out, supposing that it had for a moment revisited a coast where for a long time it had been held to be extinct, was it probable that out of the two or three million inhabitants of the district George should be the one to see the bird? It was calculated that the chances against his having made the discovery were two or three million to one. Others, with whom we were more inclined to agree, suggested that the proposal had come from David as a result of mathematical calculation, or else that Rudolph, having read some of the records of the past, had had his imagination fired by the desire for heroism, and had proposed, brave lad, a leap into what was, for him at least, the void.

It was recalled that Rudolph, David, and George had set out soon after the death of their mother, a lady who for her constant piety and former beauty had been much respected in our town, and it was surmised that her death may have had some part in the considerations which led her children to find a new occupation. A midwife, who had attended this good lady at her deliveries and at her death, was bold enough to tell a curious tale, which few of us believed but which, if true, might be held to explain something while adding to the story much more that is unexplained. According to the midwife the lady whom she attended had revealed in childbirth and at the moment of her death a curious red mark upon her belly, not unlike the imprint of a webbed foot. This she had shown to her children and had at the same time whispered to them something which was inaudible to others in the room, but which seemed profoundly to affect the brothers, although Rudolph had for the moment appeared puzzled. It was hinted by the midwife that there were other ladies in the town marked in the same way, and, which is odd, that their husbands were quite unaware of it.

David too, it was recalled, had once lectured on 'The Goose as a symbol in our early mytho-poetry', but it was difficult to see anything more than a coincidence between this lecture, delivered a long time ago, and the discovery which the old midwife pretended to have made. But, for all that, the story made a great stir in our town and there were many, particularly amongst the women, who let it be understood that they had by no means made up their minds that the story was not true, allowing it to be supposed that they too perhaps were acquainted with some things of which the rest of us were entirely ignorant; and it was Mrs. Garlic who said openly that there are things which cannot be explained in words, asking us with a smile whether we had never heard of Leda and the Swan. Her husband had clearly resented his wife's treatment of the subject and in a public address took occasion to censure gossips and busybodies in general, and in particular the old midwife, since at that time the town talked of nothing but her story. Incisive as his intellect was, the Prebendary did not entirely succeed in rooting out what he characterized as the grossest superstition.

'What, after all,' he had said, 'is all this mystery and whispering about? A red mark on the body. How is this mark explained? Ah-ha. It is not explained. And yet people whisper in corners, going sometimes so far as to recall the story of Leda and the Swan. (We admired our Prebendary for the frankness with which he dealt with a situation of such extraordinary delicacy.) Now I put it to you: either a bird is the father of boys, or something quite different has occurred. The first supposition is not only blasphemous, but is categorically denied by the known probity of the deceased. Let it be understood that I speak with all due reverence. Let us, then, dismiss once and for all from our minds all vestiges of an idea so repugnant alike to reason and to morality. I shall be sorry to hear any more about this. Good night.'

It was a moving address, but the whispering did not altogether cease. There were still some who were not unwilling to suppose that some relation of great intimacy subsisted between the brothers and the object of their pursuit and, further, that for others amongst us the same thing, for all we knew to the contrary, might hold good. The women in particular were reluctant to abandon the idea that, at any rate in the past, some extraordinary distinctions had been conferred upon their sex. But in time rather less was heard of the midwife and her story; people even began to mock openly at views which no one had ever perfectly understood, and, although some people may have kept in their hearts some lingering disposition to a dim belief, most of us looked elsewhere for an explanation of the origin of the Wild Goose Chase.

There had been, we knew, occasions in the past when the bird even in our own territory had been heard, if not seen. What more natural than for men, especially men of unusual talent, to attempt an experience which may not have been withheld from others? That the advantages to be gained were immense we were all agreed, although people differed in their opinions of what precisely those advantages were. Science would certainly be furthered, and in any case honour was assured. Some of Rudolph's messmates spoke vaguely of lottery tickets that had been attached to the legs of birds and would bring to their discoverer riches beyond dreams, and a despotic control over armies and women of other states. There was talk too at the High School of philosophical speculation and of the possibility of the enrichment of our Museum. But in all the town no one, as was natural, could speak with confidence of the precise benefits which the brothers had proposed to themselves or which were likely to attend their success in an enterprise which, even if it was of a kind that is difficult to understand, was certainly, we reflected, glorious.

And so for some time after their departure our thoughts and our conversation were concerned with those whom we would never, we

31

supposed, though we debated the point, see again now they had gone to countries whose very names were unknown to us, along roads which we believed to be difficult, through tribes of men who, for all we knew, were different in many ways from us who had been left behind. We longed for news, sitting through the long evenings in bar parlours, estimating the speed of Rudolph's motor bicycle, hoping much from David, expecting, though we wished him well, little from George. Others have been before, we reflected, but little or nothing has ever been heard of them, and, grasping glass handles, listening to sea and wind and the crackle of fire, we were inclined to shrug our shoulders and might in time have come to forget the expedition, if it had not been that one day, many years after the brothers had left us, there arrived news of a character and in a form so surprising that it was for some time the only topic of conversation in the whole town.

On a winter evening walked into a public house a man, elderly, with wild gestures and unusual eyes that seemed to run about the room like rabbits and burrow into objects of vision. He was dressed in a very old workman's blouse and corduroy trousers; his face would have been pleasing if it had not been for those rapid eyes and an expression, when he looked at us, which seemed either insolent or bewildered; and all the time he clenched and un-clenched his hands, fidgeted with feet, darting quick glances here and there, as though he were some wild animal in a trap or a man in his own house in great mental conflict.

We put down our mugs and stared at him, perplexed ourselves, wondering whether to laugh or pity or consult the landlord, when suddenly, increasing our confusion, the man turned his back on us and, looking into the wall, said: 'Do none of you recognize me?' Then, turning about, he darted towards us those unusually pointed eyes inquisitive with neither love nor hatred. We, naturally dumb-founded, hesitated to reply, till one of us, renewing his confidence,

32

winking at his neighbour, stretched a hand to his mug and said: 'I'm sorry, sir, but we don't.' The stranger looked at him gravely, it seemed with a kind of disapprobation, and in a level voice: 'I'm George, come back from beyond the frontier.' For a moment he seemed to relish our perturbation, then laughed loudly in a high-pitched voice, threw his arms in the air, and fell down in a fit.

For days we tended him while the town talked of nothing else, bewildered, almost frightened, excited at the prospect of news, anxiously uncertain of the true identity of this maniac. Our best doctors were employed, and Prebendary Garlic, now a very old man, administered spiritual consolation, while his wife, awkward in her hesitation and pitiable, unavailingly endeavoured to recognize the invalid. But with all our care we could only give the mad-man about two lucid hours a day and even during these two hours, when complete relaxation was to be desired, he would still shock us with the uncanny violence of his glances and restless movements of hands and feet. Yet with all this, and though he was never to regain his health, he was now able in some measure to satisfy our curiosity by telling us an extraordinary story which none of us could candidly suppose either completely true or completely false. Much turned on the questions whether the man was, as he some-times pretended to be, George, whom after all we might have been expected to recognize, or whether he was some quite different person or, as a third hypothesis, someone who, while not George himself, might have been at some time intimately connected with George, and so capable of relating a true story of events. All our efforts at identification were contradictory, although the police investigated every clue. The few photographs of George that still existed were found quite unlike the maniac; but that was to be expected since the photographs had been taken some time ago and in any case the strained expression of disease was quite capable of obliterating earlier and more natural traces. It was regretted that

33   C

there was no record of George's finger prints, but finger prints of the maniac, as we called him, were taken with a view to a possible future reference.

The next step was to confront the maniac with people whom George had known well, but here his conduct was ambiguous, for though he could remember no names and showed no interest even in those of whom we had thought George had been extremely fond, he did seem sometimes to smile in a knowing way when certain past events were recalled to him, and particularly when the Prebendary took occasion to announce that he had long ago forgiven and forgotten an incident of which he was sure George himself had lived to repent. The Prebendary was one of those who was inclined to believe the man's story. He had reserved his opinion until the whole narrative was put before him and had then unhesitatingly pronounced that the maniac was indeed George. He begged us to take warning, and later suggested that the poor lunatic should be painlessly destroyed, a sentence which would probably have been carried out if it had not been that one day, after he had been with us for a fortnight, the lunatic unaccountably disappeared.

But before he disappeared he was recognized by one other person, and that was the girl from the coastguard station, elderly but still unmarried, who threw her arms round his neck, calling him her George, returning the vasculum, regretting that there was no room for him at her house, while the maniac looked at her blankly as at something else, a fact which made many of us wonder whether the Prebendary's identification had been correct.

Mrs. Garlic, whom we knew to have been a particular friend of George, gave very doubtful evidence, hesitating, and refusing to express a definite opinion. She seemed anxious but unable sincerely to recognize the boy whom she had known. Certainly the maniac, for his part, seemed easier in her company than when he was with others, but that, we agreed, was no proof of a previous acquaintance, Mrs. Garlic's kindness being enough to gratify even complete strangers. And so, to the last, we were unable to make up our minds about this pretended George, but most of us were inclined to believe him to be a person with first-hand knowledge of events; for when he came to describing what had occurred beyond the frontier he was as lucid as we could desire him to be, speaking easily as of what he knew well, the details and the whole and the local colour. No one could catch him contradicting himself, and he was never incoherent until he got to the last stages of his narrative and we asked him about the Wild Goose. At such times his conduct was often extravagant, and the stories he told were so wild and contrary that they weakened the effect of what he had said before, so that many people refused to believe anything he said. But, knowing that mania is a disturbance at a fixed point, like a small area of a placid pool into which always in the same place stones are continually being dropped, and that however unrecognizably ruffled the storm centre, there are concentric circles of gradually diminishing intensity and finally an indistinguishable circumference, some of us were prepared to believe the greater part of the narrative which we heard, and even to make conjectures about the events which may have led to the hysteria which made the close of the story difficult or unintelligible.

It was the name of the Wild Goose that was apt to excite the maniac. On the first occasion when, towards the end of his story, someone asked him tactlessly point-blank: 'And did you see the Wild Goose?' he had shuddered and shouted at us. Then he would curse the question, affecting ignorance, asking us what the hell we were driving at, saying with oaths: 'Go into the marshes yourselves. Reclaim the land. That's where you will find George.'

These and similar remarks made us incline to believe that we had to do with a friend of George's and not with George himself, but when he began to tell the earlier part of his story, he spoke with such candour that our minds would again waver and we were willing to believe that all which he said was true of himself. And after his disappearance, there were a few people who put forward the suggestion that this had been really George who, under the disguise of a feigned lunacy, had given us very useful information, deterrent certainly but of great interest, and had now, still insatiably ambitious, returned to the strange scenes in which the best years of his life had been spent. But it was difficult to understand his object in appearing to us as mad, unless indeed his sojourn among different races of people had made him in a manner unfit to renew his relations with us.

Still, whatever the identity of the narrator, the truth of origins, and the precise character of the evidence, the story is memorable. In relating it I shall claim some licence in not using the exact words of the maniac, partly because many of them were unintelligible, partly because his story was told at various times and in various ways, sometimes as a strict sequence of events and sometimes he interested us by disclosing small details, irrelevant to the main history, with his reflections at one time and another. I shall tell his story in the simplest possible way, relating events just as they happened, but I shall be allowed to be able to look into his mind since, in his comments on what befell him, he gave me ample opportunity of so doing.

PART ONE

THE ONE REMAINS

CHAPTER ONE

As rapidly as the antiquity of his bicycle would allow, George pedalled down the esplanade, listening recede hoarse oaths of the Commissioner of Police, Prebendary's complaint, the hue and cry. He did not fancy that there would be a serious pursuit, and laughed as he felt the muscles of his legs stiffen, lunging at the pedals, the salt breeze in his hair, and heard the gulls cry wheeling over the pebbles where the sea broke not ten yards from his right hand. Without looking back he saw again in his mind's eye familiar buildings, the church and High School, Town Hall with Public Library and Museum, and the coastguard station on the hill. This seemed, though he was conscious of the gravity of his proceeding, holiday and a new life beginning, though he knew he was far from achievement, at the first turning only, in fact, as he swung his bicycle sharp to the left, having reached the end of the esplanade, dismounted, and began to push the machine up a steep hill, the road to the moor.

By night-fall, he thought, he might overtake his brother David who, in spite of the excellence of his machine, was a deliberate cyclist and likely to travel warily; but here George was reckoning without his own bicycle, which he remounted, when he had reached the top of the hill, after pausing a moment or two to examine the stretch of country. It was a dismal and magnificent view, brown heather rolling as if interminably extended, fading in some directions to the horizon, in others blocked by brown hills, with here and there the shining triangles, edged as though with a knife, of heaps of mineral matter cast up long ago from deserted mines. The heather was not yet in flower, and the grass, even at this time of the year, showed no signs of life, but coarse and brown lay draggled in tussocks that projected from the black mud which could be seen below the roots of the heather. 'This area,' George thought, 'will never be subdued to cultivation, but it has a grandeur and solemnity worth preserving, and possibly one day those mines might be worked again.' He got on his bicycle and continued his travels, making fairly good progress, though he stopped once to watch through his field-glasses a family of ravens flapping and bouncing, glossy purple birds, among the heather, and once to admire a kestrel swinging over a hollow. It was after he had seen enough of the kestrel and was preparing to set off again that he was disconcerted to find that, what with the machine's age and the rough roads that it had been over, his bicycle was now useless, the rim of the front wheel, eaten by rust, having given way; so he left the bicycle by the roadside and went on foot, giving up all hope of overtaking either of his brothers, whose tracks he could recognize in the dust of the road before him.

He walked for several hours till the sun was low and he hungry. The character of the country was still the same, and he began to despair of reaching the frontier that night or of getting anything to eat; and, though he would have to quench his thirst, the red-brown liquid in pools among the heather looked exceedingly unwholesome. He was passing a small wood of birch trees driven into odd shapes by the wind, when from within the wood he heard the notes of a steel guitar, and stopped inquisitive, when he heard a voice calling him and soon after twigs breaking as there appeared from behind a bush a young man dressed oddly in a torn dinner jacket, with a dead carnation in his button hole and on his head an opera hat in a covering of purple velvet. His shirt front, which was

38

very dirty, was covered with scrawled pencil signatures, many of which purported to be of the Prince of Wales, and remarks such as 'Good boy', 'Don't tell Ma,' 'Good show,' 'Oh! Sailor.'

'Hullo, sonny!' said the young man, whose face was like rubber, prematurely wrinkled, perhaps because he was always twisting it into different shapes, and whose round eyes seemed continually to be rolling or oscillating in their sockets. He grinned and gave every sign of pleasure at the meeting, then, peering into George's face, stepped back and began to dance on the road, moving his feet at an incredible speed while he accompanied his movements by a dance tune from his guitar. George was so surprised at this strange encounter that he said nothing, though he liked the jollity of the young man, who, by appearing very well fed, gave him some hope of finding nourishment before the evening. Finally the dance ended and the young man, still strumming his guitar, advanced to George and said: 'Don't say you don't recognize me. Don't say that.'

George looked at him carefully and said: 'I'm very sorry, but I can't remember your face; but of course it's very odd meeting anybody here. I thought I was alone on this moor. What's your name?'

The young man thrust one foot forward, threw back his head, having tilted his opera hat backwards and, after playing a few notes, began to sing in a very pleasant voice:—

> 'I'm Bob,
> no lob-lie-by-the-fire.
> My only job
> is just to minister
> to minister to your desire.'

Then quickening the tune, and rolling his head from side to side:

> 'Oh my! those diamond eyes!
> That coral cheek!
> There's going to be a surprise
> this week next week.'

He muted his instrument suddenly and said: 'There's a lot more of that. That's a good one.'

'Yes,' said George, 'that's not bad. But I wish you'd tell me who you are, apart from being Bob, and how you expect me to recognize you.'

'Well,' said Bob, somewhat gloomily, 'of course you wouldn't know my new songs, but surely you remember the old ones that I used to sing in the Town Hall,' and still with a disappointed expression he looked inquiringly at George.

George was sorry for the musician in his evident disappointment at not being known, so he shook him by the hand and told him, which was true, that in any case he was glad to have made his acquaintance, as he had wandered on the moor all day, and had given up all hope of getting anything to eat or of reaching the frontier till to-morrow at least. Bob, who seemed very vain, was exhilarated by George's politeness, and, taking him by the arm, began to congratulate him on his family which he pretended to know well, offering to tell him his story. They then had some such a conversation as this.

GEORGE: 'I'd love to hear your story, but forgive me for seeming very rude if I inquire first whether we can't get anything to eat anywhere.'

BOB: 'Eat! Of course we can. We'll go to the house.'

GEORGE: 'Good. But I had no idea anyone lived on this moor. Is there really a house here?'

BOB: 'What said the Duke of Wellington in 1832? If everyone's as good as me, they won't know what to do. But that's rather off the point. House? Of course there's a house. I've been there in an unofficial capacity, sort of manager, not a servant, you understand, for five years. Queer old chap lives there. Keeps me to play to him. Not the do-do-de-o, but the classical stuff. I can do that too. Easy as drinking tea.'

GEORGE: 'What sort of a fellow is he?'

BOB: 'Oh boy, don't ask me. He's always reading books. Hardly ever speaks a word. Retired, I suppose. But if you're one of these clever chaps he may like to talk to you. As for me, he seems to think I'm batty. Same to him, I say, and many of them. But are you really going across the frontier? My, you are brave.'

GEORGE: 'I started this morning. Didn't you see my two brothers? They left just before me.'

BOB: 'I saw a chap on a motor bike and stopped him. I thought perhaps he'd take me for a bit of a ride. But soon as he stopped he looked fierce and told me to put my hands up. As a matter of fact I did put my hands up, although it would have been all right because he couldn't get his gun out of his pocket, and by the time I got them down he saw I wasn't dangerous.'

GEORGE: 'Did he take you for a ride on his carrier?'

BOB: 'No, he didn't. He just twirled his moustache and said, with a great roar: "I'm travelling light, damn your cheek. I'm going to see this thing through." Then I had to push his bike to give him a start.'

GEORGE: 'That must have been Rudolph. I wonder whether you saw David.'

BOB: 'May be that was the boyo on the blue bike. Looked more like a clergyman to me. He asked me whether there was a shop in the district where he could buy a map and I said what did he want with a map when there was only one road. Then he went.'

George sighed, 'They've got a long way ahead of me,' he said.

'Never you mind,' said Bob. 'You're a regular fellow. I can see that. You're not one of these twisty-turny ones. Had quite a good education myself. Cheer up and sing this one.' And though George, who became hungrier every instant, was eager to get to the house with the least possible delay, he had perforce to stop among

41

the heather and watch Bob who was at his antics again, looking upwards as though to a moon and singing in a falsetto voice:—

> 'O say!
> though skies are grey,
> there are birds on the way
> singing for you;
> not blackbirds, not greybirds,
> not ravens, not crows,
> these birds are Oh-come-away birds,
> blue birds that nobody knows.
> > Blue birds that you never knew,
> > blue birds are coming for you.'

At the end of his performance, Bob bowed, and with the least trace of hesitation (for he had evidently conceived a feeling of respect for his companion) slapped George on the back. George complimented him on his singing, shook his hand and proposed that they should put their best feet forward in an effort to obtain a meal as soon as possible; but in stretching out his hand he had bared his wrist on which was crawling a small red spider of a kind which George had never seen before. No sooner did Bob observe this than he started backward, raised his eyebrows, distorting his whole face to one expression of surprise; then in a reverent voice: 'My! what did I say? You're the lucky one. Oh it's too cheesy to be true.' While he was speaking a feather, one of the bright wing feathers of a jay, fluttered from the trees and rested in George's hair. The effect of this event on Bob was even more notable. He fell on his knees, and looking up to George in a kind of adoration, burst into tears, while George, too mystified to believe anything but that the poor fellow was mad, patted him on the back, puzzled, asking what was the matter. At last Bob found himself able to speak. 'O sir,' he said, 'please sir, take me with you. That spider and that feather. Don't you see what it means? You're going to bring back a heap from beyond the frontier. Let me come too. I'm so lonely. I'll carry your luggage, only you haven't got any.'

With some difficulty George raised Bob to his feet and began to laugh. 'Don't be so absurd,' he said. 'It's all superstition, all this about spiders and feathers. And, as it happens, apart from meeting you, I've had very bad luck so far. Of course you can come with me, if you like, but I can't promise you anything. I've only two shillings left in my pocket, and I haven't the least idea of what I'm going to do when I've crossed the frontier.' And for some time he endeavoured to drive superstition out of Bob's head and to persuade him to give up his mad idea of uniting his fortunes with those of a vagrant who had only the haziest notion even of where he was going; but Bob clung firm to his intention and, with tears of gratitude in his eyes, thanked George, whom he now would call nothing but 'Sir', for his generosity in favouring him by allowing him the position, which he selected for himself, of factotum, or, a term for which as his confidence returned he showed a preference, general manager. Nothing could alter his opinion that George was safe for fortune, and he hinted that at his own birth there had been favourable omens for his success, that he too had aspired to cross the frontier but had been deterred by the dangers and difficulties of the enterprise. George began to realize that he had obtained a jolly coward for his companion, and wondered how much of Bob's enthusiasm was due to his belief in spider and feather and how much to his wish to have an escort to carry him to the richer countries beyond the border where, as he constantly said, his musical talent was bound to receive a fitting recognition. In order to check the flow of prophecy and to satisfy his own curiosity, George, having discovered that they were still some way from the house, asked Bob to tell him the story which he had promised.

Bob informed him that his profession of having known George's family and town had been only a bit of fun, and a way of making everyone feel at home. Actually he had been born at a town many miles distant along the coast, the illegitimate son of, he believed, the Mayor, though his paternity was never fully established. He had however received a good education for which some unknown person had paid. He had not been, he said, better than the rest at his lessons, but had very early shown a great aptitude for music, and, owing, to the influence, he suspected, of his father, had left school before the usual age, and been given a good job in the town orchestra. So young was he at this time that people came from all over the surrounding country to hear him play, and he was surprised that George had never been among them.

After a time he had begun to despise his fellow musicians in the town orchestra, there being none of them, he said, without a beard three feet long, and, classical music palling on him, had set up by himself in the do-do-de-o business. It had been a tremendous success. He had been the composer of all the popular tunes for some years; his dance hall was packed with all the best people in the town; the dancing partners whom he had engaged were sought after by the sons of City Councillors; and he began to lay the foundations of a substantial fortune.

Everything, in fact, had gone well until he had become engaged to a rich widow, feeling that it was necessary to have a woman about the establishment to look after the girls. This widow had been content to overlook the accident of his birth, declaring that she had long been delighted with the vigour of his hilarity. The wedding day had been fixed and all arrangements made, when the widow, during an evening that he had agreed to spend alone with her, demanded, somewhat indelicately, he thought, a foretaste of those joys which should rightly succeed their marriage. He had fobbed her off for a time, declaring that such a course of action would be to take the gilt off the gingerbread, but as she grew more importunate, he was compelled to confess that he was unable to satisfy her, never having felt much inclination to all that.

Here George, genuinely sorry for him, interrupted him and,

44

pressing his arm, attempted to show sympathy, hoping that by this time the musician had recovered his virility.

'Sorry my hat,' said Bob. 'Why, the do-do-de-o business would be ruined, if people took it into their heads to recover their virility, as you call it. The wonder of it all is that anybody ever gets born. Wild oats, I suppose.'

George suppressed his astonishment and listened as Bob went on to tell him that as soon as the story got about the town, which, thanks to the widow, an eccentric lady, had happened very quickly, his business was ruined. Though, according to him, the majority of his clients would never demean themselves by entering into any intimate connection with members of the opposite sex, they were all rather touchy when it came to a question of a possible scandal. And the police and religious authorities were anxious for a case, in the course of which they thought themselves capable of securing not only a return to the simpler life of their ancestors, but also his whole fortune, which was considerable.

He had been imprisoned and his goods confiscated. In order to avoid a scandal which might involve several important personages, he was tried and found guilty on a charge of bigamy and condemned to perpetual exile. If anything was wanting to make him the most despised man in the state, this wholly unjust reflection on his character sufficed. It was, he cynically supposed, the reward of what might be called chastity, if he had ever considered it as such; but he had been much too busy with his music and the making of money ever to think of all that dirtiness.

George again attempted to expostulate, saying that, since people were created male and female, they should make the best of their lot and he had reason to suppose that a very good thing could be made of it; but Bob looked at him in amazement, shrugged his shoulders, and went on with his story.

He had wandered about the borders of different states, but had never found a place where the do-do-de-o was so well developed as it had been in his own city, though he was just able to make a little by performing in country villages and fairs. Even here, however, he had been hard put to it by the odious and disgusting advances of women and of some men, who seemed always ready entirely to misunderstand the gaiety of his disposition. He had often longed for a dance hall of his own, where this sort of thing could be confined to his humblest subordinates.

Finally in disgust he had wandered on to this moor, though he confessed that he had been terrified by the gloomy character of the country and by the unlikely, but still just possible, supposition that wild animals might exist on so deserted a piece of ground. He had almost resolved to lie down and allow himself in the night to be eaten up by something fierce, when he had had the good luck to meet the philosopher whose house they were now approaching. This man had frightened him at first, because he dressed in clothes of such an antique cut that he might be the ghost of somebody's grandfather, but he had been reassured after a hearty meal, had performed on his instrument and been invited to stay on indefinitely on the condition that, when required, he should play the Nocturnes of Chopin on an aged grand piano that was irreparably out of tune. Of late he had been growing discontented again and so was as happy as a sand-boy at the chance of attaching himself to a person like George, who was, after the omens that had already been noted, bound to succeed across the frontier and in the time of his success would not, he hoped, forget a poor dependant.

George assured him of his friendship, though he remarked that he seemed unbalanced and had put forward views which appeared to him thoroughly muddle-headed.

Bob smiled at this and said that he was a modern; but their conversation was interrupted as they turned the corner of a wood and saw the house in front of them, a large building of white

46

marble covered, somewhat incongruously, with a heavy thatch. George was about to inquire into the character of its owner when they observed the philosopher himself, coming towards them out of the wood, holding in his hand a white root. How they were received by him will be told in the next chapter.

CHAPTER TWO

THE philosopher was a man of imposing stature and features of face. His forehead was high, nose prominently hooked, jaw like hatchet, with high cheekbones, and pimples on those parts of the face which were left exposed by growth of black side whiskers and square black beard. His eyes, when he was directing attention to some object of an abstract nature, were straight and piercing, but in ordinary conversation they would oddly waver, grow dim and give to the whole face an expression almost of stupidity. As he stood there in his check trousers, top hat, and frock coat he would have appeared ridiculous if it had not been for his upright carriage and the severity of his countenance which seemed, from the eccentricity of his dress and features, to derive an additional authority.

George, who had felt at first some diffidence in intruding himself on this man's hospitality, was soon reassured by the philosopher who, while not appearing exactly pleased with his visit, bowed to him from a distance and then, still holding the white root in his left hand, extended limp fingers for George to grip, saying at the same time in a voice unusually gruff:

'The traveller is always welcome to the sage.'

George thanked him and explained that, having wandered all day on the moor, he had given up all hope of reaching the frontier before nightfall and, what with his fatigue and hunger, he would be exceedingly grateful for one night's lodging; then, observing that at his mention of the frontier the philosopher had started with surprise and dropped the root to the ground, he paused, picked it up again and said:

48

'I think you have dropped this root.'

The philosopher sighed and said: 'Perhaps it would be as well to leave it where it is. *Non omnia possumus omnes.*' And for a time he remained silent, seeming so upset by grief that, after a few seconds had passed, George asked him whether inadvertently he had happened to say anything to offend him. With this query the philosopher was pleased and, rubbing his hands together, though his face was still full of melancholy, he said: 'Not at all, not at all, my boy. Your methods are bad, but your heart, I believe, is good. We will talk further of this, and as for the root, in time perhaps I shall find another. At the moment I cannot tell to what use it would be best to put it.' And he proposed that before dinner he should show George round his garden, to which George agreed out of politeness, being unwilling to offend this remarkable old creature, although he longed for rest and food.

The philosopher took George benevolently by the arm and, after he had satisfied himself that he was speaking to a man of some education, he dismissed Bob, who grinned and winked at George as he ran away to the kitchen, and began to speak.

'First,' he said, 'let me tell you that my name is or was Don Antonio of Castelfiore.' He paused, waiting for George to make some comment, and George said: 'I come from an obscure district some miles away from here, and it is therefore not surprising that I have not heard your name before.'

'No,' said Don Antonio, 'that is so. Though it is likely that some rumours of my unhappy story have reached even the remotest villages. But now it is sufficient to inform you that I live a long way from the scenes of my early follies and disappointments. I live, as my curious retainer must have told you already, the life of a recluse, a life devoted in the main to philosophical speculation, though I also take a keen interest in science, the mathematics, literature, and the arts. Admire this prospect. In front of my

D

house, which is, as you see, built of marble and thatched in the way that the cottages in this part of the world have been thatched for generations, I have had laid out two flower beds of which one bed contains all the flowers mentioned in the Eclogues and Georgics of Virgil, the other all those old sweet-smelling posies that in happier times were culled by Elizabethan lovers.' Here the philosopher sighed and with a solemn face continued: 'Between the flower beds is a fountain. I call it my Pieria, for there I sit in the evening and refresh my mind with the cooling streams of poetry and romance. Sometimes it is a Homer that I peruse, sometimes a Boccaccio.'

The old man smiled sadly and laid his hand on George's shoulder. 'Even now,' he said, 'we may be happy to catch the aroma of the Golden Age. Old Faunus I declare is not dead.'

George had smiled at the incongruity of Don Antonio's mansion, had glanced quickly at the flower beds, empty at present (a thing which surprised him) of flowers, and the cool pool into which the fountain played. Now his eyes had wandered to the country beyond the garden, dark woods falling precipitately, tree trunks grappled by a fierce green undergrowth, and beyond the valley the forest rising again rolling over the crest of a farther hill. 'It's fine country,' he said, 'and a lot of timber.' Then, sorry for the old man, who was evidently anxious to please, he turned to him with a laugh: 'You'll find Pan too in those woods.'

Don Antonio pointed out to him the dome of his Observatory, appearing above the roof of the kitchen, promised him a look over his library and began to walk towards the house. On the way they passed many statues of stone or bronze, some Chinese, some copies from the Greek. By one of these, a bronze figure of an athlete, the philosopher paused. Laying his hand on the sleeve of George's coat, he spoke kindly: 'Can you, you who look for novelties beyond the frontier, find anything to repay your work as this little figure can regale your leisure? Can you improve on this? Look at these green limbs, this strength caught exquisitely in repose, not lethargy. The artist who made these limbs, don't you think, must have seen life more steadily than it is seen now. And why? Because his eyes were beautiful.'

'Or because what he saw was beautiful,' George ventured, and Don Antonio, gently smiling, replied: 'It is the same thing, my boy. Even to-day we can so purify our vision that we shall behold nothing unlovely, nothing that is loose or unpoised. Viewed aright, each common object can stand out, deliciously poised, against the flux, a statue, a poem, or a jewel. Look again at those lovely limbs, so naked, so pure, beyond touch. And why so? Because they are of the spirit, the joyous free spirit of Greece.'

George glanced at the harsh Victorian face, the pimples, the side whiskers of his companion. 'But to us,' he said, 'happily or unhappily, these things have lost meaning.'

A quick nervous shudder ran, like the shadow of a bird, over Don Antonio's face. He blinked and then, with a still more melancholy smile: 'Ah, intolerance! But you don't mean it. Beauty I declare is immortal. The old gods are not dead.'

George was embarrassed for a suitable reply, but was saved the trouble of answering the old pedant by the apparition of Bob, who, having discarded his top hat and changed his shirt to one that was white, so that, if it had not been for the age of his dinner jacket, he would have seemed quite smart, came running out of the front door, strumming his guitar and in glee crying that dinner was served. Perhaps it was his pleasure in having made a new acquaintance that made him disregard for this once the gravity of the philosopher. Certainly his exuberance was unbounded, and while Don Antonio escorted his guest at an easy pace towards the house, Bob, after a little preliminary shuffling with his feet, struck his guitar and sang:

'Bow wow, let the old dog bark.
We're quite happy spooning in the dark,
And in the moonlight, Oh this is a new moon,
A none-too-soon night for singing this tune.
    Sugar my Venus
    Nothing's between us.
    There's no cloud, Oh you know
    What I mean, my Juno.
Then quick Oh quick we know what to do.
Up in heaven they're putting the light out too.'

'Sickening,' said the philosopher, and, turning to Bob, he informed him that he could have dinner to-night in the kitchen, a suggestion with which Bob seemed very pleased, winking at George, and shaking his head, indicating that he did not wish his friend to intercede for him. So he gambolled away to the kitchen, still singing.

'A strange, and often an irritating fellow,' remarked Don Antonio, when Bob had disappeared round a corner of the building. 'He has quite a talent for music, but a talent that deplorably he desires to waste. Well, well, what heart alike conceived and dared?' He looked up at George, almost with nervousness in his eyes, and said: 'You see I have read some of your modern poets. But they are not the same thing, not the same thing at all. Even Browning.'

And now at last they were in the dining room, a long room lit by torches, windowless, with velvet curtains of purple hanging along the wall. What ventilation there was must have come from a high skylight in the roof, but the atmosphere was far from pure, smelling of roses and of sweat. At the threshold of the door they paused, George interested, Don Antonio rubbing his hands together, and surveyed the glitter of torchlight on the silver and white linen in the centre of the room, a pleasant focus for all the flambeaux which seemed themselves beacons isolated in a great darkness. The table was small but loaded with plate, decked with garlands of roses and of parsley. There were two couches facing each other across the narrow strip of white and silver, and George when ushered to his seat was doubtful how to deport himself till Don Antonio demonstrated his manner of dining by reclining on his couch and with his disengaged hand (the other being occupied in supporting his considerable weight) taking a garland from the centre of the table and placing it upon his head. George, in spite of his fatigue, was constrained by the politeness which he felt due to his host to arrange his limbs in the same uncomfortable positions, and then Don Antonio, who appeared happier than he had been previously, looking at him with dim eyes beneath which hung the flesh in loose-folded pockets, said in a reverent voice:

'I shall hope that my entertainment will gratify you. Old Epicurus, I like to believe, must have dined in some such a way as this.' He clapped his hands and there entered the room two women, both naked, at whom the philosopher gazed. 'Cleobyle and Pyrrha,' he introduced them, 'my devoted attendants. Admire their limbs. I have been ever an amateur of the female form divine.'

George glanced at the two women, neither of whom could now be called young. Cleobyle simpered, smoothing back her yellow hair, tousled and dirty. The skin was wrinkled on her arms, and her breasts hung down like grey purses. The other woman, Pyrrha, was growing fat and seemed in some way anxious to hide her body with all she had to do it with, her hands. Fat and lean, they both seemed unsightly to George, and he frowned as Don Antonio went on to describe more minutely their charms of person and disposition; while the two women stared at him inanely, the one simpering and the other scowling. But the philosopher was by this time unaware of his guest's feelings, and, clapping his hands together he demanded wine, which the women brought. 'Ah, *pia testa*,' exclaimed Don Antonio, when he saw the bottle, 'reverend jar! I think this will please you, my friend. I think this would have pleased Anakreon. And now, Pyrrha and Cleobyle, my dears, we shall both be gratified to hear you read to us.'

The two women went out of the room and returned with volumes of Horace. They read the Odes, with great exactitude, although, as Don Antonio said, they did not understand a word of what they were reading, and a silence was maintained during the performance, broken by an occasional interjection from the philosopher, 'εὖγε' or 'optime!' George was far too hungry to pay much attention, though he was at first rather irritated by the staid uncomprehending voices, reciting in dialogue passages which Don Antonio had painstakingly arranged for them.

All this time there was good drinking of excellent wine, and varied food to eat, red mullet, larks, thrushes, and roast beef; and, when the port was on the table, and the two women, having laid aside their Horaces, had sung in accurate low voices several of the songs of Schubert, Don Antonio called for cigars, dismissed Pyrrha and Cleobyle, and turning to George: 'You have shared the table of a sage,' he said. 'I hope the memory of this evening will not lie too lightly or too heavily upon your mind. The entertainment has been as graceful as art will allow. The rest is for the entertained. As I attempted to explain to you this evening, it is eyes that we need, not objects. I will maintain that point. It is, indeed, the corner stone of my system. From that beginning the edifice, now almost completed, the work of thirty years, has been raised.'

George perceived that, under the influence of the large quantity of wine that had been drunk, the sage was growing quarrelsome. He sat bunched up on the couch, blinking his eyes, which were a little bloodshot, and over which tilted precariously askew a garland of withering roses. And George too felt himself becoming lightheaded, though, as was usual with him when in this condition, he was far readier to make friends than to make enemies. Consequently, when Don Antonio, looking at him as fiercely as he could, pronounced in his gruff voice: 'Let us dispute,' he merely smiled, hardly even curious about the next item of this extraordinary entertainment. He was aroused by the renewed voice of the philosopher, who, after he had removed the rose garland from his head and had refilled the glasses with port, reclined his body, that was too big and awkward quite to fit an attitude of repose, farther back on his couch, and, with a new solemnity, said: 'I shall maintain that always the sage is happy. You, if you will be so kind, will maintain that there may exist circumstances capable of refuting my thesis.'

'Very well,' said George, 'you start,' and the following dialogue took place.

DON ANTONIO: 'Scorched inside the brazen bull the wise and virtuous may still, I declare, be accounted fortunate. For on what is the mind of the sage set? On the contemplation of abstract truth; and the more closely he approximates to those heavenly patterns which in a daily increasing clarity he perceives, or (for it is here that my philosophy differs from that of the Master), which he creates, the more indifferent will he become to the whole charivaria of sense unguided by philosophy. Earth and water will be sufficient for him whose mind is fire and ice. He will need no palaces, no conquests, who is always and in every way secure in his own soul.'

GEORGE: 'Why then do you live in such luxury? I can hardly believe that your maids, wine, books, and furniture are quite meaningless to you.'

DON ANTONIO: 'Let us, if you please, avoid particularities. There is nothing so dangerous to the elucidation of truth.'

GEORGE: 'But actions, or conduct, are a good test for the

sincerity of a mind; for when the mind overgrows itself, the body will pull it back.'

DON ANTONIO: 'Newfangled nonsense, my friend. It is just the opposite of this that I maintain. The mind can and does rise so far above and beyond its corporeal territory that it inhabits carefree a world of its own, a world more real than that which ordinarily we perceive with our senses, yet a world which is the perfect exemplar creative in a sense of the imperfect world in which we live.'

GEORGE: 'With all this knowledge you should be capable of transforming our present unsatisfactory conditions. It is a pity that you live so retired a life; for a knowledge of the kind which you have mentioned cannot, surely, be quite useless to everyone but yourself. And if, on the other hand, your opinion is that the knowledge of the sage is purely contemplative, are you not running a risk? Is not experience at all events a good test? Is not humanity one? And finally is not an individual whose life is wholly unrelated to the lives of others almost a maniac?'

DON ANTONIO: 'Pertinent questions which might embarrass another. I realize the force of the objections to solipsism. I appreciate the stern imperative of morality. And for these reasons I blend Plato with Epicurus. So as not to go astray in the airy regions of speculation I drop, as it were, an anchor to earth, gratifying my senses with agreeable objects. While Pyrrha and Cleobyle, charming creatures, are with me I cannot neglect the flesh and the blood, nor lose myself in too spiritual a trance. But these are precautions, not essentials.'

GEORGE: 'I think that you misunderstand my meaning and I seem to detect some confusion in your principles. You must be aware that over most of the world there is more misery than happiness. Can one ever, I wonder, be quite at ease this side of the frontier?'

At these words Don Antonio showed impatience, half-sitting upon his couch. For a moment he stared angrily at George, allowing cigar ash to fall into his waistcoat, then his bloodshot eyes wavered and he burst into tears, burying his face in his hands, while his big round shoulders heaved and shook. After a second or two he looked up timidly. 'No sympathy,' he said. 'I get no sympathy, not even from the young.'

George was surprised and shocked at the sight of so much dignity, severity, and apparent content collapsing like a pack of cards, although he had noticed in the philosopher's speeches a lack of daring and a tendency to the repetition of meaningless phrases. He was inclined to pity the moral bankruptcy of the old pedant, and assuring him of his sympathy, begged him to continue, though it was late, and he was becoming a little tired of the conversation. The philosopher, for his part, was easily reassured and, looking sternly at George, said: 'Dispute with you I will not, as it is already evident that you are ignorant of the rules which govern disputation. You seem only capable of making irrelevant remarks about a frontier whose importance is, I declare, greatly over-estimated. Let me tell you something about that frontier. You cannot, I fear, support a dialogue. I, at least, will provide a Mythos.

'This, then, is the story of my early and lamentable life, from the follies of which I desisted none too soon, and retired to this state which is, whether you agree with me or not, a state of perfect felicity.'

The last words were pronounced with an air of defiance, at which George smiled, remembering the philosopher's tears and his inability earlier in the evening to decide what he was to do with the root which for no purpose he had extracted from the ground. But he was interested enough to attend to Don Antonio's speech which follows.

THE STORY OF DON ANTONIO OF CASTELFIORE

"My father was the greatest landowner in the district and had three sons of whom I was the eldest. He had also a beautiful and devoted wife, my mother, to whom he was not so attached as he should have been, but for whom, during her life, I had always an extravagant affection. My father's conduct towards his wife was partly, perhaps, excusable from the fact that he was seldom at home, being a busy and distinguished diplomatist, always travelling from one state to another. I remember him as a big jovial man, who on his rare visits to our house cursed us all, when he was in a bad humour over some trifle, but as a rule regaled us with his improbable adventures, many of which were of an amatory nature and thus, of course, very disgusting to my poor mother.

'He told us once, I remember, that his fingers were not numerous enough for him to count the royal princes of whom he was the acknowledged father, and such stories he used to accompany by winks and coarse descriptions which affected my mother, who had long ceased living with him, almost to the point of tears. Other strange stories he told, which were generally disbelieved, but which I, always an amateur of the marvellous, accepted with a credulity of which I should now certainly not be capable. He related to us once that he had saved the life of an eastern potentate by grappling barehanded with thirty crocodiles, which had been introduced into the harem by a revolutionary agent. He added, much to my mother's distress, that his reward had been the experience of the richest beauties that the harem contained, a distinction, he said, very rarely granted to an outsider. Often too he announced his intention of going beyond the frontier which you have in mind, but my mother, with tears in her eyes, begged him, even if he had long lost all consideration for his wife, at least to consult the interest of the little children.

58

'Finally, I believe, my father unaccountably committed suicide. A letter was found in which he stated that having long lived on lies he had discovered them to be as barren a diet as reality. It has always seemed to me a pity that such a man, whose energy and vivacity must have denoted some real merit, should have died without the consolations of philosophy.'

Here George interrupted and said: 'But at one time the poor man must have been happy with his wife, if not in his profession.'

'Yes,' said Don Antonio, 'I can inform you about that, for from this time I became my mother's confidant and she often spoke to me of my father's early affection for her and of the brutality with which he fed it. My mother was a cultured woman of delicate sensibilities and you can imagine how she must have been disgusted at discovering her husband in the light of a lover. Three rapes (I can give them no other name) were perpetrated on her milky body, and of these myself and my two brothers were the fruit. So delicately and so affectionately did she speak to me of these events that my own conduct has been affected by her example, and I have never debauched anyone whom I could not despise. With women of my own rank and culture I have had relations of tenderness, but for me as for them a pressure of the hand has sufficed.

'On my father's death I, as head of the house, was left in possession of a considerable property. I gave my two brothers suitable allowances of £50 a year each, intending to preserve the family circle intact. But, unfortunately for my plans, my brothers became too arrogant to be supportable. I was my mother's favourite and they took after my father, being loud-voiced and irresponsible. They would quarrel with me in my own house, and, when I remonstrated with them, would, even before my mother, reproach me with certain incidents of my own life in the town; for I was a wild young fellow in some ways. My mother, for her part, easily forgave me these delinquencies, when I informed her that I was simply gratifying the desires incident to youth, and that for this purpose I went only to the best houses; and naturally there was no question of a permanent relationship. And it was on this very score that my brothers irreparably offended both my mother and myself. One of them was foolish enough to marry a poor girl whom he had previously seduced, and the other not only would not support us in disowning the match, but even presented his brother with the half of his own annual allowance as a wedding present.'

'It seems to me,' said George, 'that he must have been an exceptionally generous man.'

Don Antonio interrupted quickly. 'My dear fellow, you cannot possibly appraise the situation. My mother was heart-broken, not only because her consent had not been obtained, but because the marriage was of a kind without any delicacy or fitness. It could only lead to the coarse and the inappropriate. I, who was already a philosopher, fully agreed with her, and from that time to this I have never seen my two brothers. The married one, for all I know, still lives in reduced circumstances and, such was the grovelling nature of his mind, he was, by all accounts, quite content with them. It is the content, not of a sage, but of a savage. The other brother did, I believe, cross the frontier. Naturally he has not been heard of since.

'But let me return to matters of more interest. It was not long after this when I lost my mother. She died in delirium, constantly calling out the name of her husband, and on her death-bed was unable even to recognize me. It was a scene which afflicted me greatly, though I could pardon her for her ungracious conduct when I reflected that she was quite unversed in philosophy, and indeed her only reading had been in fashion magazines and in modern poetry.

'For some years I gave myself entirely to the pursuit of truth, but, happy as I was in my own house (Cleobyle and Pyrrha, just children, were with me even then), I was constantly disturbed and perplexed by the vagaries of my fellow citizens. Naturally I avoided any profession or public position. 'It is a swineherd,' I said to the Mayor when he asked my permission to propose my name for a City Councillorship 'who gives laws to swine.' And from the earliest years of my life I have been averse not from the congeniality of the dinner table, but from the press of the market place. I lived remote, injuring none, pleasing myself with sensual and metaphysical delights.

'But alas! even the sage is exposed to the frenzy of those who with him have the appearance of rational human beings. There was a tendency towards democracy in the state. Laws were passed which seriously impeded me in the enjoyment of my own legitimate wealth and so jealous were some of our demagogues of my natural eminence that a proposal was made that I should be forced to support my brothers.

'For some time I had been making my preparations. I had bought an estate on this sequestered moor and caused a house to be built and furnished, gardens to be laid out. Already my chef, with Pyrrha and Cleobyle, had been secretly dispatched to their agreeable hiding-place and I myself was making a few final arrangements before leaving for ever the society of ungrateful man, when an event occurred which by the shame and suffering that it produced confirmed me in my resolution, although for some time it left in my heart, a heart now fully steeled against the blows of fortune, room for some trifling inklings of regret.

'In a word, I fell in love. The death of my mother had left such a gap in my heart that I longed to fill it. I sought some woman of an exquisite tenderness, who would condole with me in my misfortunes, would sympathize with me in my learning

61

and would, out of a respect for the Greeks, be content to overlook my dalliance with Pyrrha and Cleobyle, pets. Believe me or not, such had always been the purity of my mind, that I desired nothing else.

'Well, one day shortly before my intended departure, I was introduced to a woman from another country, the daughter of an ambassador, a creature as learned as she was beautiful. It was her learning at first that caused me to favour her in my mind. It conferred on her distinction and a kind of equality. I declare that a man should, if it is at all possible, regard two women in the world as his equals, his mother and his wife. Miss Harrison (for this was the young lady's name) had sufficient learning for her to become a fitting help-meet to me, and in addition to this her beauty was really alarming. Some thoughts I had (I confess it to you now) which I should hardly have been able to confide to my mother; and it was this weakness of mine perhaps which led to the disaster which I am going to relate, for Miss Harrison herself, I have reason to believe, was a lady of a naturally lewd disposition, fitted perhaps to some parts, but hardly to the position of a wife.

'To bring matters to a conclusion my addresses received a favourable reception and I can still remember the strange fervour with which Miss Harrison, after I had asked her for her hand, flung her arms round my neck and said, half-sobbing: "Yes I will marry you, and I'll make a man of you." Disengaging myself from her embrace, I bestowed a soft pressure on her hand, asking her to name the day on which I should be able to call her mine. She named a day in the same week and I, with some hesitation, communicated to her my decision to retire, after the marriage, to this very house where we are now sitting, a place solitary, I informed her, for a young lady, but adequate for a wife. At this she frowned, anger giving to her face an inexpressible charm, and promised to abide by my decision on one condition which was that our honeymoon was to be spent beyond the frontier. It is impossible to describe to you the perturbation into which I was thrown, not because there was any real reason why I should not take a trip in the direction indicated, not because I was afraid of the difficulties and dangers which I had always believed to be exaggerated, but the proposal was against the tenor of my life and there was something within me which declared No. Miss Harrison however won my assent. She felt the muscles in my arms, bade me hold up my head, and provoked the imagination of delights which I had never intended to secure from her. Unwillingly I agreed to her mad suggestion, and she held me to my promise.

'Many times I disturbed my ordinary tranquillity by cursing myself for a fool, but I was carried away by my feelings for Miss Harrison, whose behaviour at this time was invariably most cheerful, and provocative of my worst desires. It seemed to me almost that I was about to enjoy some quite new experience and, although I often demanded from my fiancée what more could be desired than a life modelled on that of the wise and virtuous in older days, a life where Homer would be at our elbows and Praxiteles before our eyes, while in our mental prospects would shine the clear luminaries of Plato and Aristotle, all the time I, in my folly, hardly believed in my own arguments.

'And now the great day arrived. Miss Harrison was led to the altar, more beautiful than I had ever seen her, and something of her over-assertive vigour seemed to leave her as the good priest joined our hands together. I believe that in all the town there was none who did not envy me; but I myself was far from comfortable, reflecting with pleasure on the performances of my past life, and contrasting them with the dubious and unnecessary adventure to which that evening I was pledged. After the marriage ceremony I was reassured or perhaps I should say lulled into forgetfulness by the tender glances and rapturous excitement of my bride, and, rather forced than willing, immediately took my place in the car which was to convey us to the frontier. All the way I endeavoured vainly, by praising the avocation of a sage, to dissuade her from holding me to my mad promise, but she remained firm and even affected to be disappointed by what she termed my irresolution. Still arguing we reached the Customs House where our passports were examined, and across the frontier I saw buildings of an unusual size and shape and heard the natives talking in a dialect that was incomprehensible to me. My wife stepped quickly through the turnstile, which clicked as she went by, and without turning her head walked slowly forward, waiting for me to catch her up. At that moment she appeared to me so remote that I began actually to conceive a distaste for her society. Some god preserved me. I turned quickly, retraced my steps to my car and drove to this house which from that day to this I have never left. I caused it to be reported that I had crossed the frontier, and no doubt it is still the general belief that I did so. Of my wife not a rumour has been heard, and I implore you, my dear friend, to take the advice which I have bought with experience, and not to hazard your success in life by losing touch with what is best and most estimable in human history, I mean pure thought and Graeco–Roman civilization.'

At the conclusion of his narrative Don Antonio sighed and looked at George with a curious expression in his eyes, a mixture of timidity and confidence. George, although he pitied the old man for his stupidity, had been inexpressibly disgusted by the futility and self-conceit of the impossible pedant, and so he simply asked to be shown his room.

CHAPTER THREE

THAT night nothing remarkable occurred, and George was pleased to find himself able to sleep well, unencumbered by either Pyrrha or Cleobyle; for earlier in the evening the philosopher had hinted that his guest might expect some such complaisance. George concluded that Don Antonio was angry with him and had countermanded any orders of this kind which he might previously have given; and so, after reflecting for a time on his next day's journey, he prepared himself for sleep, and slept well till he opened his eyes to the sun streaming through the high window and glancing through the room reflected from twenty or more marble statues of Venus, of which he had been so unmindful the night before that round the neck of one of them he had hung his trousers and had put his coat over the head of another. 'That would keep them warm in the winter,' he thought, waking slowly and smiling at the chiselled limbs.

Soon he heard the twanging of a guitar outside his bedroom door, and laughed as he envisaged Bob standing outside, shuffling his feet, clearing his throat. The sunlight was warm on his face and in woods beyond the garden were singing birds. Bob's voice came:

'Here comes the sun through a castle window in Spain.
Jolly old sun, give him a chance once again.
   Go on seeking, you'll be finding,
   Fortune making, and Oh that silver lining,
      sow's ear, silk purse,
      for better or for worse.
Here comes the sun once again.'

George sprang out of bed and ran to open the door.

'Good morning, sir,' said Bob, who stood outside, dressed again in signatured shirt and dinner jacket, holding the guitar under his arm, and then in a pleading voice: 'You're going to go, aren't you, sir?'

'Of course I'm going to go,' said George, 'and for heaven's sake stop calling me "sir". What have you been doing all this time? Did you get a good dinner last night?'

But Bob was so pleased at the news that George had not given up intention of travel that he could think of nothing else, capering about the room, saying 'Of course, sir. Very good, sir. After all the highbrow talk you had last night I thought the old man might have got you to go back. There've been lots of others he's persuaded to stay with him, and then no one knows what happened to the fellows. But now we're really going. O my, it's too good. The sun's shining, and I wish my old mother could see me now.

> 'We're going to go,
> Oh my! we're dying, we're sighing, we're crying to go,
> Go where? Oh nowhere, nowhere, you know,
> But still we're going to go,
> Not going to stay,
> > Oh no, we're going to go,
> > going to go right away.'

'That's right,' said George, who had now got his clothes on. 'Stop calling me "sir" and we'll start directly after breakfast.'

'Good biz, sir,' said Bob. 'How do you like sleeping in a museum?'

'Glad to be out of it,' George said, turning his back with relief upon the marble Aphrodites with their public school faces. 'What about breakfast? Will Don Antonio be up yet?'

'Don Antonio and his ice-cream cart,' Bob replied. 'I'll be glad to see the last of that blighter.'

And he had seen the last of the philosopher in a live state, for after they had passed along the long landing whose walls were covered with a frieze depicting the battles of the Amazons, they heard at the head of the staircase howls, and descending to the dining room discovered Don Antonio, lying in a pool of blood, long lifeless, with on each side of his body one of his two women, both of whom were naked and sat back on heavy haunches, Cleobyle with a vacant expression almost of dull pain and Pyrrha frowning, every now and again spitting at the dead man's face. Don Antonio himself lay stiff upon his back, still in a frock coat. His whiskers were congealed with the blood that had spurted and was still slowly draining from his throat, which, it seemed, he had himself cut with a razor.

As George and Bob came into the room the two women had turned their heads towards them and had then turned away, resuming their attitudes of terror and of distrust. Bob's hand nervously clutched his friend's arm, and his eyes opened wide in terror. 'O sir,' he said, 'it's awful. Let's get away quick from this place. And besides the police may be here any minute.'

George was still looking at the dead man's face which held a ghastly expression of panic, maniacal, although the lines of the forehead were noble and in death he had lost the appearance of furtive pride which had often made his features unpleasant in life. Anyone would have been moved by the spectacle of the owner of so much wealth, the amateur of so much learning, lying, after a worthless life, dead in so repellent a posture.

George, with Bob timidly following him, approached the two women and asked them how it had happened. Pyrrha shrugged her shoulders, but Cleobyle, with an inane look upon her face, began to weep, repeating: 'Master dead. Master dead.'

'I can see he's dead,' said George, 'and I'm not sorry.'

At this Pyrrha looked up at him distrustfully and said: 'Master old rat's tail dead good,' but Cleobyle still wept, muttering: 'Came little live with master little in bed now dead.'

Bob with horrified wide eyes turned to George. 'Good Lord,

sir, the girls can't speak our language, and yet they were always reading out Latin or something. I don't suppose they know a single thing thanks to their nice ice-cream-man.' He gave the body a kick and looking sternly at Cleobyle said: 'Now then, my girl, what do you know? Ever heard of God, for instance? Don't be afraid.'

Cleobyle, severely frightened, simpered at him in a way calculated to please, and Bob started back a pace, saying: 'Did you ever see? I was asking you about God.'

His change of manner seemed to reassure the woman and she puckered up her face. 'Not remember God. Heard God was bird.'

'Well,' said Bob, 'isn't that shocking? I don't know what we can do with the poor babies. Have to put them in a loony-hole, I reckon. Bad luck, all the same.' He turned to George. 'Don't know about you, sir, but this corpse makes me feel all funny. And all the blood. Goo. I'm going to see about breakfast,' and he sidled out of the room, one eye askew, winking nervously.

George looked at the two women, and was very sorry for them. They must both, he reflected, have once trusted the philosopher, their 'Master', and the philosopher had ruined them utterly, teaching them the pronunciation of Latin words and some notes of music, coolly debauching bodies that were servile to him, rendering them idiotic and animal. For a moment tears filled his eyes as he looked at Cleobyle twisting nervously her hands where she sat gibbering on the floor, smelling offensively, for she was very dirty. It was obvious that she was dying fast, now that the hollow foundation of her stupid ill-considered life had collapsed. She could have had no affection for him, for when Pyrrha from time to time spat at the dead philosopher, or pulled his hair, she interrupted her scarcely intelligible murmuring, watching with furtive satisfaction, bestial, the doings of the bolder woman, who still scowled, preoccupied with her task and showed no signs of the collapse and disintegration that seemed to be threatening Cleobyle.

George realized that it was Cleobyle who must first be attended to and, going over to her, he pulled her to her feet, trying, though his emotion made it difficult for him to speak, to assure her that he only meant her well; and perhaps it was the tears near his eyes and the agitation which gave his voice a note of tenderness that reassured Cleobyle, for she rose willingly to her feet and, letting her head fall back, with glucous lips parted, clung to George's body, while Pyrrha squatting above the bloodless head of the philosopher, morosely watched them through slots of sleepy eyes.

The body of Cleobyle was slippery with cold sweat and shook like jelly. In high fever, hardly capable of standing, she still leered with face fatuous wide at George, who, feeling unreasonably perhaps a general dismay, clenched his teeth, holding back tears with difficulty, and, putting his arm beneath her knees, picked her up and carried her out of the room, though he had little hope that he would be able to save her life. He carried her upstairs and put her to bed. There she lay quiet, still fixing on him large watery eyes, while he stroked her hair and, trying to keep her calm, said: 'Be quiet now and go to sleep. You'll never see your master again.'

Her slow eyes became dimmer, seeming to look beyond George and beyond the walls of the room. It was a voice alone that said softly:

> *'Integer vitae scelerisque purus*
> *non eget Mauris iaculis neque arcu,*
> *nec venenatis gravida sagittis,*
> *Fusce, pharetra.'*

And at the sight of the poor nincompoop, irreparably ruined, reciting Latin verses, George, in an agony of grief, flung his arms round her, pressing her close to him, wildly crying: 'Don't die

69

now. Don't die. Oh please, Cleobyle, don't die.' But she was already dead, her face composed to something like beauty.

He let the dead body fall away from him and sat still for a moment with hard eyes, metallic, envisaging nothing but a cruelty which he had not found in nature. For a second his mind was red with fury at the philosopher, his vindictive cowardice, puny conceit, and accidental enormous power. He looked at the body of Cleobyle and saw waste matter, never so beautiful as when inanimate, a thing that had lived diabolically, the parody of an ape. Then he went out of the room, since nothing more could be done there.

On the way downstairs Bob, white-faced, wide-eyed, ran into him and clung to his arm, almost sobbing, such was the state of his terror and agitation. 'Sir! Sir! Let's go away. I can't bear it, this house.' George went to the dining room and, on opening the door, saw Pyrrha still squatting on the floor, and by her side an axe, some savage instrument which she had taken from the wall. She looked up at George, then, for the first time smiling, said: 'Had good time?'

Despite her attitude, there was in her smile a kind of cynical appreciation of others which convinced George that she was perfectly sane and so he sat down in a chair and, looking at her sternly, said:

'Cleobyle is dead. I didn't want her. I was just trying to keep her alive.'

'Well, leave *me* alone,' said Pyrrha with an expression on her face only slightly less surly than before.

George, although he was greatly surprised at finding this woman able to speak intelligently, saw no possibility of satisfying his curiosity or of making her understand that he was not an enemy, and for a second or two they looked at one another over the body of Don Antonio, until George, hearing the door open behind him, beheld an amazing change in the face of the woman, who sprang to her feet, holding out her arms, while all the surliness of her expression became as if wiped away by a sweet smile rounding her bitter lips, and softening the tense muscles about her eyes. George turned, and saw running through the door a man in a white coat with a chef's hat upon his head. As he ran he pulled away a false beard from his chin, and, with a look of rapture, clasped Pyrrha in his arms, crying: 'My wife! My wife!' while she, burying her head in his breast, sobbing, with heave of shoulder, sighing: 'My Albert!' relaxed her whole body in his embrace.

When after some time the first fury of their mutual emotion had been satisfied, the chef (for so he was) observed the ghastly spectacle upon the floor. Pyrrha, interpreting his look of horror, sobbed again, and clung to him, while the chef, still with an expression of rapture upon his indeterminate face, pink, where no feature except pale blue eyes was remarkable, raised his hands up, exclaiming, 'There is One, you know, who will forgive.' Pyrrha, still clinging to him, turned upwards her eyes in admiration. She then freed herself from his embrace, and ran upstairs to get dressed. There was now almost a sprightliness in her gestures and in her face such a look of resigned happiness, that George found it hard to recollect her former appearance. He turned to the chef, who was kneeling on the ground, raising his hands as if in thanksgiving, but whose religious exercise was broken in upon by Bob who, still with a face as white as a sheet, came running into the room, crying: 'She's escaped! She's escaped!' and, clutching George's arm, he pleaded: 'Come away, sir, now. O do come away!'

George seated him in a chair, gave him some whisky, and told him that Pyrrha was quite harmless. He implored him to keep quiet, as soon everything would be explained. He then approached the chef, who had now risen to his feet, and, congratulating him on his happiness, asked him to be so good as to tell who he was and how he had succeeded in bringing about this extraordinary change in Pyrrha.

The chef smiled and said: 'Sit down; for it is I, I think, who should now be doing the honours of the house. I listened to your conversation last night, and although I cannot approve your decision to cross the frontier, I can see you are a generous man and are sincerely interested in the misfortunes of my wife.' He glanced again at the body on the floor, and sighed. 'Poor child, it has been too much for her; but she will be happy now.'

'Do you know how he died?' George asked.

'Yes,' said the chef. 'He died because he had no faith. And you, I think, by not flattering him, were the immediate cause of his death. By your evident distaste for him you sapped his confidence in his own atheism and, after you went to bed, he took a razor and, going over to a looking glass, held it to his throat, reciting a speech from Shakespeare. I don't believe that he intended to kill himself, but, in turning back to the room, he stumbled over the corner of the carpet and, as he fell, the razor penetrated his throat. It was not for me to interrupt the vengeance of a God whom he had so long despised. I went to the woods and prayed for his soul, since it was in that way alone that I could hope to benefit my brother.'

'Your brother!' exclaimed George. 'Are you his brother?'

'Yes,' said the chef, 'I am the brother of whom he told you last night. I was driven from Antonio's house by his harsh treatment of me and sinned with a woman, whom I devotedly loved and married. Since then I have hoped that my marriage has done something to atone for the sin which preceded it. For some years we lived in poverty and content, but preyed upon by the ambition of seeking further happiness beyond the frontier, whither my younger brother was always urging us to accompany him. From this we were saved by the inspired preaching of a clergyman, Prebendary Garlic, who chanced to stop in our town for a few days, and whose address in the Cathedral we were fortunate enough to hear. He told us, what we knew, that wealth and earthly honour were unimportant, and, though we were surprised to notice so many diamonds glittering upon his fingers and his pleasure at the enthusiasm with which everywhere he was greeted, we had sense enough to be ashamed of these unworthy thoughts. He put into our hands a book of rules, by the keeping of which, he said, we should be happy both here and hereafter. We were to love our enemies, to resent no injuries, and to do good wherever we went. So impressed were we both with this way of bettering not only ourselves but the whole world, that I offered to give up my market garden and preach, as well as I could, all over the country, but the Prebendary, doubtless for excellent reasons, advised me not to do this and indeed censured me for suggesting that the Church was not at present in hands fully capable of preserving it and increasing its sphere of influence.

'For some time things went badly with us, for, when my views became known, young fellows from the town would, when they were drunk, often plunder my garden and beat me, since they knew that I would neither prosecute them nor defend myself; and when I tried to argue with them, they merely laughed. But I was happy in the fortitude and affection of my wife who, I think, never had loved me so much as then, when I was so disdainfully treated by others.

'Before long we were reduced to the extremest want, and one evening, I remember, were discussing what, if any, was to be our future (for, though we were happy, we were hungry), when there came to our cottage a fugitive, a girl of about twenty-five years old, a miserable sight, uninstructed spiritually and indeed scarcely able to speak intelligibly. She was my wife's twin sister, who at the age of eight had disappeared and was now restored to us in a condition bordering upon lunacy. It appeared that with another girl of her age she had been procured for the terrible and furtive pleasures of my brother. That wretched man had not only debauched their bodies but had stifled their souls, instructing them only in the recitation of Latin verses, which he was careful that they should not understand, and the singing of German songs. They were taught to regard him with a veneration which should only be paid to One above. And this, he used to say, was the state of innocence which he required.

'How my unhappy sister-in-law was able to escape, and by what means she found out her relations I cannot guess, but I seemed to see in her deliverance a decree of providence. We sent her at once into the country to the house of an old serving man of my father's, from whom I have heard since then that she has made a slow but a complete recovery. Of our whereabouts she was ignorant, as I intended she should be, and the kind wishes she sent me were, I can assure you, very bitter to me in the situation in which I found myself.

'From the first, I think, we must have known the task that was allotted to us. It was hopeless to think of evading the anger and the discovery of my brother, for his wealth was immense and it would have cost him little trouble to investigate the whole affair and bring back to slavery the poor girl who had been enabled to escape it. It was my wife, her twin, who with tears in her eyes, proposed that she should go in her sister's place, though she knew the agonies and humiliations which awaited her. She had been, she said, a sinner in her first youth and here was an opportunity, perhaps heaven-sent, of atoning for her sin. I could not but applaud her resolution, though the knowledge of what she must suffer was a red-hot iron in my brain. We packed with tears, both, I think, almost heart-broken, and on the next day I disguised myself and, as I had reason to believe would be the case, was accepted at my brother's house as a chef. Of this my wife knew nothing, for I could not bear to add to her misery by making her acquainted that I was to be the spectator of it.'

Here George could contain himself no longer. He had been indignant at the recital of every event in the poor man's life, and not least at the thought of the reverence which had been paid to a Prebendary whom he knew to be luxurious, inefficient, and hypocritical. Now in tones of urgency he demanded: 'Why didn't you kill the man?' But the chef, smiling at him, stopped further words by saying: 'Is it for you or for me, my friend, to execute judgment?' George sank back in his chair, profoundly agitated, impatient to hear the rest of the story which continued:

'For fifteen years I lived at my brother's house, and most of that time was spent in this wilderness where his conduct, as he was further removed from his fellow men, became daily more arbitrary. If I tell you that in these years I have passed through more sorrow than I could ever have imagined it to be possible to feel, I shall convey to your mind only a faint image of my actual suffering. It was terrible at first to see my wife, a naturally modest woman, go without her clothes and submit to the impudent attentions of my brother, terrible to see her forced to learn the pronunciation of Latin from the poor idiot creature who was her only companion, terrible to see her shame and abjection, but wonderful to admire the spirit in which she bore it.

'For some time, known only to her as the chef, I was a welcome friend to her, and I took every opportunity of seeing her and condoling with her; but soon even this comfort was taken away from us. After a few months her heroic spirit became weaker. Most of the day she would spend in tears, and often in my hearing would sigh for her husband, praising him for his goodness, often would gently reproach him for having allowed her to make this sacrifice of honour and of love. How inexpressibly bitter such moments were to me! But I could not reveal myself without incurring the risk or the certainty of distressing her yet further and of giving some hint of our identity to my brother, whose temper I knew. Would it have been wise of me to have imperilled not only ourselves but also my poor sister-in-law?

'The distress of my wife gave her an additional charm in the eyes of Antonio, whom she was forced to address as "Master", and to whom she had to speak in the childish language which the other wretched girl used. It was one night, I remember, when she was returning late from his room, that I, who had been waiting for her, stopped her, as I always did, to talk to her for a few moments in an endeavour to efface from her mind some of the memory of her horrid violation. This night she simply looked at me with blank unseeing eyes, scowling in my face, and went on to her room, muttering curses; and from that moment she never spoke to me again nor to anyone else in the house.

'If it was terrible for me to see the humiliation of her body, how much more terrible was it for me to behold the mutilation of her soul! In hopeless resignation, dulled and deadened, she has passed through ten years before deliverance came to her. I am afraid that even her faith has broken in so terrific a strain, and that it was only out of loyalty to me and her promise to her sister that she has been able to undergo the sufferings of a slave, a maniac, a whore, and a bullied child. And I, thinking of the wreck not only of our domestic happiness, but of her great beauty and of the delicacy of her mind, have often been in doubt of my own sanity.

'All last night I prayed for her, and now our affection for each other is unchanged, and in time we shall come to think without bitterness of these years of misfortune.'

He ceased, and his wife entered the room dressed in clothes that were somewhat too small for her, being indeed the same clothes in which she had left her home fifteen years ago. Bob gasped as he saw her smile at her husband and come running into his arms; for indeed she was scarcely recognizable, so pleasant, soft, and trusting was the face that had been like a dark wood or savage rock.

After the good man had pronounced a prayer, they went in to breakfast and a very happy meal it was, though George and Bob felt intruders as they listened to the reunited pair planning their future. The chef or, as he must now be called, the head of the house of Castelfiore, implored George to give up what he stigmatized as his impious design of crossing the frontier, and begged him to stay with him and his wife in this house, whither they proposed to summon all in the district who needed food or clothing and to found a community based upon the book of rules which had been distributed by Prebendary Garlic. And George, for his part, in spite of the agonized prohibitive and appealing winks of Bob, was for a moment half-inclined to agree, for he admired the good man's simplicity and the almost unbelievable devotion to him of his wife who by his presence alone had shed not only her appearance of brutality, but, it seemed, all memory of her sufferings. But finally, with many expressions of gratitude and good wishes for the future, he refused the offer of hospitality, and shortly after breakfast, much to the delight of Bob, who accompanied him, skipping along the road and even before he was out of sight of the house singing snatches of songs which disturbed woodpeckers green and scarlet among the trees along the path through the woods, set out still bitter at heart because of Cleobyle and the sufferings of his friends, towards what he hoped to reach before nightfall, the first stage of his adventure, the frontier.

CHAPTER FOUR

I<small>T</small> may have been their animated conversation in which George defended the good chef against the incredulous ridicule of Bob, saying that it was quite evident to him that he was a sincere professor of the Prebendary's book of rules, and, however mistaken his conduct might have been, it had at least been of a wonderful fidelity to belief; for, said George, though I quite agree that it was a wicked thing to allow a wife to go through such sufferings without seeking a bolder remedy, nevertheless I admire his constancy to his book of rules, in which all violence is expressly forbidden, and I don't see how he could have remained constant to his beliefs and acted differently: and Bob said that for all he knew or cared George might be right about the loony, but he was a loony all the same, and in this opinion he persevered, although George continued to speak favourably of the chef, while renouncing his doctrine, declaring that such absolute resignation was just what people like Don Antonio grew fat upon and that, although for many years the book of rules had been circulated by the Prebendary and by his predecessors, they had never been followed in any one generation by more than one or two people, who had usually been made to suffer for it; and consequently George said, it would be a much better plan to shoot Don Antonios and pray for them afterwards, than to flatter their incredible self-conceit by passivity, allowing them to continue, to the great detriment of everyone else, in their stupid notions of a self-sufficiency which entailed the ruination of others; to all of which Bob made guarded replies, being anxious out of his natural timidity not to offend his escort, and so the conversation continued perhaps for a long time with, on George's part, so much animation that they hardly noticed the road on which they were travelling until they found that it had led them into new country, where, instead of the black moor, and heather squatting on the mud, were trees and huge fields waving already with the young corn, separated each from each by choirs for birds, high hedges along the tops of which slanted the nearly horizontal rays of the setting sun, and not very far ahead was a building of red brick which seemed, from the barns with which it was surrounded and the noise of cattle which the travellers could hear, to be a farm and almost certainly inhabited. They stopped still, surprised at the speed with which time had passed, but soon were put still more out of countenance by the passage of space, for Bob noticed by the road in front of them a milestone, which they approached and read inscribed the name of George's town and the distance—30,000 miles.

Bob laughed, demanding who was the speed-king now, but George was puzzled, for the strange information of the milestone seemed to denote a different way of measuring space, and yet how could they have crossed the frontier unknowing? Where were the gigantic buildings, the Customs House, the turnstile which Don Antonio had mentioned? He determined to approach the farmhouse and make inquiries, although Bob began to be afraid, saying that you could never trust a countryman and for all one knew these countrymen might be cannibals, advising a quick march forward to the nearest town where, he was sure, his talents would provide them with food. George laughed him out of his timidity and told him that peasants were perhaps more likely to approve his songs than townsmen beyond the frontier who, for all he knew, might have already carried the do-do-de-o to a height of perfection which Bob could never attain. So in a short time they reached the farm.

It was a long building of two storeys high and must once have been handsome, though now the roof needed repair, the paint on the windows was peeling, and of the outhouses which surrounded the courtyard many were in a state of collapse. It was surprising to hear the lowing of so many cattle, the gutturations of so many hens, geese, turkeys, and guinea-fowl, to see so wide an expanse of pasture and cornland, and yet find the farm so dilapidated, with tiles off the roof, glass out of windows. But, for all that, the building was a pleasant sight glowing red in the setting sun, with boughs of cherry blossom visible behind angles of brick, wistaria on walls and, so far as was possible in such a state of disrepair, an air of tidiness, and a sense of comfort that came to the nostrils from the rich smell of animals, milk, and vegetation. There were swallows gliding in long curves in and out of the sheds; overhead rooks flapped cawing black to tree tops, a natural scene.

George knocked at the green door in the centre of the building, while Bob stood at his side on one foot, nervously fingering his guitar. Soon they heard slow steps inside and the door was opened to them by a man not above medium height, but immoderately fat, so fat indeed that his belly seemed to hang in front of him, hiding away knees, and it was with some difficulty that his short legs staggered under what was almost a sphere. His head was round as a bullet and his face so wreathed in fat that little twinkling eyes were almost lost. Shrewd and merry his eyes surveyed the travellers. Then he turned abruptly and waddled down the passage, saying: 'Come in, gentlemen, but don't make a noise. I'm listening to the news.'

They followed him into a clean kitchen, a large room, with white-washed walls where pots and pans were hanging, stooping to pass under a piece of rope from which swung the dead bodies of a hare, a chicken, and a duck, with a bunch of sage. Bob opened his mouth to speak, but thought better of it, as he noticed the farmer's preoccupation with his wireless set, which was on the table in the centre of the room. The farmer pointed them to chairs and they sat silent close to the great fire glowing in the hearth, listening to the voice of an announcer, who said:

'This is the All-you-need Programme for the farmers. The town news will be broadcast later on a wave-length adapted for sets H and HX issued by the Government.

'First of all an S O S to which those living in the country districts are required to give their special attention. The Commissioner of Police requests us to make it known that the man who crossed the frontier two days ago on a motor bicycle has fled, having stolen an aeroplane belonging to the Ambassador. The Police are particularly anxious that no attempt should be made to recover the machine, but would be interested to receive information as to the direction taken by the runaway, who is believed to be of unsound mind.'

Here George and Bob looked at one another, wondering both of them, into what risks Rudolph had already run; and the farmer, somewhat to George's surprise, turned in his chair and winked ponderously, then attended as the announcer's voice continued: 'Here is the All-you-need News.' There was a short pause and something which seemed like laughter from the broadcasting station, at which the farmer brought down his fist angrily on the table and then buried, as far as he was able, his face in his swollen stumpy hands. The voice proceeded: 'Rumours that there is any danger to the financial stability of the country are malicious and should be discounted by all men and women of good will. Never has the country been in so prosperous a state, and we are glad to be able to announce, for the special benefit of the farmers, that in exchange for their last year's harvest we are dispatching to the country districts either to-morrow or next month a large consignment of cigarettes and of those blue beads with which, as we are

informed, the honest wives and daughters of our sturdy agricul-
turists have been so well pleased in the past.

'An ugly incident occurred to-day in one of our frontier
provinces when a brick wrapped in cotton-wool was thrown at the
Hon. Mrs. Batter, the wife of the Minister of Finance, while she
was, in the interests of Individualism (a cause that has always been
dear to the farmers), officiating at the ceremony of suppressing a
hospital which has been raised by subscriptions obtained through
all kinds of intimidation. Her assailant, who is thought to be of
unsound mind, was grappled by the lady's dog until the police
arrived and seized the malefactor. It is expected that all good
citizens will demand that some signal punishment be inflicted.

'There is one further item of news which may be of interest to
some of you. The young man who arrived at the capital to-day on
a blue bicycle was received into the Convent and expressed himself
delighted at the opportunity of living under so enlightened a
government. He has informed us that his brother, who is thought
to be of unsound mind, is travelling in the same direction. Anyone
who may meet this young man is requested to give him every
assistance and encouragement to continue his journey.'

This last item of news surprised and delighted both George and
Bob, neither of whom had imagined that this journey would have
been made so easy for them. But the farmer, after looking George
over shrewdly, said: 'Don't you believe it, squire,' and sorrow-
fully shook his head. He then turned off the wireless and looked
inquiringly at his guests, his mouth conveying a pleasant sense of
welcome, though his eyes were very shrewd.

George said: 'I'm sorry to have troubled you. We only meant
to ask the way to the frontier,' and at this the farmer began to
laugh. 'God, sir,' he said, 'you crossed the frontier miles away
back.'

Bob, who by this time had recovered his confidence, said:

'Come, come, old man, you're batty! We've not passed the Customs or the skyscrapers or anything.'

The farmer gave Bob a look which startled him. 'No "old man" to me, you little ape!' he said, and Bob said: 'Yes, sir. I'm sorry, sir,' and sat very quiet for the rest of the conversation.

George inquired again how it was that they had observed no visible marks of the frontier, and the farmer told him that the Customs House and the big buildings, of which he had heard, were in a quite different direction on the main avenue to the town. This part of the country was predominantly agricultural.

'There was another thing,' George said, 'which puzzled us. Not far from here we saw a milestone which informed us that the town from which I came yesterday and for most of the distance on foot was 30,000 miles away. What exactly is a mile in this country?'

The farmer laughed and looked kindly at George, as though sympathizing with a simplicity in which there was some charm. 'That's what you must ask the Government,' he said, 'or the Commissioner of Police, or some of those scientists in the Convent. I don't know myself. It depends where you're going to and whether you're going or coming. Perhaps there are more miles on a backward journey than on a journey forward.' He got heavily up from his chair shrugging elephantine shoulders and, waddling to a cask that was set against the wall, filled three tankards with beer and set them on the table. 'Very good health, sir,' he said, raising his glass. 'I know your name's George, though I don't know who the little jackanapes is. All I know is (he winked at George) that he's likely to have a hot time in these parts. There's going to be none of his jingling in my house. There's enough anyway which we get from the Government. So sit still, young man, and don't go kicking your feet about.'

Poor Bob was terrified by this speech and sat hugging his guitar, almost at the point of tears, looking despairingly at George, who, being assured by the farmer's wink that he was really quite well disposed, smiled at his friend and said to the farmer: 'His name's Bob. We met on the road and he's a friend of mine. I'm sure he won't sing here if you don't want him to, and both he and I are anxious to go on to the town as quickly as possible. We were delighted to hear on the wireless that things are being made easy for us, though I don't like to be thought of unsound mind.'

The farmer's face set grave. 'Look here, squire,' he said, 'no offence to young Bob. I only want to see he behaves himself in my house. My name's Joe and I'm pretty well known in these parts. One of your brothers was here the night before last and one last night. You must ask Joan about them. She's my little daughter,' Here he chuckled for some time, rubbing thick hands, and then continued: 'They're both in queer street by now. Don't you go on to do the same thing. Stay with us here for a bit and look round.' A glow of genuine kindness made beautiful his great face as he added: 'I oughtn't to have said that; but you take my advice. Bless you, sir, I know what you're after, and you're welcome.'

George thanked the farmer for his kindness and puzzled his brain to think why he was trying to keep him back. Many aspects of Joe's behaviour and conversation had been perplexing. What, he wondered, were the exact relations between the town and the country, remembering the strange wireless programme and Joe's apparent disgust with some items of the news. And why should his brothers be in queer street? And how could the farmer possibly guess the object of his journey? How, too, could Rudolph have stayed here the night before last, when he had only set out the day before yesterday? There were these questions and others, as for instance what was the Convent into which his brother David had been received, which he would have liked to have answered, and so he attempted to find out something more about the town, asking first who were the Government and whether he had any reason to be afraid of them.

Joe looked at him cunning-kind, unwilling evidently to say more than he considered necessary. 'You'll find out enough about that yourself,' he said. 'I'm only a farmer, living as best I can. How do you expect me to know?'

Already George had begun to suspect that there was something not ordinary in Joe. He spoke heavily with a coarse voice, and his appearance was certainly more jovial than refined, and yet he did not speak exactly as a countryman, being capable of expressing himself somewhat more sharply than the farmers with whom George had consorted when he lived in the vicinity of the coast-guard station. George saw that he had to do with a man of rural cunning and probably of rural kindness, but a man whose mind was, through all disguises, subtle and appreciative of much more that the normal routine of the countryside. Until he had won his confidence it would be useless, he saw, to expect any answers to dangerous questions about the Government, and so he contented himself with asking whether the townsfolk ever came to the country or whether one's knowledge of them was confined to what they chose to say over the wireless. With this question Joe seemed better pleased. 'No, sir,' he said, 'we don't see much of them in these parts. But we had one not so long ago. God, sir, it was a laugh. He came down here on his honeymoon. Thought he'd like to see a bit of the country. Well, sir, Joan and me (both of us like a bit of a practical joke) we tied a great big bell under the spring of the wedding bed. Soon as his lady got in, clankety-clang goes the old clapper and out she jumped as though the house was afire. Then up comes her husband (he was a weedy looking young lad. Used to give lectures on literature, he said) and into the bed he goes. Clang! Clang! goes the old clapper and out he springs, as if he's been burnt. Never occurred to them to look under the bed.

Thought the bell was inside them, I suppose. And at last they crept into the bed and lay awake, not daring to move. No bouncing about that night, and in the morning they were talking about a divorce. God, sir, we had a good laugh over that.'

This story was perhaps more informative that George thought at the time. As it was he laughed with Joe, watching him shake his huge shoulders and throw back his round head, every now and then bending forward and wiping tears from his eyes.

Before the laughter had subsided there was a knock on the door which gradually opened and a long thin hand was thrust through the aperture. Very stealthily a strange figure entered the room, squeezing through the door without opening it more than was just necessary and then, with his back to the company, securing the bolts. The man turned on tiptoe. He was tall and emaciated, dressed in cheap clothing, a threadbare purple jacket, and brown trousers. He paused with finger on protruding lips, and what was most remarkable in his appearance was his glowing fierce eyes and the nose which stuck like a great rock out of his sunken cheeks, away from a low forehead and crop of thick disordered ginger hair. While Bob remained fixed in terror, the stranger made various signs with his long fingers to Joe, who, somewhat impatiently, answered with corresponding signs. The man then advanced to the table, setting grimly his jaw, and leaning lightly on his extended finger tips, glancing quickly round the company, 'I can speak freely?' his hoarse whisper was directed to Joe.

Joe rose to his feet and introduced his guests. 'This is George,' he said, 'the young man they mentioned in the news,' and the stranger directed a grim stare to George's eyes, before stretching out his hand which George took, smiling, though he was perplexed by the atmosphere of secrecy and intrigue. 'And this,' said Joe, indicating Bob, 'seems to be a sort of strolling ninny. He's called Bob.' 'Sh!' said the stranger and then whispered into Joe's ear so loudly that everyone in the room could hear: 'He may be useful.' He then shook hands with Bob, who grinned sheepishly and said: 'Anything within reason, sir.'

The stranger then walked, still on tiptoe, to the centre of the room, and, drawing himself up to his full height, said: 'Call me Pushkov.' He ran quickly to the door, flung it open, and looked outside: then, closing it again and barring it, he returned to the centre of the room and pronounced: 'I am an agitator.'

George had so far been too much interested in the behaviour of this fantastic to reflect upon his own position. He now was astonished to find that not only was his name and destination known, having been proclaimed over the wireless, but also that he was treated with a kind of confidence by Joe and by this agitator, while the Government, for reasons unknown to him, had already stigmatized him as a person of unsound mind. Was there, he considered, any connection between the behaviour of the Government on the one hand and of Joe and the agitator on the other? Did they imagine, on the strength of what they had heard on the radio, that he had some quarrel with a Government of which he knew absolutely nothing, and were they consequently hoping to enlist his support in come kind of revolutionary activity? But, so far as the evidence of the radio was concerned, the Government had, apart from a curious mistake about his sanity, shown themselves much more friendly than hostile to him, and it appeared that already, although Rudolph had got himself into some scrape or other, they had done everything in their power to satisfy David. What, he wondered, was this plot, if plot it was, and how was he concerned in it? Completely mystified, he attended to Pushkov, who sat down at the table and, leaning his body forward, shooting out his long jaw, drummed nervously with his fingers and began to speak in a harsh exact voice, clipping his words short. He said: 'Last night a certain person was staying somewhere not very far from here. That person shall be nameless. Suffice it to say that he had been riding on a bicycle. Certainly he was very well known to at least one of us. Perhaps you can guess whom I mean.'

It had long been apparent that the agitator was speaking of David, but before anyone could mention the name he continued: 'I gave that person, whom we will call Mr. X, some advice. He did not follow it, and we heard to-night what has happened to him.' (Here Joe nodded his head sadly.) 'I shall repeat to you, sir' (he turned to George) 'the advice which I gave to Mr. X, who was, as perhaps you may have guessed, on an errand very similar to your own.'

'I'm very much obliged to you,' said George, 'but if, as I suppose, you are talking about my brother David, how do you know that he is anything but well pleased with himself? According to the wireless he is delighted to be in the Convent. I wish you would tell me something about that Convent.'

'Stop a moment,' said the agitator. 'Don't let us go too fast. First of all I have said nothing, and I have two witnesses to prove that I have said nothing, about your brother. I only mentioned a Mr. X.'

George nodded his head, endeavouring to discover a reason for this mystification.

'Good,' said Pushkov. 'That, I think, is agreed. Secondly I can give you no information, at least, not to-day, about the Convent. A time will come, believe me, when we can talk about these things. If you had lived longer amongst us, you would appreciate our difficulties. What I said was that I would give you some advice. I shall do so in the strictest confidence, of course.'

George signified assent and Pushkov leant still farther across the table, extending one finger with which, by moving it up and down, he emphasized his words: 'Don't go to the town,' he said slowly in a low rasping voice, and then, as George was waiting eagerly for his next words, he rose quickly to his feet, went to the door, unbarred it, and stealthily stepped outside. A second later his head was thrust once more into the room; then he closed the door and disappeared.

Bob was now shivering with fright and ran over to George whimpering: 'O sir, let's go back, let's go back.'

'What!' said George, smiling, though he was disturbed by the scene which had just passed, '30,000 miles?' and he succeeded in encouraging Bob to the extent of persuading him to sit down again on his chair. But before he could question Joe, whom he trusted instinctively, about the warning which had been given him, his attention was distracted by the entry of the farmer's daughter, Joan, who came quickly into the room, carrying a basket of eggs, a beautiful girl whose appearance and conduct will be described in the next chapter.

CHAPTER FIVE

INTERESTED in the sight of visitors the girl stood still with basket in hand, bearing butter and eggs. Hair like butter, but corn-furry, lay smooth glistening on back and side of head, on forehead strayed in wisps, a low forehead sweat-pearled, beneath which began a straight nose, a short one, set between fresh cheeks, sweet apple flesh, and then the calling soft mouth, retentive chin—soft material, no more plastic than the sea. Mouth broke to smile and eyes spilt sparkles (Oh, lovely, thought George, that warm mouth, the burstingness of) as she stood still holding the handle of a basket, holding back, knowing the life coiled within, braced and barred by cloth (Oh, long, lovely the straight limbs, George thought, must be, with shapely catenation of breast curves and the flank and sweeping of buttocks), unreluctant to be cloistered, conscious of the oceanic soul tide-heaving through athletic limbs, of the million-volt spark to be generated later, the live maiden, carrying butter and eggs, with no pronounced singularity in gesture or appearance, wearing a green dress rough-woven and clinging to the body, with a yellow collar, through which rose stalk of firm neck, sap-filled columnar, poising head and not flower, a face. Nor was Bob unmoved, but sang:

> ' Ripe corn acres where I was born!
> I understand that's a very nice land, a Paradise, and
> I'm going away South, no more delaying,
> Going to get the honey in my mouth.
> Oh, hist! listen what the wind is saying:
>> "I blow dust in your eyes,
>> gold dust and spice
>> and cherry showers of spray,
>> windflower of orchards on my way,
>> cornflowers and golden dust.

Forlorn no longer must hesitate,
must pack bag rucksack and go,
(not hesitate) but take in your arms
the corn growing high,
the sun in your eye,
and find a nice land." '

and would have continued to sing, forgetting his situation, had
he not heard the farmer ejaculate an oath and found him malevo-
lent the only listener; for George sought the girl with deep looking
below the eyebrows, and she answered him with an inclination
of lids, laying the basket upon the table, while from her ten fingers
seemed to irradiate currents of desire twining, festooning the air
till they met with and gripped some corresponding ectoplasm from
final promontories of George's body. So seemed the blood flow
a wave of force, spangle of live sparks, till they both smiled, deep
knowing the soon effect, and bowed their heads, not wishing now
to shake hands.

Was dusk already and the table spread for supper with cheese
and butter, bread, potatoes, and salt, and rang from somewhere a
great bell warning the countrymen, so Joe said, to be indoors.
Still, helping himself to salt, moved vague across George's mind
the figure of Pushkov and his finger outstretched in warning, but,
conscious as he was of his purpose, he was more immediately
aroused and did not remark the farmer who, in isolation, winked
even at Bob, amused and pleased with his guest, a sign of intimacy
which did much to revive Bob's spirits and encouraged him to eat
enormously and even to address to the farmer some observations
about the weather and about the state of the roads. Soon calmer
George too spoke, provoking Joan, who looked at him with eyes
sad in general, though mouth wavered to smile, foretasting an
instant bliss, but anxious for universal satisfaction. So she asked
for a potato, wide-eyed, rock-faced, though the lips were cracking
to grimace, maidenly, an O, an ocean to be filled by spurtings of
desire.

Supper was soon done, and, with Joe winking at Bob, his satisfied companion without the circuit, they sat for some moments about the fire, not asking many questions, as Joe nodded, guffawed pleasantly, not a pimp, and Bob, outlawed now from George's notice, still was proud, an understanding man ushering, in his conceit, an event; but Joan stared in the fire, in the last embers, cozening what she did not want, delay, reflecting arrogant in her mind a procession of past events, of which George knew none, confident of a future into which she did not peer; and George now easy in a little of his soul, talked, asking the meaning of the bell, and was informed that it was a curfew, driving betimes to bed, as Joe rose, saying daybreak was time to rise and now, the sun having set, the firelight dying, was hour for sleep or something like it; and he led the way upstairs, accommodating his guests, summoning, with wink, good night.

Bob, undressing in room with George, slung guitar on hook behind door, and awestruck did not sing, but remarked sheepish in reprobation: 'You won't be here long,' and 'No' said George, laughing, pulling off his trousers, ready naked to step into the landing, where soon he stepped, when Bob was huddled between blankets, disapproving but resigned. On creaking boards George went on tiptoe, knowing not why, opened door and saw Joan standing upright before a long mirror, naked, fingers plaited behind head, not admiring herself, but sleepy-eyed surveying; and motionless she stood as he entered, raising only heavy eyes in ordinary welcome. Closing door swiftly, swiftly instepping George confronted and circling arm encountered warm curve. He pressed close and his arm gliding upward sank into the waist dip. Kisses are like iron in flowers, and soon they lay lovingly at ease, having exchanged something not them, with minds swirling gradually to peace and a deep a far calling from dear blood to blood, a redintegration.

And before long, opening their eyes, they gazed with greater freedom in each other's faces, and finger tips lightly, as in a childish reverie, traced patterns on flesh that coy shrank from lightest touch, and smiling they uttered endearing words, grateful each to each. At last he offered to give, she to receive, while their scattered manifold of joy rose to a broad breaking wave, delaying the crash, though it throbbed and pulsed in its suspension, then overwhelming broke, plunging them again down to a swirling darkness, a mountain top or an abyss. In ease of satisfaction they lay still; breath heaved them, indicating life, like two coiled snakes. In a long trance they followed their minds in different and meaningless volutions, leaving business to the blood which bound them otherwise together.

Joan's body stirred in delicate protest and George withdrew from her, and turning on his side thrust his arm beneath her neck. So they lay, heads separate, till Joan in a low voice, without stirring, said: 'You do love me, don't you?' Irritated slightly, George grunted 'Yes', and she went on, 'Even though I'm not a virgin.'

George laughed, slowly kissing her eyes, conscious of the warmth below, and she raised her head suddenly, darting a smile, saying: 'You're different from your brothers,' raising her mouth up to his. And her face was so easy with so much friendliness, and yet in the flickering light of the fire that was nearly extinct in the bedroom hearth took on so strange a remote look, softened by shadow and momentarily sharpening in light, that George was bewildered looking at her, for he had communicated with her blood, and was grateful, yet saw in her face something other than their common pledge, a secrecy of her own, which, while it separated her from him, endeared her much more with a fascination in which was reverence, and did not interrupt, but rather furthered, passion. She too, exploring his face with her eyes, then following the lines lazily with her finger tips, saw in it a nobility which she had not suspected, something not from the body which she held, nor from the mind of which she was careless, and pressing close to him she was eased to find him responsive to her embrace. 'You're tired,' she said, 'Don't you want to go to sleep?'

'No,' George said, while his hand passed over, meditating upon, the skin of her back. Then, 'Tell me about yourself, Joan. Did you sleep with my brothers?'

She disengaged herself from his embrace and they lay on their backs, watching the room grow dark. Joan said: 'In the last three years I've had many of the men who've stopped here on their way, but I've never liked any of them. Some are cruel and some are afraid.'

George, contented, opened one eye and said: 'But you didn't have to have them, did you? Not if you didn't want it.'

'I did want it,' she said. 'I don't know why. But I was getting tired of it, and was so glad to see you to-night. You're much the nicest, and I want to marry and settle down.'

'We'll see about that,' George said. 'I don't understand this country yet, or you people who live here. I have some business in the town and intend to go there, although a man called Pushkov has warned me not to go. It's all very mystifying, and I wish you'd help me.'

Joan sat up on the bed and pointing towards her belly said: 'Look! it's white and clear isn't it?' and George stroked the warm softness with finger tips finding firm muscle underneath. She went on: 'If you'd seen any other women in this country, you'd be surprised, because there are very few people whose bellies are like this. Every child born from registered parents, in the country at all events (I don't know what they do in the town), has an owl tattooed just here.' She pointed to the space below the navel, and

94

spoke bitterly: 'It's a sign of slavery, and we'll never be happy while things like that are allowed.' Then, since it was getting cold, she lay down again, pulling the bedclothes over them, and seeking warmth from George's body. She continued: 'So I'm different from the other girls in these parts. My father wasn't always a farmer and, though he never speaks about his early life, I think he once came from abroad and has been to the town. My mother died soon after I was born, but she too, I think, was not a native of this country. If she had been, I should have been branded, because my birth would have been registered. I've often wanted to find out more about my parents, but my father will say nothing, and I can hardly blame him, considering the danger that there is in making indiscreet remarks, and particularly would it be dangerous for him, who is a powerful man in the district, already suspected by the Government.'

'This is all so mysterious,' George said. 'I wish you'd tell me something about the Government.'

Joan sighed. 'It would take too long,' she said, 'and besides you'll hear all about it to-morrow. You will stay, won't you? It would be so nice to get married. Will you promise?'

'I'll stay for to-morrow,' George said, 'and I'll make inquiries. You can't expect me to promise any more than that. You know what I'm after.'

'Yes,' she said, 'and I think it's very brave of you. But, oh I'm not certain that you're going about it the right way. Dear George, I wish I could help you. There's so much you don't know.' And she wept silently for a few moments, till George, a trifle angry, asked why she did not give him some enlightenment.

'No', she said, 'you'll have to wait till to-morrow, and then you'll be able to judge better for yourself. Besides I really don't know how to advise you. But if you're not tired I will tell you something.'

'I'm not tired,' George said, and she laughed: 'I'll tell you about your brothers, shall I?'

'Yes,' said George, 'tell me about them.'

'Rudolph came here two days ago,' she said, 'on the fastest motor bicycle that I've ever seen. He behaved in a courtly and magnificent manner to my father, who was, I'm afraid, rather rude to him. Dad is rude to almost everyone, even to Pushkov, but he seemed to like you. Anyway he began to laugh when Rudolph was telling him of the dangers he had been through already, and of his plans about what he'd do when he made his purpose clear to the Government. Rudolph didn't notice that we were laughing at him (we could see at once that he had no chance), and I saw that he liked me.'

'Doesn't your father ever object to your going to bed with so many people?' George asked and she replied: 'Oh no. Why should he? He knows that there's no risk of any kind. All who come this way are sterile. Even you, my dear,' she said, hugging him, 'though I hope you won't always be.'

'But I'm not,' George protested. 'Does it seem as if I am?' and she could give him no further reply than a shake of the head, telling him that it took some time to get used to the climate, and George pondered on this strange information, conscious of his virility and not at the moment at all disheartened by the reflection that at present there was no danger of his having to provide for a family. Yet all the same, he thought, its very odd and a little humiliating; but of one thing he was quite sure, namely that his success in this article as in much else depended on his conduct in the city, and he began, almost without acknowledging it to himself, to suspect that the Government could dispose of unusual powers over those resident in or entering the country. Joan hugged him again, saying: 'Never mind. I don't love you any the less for that, because I'm sure it will be all right later on. That is, if you will stay and help us. But I'm not to talk about that now, so I'll go on telling you about Rudolph.' She moved closer to him and continued: 'When it was time to go to bed I knew Rudolph would come to my room, but somehow he missed his way in the passage. For a long time he knocked on my father's door, and, though Dad was snoring loud, he did not realize his mistake for some time and he never thought of opening the door. Then I heard him creep down the landing to the door of the lavatory and I think he would have knocked on that door all night if I had not opened my own door, as I was getting cold, and called out to him. He was funny, because he just bowed to me and then waited till I got back into bed, before he came to knock for the first time at the right door. He was still dressed, and he carried a large suitcase. I was going to laugh with him about all the mistakes which he had made, but he was very grave, kissing my hand, as he turned his eyes down to the floor. "Passion knows no laws," he said and then began speaking to me in Italian, and I said "Hadn't you better hurry up?" He bowed again, but I think he was rather shocked. Then he began unpacking his suitcase, and it seemed to be full of revolvers. He took them out very carefully, though I was getting colder and colder, and told me what he had done with each of them; I forget what, but I think he had won a shooting competition somewhere. Anyway he wouldn't come to bed. He put all the revolvers back again and unpacked a silk dressing-gown, and then he took off his coat and waistcoat after he had apologized for undressing in my room. He said: "By Heaven, you have raised such a flame, that I am blind to all else," and he walked backwards and forwards saying much the same things, till I began to despair and said: "Aren't you coming to bed," "God!" he said, kneeling by the bedside, "how can I take advantage of so much beauty, so much purity?" and I saw that he was afraid to take his trousers off. "Some day," he went on, "I shall ask to be allowed to call you

G

mine. I shall work for you, though it's going to be hard. Let me leave you now a tender memory, upon which you will be able to look back with pleasure. I'm a rough sort of a fellow, but my heart is as tender as any woman's"; and he ran out of the room. Poor young man, he was scared nearly out of his wits, and he forgot to take his revolvers with him. But he must have come back for them in the night, because they and he had gone in the morning. He heard what David heard, I expect, and went away to steal the Ambassador's aeroplane. I'm glad you're not like he was, because it's been so nice, hasn't it?'

George kissed her, straining close to her, and then, with muscles relaxed, laughed as he thought of Rudolph's escapade. 'What was it" he asked, 'that David heard?' and now she pressed his arm convulsively, as if in misgiving, and began to speak again: 'David was here last night, and Dad was even ruder to him than he had been to Rudolph, because this time all the conversation was about philosophy. Dad kept asking: "How much bread does that put in your belly?" and David grew quite testy, replying: "I'm not talking about bellies, my dear sir," and Dad said: "It would be a great deal better if you were," till finally we all became silent, but I noticed how David was looking at me, greedy, but pretending not to notice. He never spoke to me at supper and after supper he went to the window and began to read a book. I think he was angry with us because we didn't treat him in some special way; but I quite liked him in his blue suit. When Pushkov called, David didn't think much of him and said that he supposed that even an agitator might get his hair cut. He was always making silly remarks like that, which was the reason why Dad was so rude to him, but he was handsome and I didn't mind.

'As I expected he came to my room. He wore a silk dressing-gown and carried a book with him. There was a nasty expression on his face, partly greedy and partly it seemed as if he were ashamed of himself. He walked straight to the bed and stroked my hair, and then pulled it till it hurt. "Well," he said, "how much do you want?" and I told him that I didn't want anything. "An amateur?" he said. "What a bore!" and then he said that before we started he'd like to try an experiment. So he recited a piece of poetry to me about a nightingale and asked me what I thought of it. I said that I thought it very beautiful, and he said that we were all the same, pretending to admire what we could not possibly understand; and the poor boy was so unpleasant that I had half a mind to go to sleep and tell him to go away; but I saw that he was just being silly.

'He talked even more than Rudolph, saying that he supposed that all this was necessary, though it did seem to him very stupid. He said that the shape of my body was all wrong, and I saw that he didn't really want me any more than Rudolph had done. He said that women always smelt of iodoform and asked me whether I would put on boy's clothes because that, he said, was the only way of making women at all attractive. So I got rather annoyed, and told him that he could take me or leave me, but if he was going to go on talking I was going to sleep. And then I think he was really going to take off his dressing-gown when he heard—but listen, there it is again! O George, don't leave me!' And she clutched his arm, shrinking beneath the bedclothes, while George started up in bed hearing a noise that gradually grew louder.

From a great distance a honking, and mingled with that some harsh metallic notes, a yelping almost of hounds, a strange concert was heard to approach quicker and quicker, and soon a rushing of wings beating up furiously the air was audible and the unearthly honk-honk of the meteoric birds seemed to shake the window panes and the backwash of driving feathers to dispel the room and all visibility, leaving only that dreadful sound of churned air and of demonic voices. Now they were passing the window and the room trembled, quivered as though about to be swept away by that deluge of air and sound, and the voices pierced the brickwork, baying, clanging, honking, with every now and again a clear musical note of an overpowering sweetness. George sprang out of bed, though Joan clung to him, and swung back the window letting into the room a high wind which blew the clothes off the bed, the ornaments off the mantelpiece, and buffetted him backwards till he had to cling to the bedpost, his body whirled in wind arrowed from flying wing-tips, riddled with sound, awed, anxious and delighted with the power of the thing and those notes of clear music. 'Wild geese! wild geese!' he shouted, not thinking of what he meant, his heart bursting with joy, feet eager on the floor, and heard pass away as quickly as it had come the sibilation, the swishing, the strong jangle, and the music.

Then he turned and saw Joan huddled up on the bed, her hands covering her face, in an attitude of utter desolation, and he ran to her, throwing wildly his arms round her, covering her cold body with his kisses, still crying: 'The wild geese! Oh the wild geese!' and she looked up at him doubtful, in need of reassurance, then gladly turned to him, crying out in joy, close clinging. She said: 'Oh, I thought you were going. David heard them, and he cursed me, dragging me about the room by my hair, saying that it was I who had kept him back from what he wanted. And he left at once, when he had kicked me.'

But George, lying still, hardly listened to her. He was saying in a low voice: 'Oh my dear, did you see the room shake? Did you hear those voices?' And she pressed tighter to him, asking with some misgiving: 'And you don't want to go away? You don't want to go after them?'

George laughed, as one with knowledge. 'What's the good? They're miles away. They don't feed near here. It's the marshes they're going to; but first there's the city,' and in delight he gripped her and found her responsive to his embrace.

100

CHAPTER SIX

IT was early when George woke up, but early as it was, he found himself alone. 'Perhaps she has gone to milk the cows,' he thought, glad to notice the scent of her still clinging to the sheets and pillow. He soon got out of bed and, crossing to the window, looked through mist at a sun that had not yet fully risen. The fishy-pink sky, the cool air on his throat, the skeins of mist were familiar to him, and the lowing of the cattle, the trumpeting of cocks he had heard before; and yet, he thought, this is a new land, familiar as it seems, rich and perhaps treacherous, but certainly in the track of events; and he remembered with glee last night's passage of birds. Looking from the window he was surprised to find that the farmhouse was not, as it had seemed to him on his arrival, isolated from other dwellings, but was on the crest of a hill up which climbed the moorland road, while on the opposite side, towards which this part of the building faced, was a gentle declivity, misty now, but not so misty as wholly to disguise branches of cherry trees and the chimneys of cottages. For some time George stood staring at the village, waiting for some sign of life, while the vigour of sunrays increased and revealed more clearly here a patch of grey wall and there a glitter of tiles; fires were being lit within some of the low buildings from which coiled gently little wisps of smoke, and, as the sun rose higher, the lowing of unseen cattle, the crowing of hidden cocks, became more and more insistent, but the inhabitants of the village were not abroad yet or else they were out of sight lower down the hill, and George began to smile at his own unreasonable eagerness to see figures going in and out of doors. 'Of course the men have been up and about for hours,' he said to himself; 'only the women are indoors lighting fires to cook breakfast,' and he ran quickly along the passage to his own room, where Bob was still asleep, and, when he was dressed, went downstairs, noticing on his way that Joe's bedroom door was open, and concluding that he too was busy about his work.

He found his way by the back of the building to a rough paved track which led down the hill into the mist, and was soon walking between rows of grey cottages variously dilapidated. Some of the doors were without hinges and were either leant-to or propped against the sides of the houses, leaving views of empty rooms; thatches were thin and, where roofs were tiled, many of the tiles were missing; in almost every window the panes were broken or cracked, and it was only the carefully cultivated flower-beds in front of the cottages, and the few wisps of smoke that rose from some chimneys, which offered any reason to believe that the place was inhabited.

George went farther down the hill into deeper mist, neither seeing nor hearing any living beings, but when he had passed the last of the twenty or thirty cottages he heard from below him what seemed to be the sound of a steam-siren and at the same time was aware of steps approaching him up the hill. There came into view a figure dressed in a policeman's uniform of blue serge wearing on his head a helmet of some transparent crystal material, while at his side swung a truncheon that was the oddest truncheon which George had ever seen, for it appeared to be made of straw. What was equally remarkable was that this policeman (for his clothes and the initials C.I.D. on the lapel of his tunic seemed to indicate him as such) had a face that was continually being ruffled by the drollest possible expressions; at one moment he was grinning, then smiling, then laughing heartily and then grave as a judge about to make some excellent joke. The policeman looked carefully at George, and while his attention was concentrated there was intelligence and cunning in his idiotic face; then he stopped, clicked his heels together and saluted, at the same time winking with one eye. George looked at him in astonishment, while the policeman turned aside and laughed behind the shelter of his hand, though, without any doubt, he was not really reluctant to allow George to see that he was laughing at him. He spoke in a casual, drawling, well-educated voice: 'Coming with us?', then bent forward in a paroxysm of laughter, straightened up again and looked with a mock gravity at George's ears.

George had disliked the look of the man from the first, and now said sternly: 'Coming where to?' and the policeman, as he said: 'Why to the town of course,' endeavoured to compose his face into something amiable and stood still for a second or two without laughing.

George was half-inclined to accept the offer of assistance on the next stage of his journey, but several considerations held him back. First of all it would have been ungracious to depart without having seen Joan and her father; then George felt that, whether wisely or unwisely, he had undertaken a responsibility for Bob at least until he had seen him safe to the town; and finally what influenced his mind more still, perhaps, was a suspicion that he might be entering upon difficulties with which, in his present state of ignorance and unpreparedness, he would be unable to cope. He was pretty well aware that hostility existed between the Government and at least some sections of the agricultural population, and saw that, before he went farther, it would be advisable for him to discover, so far as he was able, the reasons for and the extent of this hostility. He had been assured over the wireless that his brother David was content in the town, but could he trust either the wireless or his brother David? On the other hand Joan had begged him to remain with her, and, though he had no intention of terminating his travels until he had attained his object, he had enough respect for Joan's advice to make up his mind that he would stay in the country at least until he was better informed of what was at the back of her mind, when she urged him not to follow the example of his brothers. So he said to the policeman: 'I'm sorry to have troubled you, but I don't expect to go to the town to-day. There are a few things I have first to do here.'

At these words the policeman trembled all over and looked at George as though he were some monster. He then bowed and, attempting to kiss George's hand, which was withdrawn, said: 'Kindly accept, your Majesty, my profoundest respects,' and went dancing back down the lane, tittering. He went with such rapidity that George, who, after having stood still for an instant, had followed him, was quite unable to catch him up, and could not even hear the sound of his steps through the mist, which became denser as he descended.

The departure of the policeman had been even more startling than his first appearance and George was inclined to be despondent as he recalled to his mind that ironic laughter, wondering whether, perhaps, he had not been stupidly cautious, whether, perhaps, he might not have made a miscalculation likely to cost him dear; but he soon shook off his depression when he considered that by accepting the invitation he would not only have put himself into the hands of a police force whose representative appeared to be thoroughly untrustworthy, but would also have been guilty of great ingratitude and unkindness to his friends at the farm house. Still he was puzzled and was still seeking some explanation for the unsolicited attentions of the police when he heard with greater distinctness the sound of a siren and now could distinguish through the mist shapes in front of him, some stationary and some moving figures.

Abruptly the mist gave way and he stood before a visible landscape. Directly in front of him stretched as far as his eyes could see a broad cemented road, running into a remote distance between wide fields of young corn. Along this road moved a procession of the beetle shapes of lorries, an innumerable quantity of them, of which the nearer ones, he could see, were loaded with milk cans, meat, vegetables, and dead rabbits. The last of the lorries was, apparently, just being loaded, for it stood at the terminus of the road, alongside a raised platform on which jostled and shouted a crowd of country folk, men and women, amongst whom George recognized the burly figure of Joe, who, aided by his daughter, was hoisting a large milk can on to the lorry. There were shouts as some bale, package, can, or parcel was packed in its appropriate position, but otherwise the work went on silently, and the men and women stood, handing articles to each other in a chain, dumb and automatic, performing what was evidently a routine task under the supervision of two or three of the oddly dressed policemen who stood in a group, laughing at the peasants as they pointed out to each other features or gestures which might appear ridiculous. And, indeed, George thought, there was a curious contrast to be observed between the straight excellently constructed road, the long capacious lorries, the efficiency of organization, and the hard dumb faces of the farmers, their hastily thrown-on clothes, their harassed wives; and he thought with wonder of the poverty of their cottages and of the amount of work they must have done already, if they had loaded that vast train of lorries that was vanishing into the distance, bearing fresh farm produce towards, he supposed, the town.

Joan saw him and waved her hand, smiling, and George walked across the platform through the crowd of peasants, of whom some looked at him with interest or mistrust, whilst most seemed not to notice the stranger, so busy were they in putting the last loads on the lorry. By the time that George had come up to Joan and her father the work was finished, and the police officers, blowing kisses

105

and laughing, sprang into positions by the side of the driver or on top of the freight. George found it impossible to recognize the officer with whom he had spoken, so alike were they all with their distorted faces and empty-looking eyes. He felt a great repugnance for these apparently pleasant fellows, and when one of them, just as the lorry was about to start, leant out and, making a clucking noise, began to pull Joan, who was standing at the edge of the platform, towards him, he stepped forward and aimed a blow at the policeman's face, while the crowd, showing no emotion of any kind, took one step backward and observed the policeman dodge so that George's fist crashed into the hard wood of the lorry, which immediately moved forward. George was nursing his damaged fist when the police officer peered out and, with an expression that was as near to being genial as was possible in an almost completely characterless face, made a long nose at the company.

Till the lorry was out of sight, the countrymen stood silent, shading their eyes, as they watched the procession of their produce; then they turned hurriedly to go home, though many of them looked, as they were turning, at George and winked approvingly, and one or two came up to shake him by the hand. George, when he realized that by mishitting at the policeman he had performed an action likely to be regarded as meritorious, began to make light of the affair, though he was glad that he had done something to make himself a figure of some importance among the country folk, and did not stop to think that, while he had hurt his own hand, he had in no way injured the person he had assailed and that, for all he knew, the policeman might have been restrained by official orders from doing anything but deride the affront which had been offered to the force. So he easily accepted the felicitations of two of three young men who, after having shaken him by the hand, began to compliment him on his courage. 'There's nothing in that,' he said. 'What I can't understand is why you don't knock these fellows on the head yourselves. Look at the way they behave.'

Here he was disconcerted by hearing Joe's voice at his elbow, 'Come away, you fool!' and by Joan pulling his coat from behind. He turned round, but not before he had seen the two young fellows with whom he had been talking exchange a significant look and hurry off in a direction different from that followed by the rest of the country folk.

'You young fool,' said Joe, and interested George by speaking without any hint in his wording or intonation that he was in reality what he pretended to be, a farmer, 'can't you see that you're talking to spies? Do you think any of us would congratulate you on behaving like a perfect lunatic? Lucky for you you only hurt yourself.'

George, recollecting at the same time the pain in his injured hand, was a trifle indignant to find his exploit treated so contemptuously and said: 'Why? I'm not scared of a policeman, even though all of you seem able to put up with a lot.'

'Able to put up with it,' Joe repeated, relapsing, as he wrinkled up his fleshy eyes in a kind of grim amusement, into his old bucolic voice, 'Mind what I say, squire. One or two men can't declare war.'

'There's no need for you to go on calling me "squire",' said George. 'I can see that you're not a farmer yourself. And how do you know that the police are so dangerous? I don't believe anyone has ever been near them.' He stopped and noticed Joan looking at him sadly. 'Shall I bind up your hand?' she said, and he realized that his knuckles were bleeding freely. But he was irritated with her (unreasonably), with Joe, and all the other country folk who were plodding ahead of them up the lane, now laughing amongst themselves, and occasionally stopping to look round and stare at him. They were fine creatures, the men in big boots, trousers, and shirts of blue, red, and black, with massive shoulders, and the women buxom, broad-backed; but in spite of strong jaws and steady eyes their faces in apathy were, thought George, disheartening to look at, and sometimes unpleasant when a little point of suspicion would seem for an instant to slit across their beautiful eyes, a wound soon healed, but an indication of dissolution. Between these ordinarily simple faces and the shrewd honesty of Joe's fat-ringed features there was a marked unlikeness, and George was more certain that ever, while he studied the peasants, that Joe was not quite one of them. Consequently he was more than ever angry at Joe's refusal to take him into his confidence and made no reply to his remark : 'Seems like there're some things the young squire don't know yet,' though the remark was accompanied by a jolly laugh and a slap on the shoulder.

So they proceeded to the house in silence. On the way Joan looked at George reproachfully and Joe occasionally chuckled to himself, but George paid no attention to either of his companions, being strangely upset by his encounter with the police, conscious of the pain in his hand, and angry with Joe and the whole village for their baffling behaviour. However as they climbed up the hill into the sunlight his temper became easier and he reflected that he was being angry for no good reason, since, for all he knew, everything that Joe had said and done had been with the kindest possible intentions, while Joan, who had given him signal proof of her confidence, was undoubtedly his friend, and, as for the peasants, how could he expect them to show much interest in a stranger? Yet his mind was disturbed (a fact which he put down, perhaps correctly, to the irritating conduct of the police officer) and he had lost the joy with which he had begun the day that succeeded so delightful and promising a night. He determined that, after breakfast, he would insist on some kind of an explanation of the state of affairs in this district.

CHAPTER SEVEN

AT the threshold of the farm George ran into Bob who said, 'I'm in on this too,' and then, pointing his thumb towards the front room, 'Who's the mystery man? I wish they'd cut that part.'

George looked into the room and saw standing by the fire-place a man in a chauffeur's cap, coat buttoned high, motor goggles and a black beard. His long fingers drummed the mantelpiece and every now and again he stared sombrely at Joe who was sitting in an arm-chair, smoking his pipe.

'Come in,' said Joe, when he saw them. 'Now's the time to talk,' and he seated them at the table, himself drawing up his chair opposite to George and leaving the chair facing Bob, who smiled contemptuously at the proceedings, vacant for the stranger who, after he had secured the doors, sat down and removing cap, coat, beard, and eyebrows revealed himself as Pushkov.

'Well, if that's not a quick change!' said Bob. 'Reminds me—'

'Keep quiet!' said the farmer, but Bob, knowing that his host was not dangerous, no longer was frightened by his words, and simply shrugged his shoulders, muttering something about clod-hoppers and that he wouldn't be there long anyway.

'Let him stay,' said Pushkov, in answer to an inquiring glance from the farmer. 'He may be useful and deserves a chance. He turned suddenly to George. 'And now what are you going to do?'

George said: 'You seem to know a lot about me, and you must know that my way lies through the town. I'm going there certainly.' Here Joe, nodding his head, looked at Pushkov, who tightened his lips and said: 'Ah-ha.' George continued: 'But before I go I want to have all the information that I can obtain. I can see that there is a certain amount of hostility between some of you people here and the Government in the city, and I'd be very grateful to you if you would explain to me what it is all about. I don't promise to take sides, but I should like to know whom I can trust, since, as you must be aware, it is exceedingly important for me not to act mistakenly once I get to the town. But if you can convince me that I should be doing best in helping you, naturally I shall help you as best I can. May I ask a few questions and be sure that you are willing to take me into your confidence?'

Pushkov brought his fist crashing to the table. 'We want men like you,' he said. 'I will tell you for why. I will tell you,' he continued, puckering his eyes and leaning across the table, 'a story which—'

Joe interrupted. 'Let him ask his questions. Time enough for all that at the meeting,' and Pushkov sat back silent, gloomily nodding.

'Well, first of all,' said George, 'I should like to know how Rudolph could have been in two places at once. You say he was here two nights before I arrived, but two nights before I arrived he was getting ready to leave our town, which, by the way, is, according to your standards of measurement, 30,000 miles away.'

Pushkov looked puzzled but Joe smiled and said, speaking in the voice unlike that of a farmer which sometimes he affected or resumed: 'I can do my best to answer that question, though you'll probably have to go to the town before you're much wiser. We here live by the sun and seasons, and walk from house to causeway or barn. These are our normal directions, and that is the kind of people we are. So to you we must seem quite ordinary and you don't notice that our times and spaces are calculated in a different manner from any which you know. With us space is a matter of direction. In some directions the going is good, in others more difficult. It is 30,000 miles from here to your town, if, that is, you are going backwards; but you got here quite easily.

'Time, too, depends on the person. We simple farmers see the sun and follow him, but in the town the sun matters very little. It is only the wireless authorities and those responsible for the food supply who pay any attention to our day. In other districts time is quite different, being interwoven with space and depending, as you can easily see, on the direction which each individual takes. So there are results which would surprise you and used to surprise me till I became a farmer. You will find men whom one might have expected to be old, babies or unborn, because having reached a certain point they have from then onwards turned backwards in our space-time. There is nothing, then, surprising about your brother Rudolph. He was here before he started, going forward in space and backwards in time. The motion of his bicycle was contrary to the motion of his own self. Some would say that he had never been here at all, but of course we know that he has. That young man travels great distances, but so slowly that he gets to his destination long before he has started. Its a great pity and I prefer to take sun and seasons for my clock and mind the animals. Do you understand?' He spoke clearly, but with a great effort as though he were remembering some useless piece of knowledge, learnt long ago, and now painfully dragged to mind from below memory. Pushkov looked at him respectfully, though at the conclusion of the speech he had said: 'I wish to make it quite clear that this has nothing to do with me. I am not responsible in any way.'

George answered Joe's question: 'No, I can't say that I do quite understand. It seems to me that we are talking about different things. But there must be some common standard, a foot-rule, say, for space, and the sun, which you seem to think belongs to you, for time.'

111

Joe sighed and went on speaking laboriously: 'No foot rules here,' he said, 'and most people don't like the sun. Why should they? They're not farmers. But you miss the point. We think that we are more important than bits of metal. Space is regulated by possible acceleration, time by exactitude of direction. That's what I learnt. We're all right here, but I don't know what they do in the town.'

'Then,' said George, 'there's nothing for you to go by.'

'Sun and seasons, sir; sun and seasons,' said Joe, relapsing into his old voice, indicating that he had said all that he had to say on this subject.

George smiled at him and said: 'I don't quite understand, and perhaps I needn't bother about metaphysics just yet. But when did I arrive here?'

'You slept here last night, squire,' said Joe. 'That's all I know, and for you it may not have been what I call last night. Sure I don't know how much older you are than when you left your town; but I shouldn't say you're much younger.'

George shrugged his shoulders and Bob leant towards him across the corner of the table: 'Say, let's leave these loonies and get along to the big city,' but George was far too interested in what he had heard to think of anything but further questions so he said to Bob, 'Go and practise your songs outside. There's more I want to hear.' And Bob sprang up and went out strumming his guitar, after he had bowed ironically to Pushkov, who glared at him and said in a whisper to George, after Bob had left the room, 'Wants watching. Mark you that.'

George laughed and said: 'Bob's all right. But let me ask you another question. What were you all doing so early this morning? Who were those policemen, and were all the lorries going to the town?'

'That's a long story' said Joe, and Pushkov sprang to his feet

112

and paced twice or thrice across the room. He seemed to be deliberating in his own mind, and, as if in mental agitation, ran his fingers through his thick upright hair, while his eyes searched every corner of the room. Finally he stood still, and, propping himself on fingers outstretched to the table, stared sternly at George. 'It is a story,' he said, 'of death, a story of what to every woman is worse than death, a story, which, if you please, I will relate.'

Here Bob's head appeared above the window-sill and his beautiful clear voice rang out:—

'Don't tell stories until it's dark.
Don't tell those stories you love so to tell
Until it's dark, till hark! there goes the bell:
    Nine, ten, eleven!
    Isn't it heaven
To hear those lovely stories you love so to tell?'

At the unexpected interruption Pushkov had hastily resumed his disguise and had then concealed himself in a cupboard, from which Joe pulled him reluctant, and then, cursing at Bob, drove him away. George was concerned to notice in the agitator's face no amusement at the trick which had been played on him and no enmity towards its author, only a terrified surprise, which convinced George that he had to do with a man used to the imagination of danger, though whether he was more idealist than charlatan was still, in George's opinion, a doubtful point.

Pushkov sat down and wagging his long finger in George's face, began to speak: 'You may laugh at me, but if you knew what I know you would do something else. I will tell you for why. Certain measures may at any moment be taken against certain people and there are other people who are always ready to provide the right moment for the taking of those measures. Ah-ha, it cuts both ways, though.'

'How do you expect the squire to understand you?' said Joe. 'Cut it short.'

Pushkov seemed to lose some of his nervous agitation when he heard Joe's friendly voice. With great dignity, he bowed and began to follow his advice.

'Many years ago, he said, 'there were living in this district hardy husbandmen, people like ourselves, though I, for one, in the present state of affairs, have certain other tasks to do. Enough of that. These people lived in innocence and plenty, happy with their crops, their wives and children, pious and industrious without kings or priests. And why were they happy? I will tell you for why. They had not heard of the town. One day, and it was many years ago (don't ask me how many), certain visitors, oh very interesting people, came into the country. They offered, what do you think? blue beads to the country folk and announced that their visit could be accounted as good fortune, since they were subjects of a powerful king who would confer the greatest possible benefits on those who would swear fealty to him and embrace the religion of his forefathers. Then they did, oh the kindest possible thing. When from their packing-cases they had distributed all the blue beads, they began to unpack their Lewis guns, with which they killed those countrymen who would not swear allegiance to their king. There were then (and perhaps there are now) two parties in the country, of which one was for resisting to the death, and to the death it might well have been, for the townsmen had better armaments and, though numerically the weaker, had (and have) enormous mechanical strength, while the other regarded the townsmen as gods, as superior beings, likely to be beneficent. Traitors! Oh worms! They sold our liberty. And for why? Ask the sixty-pounders.'

Here Pushkov rose from the table and, taking his head in his hands, shook it, a gesture which would have impressed George had he not fancied that he detected in the agitator something too much of the histrionic, though when he looked at Joe's grave face, he was not so sure that Pushkov's frenzy might not have some important cause with which he would be to his advantage acquainted. Pushkov sat down again and his eyes were wilder, while he thrust out his rocky lean sensitive jaw.

'The rest is easy, he said. 'We received the benefits which had been promised us. No sooner had the first townsmen established themselves in the country than they sent for what we might have expected, their guns, their police, and their priests. We were told to respect the deity of the town. Perhaps you know what that deity is?'

George shook his head and Pushkov, leaning farther forward, whispered through restricted lips: 'It is a Wild Goose.' He paused while George stared at him in incredulity, then brought his fist down on the table and shouted: 'But it's stuffed!' He was silent again and to George's eager questions would only reply: 'I can say no more. Not now at any rate. Perhaps there will come a time. But I ought to know. I have been in the Convent.'

Joe, taking his pipe from his mouth and shifting uneasily his great weight, interrupted: 'Tell him about that afterwards,' and Pushkov nodded and went on with the history.

'A great portion of our people,' he said, 'was taken away into slavery. Inside the town they now work in factories, making beads and cigarettes for us, and for the townsmen instruments of science, utility, and torture. Consequently, since our district was annexed, the wealth and power of the town have grown enormously. Now mark you this. Who feeds the town? We do. Every day the inhabitants of this district get up long before dawn, to pack and see carried to the town the greater portion of the produce of their farms. What do we get in return? Cigarettes, blue beads, and a repulsive medical attendance, things which we never wanted before the annexation.

'You ask me about the policemen. Simple fellows they look,

115

laughing at everyone, but their cunning is diabolical, and they have no notion of morality. How many of the farmers can confidently call their children their own? I have heard of honest girls raped by these villains who laughed at them continuously while they were performing their wickedness and who afterwards, laughing heartlessly, deserted those whom they had deflowered. Their laughter is a dangerous, but not always a deadly, weapon. Their truncheons, made apparently of straw, their helmets, ornamented apparently with crystal, are vehicles for the most potent electrical forces. And mark you this. These policemen are among the minor government officials. Subordinate to them are secret service agents of all kinds and above them are men of science, politicians, and ministers of religion capable of exerting terrific power. This much, for the present, I will tell you. Every agricultural instrument is magnetized and can be controlled from the town. Every child born in the country, has, by order of the medical authorities, an owl tattoed on its belly. In every household there are spies. Not far away there are prisons where some people have been tickled to death.

'You will have noticed the dilapidation of our houses. I will tell you for why. No longer can we get from the town tiles for our roofs, hinges for our doors, or glass for our windows. They send us cigarettes instead.'

Pushkov rose to his feet and, raising one hand, delivered his peroration. 'But the time is coming. I will not say it is yet come, but come it most certainly will when certain events will take place. Perhaps you will understand me when I say that, in spite of spies, there exists here a certain organization. Later in the day I will take you to a meeting. We have been training for years. Arms have been smuggled. Everything has been done with the utmost secrecy. It may be to-morrow, it may be next month, it may be five years hence. But the time will come when we shall strike and all the sixty-pounders will not stop us.

116

'I have spent my life in politics. I have, when I was a little boy, seen the police raid our village. They stripped the women naked, painted them green, and threw them into the horse pond. My friends have been shot without trial, in castles have been tickled with feathers till they were mad. Others have had their finger-nails pulled out till they betrayed their friends. Others still have taken the bribe, the gold of the town, and may their bodies stink on earth, their souls rot in hell! Willy Bright, Freda Harrison, Patrick More, Gobolov, and Abdallah! Immortal names! Slain, and by whom? By their friends. Mark you, it will not be for nothing. Even the ghosts are on our side.'

He ceased and looked at George, pathetic behind the too protuberant features of his sensitive face. George had been impressed but was still puzzled, reflecting that it was only the eccentric agitator who had given him an account of the situation and wondering how far his complaints were justified or his assertions true. The disguises, the rhetoric, the egoism of Pushkov he found repellent, but not half so repellent as the police force, about whom he had heard what he was quite willing to believe, except that he doubted the possibility of their straw truncheons being really so dangerous as they were supposed to be. He looked at Joe and saw him blowing his nose with movements that were like the wiping away of tears, and he became more ready to believe in Pushkov's story.

'Please forgive me,' he said, 'if I don't appear as affected as I might be by what you have told me. You know that I am a stranger and that this is the first coherent account that I have heard of the political situation. I can believe everything you say about the police; but I shall have to have time to reflect about the rest. I'd like very much to go to the meeting with you, so that I can have a chance of estimating the revolutionary feeling. But before we go there, I wish you would tell me something about the Convent and how you came to be there.'

117

Both Joe and Pushkov seemed pleased with this speech, 'Dear old man,' said Pushkov, 'we don't expect you to make up your mind until you've seen something more. But, mark you, there are certain people who will be doing their best to induce you to make up your mind in the wrong way. Enough! I will tell about the Convent. I was there for some years, teaching music and elementary mathematics; for (I was a foolish boy at the time) I had left my village and had promised myself a distinguished career in the town. I don't want to boast, but I would like you to meet those who have heard me play the pianoforte. My examination results were excellent and I was popular with my pupils, although I did my best to restrain the gross immorality with which that place seethes like a—' (he searched for a simile, found it) 'like a cesspool. One day I was going to give a concert in a concert room (a magnificent building) adjoining the Anserium. Not long before I was to appear the senior classical master, on his bicycle, passed me in the street. He handed me a card on which was written: "Perhaps you've forgotten about the musical show. Don't bother to come if you don't want to." My suspicions were aroused. A plot, I saw, was being made to secure my dismissal and I had little doubt of why my presence was unwelcome to the other masters. Listen to this. The brother of the senior classical master had been in the Grenadier Guards as a private. A private, mark that. It's important. But the senior classical master alluded to his brother as an officer in the Coldstream Guards. On these occasions I would keep silent, but his behaviour that morning led me to believe that he knew that I knew.

'In spite of the classical master I kept my appointment at the concert. But there was no audience. My enemies were before me and had announced that the concert would take place at another date. In the huge auditorium there was just one policeman, roaring with laughter.

118

'Next day I was dismissed. I appealed to the headmaster, but he had resigned and the new headmaster informed me that he knew nothing of the affair, but fancied that the Commissioner of Police had something against me. I saw the Commissioner of Police, who showed me a signature, covering the rest of the letter. "Is this your signature?" he said and I said "Why, yes," and found I was convicted on a charge of illicit distribution of obscene photographs, this being a monopoly of the Government. The letters must have been forged, but I was never allowed to see them. I suspected the hand of the senior classical master.

'That is the story of my career in the Convent. With one thing I reproach myself, that I did not, while I was there, make a stronger protest against the system which prevails there. Shall I tell you what that system is? It is a terrible thing." He leant across the table and pronounced his words slowly in a low voice: 'The pupils in the Convent, thanks to a scientific operation, are able to fulfil the functions of both sexes.' He paused, nodding his head. 'Terrible, is it not. Boys and girls they are called, but it is not by any means so simple as that.'

George had been attempting to adjust his mind to the complexities of Pushkov's story in such a way that he could receive some clear impression of the Convent in which, as he had been informed, his brother David was now residing, but the agitator had spoken so rapidly, had, by significant gestures, hinted at so much that he had not verbally expressed that George was only slightly less ignorant than before, having learnt only that the Convent was a kind of Academy for young people, whose morals were, in Pushkov's view, unusually lax. He was about to make some further inquiries when the door opened and Joan came into the room, smiling at him with great tenderness. She put a letter into his hands and, while he opened it, she looked anxiously at Pushkov and at her father. They all stared at George, silent, as he, after glancing in some astonishment at the expensive note-paper ornamented lavishly with monograms and coats-of-arms, began to read:—

'Dear Brother George: I should have written to you before now if I had not thought that by this time you would have been with us. Now I hear that you are being delayed by the people at the farm and am, at the request of the headmaster, writing to urge you to come to the Convent as quickly as possible.

'You will receive a cordial welcome and will, no doubt, set off at once when I tell you that I fancy that I have attained the object of our pursuit. τὰ καλὰ, I am inclined to believe are not χαλεπά. Good things can be obtained quite easily. But perhaps you have not forgotten your Greek.

'The people you are staying with are dangerous, except for the old man, who is fairly harmless. His daughter, who forced me to deflower her, is probably trying the same on you. I fancy she is diseased. You may also meet a certain Pushkov, a revolutionary, and I should advise you to keep clear of him. Everything about his activities is known to the police and in any case he is not a very interesting character. He was sacked from the Convent, I think, because he couldn't play the piano. Confident of seeing you to-day or to-morrow,

I am, dear brother,

Your devoted and I think I may say successful,
David.'

He laid the letter on the table and asked his friends' opinion. 'It is forged,' said Pushkov, 'and I think I know by whom.' 'Nonsense,' said Joe, 'that young rat of a brother of yours wrote it all right. He's just the sort they want in their convent.' Joan simply laughed and said: 'What a funny letter.' But George could not discuss it so easily as that. What, he wondered, did David mean (for he had no doubt about the authenticity of the letter) by saying that he fancied that he had attained the object of the pursuit? If he had really been so successful, George thought, would he not be more confident of his success? What was the meaning of that 'I think I may say'? Then, he reflected, whatever might be the truth about Pushkov, David's story about Joan was much less credible than the story which Joan had told last night about David. All David's remarks might be, for all he knew, equally malicious, and the fact that he was writing, so he said, at the request of the headmaster seemed to indicate that, if left to himself, he would not have been over-anxious to communicate with his brother. But against all this must be set the certainty that David was very well pleased with himself where he was, and his statement that the police knew everything about Pushkov, in spite of his vaunted secrecy, seemed to show that the town Government was quite as strong as Pushkov had represented it to be. And David was apparently in with the Government, consequently in a good position to help his brother to go beyond the city, should he find it necessary to do so (for George was exceedingly doubtful about what David had termed his success).

More puzzled than ever George put the letter in his pocket and suggested to Pushkov that they should go on to the meeting, after which he would give his decision whether to help the revolutionaries by staying on at the farm or to go forward by himself. Joan, he saw, was looking imploringly at him as he rose to his feet to accompany Pushkov and her father. He crossed the room to her and kissed her, while Pushkov looked on approvingly, but she was ill at ease, saying, 'It will be terrible for both of us, if you go, George. Oh, why can't you see that?'

'If I do go, I'll soon come back,' said George. 'I feel sure I shall want to help you and not any government which employs those policemen.' But she said: 'Oh you're so stupid. What do you think you can do by yourself? You want to get away from me, that's all,' and George went out of the room, on the way to the political meeting, irritated with her.

CHAPTER EIGHT

Leaving the room they encountered Bob, and, while Joe and Pushkov went on ahead, George endeavoured to persuade his friend to come with them to the meeting, telling him that however certain he might feel that his fortune lay waiting for him in the town, it was worth while at least to make inquiries about how the countrymen were treated by the authorities into whose hands they were about to commit themselves as strangers; and he added that, since their journey was sure to be dangerous, they would lose nothing by seeking information which might enable them to know the precise dangers which were to be expected.

At the mention of danger Bob had grown pale, and now he clung again to George's sleeve, losing the self-confidence which he had shown previously. 'Oh sir,' he said, 'you don't say. I'll come to the meeting all right, and I hope I haven't offended the Bolshie gentleman. Its just that no one likes my songs here and I didn't want to see you entangled with the young lady. I just thought that we'd make more money in the town.'

'I daresay you will,' said George. 'There are sure to be bands in the town. All I say is that we ought to know what we're doing.'

'O yes, sir,' said Bob, 'you're quite right. I'll take notes.' And he pulled from his pocket a pencil and note-book, accompanying George gladly and chattering continuously while George watched in front of him the broad back of Joe, the lean back of Pushkov, having much upon which to reflect.

He was particularly pleased at the opportunity of seeing some of the peasants other than Joe and the two young men, reputed spies, with whom he had spoken after his adventure with the

122

policeman; for, after all, he thought, how do I know that apart from Joe, who is clearly an unusual person, and Pushkov, who seems disgruntled by the way he has been treated at the Convent, the peasants are not really contented with their lives and do not regard the Government, whatever its failings may be, as a quite tolerable institution? He thought then of the poverty of their dwellings and of their hard, resigned, occasionally cunning faces and was convinced that, if the wealth and power of the town were what they were said to be, all was certainly not well. But still, he thought, if anything is to be accomplished there must be audacity, resolution, even a kind of ferocity among the peasantry, and what I want to find out is whether Pushkov and his organization have succeeded in fostering these qualities.

His reflections were interrupted by the sight of a small group of peasants, going in the same direction, who met them and exchanged short greetings with Joe and Pushkov, then nodded at George, disregarding Bob, though he bowed elaborately to them and began to play the Marseillaise on his guitar. They were strong men, with huge hands, massive-faced, except for one of them, a man younger than the rest, whose small head and alert features interested George, while his bold eyes seemed to denote unusual resolution. He was introduced as Comrade Alfred and, shaking George's hand, he smiled cordially, then, turning to Pushkov, said: 'All's well in my district, Comrade. We're holding a giant rally on Sunday and expect to enrol two more members. Things are beginning to move.'

He spoke with great enthusiasm, but Pushkov only nodded gloomily, seeming almost to resent the enthusiasm of the younger man. 'The priest,' he said, 'are we going to have that holy man at the meeting?'

'The Rev. Hamlet?' said Alfred. 'I'm afraid so. He gets on so well with the women that the comrades won't turn him out. As

123

a matter of fact some of them like him, too. He's been calling himself a revolutionary.' Alfred snorted in indignation, and Pushkov shrugged his shoulders, saying: 'When I see a priest on a revolutionary platform, I think of the quickest way to get him off it!'

By now they had reached the barn, a building isolated from other dwellings or any cover, where the meeting was to be held. The barn was full of people, men and women, huddled together, the men with pipes protruding from heavy non-committal faces, the women looking gloomily to the ground, waiting with no impatience. There was little indication of enthusiasm, some of misgiving; for every minute or so a man would peer out of door or window anxiously, afraid, probably, of police surveillance. At one end of the barn was a small table where two men, a clergyman, whom George assumed to be the Rev. Hamlet, and a stocky farmer smoking a pipe, were sitting. Pushkov and Alfred forced their way through the crowd to this table and sat down on the two vacant chairs, leaving Joe, with George and Bob, standing at the back of the barn. 'That's the Rev. Hamlet,' Joe explained, 'in the dog collar. Used to live here, but he's been to the town.' He nodded significantly. 'The other man is Comrade Stanley. He's chairman.'

Stanley rose to his feet and shouted: 'If the Comrades will be silent, we will proceed with the business.' Nearly everyone had been silent previously; indeed George thought that he had never attended so apathetic a meeting. But Alfred's appearance and enthusiasm had encouraged him to believe, against appearances, that this organization meant business. So he listened intently to Stanley's next words, watching closely the thickset man who still clenched a pipe between the teeth at the corner of his mouth, and with somewhat inexpressive eyes sought the roof of the barn while he was speaking. 'First of all,' he said, 'we will hear the district reports. I may as well give an account of my own district. Everything is going very well, I think. Very well indeed.' Here Bob clapped and the rest of the audience looked round at him in surprise; but Stanley continued, without having noticed, apparently, the interruption: 'I don't think I need say any more. Everything is going quite satisfactorily. And now—'

Alfred sprang to his feet and in a louder voice: 'Surely the Comrades have a right to a fuller account. How many new members have been enrolled? What mass demonstrations have been made? I would like to know this. Are we planning for our own lives or for our great-grandchildren?'

He sat down and George looked at the faces of the audience, surprised to find them almost as expressionless as before, though here and there lips round pipes would curl to the beginnings of a smile, and one man, in front of George, after withdrawing his pipe from his mouth and knocking out the ash, whispered to his neighbour 'Rare young lad, Alfred' and giggled.

'Order! Order!' said Stanley. 'No one has done more for the comrades than I have, and I think I still have their confidence.' (A few hands were clapped together.) 'Everything is going very nicely, very nicely indeed. I call upon Comrade Alfred to give us a short account of his district.'

Alfred rose, angrily glaring at the chairman, seeking sympathy from Pushkov, who sat with his legs extended in front of him, frowning. The Rev. Hamlet had said 'hear, hear' once or twice and listened to every word with a somewhat demonstrative attention. Alfred spoke: 'Comrades, is it to be this year, next year, or sometime never? That is the question we have all to ask ourselves. I, with the authority of Comrade Pushkov, if not of our chairman, have in my district kept the immediate future always in mind. Yet in my district I have only three members of the party, and thirty probationary members. It is not good enough. The police laugh at what we do and well they may when our chairman himself is content with evolution instead of revolution. (Cry of 'Shame!' from the Rev. Hamlet). Yes, it is a shame for us to have a priest on a revolutionary platform. It is—"

'Order! Order!' cried Stanley, while the farmers grinned at each other and winked, 'I cannot have any unpleasantness. I must request Comrade Alfred to sit down, and call upon Comrade Pushkov to deliver his monthly address.'

Alfred remained standing and sought sympathy in the audience who were, to George's astonishment and dismay, when not apathetic, merely amused, but seeing that Pushkov was already on his feet and was evidently not going to assist him he sat down heavily, banging his fist on the table, scowling.

'Quite a young fire-brand, isn't he?' whispered Bob, who was evidently relieved that the incident was over. 'But the others seem to be sensible. Guess the big city's pretty safe from these boyos.'

George was already disgusted with the meeting, having beheld apathy and the uneasy cowardice of the peasantry, like schoolboys stealthily enjoying a trifling breach of rules. What could Pushkov and Alfred do with these fellows? Indeed relations even between these two appeared to be none too cordial, and George suspected that Pushkov was not without some jealously of the rising star of the young revolutionary, while Alfred, although he reverenced the agitator at present, was no doubt quite willing to head the movement himself. As for Stanley, thought George, what could be more incompetent? and he was surprised when Joe, as if to calm him, whispered 'Stanley's all right. He's honest.' 'What about the rest?' George asked, and Joe looked at him sadly, shrugging his shoulders, saying 'That's where we need help.'

Pushkov had now begun to speak, leaning forward, propped on finger-tips. His voice was low and thrilling, and he held his audience with his eyes. 'Fred Birch,' he said, looking slowly round the room till he found a giant labourer standing uneasily on one foot, 'do you remember what happened to your wife? George Dupont, do you remember your young son? Ethel Sharp, are you quite well? Mother Avory, where's your old man? Comrades, have you forgotten Gobolov, and what happened to Freda Harrison?'

He paused and continued in a louder voice. George noticed that the peasants were uneasy while he was speaking. They showed no enthusiasm, but they listened carefully. Pushkov proceeded: 'If you have forgotten (though you, Myra Black, will not have forgotten what passed last night)'—at these words a young girl, hardly more than 14 years old, shrieked, fainted and amidst considerable commotion was carried out into the fresh air, while Pushkov went on speaking—'if you have forgotten, you have short memories. If you remember, you will know one thing. I will tell you what that one thing is. It is this—that you can expect no mercy from the town.'

'Question,' said the clergyman boldly, but Pushkov ignored the interruption. 'I have met turn-coat priests. I have met spies. I hope I shall not meet them again, because if I do, I say, if I do, by God Almighty—' He raised his clenched fist and nodded his head. 'Enough of that. I am here to tell you three things. I have told you one of them. You can expect no mercy from the town. You can be sure of that. And you are all marked men. Not only the members of the party, but mere sympathizers, you are all known to the police. What can you do then? You can, if your courage fails you, turn informer. We have ways of dealing with informers. Or you can be men, you can fight, you can be sure that this is war to the death, that no quarter will be given by either side, that you can never be your own men till the last government official, till the king himself, is rotting beneath the earth, that, if you fail, you will be no worse off than you are now, but if you succeed you will inherit the land, the power, the freedom which have been taken away from you.

'It is war to the death, with no possibility of compromise. That is my second point. Let no one lead you astray with talk of co-operation with the town, arbitration, and the rest. It is a bag of tricks. Give us what belongs to us and then we will think of these things. But they will never do that, and you know it. So let us present a united front, determined to accept nothing short of the utmost we can demand.

'My third point is this. We are bound to win. We have the numbers, we have the organization. One thing we lack, revolutionary discipline. You were not contented, Harry Heddle, when the police took your black bull this morning. You were not contented, Father Granby, when your daughter died beneath the attentions of the officer of health. Why not do something, then? Why not join the party? Why not act instead of shuffling your feet and grinning?

'Mass demonstrations must be held. Bring your friends. Bring banners. Cells must be organized even in the obscurest villages. Efforts must be made to get into touch with our brothers in the town. If we succeed there, we shall succeed all along the front. It will be a question not of decades, as some would have you believe, but of days before we come into our own, rebuild the ruined farms, drain the marshes, be free.'

He sat down and there was some faint applause, though the majority of the peasants stared silently in front of them, avoiding each other's eyes, impressed, obviously, by what they had heard, but, whether from timidity or stupidity, reluctant to commit themselves to anything. This was certainly not, George thought, material for revolution, and in spite of the strength, fecundity, and honesty of the peasants, qualities which were evident by their eyes and broad backs, he began to despise them for their unresponsive minds, their acquiescence in what, he now felt sure, was a system

128

of government almost, if not quite, as oppressive as Pushkov had declared it to be.

But, though he looked for very little from these people, he decided to wait and hear what the clergyman had to say, and Bob, too, was willing to wait, for he had been scared by Pushkov's speech, particularly by his statement that all who were attending the meeting were marked men, and he hoped that the clergyman would have some more encouraging news for those who were, as Bob was, anxious rather to make a fortune in the usual way than to be involved in any trouble. 'Oh sir,' he whispered, 'surely the parson isn't a Bolshie too?'

The Rev. Hamlet was clean-shaven, well soaped, with straight black hair brushed back, blue expressive eyes, features of great nobility, and an appealing mouth set above a wide, but somewhat loose chin. He spoke with frequent smiles and movements of arms outstretched in supplication. He was saying: 'Look here, you fellows, I want you to treat me just like one of yourselves. Because that's what I am. I am really. I'm not one of those stiff dry-as-dust parsons, who are always telling you what not to do. I'm not a bit like that. Really. I want us to all get together and have just as jolly a time as we possibly can have.

'Now, look here, I know, just as well as anyone else, that things aren't right. God knows some of us parsons haven't always done our jobs as well, perhaps, as we might have done them. And I don't think we're the only ones. Things are bad, damned bad. Well, we've got to put them right, haven't we?

'Now what's the best way of doing that? Do you know, as I was coming to this meeting to-day I passed two little children in the road. They'd been having a squabble about something and were starting to go to fisticuffs. I stopped them and said to one of them "Tommy!" (I don't know whether it was Tommy or not, but he was a beautiful little blue-eyed child. You mothers know what that is. It's a bit of heaven, I sometimes think) I said: "Tommy! What's it all about? You don't want to hurt your brother, do you?" And he said: "No. We're only playing at revolution. He's one side and I'm the other." And I left them, and I think I went away a bit wiser.

'Oh why can't we be more like little children? I don't know what you think, but I think its a damned fine thing to be only playing, to be innocent, not to want to hurt other people. You may say that I'm sentimental. My God! it would be better for us if we were all sentimental.'

By this time Bob and indeed many women in the audience were weeping profusely. A few murmurs could be heard: 'The Reverend's quite right.' 'What's it all about anyway?' 'Bless him!'—'Isn't he broadminded?' George looked towards the plat-form and saw Pushkov, apparently asleep, with his long legs stretched out in front of him, Alfred biting his lips, and Stanley still looking at the ceiling, his pipe dangling from his jaw. From the back of the room Joe shouted out 'Bunkum!'

There was a commotion, cries of 'Shame!', 'Turn him out', and, though a few peasants looked at Joe approvingly, none dared to support him. The Rev. Hamlet stretched out his fingers, 'The man who said that,' he pronounced in his smooth carefully modulated voice, 'is a bounder, an unmitigated bounder. My dear friends, can't you see that I'm only trying to help you? I'm not a prig, or anything like that. I just want everyone to be happy.

'Now I'm going to surprise you. I'm a revolutionary. Oh yes I am. Just as much a revolutionary as any of you. And I'll tell you what kind of a revolution I want. It isn't easy, but, please God, it will be effective.

'I don't want any bloodshed, any bitterness. We've got too much bitterness in the world already. My revolution won't be like that. I simply want us all to start again (that's what revolution means really), to forget the past, to get together and see if we can't make things better. Don't let's have any of this bitterness. It's a nasty feeling. If you've got complaints to make, send them in to the authorities. They'll respond. Oh you've no idea how they'll be pleased just to have a chance of doing good. Of course they have their faults. I think we all have. Don't you? But they're decent fellows really, just like you or I, and I really think that many of them would be pleased to do a little now in order to make up for some mistakes (and there have been mistakes) which have been made in the past.

'I say, lets be friends. Don't you think that's a jolly good idea? So much pleasanter, isn't it? You know, all this class-feeling is a terrible thing, when you come to think of it. It does nobody any good.

'So why don't you fellows trust me and join my revolutionary party? If you do, I'll go and see the authorities and have a chat about your grievances. Oh I know I may not be able to do much, but I'll jolly well do my best, because—oh well, you know what I mean, I'm awfully fond of you people.

'So why not do that? You wives, you don't want to lose your husbands. You husbands, you don't want your wives and little children to starve. But that's what war means. War's a terrible thing. Don't lets have it, then. I say, I do wish you'd take my advice. Just try it out. Oh I know I'm not much good, but I should feel I'd done something in my life if I could persuade you people to all make a fresh start, to get rid of all this bitterness, to be prepared to give and take, to start a revolution that way. You know, I think that would be the most splendid revolution you could possibly have. Well, who'll join up?'

He sat down amidst loud and prolonged cheers. Joe spat on the floor and then shouted 'Spy!' but only a dozen or so of the audience seemed to sympathize with him and they stared hopelessly in front of them, listening to the sobs of women, the chuckles of the older men, the applause which seemed to relieve their fellows of anxiety. No doubt that the Rev. Hamlet had effaced the impression which Pushkov had made on these slow minds so much more ready to believe in arguments for inertia than in calls to action, and George, inexpressibly disgusted, though he pitied Joe, Pushkov, and their few supporters, was about to leave the meeting, when he heard his name being called out by Stanley, who, after a whispered conversation with Pushkov, had called for silence and was saying: 'We have with us to-day a visitor from the past country. His name is George. Will George be so good as to give us his impressions of our organization and tell us whether he is prepared to join us.'

George was surprised at this sudden call and irritated by Bob who kept slapping him on the back, clapping, and crying 'Speech! Speech!', but he prepared to speak, while Bob whispered, 'Just a few words. Tell them to trust their own clergyman and not to make a rough house.' The peasants turned round towards the back of the barn, where George was standing, and looked at him approvingly, encouraging him; and the Rev. Hamlet, elated with his success, shouted out: 'Be a good chap, and tell us all about it.' George saw Pushkov looking at him almost in despair, Alfred biting his nails, and Stanley looking at the ceiling.

'One thing,' George said, when everyone was silent, 'I would never do, and that is to join the ridiculous organization proposed by your clergyman.' (Cries of 'Oh!') 'If you are taken in by that sort of stuff, it seems to me that you can be taken in by anything. What I should like to know is whether Pushkov is right or wrong in what he says about the Government. If he is right, then it seems that he'll have a job to get you fellows to help yourselves. If he's wrong, then I'm just as ignorant about the town as I was when I left home. In either case I can do no good by staying here and helping you. Your revolutionary organization appears to me to be the least promising one I have ever seen or heard of, and I am going on alone. If I can do anything for you in the town, of course I shall try to do it. Meanwhile I should advise you either to give up revolution altogether, or else to take it seriously.'

He ceased speaking, angry, and noticed Joe looking kindly at him, as though in pity. His speech was received in silence, and he was disconcerted to find that his words, so far from rousing the hostility of the peasants, had only hurt their feelings. They stared ruefully at their boots, and George could hear some of the remarks they made to each other, 'He doesn't understand,' 'Thinks he's too good for us,' 'Poor lad, going to the town like this,' and as they trooped out of the room (for the meeting was now over) many of them, passing him, touched their caps and said: 'Good luck, lad. We're sorry you won't stay with us.'

Their behaviour affected George deeply, and he half-wished he had not been so outspoken. Nevertheless, he thought, honest, strong, and kind-hearted as these people are, how can one do anything with such stupidity, such inertia? It is best for me to go, even though I offend Joan and her father and Pushkov. He saw the Rev. Hamlet coming towards him, his face smiling. 'I say,' he said, stretching out his hand, 'I just thought I'd like to thank you for your little speech. It helped me a lot.' 'Oh get out, you pimp,' George said, turning aside, and stepped out of the barn into the sunlight, followed by Joe and Bob. A little distance from the door swaggered and joked a patrol of police, pointing out to each other with peals of laughter the pretty girls and the more awkward of the men who went by them quickly, blushing, scowling, frightened. George said to Pushkov, who had now joined them, 'So much for your secrecy,' and Pushkov scowled as the policemen roared with laughter at him; for just as he was passing them his beard had fallen off on to the ground. 'Your beard, I think,' one of them said, offering it to him, but Pushkov hurried on, while the policeman followed him, still trying, with the utmost politeness, to persuade him to take it back. Finally Pushkov did stretch his hand out, but the policeman snatched the beard away, and, stuffing it into his pipe, lit it and began to smoke, while his comrades roared with laughter and clapped hands. When they arrived at the farm, Pushkov collapsed into a chair, weeping with fatigue and vexation, a ludicrous and pitiable sight, with gum on his chin, his motor goggles askew, and tears trickling down his great nose.

Joe got some brandy for him and, while Bob went upstairs to pack, George did his best to console the agitator, saying that at all events there seemed to be a dozen or so genuine revolutionaries in the country and that these in time might secure new recruits. Pushkov sat up quickly and shouted: 'Then why leave us?'

'Because it is too slow a business,' George said. 'I'm going to see what I can do by myself. Perhaps I'll come back.'

'You'll come back, squire,' said Joe slowly, 'that is, if you're alive. And you'll wish you'd never gone.'

Pushkov said: 'You have had your chance,' and walked out of the house without looking at him. Joe said gloomily: 'You'd better say good-bye to Joan,' and George went into the scullery, then upstairs, looking for her, till he heard from her bedroom the sound of sobbing and entering saw Joan huddled on the bed, red-eyed, with loose hair, heaving shoulders that made creak the wire springs beneath the mattress. When she saw him she quickly turned her head to the wall and nothing that he could say to her could make her look at him, so he caught hold of her shoulder and forced her on to her back and, bending down, was about to kiss her when she spat in his face. 'Joan,' he said, 'I must go away, so don't be silly. I'm not going away because I don't love you. You know what I'm out for. Can't you see I must go? I'll come back some day.'

'Liar!' she said sobbing, twisting loose muscles beneath his hands, 'You're only going to get away from me. And I gave you more than I gave anyone else. I've told you you're making a mistake.'

She was calmer now and spoke plaintively. George said: 'I'll come back, and then we'll get married,' and she, with a sudden effort, twisted away from him, slid off the bed and ran across the room to the window. The room seemed full of the sparks of her anger. 'Beast!' she shouted, 'I'll never marry you. If you come back here, you shall mind my pigs. Conceited fool! You're worse than your brothers. You and your silly geese! It's the town women you're after. Fresh every night's what you want, you filthy swine, you little boy that can't even have a baby, you cocky one, what will you do in the town?' And she burst into tears again as she heard George go downstairs, say good-bye to her father, and open the front door. Sobbing she saw George and Bob come round the corner of the building and set off down the hill to the high road, George silent, with tense lips, Bob skipping and dancing round him, twanging the guitar, singing melodiously as they went out of sight among the cottages:—

> 'Good-bye, horses and pigs!
> Good-bye, the little earwigs!
>   Bye-bye the farm!
> We won't come to you any more now.
> Bye-bye turkey-cock, bye-bye cow!
> See you don't come to any harm.
> Bye-bye the milk-maid all forlorn!
> Bye-bye barley, oats, and corn!
>   We're heading for the city lights,
>   We're looking forward to gay nights, half-the-day nights,
>   Heading for those pretty, those big city, lights.'

CHAPTER NINE

Soon past the grey village, from the houses of which, as they went by, some few peasants emerged and waved hands, nodded heads, George and Bob reached the bottom of the hill and the high road, magnificent for motors, but now empty of all traffic. For some miles, until the farm house on the hill was out of sight, they walked on concrete and George had never found walking so disagreeable, while even Bob began to complain of the journey, which appeared the more arduous because the straight hard road ran between fresh fields of corn, grazing land, vineyards, and plantations of olives. But gradually they came into a different country, level still, for the most part, dusty, arid, interrupted sometimes by rocky cliffs, lifeless ravines, which, being no part of any mountain range, appeared an evil and irresponsible growth upon a field of dust. There were no trees now, and, since the travellers were tired, they sat down to rest in the shadow of one of these rocks, when they were surprised to hear at a distance, but approaching, the roar of an aeroplane engine, and, coming out from their shelter, they saw flying low a huge red monoplane, flying towards the frontier. Just as the plane was above their heads the pilot, whom they could not recognize, but who was notable for his red flying-costume and a large silver-glinting star affixed to his helmet, leaned over the side of the cock-pit and dropped an object to earth, a box, or so it seemed, to which was attached a small parachute. Then, raising his hand with a dignified gesture, he swept upwards and away, soon out of sight, while the parcel which he had dropped fell slowly to ground at George's feet.

Excitedly George unwrapped the package from its covering of

silver paper, loosed the parachute, and discovered a metal box, which he opened, and found inside a note-book on the cover of which was written:—

A DIARY

by

RUDOLPH

once an Officer in the Yeomanry,

now

KNIGHT COMMANDER OF THE SILVER STAR, CHIEF OF THE BONJI INDIANS, HIGH PRIEST OF THE MA-TA-BLAS, HEREDITARY GREAT BULL OF GINKISTAN, AN ENGLISHMAN.

'Oo, sir!' said Bob, who was looking over George's shoulder at the MS, 'Cannibals!' George smiled and turned to the first page where he read:—

FOREWORD

'Copies of this MS. have been placed in bottles and dropped into each one of the seven seas—the Sea of Azov, the Sea of Marmora, the Caspian Sea, the Euxine Sea, the Arabian Sea, the Sargasso Sea, and the Sound of Harris. Other copies have been deposited in metal boxes on the summit of Katchen-junga, in Tierra del Fuego, in the Gobi Desert, and (for sentimental reasons) at Kataculipatam. This copy I propose to drop from the Ambassador's aeroplane somewhere in Terra Recognita.'

The MS. did not appear to be very lengthy, but in order to peruse it with the attention it deserved, George and Bob went back to the shade of the rock and, holding the note-book between them, read as follows:—

RUDOLPH'S DIARY

'God! its hell to be lonely! I'm the last of that old gang of mine, and it's beaten even me at last, the loneliness, the jungle, the insects,

137

the terrible splendour of the tropical sky. I've done my bit, and I've lost, as many a better man than I has lost before me. But I've seen something, more, I guess, than the stay-at-homes, and my dead pals won't blame me for trekking homewards now. I know a little girl who's waiting for me, and I'm going to settle down.'

Here Bob burst into tears, but George, remembering that these accomplishments had taken place in what for him had appeared to be two and a half days, was eager to discover what he could, and went on reading:—

'Let me begin from the beginning. My two brothers, splendid fellows, started with me, but they couldn't stay the pace, and I left them behind. God knows what happened to them. I half-hope that they turned back. Perhaps I should have stayed with them, but in the jungle it is each man for himself, and before long I was beyond the fringe of civilization, in places where few white men had ever been.

'I travelled for about a week, till my stores were nearly finished, over the desert without meeting a living soul! God! I needed all my grit. The heat of the sun was terrific. The insects, I knew, were dangerous, and there was always the risk of Indians. But the first person I met was apparently a white man, dressed in dinner clothes, and I can tell you it was a shock when I saw him step out into the road in front of me. Was this, I wondered (one learns to think quickly in the jungle), a survivor of some long-forgotten race, or was I face to face with a brigand or worse? I disarmed the fellow and found him to be a lunatic. How he got there I cannot think, and have often wondered. There are strange things in the desert. Anyway he asked me for a lift to some town and I refused, as of course I had to travel light. It was a memorable encounter, and perhaps some who will tread in my footsteps may clear up the mystery. I had more important things to do.

'But before I entered the jungle I came upon one other settlement of white people, not unlike ourselves, who have reached a high state of civilization. I don't know how much longer I went on travelling across the tundra. The machine went splendidly, and when one's alone with Nature, it's difficult to keep an account of time. My provisions were exhausted, and the mosquitoes, tsetse fly, and vampire-bats were a constant danger. I was fortunate enough to get a shot at an ocelot, and I shall never forget how good that animal tasted. Still long days went by and I was delighted when, many weeks after my departure, I came in sight of a house, built in the European style, and saw cultivated ground. To my amazement the people here spoke English, and I reflected with pride on how far afield the hardy pioneers of our race may be found. When this settlement was made I have not the least idea and all my inquiries were fruitless. Certainly it was not an affair of yesterday. Perhaps I had stumbled upon some long-lost tribe of buccaneers. Perhaps it was something else.

'Well, I may as well get it off my chest. It appears that the daughter of the old man, who seemed to be the chief of the tribe, was rather taken with me. She was a charming little thing, and did all she could to please me, but of course I couldn't saddle myself with a wife or even a woman. I had to travel light. The poor girl was heart-broken, and I felt a beast. But there it was. Each for himself is jungle law, and I set off early in the morning for the town, which I had heard was in the neighbourhood, and against which I had been warned by an odd-looking fellow, evidently the medicine man; for I soon found out that, in spite of speaking English, these people were practically savages. Still I missed my little girl.

'I reached the outskirts of the town after a long journey across one of the most dangerous deserts that has been, up to now, un-explored by man. God! it was terrific. The petrol boiled in my tank. I had some nasty moments with the army ants and had to take refuge in a tree while I watched these creatures surround and eat a party of peccaries, who, God knows how, had wandered into this desert. The screams of the wretched animals were audible for miles as their living flesh was stripped from their bones, and I thanked my lucky stars that I was out of danger.

'The town, built in an imposing style, is inhabited by hostile Indians, who speak English. They have many up-to-date conveniences, such as sanitary arrangements, and aeroplanes, and it was a good feeling to get into my first warm bath for over a year. Yet, in spite of receiving these attentions in the suburbs, I found the Indians to be really hostile and devilishly cunning. How they had learnt our language and reached such a high state of civilization I cannot tell. It is one of the secrets which the jungle is likely to keep.

'After my tub, I went before one of the magistrates of the town. I told him that I was an Englishman, and suggested that I should be made chief of the tribe. I have had enough experience of savage races to know that there's nothing like bluff in dealing with natives. The magistrate asked me a number of impertinent questions about mathematics and history, and I could see by the way in which my answers were received that my position in the town was by no means secure. Knowing what Indians could do with blow pipes, I had no doubt that these Indians, who were in possession of all the lethal instruments with which our yeomanry is equipped, could do much worse, so that night I made my escape.

'It was a moonless night, and it was a tricky business climbing down three storeys by a water-pipe, but I did it. My next job was to get to the aerodrome which I had noticed on my arrival at the outskirts of the town. As I crept through the dark streets, my heart thumping at every step I took (though in reality I was quite cool), I seemed to detect the sound of footsteps behind me, and quickened my pace. God knows whether I was being followed or not. All I know is that at every moment I expected a bullet in my back, or the explosion of a bomb at my feet. The consequences of being discovered were too terrible to think of, and, almost at a run, I reached the aerodrome, which, to my horror, I found brilliantly lighted, though God knows what else I could have expected.

'It was now too late to turn back. I fingered the mascot of our yeomanry, a little black rat which I always keep hanging round my neck, and I ran towards a big aeroplane which, fortunately for me, was standing outside the hangars. It was the property of the Ambassador. I swung the propeller and soon had the engine started. It was only then, when I was already in the cockpit, that I noticed that the aeroplane was surrounded by a posse of police. What luck one has sometimes! These honest fellows were all half-seas over and simply stood still, laughing. I didn't wait till they became serious, I can tell you. In my hurry I cleared the trees at the edge of the aerodrome by inches and I was away. For miles I was followed by searchlights from the town, but, for some reason or other, there was no attempt at a pursuit. Still, it was a close shave.

'Some people may think that I ought to have stayed to investigate a little more thoroughly the curious civilization of these Indians, but I'm not a scientist. I'm an adventurer, and I knew that I should have to go far before I fell in with the wild geese. Travel light, and full speed ahead are two of my mottoes.

'Well, I think I broke the record for long distance flights, but, owing to a defect in the registering of my speedometer, I can't be sure. Anyway I passed over mountain ranges and jungles untrodden by any white man, and finally I landed in a clearing and made there my base camp, intending to proceed on foot. I had not the least idea where I was and I was eager to see what there was to be seen.

'The jungle was almost impenetrable and I had to hack my way through the dense lianas, often sinking up to my waist in the under-growth on the surface of which I walked. The howling monkeys kept up a continuous din. There were pumas and jaguars lying on the broad branches of immense tropical trees; and I noticed frequently white-faced capuchins, peccaries, kinkajous, agouti, paca, and ant-bears. My food was tapir, when I could succeed in outwitting one of these shy and elusive beasts. Otherwise I had to put up with roots and berries and any birds I could secure. The bird-life was varied. Oriole, jacana, tanager, guan, curassow, vireo, ant-thrush, quail-dove, and tinamous. I have eaten them all, and once in the topmost branches of the trees I distinguished the harsh note and brilliant plumage of Nicholl's parrot.

'For years I struggled through jungles of this description, some-times on foot, sometimes in a canoe. The loneliness, the hardship, the giant bewildering scenery drove me into strange actions. Once I grappled with a bull-gorilla, and the victory did not go to the gorilla. I acquired such dexterity in the shooting of rapids that I would venture myself on falls greater than those of Victoria Nyanza. But I was still as far as ever I was from the wild geese, and began to wonder whether the species was not extinct.

'I met with many Indian tribes, and had some close shaves. My exploit with the gorilla, however, accounted for the fact that I was made chief of the Bonji Indians, to whom I presented a Union Jack. Many years later, when I was in mountainous country, right off the map, I fell in with the Ma-ta-blas, a race of hardy mountain-eers, who at my first arrival made me their High Priest. I dis-covered later that this position is always held by some notable lunatic, and, before I left, I had a good laugh at the simplicity of these honest fellows.

'In Ginkistan I married the king's daughter. It was a court equipped with all the splendours of the Orient, elephants, palan-quins, parrots, pearls, and chandeliers. For a time I was tempted

142

to remain there wealthy and respected with my title of Hereditary Great Bull, but before I had been long in the country I discovered that the government was matriarchal, and, worse still, that my own wife had six or seven other husbands, amongst whom I was, God knows why, almost invariably neglected. I had a good laugh at the queer customs of this tribe, and one moonless night I went back to the jungle, for the lure was upon me and I still sought news of the geese.

'It would be impossible to relate in full all the adventures that I went through after this. I have fought battles in a dozen states, civilized and savage. For my skilful handling of a machine-gun, with which I routed a large rebel army armed with bows and arrows, I was made Knight Commander of the Silver Star by Colonel Moose. While I was working in collaboration with this Colonel I became head of a secret service agency which finally rid the land of revolution. I wore a mask, and all the charms of Polish adventuresses could not divert me from my course. Alas! my old pals in that service are all gone, some by the dagger, others by the bullet.

'But that sort of thing was too dull for me. I went back to the jungle. I discovered a tin mine; but I could hear no news of the wild geese. Somewhere in the Eternal Snows a Guru informed me that I was on the wrong track and I stayed with him in a hermit's shelter, sometimes descending into the plains to play polo, until he informed me that he had taught me all that I could learn from him, and I returned to the jungle.

'I began now to be more than ever convinced that the bird which I was after belonged to an extinct species. Often, bivouacking beneath the brilliant tropical stars, I was oppressed with my own loneliness and wondered whether any other white man had lived so long as I with Nature. Great as was my affection for level sand, tinted with the rays of the setting sun, for the deathly stillness of

143

the tropical night, the glow of my camp fire, the shadows of enormous tree-ferns, the marvellous man's life of the jungle, I began to long for home. Someone, I knew, was waiting there for me and would go on waiting, even if I never returned. Somehow it was hell to think of my own country, of my chums who by this time must have wives and families, and then to think of myself, sitting by the camp fire, miles from anywhere. For the first time in my life I felt like blubbing, just like a kid, and I determined that, at whatever cost, I'd leave the jungle once and for all and get back to civilization. Already I seemed to hear the church bells ringing, to see the cool rivers with no rapids and no alligators. God! it was wonderful to be thinking of home; but I had to keep a stiff upper lip as I turned away from the jungle, remembering my old pals among the Bonjis and at the Headquarters of Colonel Moose.

'Of course I had no idea where I was. I'd kept no log; there wasn't time for that. And it's impossible to describe how surprised I was when, after I had trekked a few miles, I came out into a clearing and saw in front of me the very aeroplane that I had left years ago when I fled from the Indian town. What was still more surprising, was that there was petrol in the tank and that the whole machine was in order.

'I sat down and wrote my memoirs, listening, perhaps for the last time, to the thousand-and-one noises of the jungle at dusk, keeping a sharp look out for hostile Indians, vampire-bats, pumas, jaguas, army ants, and, more deadly than any of these, the yellow moccasin snake.

'And now it's good-bye to the trail. I've done my last trek. It's been hard, but I've had my fun, and now I'm leaving the way open for others to carry on the good work. I've failed. Yes, I know it. But I've done about as much as man can do, I think.'

CHAPTER TEN

AFTER they had read the last words of the MS., Bob rose up, and, standing at attention, sang 'God save the King', but George remained seated on the rock, wondering how much truth and how much falsehood was contained in the pages which he had just read. When time and space were regulated as oddly as they were in this country, it was difficult, he reflected, to be sure of anything but of single events (and even these might not yet have occurred), while as for the interstices between events and the emotional states appropriate to them, there was absolutely no knowing. He had had an account, accurate enough, no doubt, of Rudolph's journey, but for him such speed of travel was impossible and indeed incredible. Rudolph, so Joe had said, was apt to travel so slowly that he would reach his destination sometimes even before he started; yet it could be held with an equal show of reason that he was not travelling slowly but with an amazing rapidity. Space and time here, according to Joe, depended on the individual and upon the direction, and to compare or to estimate the times taken in accomplishing journeys it was, consequently, of the utmost importance to decide from the point of view of what object or person one was making the reckoning; for, if one were to measure the duration of Rudolph's activities by the standard of the sun casting shadows over a particular strip of land, it would seem that Rudolph had crossed jungles and deserts, married, become chieftain, assisted Colonel Moose, talked with Gurus, all in the space, or time, of two days, though even of this George was uncertain, since, in trusting Joe's reckoning, he could be by no

145 K

means sure that that reckoning was entirely objective. If, however, he assumed it to be correct (and, after all, a farmer, who is in close touch with his animals, ought to be pretty well aware of the movement of the sun), there was no means of telling whether that space, or time, of two days, had been two days for him in the same sense as it had been for Joe. He had been to bed twice, but had paid no attention to the sun, and, now he came to think of it, the times or spaces during which he had been awake did seem to him to have been very long. Even now the farmhouse and the political meeting seemed far away, and he looked up quickly at the sky to find it obscured with clouds, dimly lighted, neither apparent day nor night. He resolved in future closely to watch the sun's passage, beginning already to see the difficulties and dangers of unrelated endeavour.

As for the rest of Rudolph's narrative, it was hardly surprising. It had seemed to George that Rudolph had not kept constantly in view the object for which he had originally set out, and he was inclined to think that the fact that nis travels were not aimed continually in one direction might have something to do with the extraordinary velocity with which they had been accomplished; for he had already begun to suspect that when the direction is ill-defined there can be immense speed of transit from one irrelevant point to another. And when this was so, it was natural that Rudolph's reflections upon events which had succeeded each other so rapidly should be distorted, that he should regard the inhabitants of this country as Indians, and fancy that Joan had been seriously interested in him. Indeed, George was disappointed with Rudolph's memoirs, for they had told him nothing important about the town, and it was this subject which now entirely engrossed his mind. At the same time he could not avoid a certain uneasiness when he saw how hopelessly distorted Rudolph's views of Bob, of the farmhouse, and of the town had been; for how could he be quite certain that his own views did not suffer from a similar distortion? How could he be sure that he had himself fully understood everything that had happened to him? He had not practically adopted the creed of the revolutionaries, nor was he, as David seemed to be, prepared to think of the town as any paradise. He was shocked to realize that he was almost as isolated as Rudolph had been, having only Bob for a companion, and at the back of his mind an affection for Joe and Joan, a kind of admiration for Pushkov. For all intents and purposes he was by himself, unable to move in conjunction with others, travelling, he hoped, in the right direction, but at a velocity which it was impossible for him to relate to anything else. For a moment he half-regretted his decision to proceed alone, but thinking of the recalcitrance of the peasantry, of how easily they had been bamboozled by their priest, he was certain that his way was before him and glad, in his pride, of the opportunity to confront single-handed a state the extent of whose power he had not yet begun dimly to understand.

He sprang to his feet laughing and clapped Bob on the shoulder; but here he met with some difficulty, for Bob had been terrified by Rudolph's report that the town was inhabited by hostile Indians. 'By Jink!' he said, 'that brother of yours was brave, even though he did look a bit batty and took me for a loony. Oh, sir, don't let us run those risks. Let's go for some other towns.'

'Nonsense,' George said. 'If Rudolph thought you were a loony, he'd be just as likely to think that ordinary white people were Indians,' and to this Bob seemed to agree, though it was only after George had assured him that he was going on anyway and would let Bob go back to the farm by himself, if he wished it, that Bob showed any eagerness to go forward.

So they marched on for miles over similar country, dust and

rocks, no trees, beneath clouds, in a light that seemed to be growing dimmer and might have proceeded from either sun or moon, and at last they came to a fallen monolith and standing on a hill saw in the distance lights high up in the air. Excited they quickened their pace and now could observe that the lights shone from cylindrical towers made of some shining material, glass, or polished steel, which projected to a great height from what seemed to be an interminable level roof of concrete raised about a hundred feet from the ground. To the left, at a distance, in the open country were other lights, and from the faint sounds which occasionally reached him from the upper air George conjectured that this was the aerodrome of which Rudolph had written, and that in front of him was at last the town.

'No nigs could build those towers,' exclaimed Bob in relief, as they stood still admiring the great cylindrical structures, brilliantly lighted, with, below them in the enormous roof, slits of streaming light, ventilators, George supposed, for the life beneath the concrete.

'It's just marvellous,' Bob continued, clasping his hands in adoration, 'like the movies, those sky-scrapers, and everyone else living cosy under a roof. Isn't that the modern city? Oh that's where I'd just love to live.'

'Depends on the Government,' said George, 'and anyway it must be stuffy under all that concrete,' but he was amazed at the size and splendour of the towers, the miracle of engineering by which, so far as he could see, a whole city was roofed away from the sky under one roof.

'Who's speaking against the Government?' said a voice behind them. 'You know that won't do. It won't do at all,' and they turned round to see a policeman whose smiling face was indistinguishable from the face of the officer whom George had encountered earlier on the causeway. He blew his whistle and wa joined by three or four other policemen, all exactly alike, smoking cigarettes and swinging their batons to and fro, laughing at Bob's evident terror of them, nodding their heads wisely at George. The officer put the whistle in his pocket and going up to George whispered: 'You've got to be very careful,' then, in a louder tone of voice and with a wink towards his friends, 'I'm very sorry. My name's Cochran. Captain Cochran.' He held out his hand, which George took and then dropped quickly, for it contained a frog, on which Captain Cochran immediately set his heel, saying hastily, while the other policeman skipped up and down in their delight at the joke, 'Beg pardon, sir. Can't tell you how sorry I am that this has occurred. Frog eluded my notice. Has now paid the death penalty. Honour, I hope, satisfied. Everyone will immediately make a written report to be forwarded to H.Q.'

The other policemen sat down on the ground, took from their pockets pencils and note-books and began writing, while the officer turned quickly away from George and standing over his patrol snapped out: 'The code word is "Sugar". A prize will be given for the most original composition.' The policemen giggled, and their officer turned to George and began speaking again: 'And now, sir, that this unfortunate event is receiving proper attention, I am at your service. I hope you had a comfortable night. There's going to be some trouble before long in Manchuria, I expect. You can't trust those beggars an inch. Have you seen "Topsy-toes?" Very fine show, I'm told, though its not much in my line.'

George, infuriated with the fellow's insolence and feeling slightly sick as he observed him continue sliding the sole of his foot backwards and forwards over the squashed frog, would have liked to have demonstrated his feelings, but he was deterred from any rash action by the consideration that his first object was to get inside the city and that an affair with the police, at this stage of his travels, was, if possible, to be avoided. So he said: 'We want to go to the Convent, where, I believe, the headmaster is expecting me. Will you show us the way there as quickly as possible?'

'Ah-ha!' said Captain Cochran. 'That's awkward, isn't it? We shall have to see. We shall have to see,' and he stood as though thinking, motionless for a minute except when he turned to his patrol winking at them, while they kept up a continual giggling, like a roost of starlings. At length the Captain spoke: 'Very good. Very good indeed. But we cannot dispense with the usual formalities. I shall have to ask each of you to fill up one of these forms.' He pulled out of his pocket a sheaf of papers, from which he selected two printed forms and handed one to George and one to Bob, who, having glanced at it, exclaimed: 'O Lord, sir, I can't do this.'

George looked at the piece of paper on which was written: 'Candidates are requested to write their answers legibly and in as few words as possible. Every question should be attempted.

ANCIENT HISTORY
   1. What was the date of the battles of the Eurymedon?
   2. Name two authors (i) Greek and (ii) Latin.
   3. Do you know anything about the Eleusinian mysteries (yes or no)?
MODERN HISTORY
   1. What is the name of the present king?
MATHEMATICS.
   1. Find the square root of anything you like.
GEOLOGY
   1. What is meant by 'Geology'?
LANGUAGES
   1. Translate: *Per me si va nella città dolente;*
                  per me si va nell' eterno dolore;
                  per me si va tra la perduta gente.
OPTICS
   1. What is meant by 'Optics'?
ZOOLOGY
   1. Name two, or at the most three, animals.
ECONOMICS
   1. (Need not be attempted.)
BIBLIOPHILY
   1. Name ten of the twenty best books of the week.
MINERALOGY
   1. What is quartz?

SEISMOGRAPHY
1. What is meant by 'Seismography'?
PERSONAL
1. What is your sex?
2. Are you quite satisfied with your sex?
3. Are you fair-haired, blue-eyed, Conservative, Communist, tinker, tailor, interested in the Drama, a wearer of spectacles, aviator, good at making love, neurasthenic, a drunkard, religious, musical, able to ride a push-bicycle? (Cross out inappropriate words or phrases.)
4. Are you a High Court Judge?
IMBECILITY TEST
1. What was the number of the Three Musketeers?
2. What material goes to the construction of a wall built entirely of brick?
3. A snail is walking up a post. In every half hour it advances $1\frac{3}{4}$ inches. How long will it take to reach the top?

'What's the game?' said George, when he had read the examination paper. 'Take us to the town at once, and don't waste our time on this nonsense. It may be very amusing for you and your half-witted constables, but we've got other things to do.'

' 'Shun!' said Captain Cochran, and his patrol sprang to attention, while the Captain went into a fit of laughter, spluttering out the words: 'You know what to do, boys.'

The constables produced from their clothing the parts of a machine gun which they assembled, and levelled at George and Bob, who, in response to an order, put their hands up. Captain Cochran said: 'Excuse my laughter, gentlemen. I am only doing my duty. You will be so good as to fill up the forms immediately.'

George, who was surprised to find that the police had really the power to make themselves unpleasant (for previously he had imagined them to be harmlessly malicious and had wondered why the countrymen continued to put up with their provoking behaviour), shrugged his shoulders and began to fill up the form; but Bob fell on his knees in front of Captain Cochran, whining: 'Oh sir, I can't do it. It's so difficult.' The Captain looked at him sternly. 'You can't do it. You can't do it.' He seemed to reflect for some time, while Bob remained on his knees, shivering with

151

fright. At length he turned round: 'I'm afraid there's only one thing to do,' he said. 'You must copy your answers from what your friend is writing.'

'Oh thank you, sir,' said Bob and when the forms were completed the Captain took them and glanced over them, while the patrol, tittering, dug elbows into each other's ribs. 'Every answer is incorrect,' the Captain said, and Bob fell again on his knees to the delight of the policemen who joined hands and danced round him in a circle. 'However,' the Captain continued, 'everything is in order. We may now proceed and I apologize, gentlemen, for having kept you so long.'

'Thank you. Thank you,' said Bob, rising to his feet. 'I'm sure I'd do anything for you.'

'Well now,' the Captain said, 'that's very good of you. What about a song?' and he laughed over his shoulder towards the patrol, pointing his thumb in an opposite direction towards George, who was scowling, impatient on his feet, unwilling to delay, though Bob went up to him and whispered in his ear. 'What ho, sir! Now's my chance. These fellows may be very decent fellows after all.' He shuffled shoulders and feet, arrested movement suddenly and striking the guitar, began to sing:

> 'Don't let me pain you,
> mon capitaine, you
> are so so beautiful.
> I won't detain you,
> but I'll maintain,
> mon capitaine, you are
> my beautiful star.

To this song the policemen listened with a respectful attention, and, when it was over, they surprised George by not laughing. Instead they gravely shook hands with Bob, who, treated in this way, at once regained his confidence, and went so far as to tap Captain Cochran lightly on the shoulder after, breathlessly impatient, he had heard him say: 'I see you are an artist. We shall have to see what we can do. The Metropolitan Force has a fine band. Perhaps there will be a vacancy.'

And so they were escorted by policemen to the town, Captain Cochran preceding and Bob following, talking animatedly to the constables, who laughed at his jokes, wagged their heads, grinned, slapped backs, while George followed in the rear, smiling at Bob's success, though he felt that for his own part nothing would induce him to make friends with these repellent officers. He noticed that some of the policemen who surrounded Bob were looking in his direction, raising eyebrows, questioning Bob about him no doubt, and to them Bob was replying jauntily, shrugging his shoulders, swaggering. Indeed during their short journey over the open country, Bob appeared sedulous to avoid contact with George's eyes, and George was irritated though not surprised to find himself a stranger and perhaps a suspect, neglected by one to whom it had been hinted that he might fill a vacancy in the Police orchestra. But he had other matter for thought, approaching the city at last, observing that the towers, of which he could see four, were even more imposing structures than he had imagined from a distance, rising perhaps 300 feet from the flat concrete roof which itself was raised about 150 feet from the ground, and the towers, made of some shining opaque substance, were apparently without apertures, though their summits, brilliantly illuminated, were for that reason indistinct.

As they approached the walls they could hear from inside confused sound, perhaps of traffic, perhaps of human voices. It was growing darker, and light streamed into the sky in long slotted illumination from those slits in the roof which had been remarked before. The pervading darkness, the desert road behind, the highlights in towers, the effusions from ventilators, the confused hubbub within the high blank walls combined to make the occasion an interesting one, and George, watching defile in front of him the procession of policemen with Bob gesticulating, wondered amongst what strange people he was now to live and under what government, what truth there was in David's assurance that his journey was accomplished, how he himself would be received at the Convent, and whether he would be able to do anything for his friends in the country. That he was suspect to the police he inferred from Captain Cochran's practical joke, from the difference that had already been made between him and Bob, from the probability that, even if Captain Cochran was not the man whom he had assaulted on the causeway, the incident had almost certainly been already reported ; but he hoped that his brother would be in a position to exert some influence, and for the rest he relied upon himself to exculpate himself before any reasonable authority from unwarranted suspicion and to make perfectly plain that his intentions were strictly honourable. This city, he kept repeating to himself as they drew nearer to the walls, is only a stage on my journey, but it is a stage through which I must certainly go; that it is, as David makes out, the final stage I can hardly believe, for I have a feeling that those geese which I heard at the farmhouse were going far, to a farther and a more natural habitat than this town ; and he resolved that, while not forgetting the interests of the countrymen, he would, so long as he stayed in the city, avoid unnecessary risks and do all in his power to conciliate the lawful authorities, finding out what he could, but making it his chief endeavour to secure a safe-conduct and perhaps assistance in the prosecution of his purpose.

But they had now arrived at the turnstile, perhaps the same as that from which Don Antonio had once fled; their papers were examined by someone unseen in an office, and, as the machinery clicked behind Bob and the policemen, George, who followed last, looked back on the open obscure country before passing beneath the concrete roof into a brilliant illumination through a door of curiously carved iron, which swung silently to when they had entered.

Blinded at first by the light streaming from great bulbs over his head and beneath the glass floor, he had just time to observe that they were standing in a ballroom where couples were dancing to the music of a negro orchestra that seemed very far away, when he was blindfolded and, with the sound of laughter and music in his ears, was led a devious way until a destination was reached and he heard the voice of Captain Cochran: 'You'll need a good rest, sir. The surgeon will wait upon you shortly.' The bandage was removed and he found himself in a well-furnished bedroom, three walls of which were hung with curtains, while the fourth was one mirror.

The policeman went, and George heard him laughing from behind the door, but so tired did he now feel that he postponed reflection, and lying down on the bed was soon sleeping deeply.

CHAPTER ELEVEN

W<small>HEN</small> he awoke he had, of course, no means of telling how long he had slept, or whether it was day or night, for in the city all illumination was artificial. He was, however, thoroughly rested, and stretched his arms above his head, conscious sleepily of muscles tightening in stomach and shoulder, then sat up and was perplexed to find that the wall facing him was not, as it had appeared to be last night, a mirror, but a window through which a crowd of people was interestedly surveying him. There were men in top hats and frock coats, women in expensive clothes, women less well dressed, carrying typewriters, a person wearing a dinner jacket with a skirt, looking through a lorgnette, a judge in full dress, the inevitable policeman, and two or three workmen, standing at the back of the crowd, gazing at him, it seemed, with a somewhat wistful contempt.

George got up and walked towards the window and at once the crowd, without showing any consideration for his feelings, began to talk and gesticulate, pointing out to each other aspects of his appearance, arguing, evidently, though George could not hear what they said, looking wise, as though in the discussion of some object of science. Suddenly they all ceased talking and looked with grave faces towards the door of the room. George turned round and saw stepping hurriedly the figure of a man in a surgeon's apron, carrying in his hand a little black bag, a bald man, square-faced, shining, who smiled constantly and whose small eyes twinkled as he held out his hand to George, saying: 'Sorry to have kept you waiting, my boy. It's a busy time. Let's get it

156

over quickly, shall we? Just take your trousers off and lie down on the bed, there's a good fellow.'

George shook his hand, and preparing to clear up one point at a time, pointed towards the faces at the window. 'What are all these people doing here?'

'Ha-ha!' said the surgeon briskly. 'Never mind about them. They've just come to see the operation.'

'What operation?' said George.

'What operation?' repeated the surgeon. 'Oh-ho, oh-ho, there's a fine question! What operation, indeed? Why you're the young man who's going to the Convent, aren't you?'

'Yes,' said George, 'but I'm feeling quite well.'

'Feeling quite well? Now, I wonder,' said the surgeon. 'I think you're a bit shy, aren't you?' He thumped George on the chest, then squeezed his arm. 'Now then, be a good fellow!'

'Look here,' said George, 'I haven't the least idea of what this operation of yours is, and anyhow I don't want it.'

'Ah!' said the surgeon gravely, stroking a polished chin, 'Ah! that puts rather a different complexion on things. Are you quite sure that you're being broadminded? Must take stock of the evidence, you know. Must take stock. Oh yes. Think again, my dear fellow, I'd advise you.'

'But what is this operation?' George asked, and noticed that the crowd outside the window was becoming more and more animated, noses being pressed to glass, with careful gestures, inquisitive glances.

'A miracle,' said the surgeon, 'a positive miracle. I can't claim to have made the discovery myself. Of no, it's been done in the Convent for generations; but I do think that I and my assistants have succeeded in simplifying the proceedings, and the local anæsthetic which we use, besides ensuring an absolutely painless operation, is without any unpleasant after effects. I've

157

never known it to fail. Some of my patients have told me that they hardly realized what was happening to them.'

'But what is the operation?' George interrupted.

'I'm coming to that,' said the surgeon, rubbing his shining hands. 'It's as easy as nine-pins. Naturally I can't go into details. There are ladies outside the room. Nor can I give away professional secrets. But it amounts to this. In five minutes time you'll be able to fulfil the functions of either sex. Splendid, isn't it? See? Now then, be a good fellow and lie down on the bed. We don't want to keep everybody waiting, do we?' He turned his back on George, bowed to the people outside the window, who clapped their hands, and began unpacking his instruments.

'I'm sorry,' said George, 'but I'm quite content as I am, and nothing will induce me to have this operation.'

'Pooh, Pooh!' the surgeon said, though he dropped his instruments, 'Don't let us go on wasting time. I'm a bit older than you are, I think, and perhaps I may be a bit wiser. I don't know. I don't know, I'm sure. But, my dear chap, I know you won't mind my giving you a little advice. You want to go to the Convent, don't you? Well, in the Convent they are all very brilliant people. Oh yes. And they have all undergone this operation. It may seem strange to you, but in point of fact it works very well, very well indeed. Dominant characteristics remain, at least for a time, and you will find that in many cases there is no alteration of dress. Naturally the possibilities of mutual satisfaction are immeasurably increased. That's obvious; but what appeals chiefly to us scientific men is this, that the mind is correspondingly enriched. I may be wrong, but somehow I fancy that I am not. If I am, pray correct me; but to me it has always seemed axiomatic that the mind should control the body. Now what greater conquest over the body than this? Tell me that. Of course, the effect of the operation on cases of neurosis, hypochondria, skizothumia, traumatic cases of all kinds, is magnificent, simply magnificent. And now let's get down to business. I'll just ring the bell for the nurse.' He took George by the arm and began to lead him towards the bed. Some of the people outside were smiling.

George broke loose. 'Once and for all,' he said, 'Let me tell you that I am not going to have this operation done on me. Can't you see that the whole essence of sex is that one sex is polar to the other? I haven't seen your hermaphrodites yet, but I should imagine that, so far from being saner because of your operation, they are as neurotic as you can make them. Before I began my travels I met some people who would, no doubt, have liked to undergo your surgery. They passed their exams with honours, but they were no good at games and could only review books. You can talk as long as you like, but I'm not going to have the operation.'

The surgeon was hurriedly packing away his instruments. When he had done this he snapped up his bag and walked quickly to the door. 'The chief of my department shall hear of this,' he muttered as he went out of the room, without looking back, and George turning towards the window, saw that, of the crowd, some people were looking at him with consternation, others were laughing at him, and of these the person with the lorgnette seemed most amused, while the two workmen, who up to now had watched the proceedings with dull faces, were winking at each other, as though privately satisfied. He noticed a curtain and drew it across the window, since he was anxious to reflect upon the surgeon's proposal and he felt ill at ease, as though he were a fish in an aquarium, when he looked through the glass wall at spectators standing in artificial light.

Left to himself he wondered whether he had offended the authorities by his refusal to undergo the operation. He tried to ordinate within his mind what he knew already and what he suspected of the life in the city. And he was forced to admit that he was only a little less ignorant than he had been when he set out from his home. But at the same time, he thought, I have come already a certain distance and, ignorant as I may be about what to do next, I am at least in a position where I shall shortly have to do something.

His thoughts were interrupted by a light knock on the door, and quickly entered a figure which George did not immediately recognize to be his brother David. David was dressed in his blue lounge suit, but what made him appear strange was the skirt which he wore over his wide trousers, and the tight-fitting velvet cloche hat which covered his hair and made remarkable his pale face and bright red lips. Round his neck was a thin chain of gold from which hung the jade figure of a bird which he fingered with one hand, as he stepped delicately forward, offering George the other, smiling.

'Well, I'm glad to see you,' George said, trying to suppress his astonishment at this sight. 'I've been feeling rather lost here. How are you? And what has been happening?'

David led him towards the bed, where they sat down, and, having rung the bell, said: 'First of all, I think, a Simkin. What do you say?'

A waiter entered and David ordered a bottle of champagne, and, when it was brought in, tipped the waiter liberally.

'You seem to have made some money,' George said, and David shrugged his shoulders: 'I'd be all right if it weren't for the taxes, and they all go to those savages you've been staying with so long. Did you have the girl? She's not a bad bit, is she?' He laughed and put his hand to his face, laughter distending the coat of fard. 'Well, it's very nice to have you with us after all. We thought you were never coming.'

'I didn't know whether to believe you or not,' George said,

'when you told me that you'd been successful. Is it really true?'

David spoke more gravely, though there was something in his gestures and clothes which deprived his words of much of their force, making him seem to George, in spite of the gravity of his utterance, not entirely concerned with what he was saying. 'It's incredibly difficult,' he said, 'as even you, my dear brother, must be aware, to be sure about anything. I heard the Wild Geese, though they were a considerable distance away, when I was at the farm—or so I thought. Since then I've become pretty sure that they weren't geese at all (duck, probably, even coot), or, if they were geese, that they were not the right kind.'

'What do you mean, "the right kind"? ' George asked.

'I'll tell you. They did not seem to me the kind of bird which one would expect to find here. Now don't interrupt, my dear fellow. I know your romantic ideas. You'd say, why should I expect to find them here, but I can answer your objections. First of all I have the headmaster's word for it. He's a remarkably fine scholar, the headmaster. Aramaic's his subject.'

'But have you seen the goose?' George interrupted impatiently and David slowly smiled, then leaning towards him he whispered in his ear 'Yes'.

George shouted back. 'Show me!' he cried, 'Show me!' and then looking at David, who smiled nervously, he felt curiously his enthusiasm ebb, for how, he wondered, could this be true? Why had not David mentioned this at once? Why had he dragged into the discussion the unnecessary opinion of a headmaster on a subject of which he was himself, if he was to be believed, adequately informed? Why did he betray nervousness and hesitation? Why was he living here still, a hermaphrodite, as his skirt declared, self-satisfied yet not strong, instead of spreading the news far and wide, occupying himself with some constructive work, if it was true what he said, that he had with his own eyes discovered the object of their inquiry?

David had noticed his change of feeling. 'You don't believe me,' he said hurriedly. 'As a matter of fact sometimes I hardly believe myself. Not that it matters much anyway. One's pretty well looked after here. But on our way to the Convent I'll take you to the Anserium, and you can judge for yourself. After all it's not a subject that's easily discussed.'

He spoke too loudly, betraying the state of his nerves, and it seemed to George that David was half-consciously exculpating himself from some charge which he imagined might be brought against him, a charge perhaps of apathy, inertia, of being too easily satisfied. He now was quite unable to believe that David had succeeded and was only anxious to know in what way he had been deluded, suspecting too that he was not sorry, although there was at the back of his mind a certain uneasiness, to have reached a vague belief that he had attained his terminus.

David, pouring out more champagne, was now speaking more naturally. 'After all,' he was saying, 'it's difficult to delineate objects of pure thought. I don't pretend to have reached the *summum bonum* exactly, but I just happen to have a trained mind which even you, I suppose, would admit to be an advantage. It's good stuff, isn't it, the bubbly? By the way, you've had the operation, I suppose?'

'No,' said George, 'I refused to have it done.'

David laughed, though by the twitching of his hands George saw that he was uneasy. 'The old puritan conscience,' he said. 'Honestly, my dear fellow, I think you've made a mistake. I can't imagine that anyone should not want to be like Tiresias. It's such fun. You've no idea how valuable it is to feel the reactions of a woman. And then, of course, you can be a man at the same time. You can synthesize or analyse. Oh, it's not to be missed on any account. Grubbit's not the word. Of course you were always a bit queer, but what on earth can have induced you to refuse?'

'Simply that I prefer to stick to one thing,' George said, 'but don't let's argue about it now. I'll be interested to see how the system works. What I'd like to know is how you live in this town and how you've been treated since you arrived.'

'Well, we'll have to hurry,' David said. 'I've got to give a lecture before very long. As for the operation, you must have it done some other time. The headmaster won't like to hear that you refused. The whole thing's rather embarrassing.'

He was frightened and less well disposed towards his brother than he had previously seemed to be. George wondered what was the reason for this change, being reluctant to imagine that he was in any danger of becoming an outcast simply because he had not consented to suffer an unnecessary operation, but he listened carefully as David told his story.

'You may have heard something about me at that farm where you stayed so long. It was lucky for you, by the way, that you didn't stay there any longer. There are some Reds about in that district, and its dangerous to get mixed up with them. Of course, I've got no objection to revolutions so long as I come out on top, but those fellows in the country haven't a chance. They're much too well looked after by the police.

'But I was telling you about myself. After an hour or two in that farm I began to long for some civilized food. I got here very quickly, thanks to the police, who, I found, had a fast car waiting for me on the main road. By the way, I hear you haven't been getting on too well with the police. If I were you, I should be a bit more careful. They're very minor officials, of course, but its silly to offend the Government, even in the smallest details. Not that the Government would ever take much notice; they're

163

the kindest possible people, and very hard worked. It just seems to me rather bad form, that's all.

'Well, I got here just in time to hear about poor old Rudolph. Of course, he was ploughed in the entrance exam, and then he ran off with an aeroplane. He didn't get far according to the police, before he crashed in some woods outside the town. The Government were rather clever about it. They ordered his machine to be repaired and filled with petrol, and before long Rudolph, who had been wandering about the Zoological Gardens, which are kept outside the town by order of the Government, came back to his aeroplane and flew away.

'As a matter of fact I got full marks on my examination paper, and so I suppose I had as good a reception as most people. I was taken to the Convent at once and welcomed the operation. Perhaps you don't understand the distinction which has been offered you. It's not everyone who belongs to what we like to call the third sex. Of course, we're still men and women in a sense. Dominant characteristics remain, and in some cases there has been a reversal. Personally I'm rather more male than female, I think. But there are still quite a number of people at the Convent who are unisexual. There's Marqueta, the wife of the chief statistician, a clever girl with no male characteristics, but otherwise quite normal. Then there's the games master, who's much the same as me, but doesn't wear a skirt. Oh there are all possible kinds, and everyone isn't perhaps as broadminded as I am, but on the whole we get on very well together. I had an interview with the headmaster as soon as I had recovered from the operation, and it was at his suggestion that I wrote to you. The Government didn't want you to get mixed up in politics. I don't quite know what sort of a job they are likely to offer you. It's a pity that you haven't got better qualifications. I'm teaching Moral Philosophy, and at the same time I assist Mr. Pothimere, the

Professor of Love. Perhaps you'll be able to help with the games. There isn't really much work to do, but we spend a lot of time in thought. Well now, we'd better be going. You'll soon see what sort of a place it is.' And without looking at George he led the way out of the room and downstairs to the brilliantly illuminated street, where a large car was waiting for them.

CHAPTER TWELVE

Outside the Hospital George was surprised to find the streets so brilliant and so spacious. High up in the air could be seen patches of the stupendous roof between the flares of gigantic arc lamps, and the very height of the concrete caused that stubborn material to appear almost insubstantial, so that an inhabitant of this city might well believe himself to be walking not under a roof but under a vaulting etherial. Broad streets were packed with traffic, private cars, lorries like those which brought food from the country, omnibuses, standing stalls where, so David said, food, which in factories had been chemically treated, was sold in tabloid form. The houses were mostly of two of three stories, and on their flat roofs were laid out tennis courts, motor bicycle tracks, and artificial shrubberies. There seemed in the whole town no shadow, so numerous, so powerful, and so diversely disposed were the electric lights, and it was perhaps this fact which made George inclined to look upon the people who hurried shadowless to and fro as unreal figures, embodied but only just, and the buildings, rectangular and gleaming, appeared purposeless, as if made of sugar or of something else inappropriate for human architecture.

'Don't forget what you promised to show me,' George said, and David, starting the car, nodded his head nervously, laughing, though, to George's mind, this was not an occasion for laughter, and, as the car moved forward, he began to question his brother more particularly, eager, even though he felt that his eagerness was ill-founded, to convince himself, even against his better sense, that

166

something remarkable had been seen or heard. But David would return only evasive answers, with shrugs of shoulder, till 'Now', he said, 'you can see for yourself. We have reached the centre of the town. On my left the Convent, on my right the Anserium'; and in a crowded district he brought the car to a standstill against the curb, while people jostled on the pavement, newsboys shouted, and George looked round him to see on his left a long low building, elegantly light with sheeted glass, steel walls, and aluminium triangular shades above the windows and doors (something of a toy, he thought, though he could not but admire the dexterity of the architect who with aluminium, glass, and steel had contrived to suggest a modern restaurant, an office, and a pagoda), and on his right a dome the summit of which, because of the brilliant lights set in the concrete sky, was imperceptible. This was apparently the fashionable quarter of the town, for the people passing hurriedly in the street were dressed in expensive clothes; there were no workmen to be seen, but a number of young people who stood in groups impeding the progress of men in top hats, dressed, some of them, as David was dressed, whilst others were clothed womanly as far as the waist with trousers lower, and all these, George surmised, were students or professors at the Convent.

But their immediate concern was the Anserium, and, crossing the pavement, they passed through a heavy door of carved ironwork into a majestic interior. From the floor sprang curved ribs of steel supporting the concrete shell whose apex was high above their heads. The narrowing spaces between the bright parabolas of steel were covered with a gloss of metal that shone like gold, so that the eye would have been dazzled by the brilliance of white and yellow if visibility had not been impaired by wreathing smoke from the burning of some aromatic substance, while the lights which were placed at the bases of the curving steel ribs to run up the steel were soon lost, diffused and confusedly glomerated

167

in a cloud which hung 40 or 50 feet from the floor, just penetrable because from a great height, the summit of the dome, shone another light that beat vertically upon the upper surface of the cloud but could not wholly dispel it. Magnificent the building was, but its remote summit and the curious effects of lighting that wriggled along steel or was transferred through clouds of smoke made the architecture indistinct, the scene phantasmagorical. A blue point of light shone near the door and, passing this, David instructed George to remove his cap, then pointed out to him the great number of chairs arranged in orderly rows all over the spacious floor, telling him that on certain fixed occasions a great portion of the population would come and sit on these chairs, listening to wholesome instructions, revering, with the aid of pure thought, what could be imagined.

'But where is it?' George asked, impressed by the quiet and the large secrecy of the place, half-expecting, so serious had been David's voice and so remote from the street did this scene appear, something stupendous to be discovered, 'Where is it?' and David pointed upwards where beyond the cloud of smelling smoke could be discerned swinging from a rope of gold a golden gleam and above it something white. 'In the gold basket,' David said, 'difficult to be discerned.'

George adjusted his field-glasses and peering through mist was able to distinguish what made him laugh. 'The damned thing's stuffed,' he said, turning to David, who clutched his arm, anxiously looking round, fearing lest they were observed, 'and besides,' George continued, 'it's only a specimen of the domestic variety.'

David dragged him away, tense-lipped, whispering: 'For God's sake, don't talk so loud. Someone might hear. You damned fool.' They withdrew to the curved wall of the building and after having made sure that, apart from themselves, the Anserium was empty, David spoke again in a low voice, but in more confident tones: 'Look here, I can't help you to be intelligent, but before we leave I must have you promise not to mention a word of your suspicions to anyone. You've no idea how embarrassing this is for me. I wish to God you'd stayed at the coastguard station, playing football. Can't you see that this is, in some respects, the centre of the town? Your conduct has almost certainly been observed and will be reported. But there's no need for you to make things worse by talking about it.'

'All right,' George said, 'I won't say anything about it. But you can't make out that the thing isn't stuffed.'

David spoke in an expressionless voice: 'My dear brother, I suppose it's hopeless to convince you that you are making a fool of yourself. You have only just come to this town. Do you really imagine that everyone here is a fool except yourself?'

George laughed. 'No,' he said, 'of course not. But I can see when a thing's stuffed and when it's not. What on earth can have made you believe that this was what we were after?'

'I have the headmaster's word for it,' David said petulantly, 'and I've also got, what you don't seem to have, an open unbigoted mind and a little intelligence. Now try and think straight for a minute or two and see things as I see them.'

'I'll have a try,' George said, 'but I saw quite plainly that the thing was stuffed.'

David ignored that remark and continued, growing more animated as he proceeded. 'I suppose you think me foolish for taking the word of the headmaster and other men of experience on a subject which one cannot possibly hope to understand at one's first acquaintance with it. I might as well remind you that no one has ever questioned the fact that I have a first class brain. Our problem is not one of quality, but of identity. What we have to decide is not whether the object in the basket is of this or that kind, but whether it is the object of our inquiry. Further enlightenment will follow. I have excellent reasons for believing that all is well, and I propose to act on that assumption. If you are going to insist on being romantic and on rejecting the clearest evidence, all I have to say is, keep your mouth shut, and don't drag me into it. But honestly, my dear fellow, do try and think. Can't you see that the thing is worth further inquiry?'

'I've seen with my own eyes,' George said, 'that the thing is stuffed. That's all the inquiry I need to be sure that it isn't what I want. And besides, if that stuffed goose had any value, why don't people take more interest in it? We're the only visitors to the Anserium to-day, and when you or anyone else talk about the town, it is always about the Convent, not the Anserium, that you talk. I believe the thing's a bogus show to keep people quiet. I believe you know that it's stuffed just as well as I do, but you like being here.'

David shrugged his shoulders, surprising George by showing no anger. 'Very well,' he said. 'Form your own opinions, only keep quiet about them, I'd advise you. I'll take you to the Convent now. There's just a chance that you may become civilized.'

And as they were crossing the road George, who had never given much credence to David's half-hearted suggestions that he had been successful, found nevertheless that he was keenly disappointed. He had thought that he had expected nothing, yet now when that nothing was revealed, he was ill at ease, discouraged, wondering whether he had not after all, against his better judgment, hoped that the town might contain the very thing he sought, and reflecting on the position of the Anserium at the very centre of the town, adjoining the Convent, he began to suspect that there might be more truth than he had believed likely in Pushkov's stories of the corruption and brutality of the Government. For, he said to himself, the Government are either imposed upon themselves, which is very unlikely, or else they impose this freakish emblem upon others. Then, remembering David, he was struck with the thought that perhaps in this polity governors and governed might have their own reasons for acquiescing in what for them might be simply an unimportant fraud, an interesting hoax; but he was profoundly shocked to think that there could exist people capable of treating so lightly a subject of such importance.

But now they had reached the Convent for George to receive new impressions. Entering at a glass door they were soon in the quadrangle, walking on an aluminium path which bordered a central lawn of artificial grass. The building of the quadrangle was similar in style to the exterior of the Convent, being light and rectangular, the walls of glass and aluminium relieved from monotony by the countless triangular shades of aluminium or celluloid which covered windows and doors and directed the flow of light from the electric bulbs which seemed to shine from every angle. Against the walls lounged groups of people whom George assumed to be students, young persons of indefinite age, some wearing skirts, some trousers, some both, while the upper parts of their bodies were covered in blouses, dinner-jackets, sports coats, or military uniform. David nodded to some of them and they returned his salute, looking curiously at George, who was surprised to see how little notice David took of them as he led the way out of this quadrangle into another, remarking: 'Some of the juniors. My room's some way off, I'm afraid.'

They passed through many other quadrangles, all much alike, and George was amazed when he thought what the population of this establishment must be. In each quadrangle were the same groups of people and George followed his brother for a great distance, till 'Here we are at last' David said, and then stopped still, pointing towards an upper window, which differed from the other windows by showing a box of artificial flowers.

'Professor Pothimere's room,' David explained. 'I live next to him. But listen!'

From the window came the melancholy slow notes of a cornet and mingled with them the sound of water running out of a bath. It was 'Take a pair of sparkling eyes' that the Professor was playing very slowly, so that between each note could be heard the sound of water flowing or gurgling.

'Really rather wonderful,' David said. 'It's an exercise of which he is very fond. He lies in a warm bath and when he has adjusted the flow of water to his satisfaction he plays his cornet, often wearing a false beard, while the tears stream down his face. He has the most delicate sensations. He is, as I think I told you, our Professor of Love, a man whose theories are very daring. We'll have a cocktail with him later on. We'd better go to the headmaster's house now.'

George nodded, and followed David to the other side of the quadrangle, to a staircase marked 'Halfway House—the headmaster', and David explained the meaning of the superscription by saying: 'We've come through about half the Convent. Beyond this quad live the research scholars, and some of the philosophers who don't give lectures.' As he spoke George could distinguish above the plaintive notes of Professor Pothimere's cornet a sound from the farther quadrangles which seemed a shriek. 'What do they do there?' he asked, and David shrugged his shoulders: 'Don't know. Research of all kinds. Very valuable work, I believe.'

The headmaster's door was opened to them by a young person, dressed as a girl, tall and undulating in her movements, with loose yellow hair falling over her hand-woven dress of light green. Her eyes seemed to George to protrude from her head, so nervously enthusiastic did they roll, but her face was over-white and the muscles about her mouth were restricted.

172

'Let me introduce my brother George,' David said. 'George, this is Wilhelmina. She's a great friend of the headmaster.' He simpered. 'And interested in Art.'

'Let's leave the door open for half a minute, shall we?' said Wilhelmina, 'I do so love to hear Professor Pothimere's music. It seems to me somehow that he can interpret the pathetic better than anyone, even Victor Hugo. What do you think?' She turned to George.

'Can't say I think much of it,' said George, and Wilhelmina smiled at David. 'How witty your brother is!' Then, without listening to the cornet, she led the way upstairs. 'His Grace will soon be ready to see you. Meanwhile we'll have a cocktail, shall we?'

'Not a bad piece, is she?' David whispered as they were going upstairs. 'She's the headmaster's mistress. Just as well to be on friendly terms with her.'

'My den,' said Wilhelmina, and they entered a room furnished chiefly with divans, though on a small table were glasses and a cocktail shaker, and in one corner of the room was a book-case filled with volumes bound in soft leather. Wilhelmina pointed to the wall where a small object was suspended by a silk thread. 'What do you think of my Daudinet? You'll need the magnifying glass.' David examined the picture, which was painted on a plaque of metal scarcely larger than a postage stamp. 'Exquisite!' he said, 'Exquisite! But not quite important, I should say.'

Wilhelmina's neighing laughter startled George who was examining the books, which were all printed by the same press on hand-made paper. She was saying: 'Really, David, you're getting quite a reactionary. Art isn't a question of scale, is it?' And David had begun to say: 'That wasn't quite what I meant,' when she interrupted him. 'But it doesn't matter, does it? See what you think of my review of Coddlegut's poems. He's a charming young man, quite a genius, I'm sure. He has every alternate letter printed upside down. Quite brilliant.'

She handed David a few sheets of type-written paper and turned to George. Her face was continually being distorted by the spasmodic fluctuations of her lips, while her staring eyes remained unaffected by the breaking up of her mouth and jaw. 'Tell me,' she said, 'what books do you like best?'

'Shakespeare,' said George, 'Karl Marx, *Tom Jones* and Isaiah.'

Wilhelmina neighed and twisted her head round. '*Mais quel type!*' Then to George: 'Of course you don't understand French.'

'Yes,' said George, 'I do. That sort of thing was taught very well at our high school. And I don't see why you should be surprised at my choice of books.'

'Perfectly,' said Wilhelmina. 'It's too lovely, isn't it? Well, David, what do you think of the review?'

'Very pleasant,' David said judiciously, 'very pleasant indeed. I like particularly that bit about the fiery horses.'

Wilhelmina had become very serious. 'Ah!' she said, 'I hoped you'd like that. You don't think that it's too romantic?'

'Not a bit. Not a bit,' said David. 'I admire your style very much. Of course anyone can find the right words, but what I admire about your reviews is the way you arrange the tempo of your paragraphs.'

'Yes,' said Wilhelmina, 'it's very clever of you, I think, to have noticed the contrapuntal effect. It's not everyone who can appreciate much more than the plastic side of writing. Don't you think?'

'It is always the surface which is important,' said David, and was continuing when Wilhelmina interrupted: 'But to return to my work—' and George was surprised to find them discussing so animatedly what was only a review of some other person's poems. He was relieved when a bell rang and David turned to him saying: 'That's for you.'

Wilhelmina led them downstairs into an apartment bare of all furniture and with a rubber curtain cutting off from view some portion of the room. 'See you again soon,' she said to David, and, smiling quickly at George, left them alone.

David whispered in George's ear: 'Of course you won't see the headmaster, but you'd better tell him you're here, and ask him for a job.' He pointed towards the rubber curtain, and George, opining that this screened the official, said: 'Is it quite impossible, sir, for me to see you while I am speaking?'

A piece of paper was slipped beneath the curtain and George, after picking it up, read the typewritten words: 'Quite impossible.'

'Very well,' he said, 'perhaps some other time I may be fortunate enough to see you. I don't think I need say much now. You must be aware for what purpose I am travelling in this direction, and I should be very grateful for any help you can give me in pursuing that purpose. Before I go farther I should very much like to see something of this town, and if I can have an opportunity of speaking to the appropriate official, I'd like to represent to him some of the grievances which the countrymen feel against the Government.'

All this time had continued the noise of a typewriter from beyond the curtain, and George found it very difficult to speak not only in face of a sheet of rubber but also to someone who he was by no means sure was listening to him.

'I think that's all I've got to say just now,' he added, rather lamely. 'Perhaps you'd like to ask me some questions.'

The sound of the keys of the typewriter ceased abruptly. George could hear the turning of the roller, and then another sheet of paper was pushed beneath the curtain. He picked it up and read: 'On behalf of the Board of Governors I am very pleased to be able to welcome you to the Convent. Your work will be allotted to you from time to time. Your first task will be to deliver a lecture on English literature as soon as is convenient for everyone concerned. Later on perhaps you will be so good as to referee the football match between the Pros and the Cons. Your affairs, you may be sure, will receive proper attention.'

There followed a signature which George could not read, and the printed words 'On behalf of the Board of Governors. C. Dept. 537/XD. Confidential'.

'Not a very satisfactory interview,' George said, when he and David stepped back into the quad. 'He didn't say where or to whom I was to give this lecture, and he didn't even let me hear the sound of his voice.'

'Oh, that'll be quite all right,' said David, who appeared relieved by the result of the interview. 'All that sort of thing is arranged for one, and you ought to be able to referee the football match very well. But, for heaven's sake, don't go on talking about those savages in the country. The Government knows all about them. Still, you seem to have made a fairly good start. Now I should advise you to stick to your job. I didn't think you'd get such a good one.'

They were walking towards the rooms of Professor Pothimere, who had now stopped playing on his cornet. While David stopped to powder his face and brighten up his lips, George reflected that he was still far from knowing how he was regarded by the authorities, whether favourably, or with suspicion. Of Bob he had seen or heard nothing, and he himself had, it seemed to him, been prevented from seeing very much of the city outside the convent, though he could not, of course, be sure that there had been any plan to hurry him through the streets after he had rejected the surgeon. And now he had not seen the headmaster, and had only

David's word for it that he had been interviewed by the headmaster in person. It was very confusing, and particularly disconcerting was the fact that while he was in doubt about everybody, everybody seemed to know about him and to be satisfied that he was in an appointed position. He welcomed David's proposal: 'Come up to my room, and meet some of the staff.'

CHAPTER THIRTEEN

As they went upstairs they heard from Professor Pothimere's room the sound of several voices, and 'That's where they all are,' said David, knocking at the door and entering at once.

The walls of the room were pink, and pink shades screened the electric light. On a sofa, covered in grey satin, reclined the professor, a little man, middle-aged, to judge from his appearance, with shrewd eyes and a greyish complexion. At his side was his cornet and a false beard, coloured red, which, so George assumed, was used on the occasions when he wished to disguise his thin intellectual lips and pointed chin.

On the floor at his feet sat a young woman who had not looked up when the brothers entered the room. She was staring thoughtfully beneath heavy lids at the grey carpet, and heavily luxurious she seemed with her thick black hair, swarthy complexion and the rounded flesh of her face, though, thought George, the small fingers and the nervous suspension of the head must denote delicacy of an unusual order: and he looked steadfastly at her, welcoming her presence as of one, amongst all these unsympathetic figures, who might be familiar to him, while she continued to gaze at the carpet, having her hair stroked intermittently by a man, stocky, alert in a faded sports coat, who sat on the sofa where there was room for him by the Professor's feet. And in the corner of the room on a hard chair was a burly figure, with close cropped hair, sorting photographs of boys in games clothes.

Along the walls were pictures whose subjects and arrangement were surprising. There were pictures of all kinds of scenes of gallantry—a gentleman handing a lady out of a coach, a kiss

178

stolen at a waltz, a gondolier playing a musical instrument—
and, alternately with these coloured reproductions were photographs of the insides of animals and some photographs of vivisec-
tional experiment.

When David and George had entered the room, Professor
Pothimere with a surprising agility had sprung from the sofa and,
running towards David, shook his hand, whispering, with a slight
Scotch accent, 'I dream of something more.' David introduced his
brother, at the same time whispering in the Professor's ear a
sentence out of which George was able to pick the word 'operation', and the Professor nodded, saying 'Terrible! Terrible!' and
then shook hands with George, clinging to his hand.

David pointed to the lonely young man in the corner. 'You
must meet Harold, our games master,' and Harold morosely
packed away the photographs in his pocket and advancing to
George said in a high-pitched treble voice: 'Chippy-chippy!'

George was then introduced to the stocky man on the sofa.
'Humberto,' said David, 'the chief statistician, and this is his
charming wife, Marqueta.'

Humberto grinned from ear to ear. 'Very pleased to meet you,'
he said, and went into a run of laughter, while he nervously kicked
his leg backwards and forwards, slapping his thighs. 'I hear
you're an ornithologist. We must compare notes. We must compare notes.' Marqueta raised slow eyes, fastidiously extending
fingers. Still, she's very beautiful, thought George, as he took
her hand, gazing directly, with perhaps an indecorous violence,
into the face which seemed to welcome his glance.

'I can see,' in precise tones said Professor Pothimere, who had
been watching George closely, 'that our young friend is disconcerted to find that in our system we still retain the sacrament of
marriage. *Ah! si jeunesse savait!*'

'Yes,' said George, 'I admit I am rather surprised. It seemed to me at first that there is a great deal of freedom in your sexual arrangements here.'

Everyone laughed. 'That's good,' said Humberto, kicking his leg out, and slapping it, 'Freedom. Yes. But in direct proportion.'

Professor Pothimere played a few low notes on his cornet, and then, 'Let me explain,' he said. 'Perhaps I have suffered more than any of you young people, and in love, you must know, suffering is wisdom. I may tell you, my young friend, that for years I worked as a research student, and now with my theories developed, I do my best to guide the young to happiness.'

There was in the sound of the Professor's voice a crispness which, to George's mind, was inappropriate in one whose sentimentality seemed so pronounced, and he listened with interest to what promised to be an explanation, though he could not avoid looking every now and then at Marqueta, who, he found, was not averse to the meeting of their eyes.

'Experiment,' continued the Professor, 'has enabled me, with the aid of Humberto, to draw up a calculus of sensation. I have experimented on animals and, if you will excuse me, on the bodies of unfortunate people, malefactors or votaries of science. On such occasions I have registered by various apparatus the rise or fall in the pressure of my own blood and in the blood of others who were spectators of these operations. I have been flagellated myself, and found the experiment on the whole displeasing. Sadistically and masochistically I have done my best to explore each sense, and have found that it is the sense of sight which, by communicating perhaps more vividly with the imaginative faculties, gives the best results. I shall never forget my agreeable perturbation when I first saw a woman roasted. Almost my heart burst. But ah! my friends, this is not love! True enough that this is a part of experience which no one can afford to miss, and when you graduate to the Department of Research, I know that you will

180

enjoy yourselves. There are some indeed who spend their lives in these pursuits, and I cannot find it in my heart to blame them, but yet when every sense is continually exacerbated there is no time and no inclination for the simpler things of life, music over the water, the perfume of a rose. I find now that when I am sitting in a warm bath the notes of my cornet conjure up before me such a series of delightful images, that I would not exchange them for the more arduous distractions of torturing or of being tortured.

'And so quite rightly, I think, there is a place for marriage in our polity. What can be more delightful than the blushes, which can easily be induced, of a bride, who, by the aid of one of my inventions, can be easily rehabilitated in virginity? It seems to me, as I grow older, that it is in these simple things that the very quintessence of pleasure lies. But try for yourselves, my young friends, try for yourselves. Owing to our excellent institutions you are debarred from no experiments. But to my mind there is something ineffably sweet in the tender feelings of romance. The perversions of the body are interesting, but lasting satisfaction is to be discovered in the perversions of the mind.'

Meditatively the audience turned eyes to the ground, while the Professor in a voice rich with emotion, recited some passages from Victor Hugo's poem *Boaz endormi*; but George stared in astonishment, unwilling to believe that the Professor had been speaking seriously, for he realized that if these people were occupied in speculations of this sort, there could be no chance whatever of his getting a hearing when he wished to put before the authorities some of the grievances of the countrymen. Now the faces of his brother, of the Professor, of Humberto, and of the games master seemed to him meaningless, in spite of the enthusiasm with which they followed the Professor's recitation, and, remembering the sound which that morning he had heard beyond the headmaster's house, he was ill at ease, mistrustful of the society into which he had entered alone and powerless; but he was momentarily relieved when he met Marqueta's eyes and found her smiling at him, for there seemed to be in her face something that was not wholly artificial, and he resolved that at the earliest possible moment he would have a talk with her and ask her advice.

At the conclusion of the recitation, without waiting to be asked his opinion of the performance, he went across the room to the games master, and asked him when the football match was due to take place. 'Oh, quite soon, now, I expect,' said Harold, in his treble voice which George found extraordinarily irritating. 'It's the big match of the season, old boy. No kid gloves, you understand.'

'Good,' said George. 'I hope my refereeing will be all right. Which side is likely to win, do you think?'

'Oh, honestly, old boy, I don't know,' said Harold. 'That'll be arranged by the Government, I suppose. Of course, I've never actually seen them playing.'

'But I thought you were the games master,' said George.

'Oh quite,' replied Harold. 'You're quite right, old boy. But we never actually play any games, if you understand what I mean. And besides, this match is between the Pros and Cons who are trained by the Government.' And he walked slowly to the door, turning before he left the room, saying in his high-pitched voice: 'Chippy-chippy, all you sailor boys.'

George stood still for a moment, more bewildered than ever. In this establishment, it seemed, there was no time-table, which, when he came to think of it, was to be expected, since there was no means of measuring time; but it was certainly surprising to find that the games master knew little or nothing either about the play of his own pupils or of the other football teams in the town, and as he looked round again on the easy enthusiastic faces of David and Humberto, who, in spite of their official positions, never seemed to have any work to do, he wondered to what audience he would have to deliver his address on English literature, and what precisely was expected of him by the headmaster whom he had never seen.

Marqueta spoke for the first time. Her voice was low, musically assured. 'We're all coming to hear your lecture,' she said.

'When is it to be?' asked George.

'Now,' said Professor Pothimere, rising to his feet. 'I'll lead the way,' and they all followed him downstairs, and across the quadrangle to a large hall, filled to overflowing by students dressed in the manner of those who had undergone the operation, of uncertain age.

On the way George had found time to say to Professor Pothimere: 'What would be the best thing for me to speak about? I suppose these are fairly advanced students. Are there any special subjects in which they are interested?' and Professor Pothimere said: 'Subjects of general interest are best. You'd better not talk about Love. Talk about the Heroic in Shakespeare.'

'Very well,' said George, 'I'll do my best,' and he walked through the packed hall, following the Professor to a raised dais, thinking what to say, indignant at having to speak at such short notice, while he heard the Professor's raised voice: 'I have great pleasure in introducing to you George, our new lecturer in English Literature. I am sure you will all listen attentively to what he has to say.'

The Professor climbed down from the platform and left the hall. George raised his eyes and looked towards his audience, which seemed to him, from his elevation, much too far away. Indeed, there was a considerable space between the foot of the platform and the first rows of chairs, while it was impossible for the lecturer to distinguish the faces at the back of the hall. The lighting too was unsatisfactory, for on the platform there was no light at all, so that George had to be careful that he did not step over the edge; but the back of the hall blazed with light so brilliant that he was dazzled when he raised his eyes. Surveying the audience George noticed all kinds of dresses and hats, but whether because of the lighting or because of the distance from which he was removed from them, the faces of those who were now furiously clapping their hands seemed blurred, characterless, infantile. I shall have to shout, or they won't hear me, George said to himself, and when the applause had subsided he began to speak as loudly as he could.

'First of all,' he said, 'I am going to recite to you—' and a voice came from the back, 'Speak up!' George shouted: 'I'm speaking as loud as I can. Perhaps some of the people at the back, who find it difficult to hear, would be so good as to bring their chairs to the front, where there is plenty of room.' He paused and the silence was broken by little bursts of tittering. No one moved.

'Very well,' said George, 'stay where you are; but I must ask everyone to be as quiet as possible. Otherwise it will be very difficult for me to make myself heard. As I was saying, I shall first of all recite to you a short passage of poetry, and then we shall see what we can learn from that passage. The verses which I am going to recite were written by Shakespeare, and Shakespeare has put them into the mouth of a very wicked man, a man who has just, because of his insane self-conceit and his ridiculous credulity, murdered an excellent wife, and who, at the conclusion of this speech, in order to escape from himself, kills himself. Anyone would think that such a character must be weak and despicable.' He paused for breath, since he found it very difficult to shout continually, and he noticed that quite a large section of the audience was laughing at him. He continued: 'I don't know what you're laughing at. It seems to me that I am opening up the discussion of a very interesting point. But I'm getting tired of shouting, so I'll try to get a bit more closely in touch with you.' He jumped down from the platform, and walked across the space of about 20 yards to the first row of chairs. 'Now,' he said 'I hope you will be able to hear me better,' but he was in reality worse placed than he had been before, because the seats were arranged, contrary to the usual custom, in tiers of which the topmost was at the front, and consequently it was quite impossible for George to see the great part of the audience who were at the back of the hall some 10 feet below the level where he stood, entirely screened by the first two or three rows of chairs. However, he determined to make the best of it and continued his lecture: 'I was saying that most people would think that a man capable of acting as Othello acted cannot have been, as Shakespeare makes him out to be, a heroic character.'

The laughter was renewed, and George, examining in perplexity those members of the audience who were nearest to him, observed that they were all engaged in different tasks. Some were reading newspapers, and in front of him was a pair, a young man wearing a monocle and a more elderly person dressed as a woman, who were playing cat's cradle. In the second row he noticed his brother David, who was carrying on an animated discussion with Marqueta, whose husband, taking notes, seemed the only person in the audience who was attending to the lecture. He leant across the front row of chairs and whispered to David: 'Is this the sort of thing they're used to?' and, while Marqueta looked up at him brightly, David said: 'You're getting along all right. Keep them amused.'

George raised his voice and continued: 'What I shall try to show is that in spite of his apparently pusillanimous behaviour, Othello was after all a heroic figure, a figure of great and noble simplicity, terribly ruined by contact with a completely false system of values.'

His thesis was greeted with a roar of laughter. George, surprised and offended, went on: 'I can assure you that I'm not trying to be funny. Perhaps someone will explain to me why you find the subject of my lecture so amusing.' He looked round inquiringly, but all that part of the audience which was visible to him was hushed, and it was only from the submerged rows of seats behind that there arose spasmodic tittering.

'All right,' said George, when he had satisfied himself that no one was going to speak. 'I don't suppose that any of you are such imbeciles as to laugh at the words which I am now going to repeat. I shall ask you, for once, not to think so much of the poetic beauty of these words, but to reflect on whether they ring true, on the character of the man who would use these words, and on whether or not they are appropriate to the situation. I shall then give you my own views on those points, and finally, I hope, we shall have a general discussion. These words, I think, could be put into the mouth of any one of Shakespeare's tragic heroes, and they seem to indicate the most pronounced of Shakespeare's moral feelings, that is an undeviating contempt for people who are merely clever, for partial reports, for low aims, for split minds, and correspondingly an unlimited admiration for those who, however mistakenly, follow a grand idea and are fanatical, ingenuous, pig-headed.'

By this time it was hard for George to make himself heard above the laughter, highly pitched, which convulsed the greater portion of the audience. Only the statistician was unmoved, though it seemed to George that Marqueta was laughing only with the rest and not on her own account, for there was some uneasiness in her face, as she listened to David's facetious remarks.

'I must warn you all,' said George, 'that I am quite serious, and that the subject which I am discussing is one on which it is very important for everyone to make up his mind.

186

These are the words to which I referred:

> 'Soft you. A word or two before you go.
> I have done the state some service, and they know it.
> No more of that. I pray you, in your letters,
> When you shall these unlucky deeds relate,
> Speak of me as I am; nothing extenuate,
> Nor set down aught in malice.'

But now no word could be heard above the treble laughter, as of babies, and in astonishment George saw faces strained with hysterical merriment, wet with tears. Young persons dug each other in the ribs, and George particularly remarked a person with a lorgnette, wearing a tennis shirt and a skirt of black velvet, who was standing on a chair imitating very cleverly his voice and manner of recitation.

In anger George went out of the hall, while the audience stood upon their chairs and clapped wildly. Imbeciles, thought George, as he stepped outside into brighter artificial light, no wonder that there are agitators in the country which supports these fantastic students. But he was surprised when his brother David ran up to him and shook his hand, saying enthusiastically: 'Brilliant, my dear fellow! Perfectly brilliant. I had no idea that you possessed such powers. You did it so well that you really seemed quite serious. Everyone's delighted with you.' And Humberto, arriving at the same moment, shook George's other hand, going into a long ripple of laughter, while he kicked his leg out in front of him. 'Had to take notes for the archives,' he spluttered. 'Couldn't do justice to your performance all the time.'

Astonished George looked inquiringly at Marqueta who followed her husband out of the hall, and as the groups of laughing bisexual students went by he wondered was it possible that they thought he had been making efforts to amuse them. Was this the education at the Convent? If so, he reflected, he was in a much more dangerous position than he had contemplated, having to do with a rootless society, purposeless and powerful. But he was somewhat reassured by the attitude of Marqueta, who took his arm and in her smile seemed to convey sympathy, though even she, George recollected, had laughed with the others.

'What a strange character you are,' she said slowly, looking down on the ground, as they walked across the quadrangle. 'I think you're not very happy here, are you?' She lifted her small head, meeting fairly George's perplexed eyes, then looked away, while the perfume from her hair invaded his nostrils, and he, eagerly slipping backward into the recesses of his mind, reclined there passive but agreeably anxious for an event, while his hand, as though of its own accord, fastened in her hot hand, and she led the way upstairs towards her room, she said, where they could have a talk.

CHAPTER FOURTEEN

In the small attic room was light blue wallpaper and orange light, and against one wall a low divan on which Marqueta, having slipped off some of her clothing, lay supine, looking up at George with cloudy, confident eyes. Surprised by the suddenness of the thing, George was not backward, and when he had embraced her, kissing her moist forehead, he found her shameless in her activity, urgent for him, till her initial satisfaction gave way to a nervousness and first some laughter with words thrillingly expectant: 'Must you? Oh, aren't you going to stop to think?' and soon she drew away from him, blushing, saying: 'Oh, we can't,' and then, 'Just one kiss, but a friendly one.' Hastily she covered herself with her clothes, shyly saying: 'But aren't you ashamed?' And George's astonishment increased when he saw her walk across the room to the fireplace and heard her say, when she had lit a cigarette, 'I've never had any lovers,' and smiling 'how can you ask me to make an exception for you?'

So gravely did she speak, so peaceful and low-thrilling was her voice that George was tempted to believe that nothing had occurred between them, and he forgot his dissatisfaction with her for leaving his arms so soon. But his situation on the divan convinced him that he had not been dreaming, and 'What do you mean?' he said 'Haven't we just—'

She interrupted him: 'Don't tell me! Please don't tell me. I seem to have been dreaming some ghastly dream. Let me tell you about my husband. I'm still so fond of him, fonder of him than of anyone else, though perhaps he isn't quite as kind to me as he might be.'

189

Faintly irritated George was still interested and, suppressing his immediate grievance, became prepared to listen to her melodious voice, while he was passively impressed by her grave face and innocent wise eyes. 'I'm very sorry,' he said. 'Tell me about yourself.' But he still sought in his mind for some reason to account for Marqueta's strange behaviour in which her mind had gone in a direction opposite to that followed by her body in time, acting, so it seemed to him, mechanically, and if mechanically, he reflected, why should not the direction be reversed to provide freedom for the body and, with some co-operation from the memory, a mental assurance of virtue? He rose, still feeling somewhat confused, from the divan and sat down in one of the armchairs. Marqueta's small fingers ravelled his hair as she said slowly, smiling with infinite tenderness: 'I feel that you know me already, George. And I hate to refuse you anything. I value your love more than I can say; but I can't be unfaithful to my husband. It would hurt him so much.'

'But,' said George bewildered, 'haven't you been unfaithful to him already?'

'Never,' said Marqueta slowly, looking down at the floor, 'though I've had plenty of opportunities. You see I'm not like the other people here. I had the operation and it was terribly painful, but it didn't work with me. They say I reverted to type, but I have always been a woman and so when I met Humberto, who because he is so interested in figures never had the operation at all, I thought he was a kind of God and I was, though I pretended not to be, delighted when Professor Pothimere suggested that we should get married, though I was rather angry when he wanted to take photographs of us on our wedding night.

'Everyone says that Humberto is a genius and I know he is a brilliant mathematician. I tried to help him in his work for some time, but I wasn't really very interested. I like reading poetry, and Plato, I love Plato. Now Humberto is always working when he is not at one of Professor Pothimere's parties and I hardly ever see him by himself. I don't feel injured, though I sometimes think of all that I sacrificed for him and wish that he was a little more considerate. But I wouldn't do anything to hurt him.'

'And do you like living here?' George asked, completely mystified. With what kind of a person, he wondered, was he dealing? One who, after having compelled him, though he could not pretend that it was against his will, to enjoy her, now disclaimed all knowledge of an event which had only just taken place, but treated him with the utmost candour and tenderness, hinting to him that he was in a privileged position, but debarring him in word from those very intimacies of which they had just partaken in deed.

'Oh yes,' she was saying, 'I like this place. There are plenty of books and plenty of nice people to talk to. And now its going to be nicer still, isn't it?' She looked up at him with tear-wet sombre face: 'How grateful I am to you for your love and sympathy! It seems already as if we'd known each other for years. But we shall have to be careful, shan't we? We mustn't go farther than we have gone. We mustn't let our feelings run away with us. I know it will be difficult for you, but you mustn't mind. I want you and Humberto to be great friends.'

'Yes,' said George, rather awkwardly, and then, taking a deep breath, 'What on earth are you talking about?'

Marqueta rose quickly to her feet and quickly crossed the room to kiss George lightly on the lips. She snuggled her hand in his coat, murmuring: 'So sweet, so sweet. How good you are with your simplicity and your lovely naïve ideas.' Then slipping to his feet she sat on the floor, resting her beautiful head against his knees, saying: 'Stroke my hair. It's lovely to feel you near me,' and George found his mind overcome by a great inertia as he sat still, feeling the warmth of her head, listening to noises distant in the quadrangle, conversation too indistinct to comprehend.

Soon, stirring gently, Marqueta said: 'Tell me something about yourself,' and George prepared to speak about his travels and the hardships which he had undergone, saying first; 'It is long now since I heard the Wild Geese.'

'Not that,' said Marqueta dreamily. 'Tell me about the women you have known. Have you ever been in love before?'

'There was a girl,' said George, 'at the coastguard station near my home, and for some time I was quite fond of her. She used to come with me when I was collecting flowers and I often spoke to her about birds. One night when we were returning from a botanical expedition I tried to kiss her, but she shrieked and fainted. After that I didn't think so much of her and was rather bored when she became even more interested in natural history and wanted to hold my hand when we went for walks. I was glad to see the last of her.'

'Poor girl,' Marqueta said. 'You must think more kindly of her. And has there been no one else?'

'Yes,' said George, 'as a matter of fact I'm more or less engaged to a girl at the farm and I'm very fond of her, though she didn't want me to come here and we had a quarrel before I left.'

Marqueta's body had stiffened. She laughed, stroking with one hand George's instep. 'You can't do that,' she said. 'How wicked you are, stealing people's love and then leaving them. But of course you mustn't get married like that, you impetuous fellow. A country girl like that wouldn't understand you, and those people don't wash, do they?'

'Look here,' said George, 'before we discuss that I'd like to have some explanation of your own behaviour. Why did you act so oddly just now, as if you were doing everything backwards, and why did you pretend that—'

She twisted round quickly, letting recline back her smiling face with eyes laughing at him over her forehead, inviting lips; but 'No' said George, 'I insist on having an explanation,' and hearing steps on the staircase, she rose, kissed the top of his head and regained the chair just as Humberto entered the room.

'Sorry,' he said, laughing, swinging one leg backwards and forwards. 'I'd have been here earlier, but I had to send in my report of the lecture,' and he crossed the room to the divan where he sat down, after having patted Marqueta on the head.

George looked at him more closely than he had done before. The little man had a genial broad face and short sandy hair. His legs were too short for his plump little body which bulged from his old sports coat, and he would have appeared a comic if it had not been for his shrewd eyes and the determination of his neck and forehead. All his gestures, thought George, were nervous. As he spoke he would cock his head sideways or, if anything amused him, snap out a leg, tense always in his behaviour, however light-hearted.

Now his shiny face beamed. 'I've made a list,' he was saying to George, disregarding Marqueta. 'I've made a list of the winter migrants. Perhaps you can help me to make some additions.'

'But there can't be any birds here, can there?' said George. 'Not in this artificial light and beneath a roof of concrete.'

'Pure science,' said Humberto, shooting out a leg and slapping it, 'Pure science. Of course I'm only speaking of the birds outside the town. I've never been outside myself, and I don't want to, but I sift the evidence I get from visitors and after all I feel I'm doing quite a useful bit of research. Here's to scholarship, as Dr. Zany said. May it never be any use to anyone. Ha, Ha! Rather an old chestnut, I'm afraid.'

Humberto's laughter was infectious and George began to like the man is spite of his pedantry. After all, he reflected, compared with the other inmates of the Convent this statistician was a harmless character, and he resolved to question him, hoping for more enlightment on conditions in the town than he had received from his brother, from the headmaster, and from the other characters who, now they were remote from his eyes, seemed to him, so odd and so indefinite had been their behaviour, almost the creatures of a dream.

'I wish' he said, 'that before we discuss the bird life in the country districts you would tell me a few things about this town in which I am a stranger,' and 'Certainly', Humberto replied, 'I'll do my best. But it's not my subject. I'm only the chief statistician. Still, what is it you want to know?'

'How long have I been here?' said George.

The statistician scratched his head. 'Let's see now. That's something I can answer, because I have to calculate all sorts of relative times for various Government services. You want to know how long you've been here, judging by the sun, I suppose. I should say about eighteen months.' Seeing George's look of astonishment, he added: 'Of course it hasn't been eighteen months to most of us. And of course you may succeed in making it a shorter time.'

'How can I do that?' said George. 'It's extremely difficult for me to believe that I've been here for eighteen months. It has seemed more like a day to me. But, supposing that I have been in this town for that time, I don't see how I can make it any shorter.'

'How extraordinary,' said Humberto, chuckling and slapping his leg. 'You don't see that? Why, don't you understand that you can go backwards just as well as forwards? It's a little more difficult, of course; and in your case it might be necessary to get a written order from a Government Department; but, Crikey! for some people it's child's play. Pothimere can grow backwards to the age of 10 whenever he wants to, but of course he's a research student. Still anyone can do it up to a point. I've known people of both sexes have passionate affairs with each other, sometimes against the rules, and afterwards they have protested that they would never do and have never done such things. Rather amusing, that, don't you think? Of course their minds have just ended at the starting point. Quite simple.'

'All the same,' said George, looking sternly at Marqueta, who appeared unconcerned with the conversation, 'something has taken place, whether they remember it or not.'

Humberto laughed. 'What an extraordinary thing to say! Now, I wonder why you said that. It's very interesting, because you must have some queer way of looking at things. I must make a note.' And he took from his pocket a note-book in which he jotted down a few words.

'I should have thought it was pretty evident,' said George, 'that if a thing's done it's done, and nothing can undo it.'

Marqueta smiled, showing for the first time that she had been listening. 'Isn't he charming?' she said to Humberto. 'I know that you and he will be great friends.'

Humberto was looking very serious, scratching his head vigorously. 'It's a very interesting point,' he said. 'But I'm afraid you're getting a bit too metaphysical for me. You ought to talk to Professor Wonder. Those theories of yours would be sure to interest him. I'm only a statistician and am content to take the commonsense point of view. I mean I believe in what I see. It seems to me that its as easy to go from 3 to 2 as from 2 to 3. But perhaps I don't quite follow your meaning?'

The friendliness in his look of query was disconcerting to George, who, without much hope that anyone in this city would understand a simple remark, said, 'You can't leave bodies altogether out of account.'

'Bodies?' said Humberto. 'I don't understand,' and Marqueta in a low voice said, 'Aren't you being rather vulgar?'

George looked at her angrily. 'I must say that that is rather thick from you,' he said. 'Have you forgotten your own body on that divan? I can assure you that it was there.'

'Shame!' said Humberto. 'Oh, shame! You'll really have to leave me out of this discussion.'

'Oh well,' George said, spreading out his hands hopelessly, 'we'll talk about something else. I'm beginning to realize that I shall never be able to make my meaning plain to you people with your reversed actions and controlled memories. But I should like you both to know that I think it a very wicked thing not to take the responsibility for what one has done.'

Marqueta was smiling tenderly at him. She turned to Humberto. 'I love to hear people talking like that. He's a brilliant thinker, isn't he? I knew we should be friends.'

Humberto laughed, and his red screwed-up face beamed upon George. 'He's too deep for me,' he said. 'As far as I can understand he wants people to move constantly in one direction. It's a bright idea, but a bit decadent, isn't it? And there'll be a few rather awkward consequences. If I understand George's theories rightly, it seems that one result of putting them into practice would be that we'd have to be controlled by the things we do. They'd guide us instead of us guiding them. In other words, we'd revert to pure determinism. Of course I've probably misunderstood you. I hope so anyway. Because, as no doubt you know, that sort of thing is High Treason.'

Marqueta looked at George gravely. 'I don't think he means that,' she said. 'I think perhaps I understand him better than you do, Humberto,' and Humberto said: 'Very likely, my dear. Very likely.'

George who had hoped for some explanation of the conduct of Marqueta, who had acted her part in a seduction backwards, beginning with the consummation of passion and ending with a protest of fidelity to her husband, was now convinced that no explanation would be forthcoming, and, though he liked Humberto and Marqueta better than the other characters whom he had met in the Convent, he was so offended at their inability to grasp what to him was a perfectly simple argument, at Marqueta's delicate behaviour, and Humberto's empty enthusiasm, that it was only his desire to receive some information about the Government which kept him back from leaving the room and attempting unsupported and without official sanction to go out of the Convent to see what he could for himself. He reflected that even if the inhabitants of the Convent did behave like babies, only at ease with the abstract, unable to give any definite opinion on matters outside their system of government, the Convent was nevertheless the centre of the town, and the Government which had imposed such sufferings on the peasantry must have something positive about it with which it would be well for him to become acquainted. Perhaps, if he stayed here (though he was alarmed at the speed at which his time went) he might meet the headmaster in person, perhaps some higher official; whereas to run away would be to put himself into the hands of the police from whom, he imagined, he could expect no mercy. And so, disregarding the remarks of Humberto and Marqueta, he said, 'I wish you'd tell me something about the Government. Do you think it's a good Government?'

'Of course,' said Marqueta, looking up at him softly, 'we all love the king,' but Humberto, rising to his feet and thrusting his hands into his trouser pockets, said 'Stop a minute, my dear' and strutted once or twice across the room, wrinkling his forehead. 'He's asked us a very difficult question,' he said at last. 'I'm not at all sure whether we'll be able to answer it. After all, Marqueta, what do we know about the Government?'

'Why,' said Marqueta, 'of course we never talk about the

Government. We've got such a lot of other things to do. But we know how good the Government is don't we?'

'Oh yes,' Humberto said quickly, 'naturally I wasn't questioning that for a moment. Good Lord, no ! I was speaking simply as a scientist, and from that point of view it occurs to me that we know nothing at all about the Government. Of course we all hold posts under the Government and Pothimere told me once that he had seen the headmaster who is, I suppose, in touch with some of the higher officials. But you and I, Marqueta, have never seen the headmaster, have we? So it's really rather difficult for us to describe the Government to George.' He turned abruptly to George. 'By the way, why do you want to know about the Government? It seems an extraordinary thing to be interested in.'

'It seems extraordinary to me,' said George, 'that you're not more interested in it yourselves. How do you know that the Government is working for the good of its subjects ? You may be entirely ignorant of the higher officials, but I don't suppose they are ignorant of you, and all the time, for all you know, they are setting you to dangerous or futile tasks. I've seen something of the police both here and in the country, and I must say that that Department at least could do with a thorough overhauling. Then look at your education. Everyone is simply being amused. I believe that very little, if any, serious work is done, except in your Department. As for your Professor of Love, he seems to me to exercise the worst possible influence on the minds of young and inexperienced people. What right has he to teach things which each person must teach himself? With what face can he recite the poems of Victor Hugo? He seemed to me a dirty old man.'

Here he was interrupted by Humberto who so far had been listening carefully, with a puzzled expression on his face. 'Look here,' he began, 'aren't you—,' but before he had time to continue the door of the room was softly opened and appeared the head and shoulders of a man dressed in clerical clothes whom George was surprised to recognize as the Rev. Hamlet. He recalled Joe's shout of 'Spy!' at the political meeting and was alarmed to think that the clergyman had probably been listening at the keyhole to a speech of his which, for all he knew, might be considered seditious, but he had no opportunity for testing his suspicion as the Rev. Hamlet gave no sign of recognition and withdrew his head after he had looked round the room, smiled, saying: 'Sorry, people! I just wanted to make sure.'

When he had gone both Humberto and Marqueta looked at George in alarm, but said nothing because of the sudden ringing of a bell, and hurrying of feet down the staircase.

'The football match!' voices were shouting, and they rose to attend it.

CHAPTER FIFTEEN

LEAVING the room Marqueta smiled at George, but Humberto said quietly: 'Look here, George, you'll have to be careful. I like to keep an open mind, but that was one of the Chief Constables.'

'What! The clergyman?' said George, and Humberto nodded, disinclined to pursue the subject, asking 'Have you got your whistle?'

'No,' said George, 'but I expect they'll give me one on the ground. Where is the ground, by the way? Outside the town, I suppose. You can't have any turf here.'

Humberto, relieved to be talking about playing-fields, shot out his leg and laughed. 'This way,' he said, and they followed through several quadrangles the crowds of oddly dressed students until they came to an open space, a grey field with posts and crossbars, surrounded by gigantic stands, lit brilliantly by swinging arc lamps, and here George was left alone, while Humberto and Marqueta went to take their places in one of the stands.

George went on to the playing-field, testing it with his heel, and found it to be made of soft rubber. I shouldn't like to play on this, he thought to himself; the ball will bounce in an extraordinary way; but I suppose they're used to it, and he was startled by a sudden blare of music from the centre of the field, where a band had just started to play. Over their heads was displayed a banner on which George could read the words 'Metropolitan Police', and, anxious about Bob's safety, he walked to the band stand and soon distinguished Bob in the centre, playing his guitar, shrugging his shoulders and shuffling his feet in time to the music. At the same moment Bob saw him, but, to George's surprise, gave no sign of recognition and not even when the piece was played and George advanced saying: 'Hullo, Bob' would Bob own his old companion. Instead he turned to the policeman who, sitting next to him, had been playing the trombone, and said: 'That guy's the ref. Wonder what he's doing round here.' The whole band looked George over and George, having got used to the police by this time, was not disconcerted to find them laughing at him, but walked close up to Bob and said: 'What's the idea, Bob? You know me well enough.'

Bob half-turned his head to his laughing colleagues. 'Well, if that isn't a fair slice!' he said. 'Here's the ref. saying he knows me and calling me "Bob" when my name's Robert Caraway, as all you guys know,' and George walked away indignant but suspecting that Bob's refusal to recognize him implied that he was in some danger, a suspicion which was confirmed when he heard, as he was turning his back, a quick whisper from Bob to the bandmaster: 'That's the man you're after.'

Puzzled, George made his way back towards the main entrance hoping to find the games master or some other person who could supply him with a whistle, and as he went he reflected on Bob's strange conduct. No doubt, he thought to himself, Bob has been currying favour by revealing my political sympathies and by telling stories, probably exaggerated, of my connection, which I severed myself, with the revolutionary movement in the country. The Rev. Hamlet is also on my track, but why, I wonder, don't they do something? I have been treated in two opposite ways, with suspicion and contempt by the police, and with a certain amount of respect by the inmates of the Convent. How am I to account for a policy which appears self-contradictory? Have the Government perhaps given orders that I am to be treated well inside the Convent (though the behaviour of the students during my lecture was far from satisfactory) and badly outside the Convent, to the end that I may be induced to spend my life there, change my manner of thought, and perhaps undergo the operation? Or, for that matter, are the Government aware of my existence? If even their chief statistician is unacquainted with them, how can I suppose that they are likely to have taken much notice of me? And yet the headmaster, or at least some deputy of his, interviewed me from behind a rubber curtain, and the eavesdropping of the Rev. Hamlet is not a fact lightly to be dismissed. True, these men may be very subordinate officials, but they are in touch with their superiors with whom I, through them, must also have something to do. But my time is slipping away, and so far I have achieved nothing notable.

He resolved that as soon as the match should be over he would, either through Professor Pothimere or through the headmaster, endeavour to arrange an interview with some senior official to whom he could represent the object of his journey and the grievances of the countrymen, and that he would excuse himself for taking up the time of the authorities by pointing out that at present he seemed, owing to some misconception about his real aims, to be in imminent danger of arrest.

He looked round at the stands which by now were packed with people clapping their hands impatiently, shuffling their feet, drowning the music from the band in the centre of the grey field. The glare of the arc lamps made his eyes ache and the atmosphere was rank with perfume and the smell of tobacco, the strangest possible arrangement, George thought, for a game of Rugby football. At each end of the ground, behind the goal posts, was a large board covered with rapidly changing lettering in electric lights. George read some of the succeeding items of local news and began to pay more attention as matter relating to the match was flashed in red letters over the green background. He read: 'To-day we are assembled to watch the annual match between the Pros and the Cons. A running commentary will be broadcast from the town station, and will be relayed from all provincial stations. It is thought that some of our loyal farmers will be particularly pleased to hear that this important match is being refereed by their old friend George, who expresses himself as delighted with his first few years under our enlightened government. Kindly listen for the loud speakers in a very short time.'

George looked angrily at the blank green board. So this was the idea, to discredit him with his friends and at the same time, perhaps, to flatter him into a belief that his real feelings were what they were broadcast to be. He thought with pain of what Joan and Pushkov would think of him. Joe, he half-hoped, would understand, and yet what was there at all creditable to himself to be understood? Dwarfed on a grey field, beneath arc lamps and half a million eyes, alone in a gigantic stadium, the property of a Government of which he knew nothing, he felt more strongly than ever before the inequality of his status, his lack of foothold. I must get this over, he said to himself, and then—but he was interrupted by the voice of the games master: 'Here's your whistle, old boy. Use your discretion, of course. That's the final score,' and he pointed to the electric board where George read the words: 'Final score. Pros—Nil. Cons—3 points.'

'What do you mean, the final score?' said George.

'That's what the Government have decided,' replied the games master. 'They know best,' and the conversation was ended by the roar of the loud speakers, through which a voice announced: 'The match between the Pros and the Cons is about to commence. The players are now shaking hands with the King. In accordance with the usual custom the winning side will receive a plum pudding and the losers will enter the Research Department as specimens. After a close game the Cons beat the Pros by a try to nothing. Here they come, a fine looking lot of fellows. We're going to see some good football this afternoon.'

'Why aren't I shaking hands with the King?' George asked, as he watched the band hurriedly pack away their instruments and make way for the two teams who came running on to the field, and the games master stroked his arm smiling, 'That was a jolly good one, old boy.'

George turned away from him and walked back slowly to the centre of the field where he shook hands with the opposing captains. The Cons seemed to him the heavier side, lumpish fellows indeed in their putty-coloured jerseys and large boots, but the Pros, he thought, would have the advantage in point of speed, for they looked a lively lot, laughing among themselves and passing the ball rapidly and cleanly from hand to hand. They wore red jerseys and, so far as he could judge, seemed to be male, whereas several of the massive Cons had figures which led George to suppose them to be of the female sex.

He blew his whistle and beckoned the two teams towards him. 'This afternoon,' he said, though, beneath the huge arc lamps in thick atmosphere, it was no afternoon, 'I want to see a clean open game. I'm going to use the whistle as little as possible and advise you to remember the advantage rule. But first of all, would one of you mind getting a watch for me? I suppose you're playing forty minutes each way.'

'That's all right, sir,' said the captain of the Cons, whose figure and the whisps of grey hair which escaped from scrum-cap indicated her to be female. 'The bells will ring at half-time. It's all arranged by the Government.' She laughed, nodding towards the score board, and took hold of two other huge forwards by their shoulders, explaining some detail in the formation of the scrum. George, before blowing his whistle for the kick-off, listened to a speech which the captain of the Pros, a small nervous man, a wing threequarter, was making to his men. 'Chaps!' he was saying, 'We're up against it all right. You see that

204

the final score has already been announced. But we'll give them a run for their money before we're finished, even if we have to go into the Research Department afterwards, like last year's first XV did. Hustle them, boys. Give the ball plenty of air. And you forwards, shove like hell. Let's have that ball back all the time, even if we're scrumming on our own line. It's our only chance. Put those fat aunts down wallop. Hustle, boys, hustle. Now let's go.'

George blew his whistle and the two sides lined up for the kick off, the Cons lazily shifting their huge bodies, the Pros hopping eagerly up and down, rubbing their hands together, on their toes. George had found time to whisper to the captain of the Pros, 'Don't worry about that final score. There's going to be fair play while I'm refereeing this match,' and the captain had smiled sadly at him, before running to take up his position on the left wing.

The Cons kicked off while the air was full of the cheers and plaudits of the crowd. Very slowly the heavy forwards ambled up to the line, but their captain, who was taking the kick, ran more slowly still, and by the time the ball was kicked several forwards had crossed the line, and George blew his whistle ordering a scrum in the centre, while the Con forwards grinned heavily at each other, leading George too late to suspect that their infringement of the rule had been a collusion in order to have an opportunity from the very start of the game for taking advantage of their great weight; and indeed it soon became evident that in the tight scrums the light Pro forwards were no match for their heavier opponents. As the ball was put into the scrum, the Cons, with what seemed the lurching lunge of a tortoise, pushed the Pros back a yard, and, keeping the ball between the second and third ranks of their pack, began to move slowly down the field, carrying the struggling Pros in front of them. 'Shove, boys! For God's sake shove!' shouted the Pro captain, with tears running down his face, as he saw the slow moving mass bearing down upon his goal line, and the vain efforts of his hopelessly outweighted men, and George too, though he could not but admire the accurate formation of the Cons, was on the whole disgusted by so unambitious and so overwhelming an attack. A score seemed certain, and some of the big Con threequarters had sat down in the centre of the field and taken out sandwiches, grinning as they watched the tremendous scrum move nearer and nearer to the line. By now all the Pro outsides had hurled themselves into the scrum, but for all their desperate efforts and the frenzied exhortation of their captain they were unable to stay their opponents' advance and the Cons would certainly have scored between the posts, gratifying the frantic applause of the crowd, if one of their forwards had not, from a lumpish satisfaction with victory, bitten the ear of a Pro forward in the sight of George, who blew his whistle and awarded a free kick against the Cons. 'I shall watch you closely,' he said to the offending forward who stood sheepish while his companions kicked his shins in anger, 'and if I notice anything of the kind again I shall send you off the field.'

The crowd was howling viciously and George had to incline his head to escape an empty bottle thrown at him by some sympathizer with the side which he had penalized. The Cons were evidently favourites and George began to foresee trouble from the excited crowd, at the same time reflecting that he could look for little or no assistance from the police. He set his jaw and attended to the free kick, and soon was to admire the dash and the dexterity of the lighter side.

The scrum half, the smallest man on the field, took the kick, and punted over the heads of the Con forwards who stood stock still in a straight line; then, running past them to the right and gathering the ball before they had turned round, he swung out a long pass to the left wing which was well taken by the captain who, having caught the whole defence on the wrong foot and being a faster runner than anyone else on the field, easily swerved round the opposing wing and the full back, and, while the crowd hissed and George could hardly refrain from applauding the speed and certainty of the manœuvre, ran with the whole field clear for him towards the try line.

But when he was 5 yards from it, to the delight of the crowd a bell rang and the loud speakers roared 'Half-time'. George indignantly blew the whistle, shouting 'Play on', and the wing threequarter on the point of scoring looked gratefully at him and was just grounding the ball between the posts when a shot cracked and turning up his eyes he fell crumpled on the wrong side of the line. A policeman came forward from the crowd, coolly setting back a revolver in his belt. 'We have to be very careful,' he said to George, 'to see that the regulations are strictly observed.'

George was on his knees beside the body of the young threequarter whom he discovered to be stone dead, shot through the heart. 'You bloody swine,' he said, looking up at the police officer, and he turned his back while the body was being removed, then returned to the centre of the field, calm no longer, his mind sick and swirling, will-less, mechanically to direct an evil game. The two teams were standing in separate groups, and passing by the Cons George heard the fat captain say: 'Keep it fairly clean, fellows. We know the final score,' then going farther to where the depleted team of Pros were standing he heard the speech of a tall forward who, after the murder of their leader, was to assume the captaincy. 'Conrad is dead,' he was saying. 'Let us, before this game is over, so conduct ourselves that if he were alive his eyes would be delighted. Let us call to mind what manner of man he was and strive to be worthy of our places in his to-be-defeated team. He had good hands. His passes were fast and low, to be taken at full speed. There was an agility in his ankles and his instep was high. He would catch his opponents on the wrong foot. He could swerve like swallow and vary his pace like any bird. He never shirked a tackle. In the grovel his eyes were open. Dear chaps, let the swiftness and courage of our dead captain inspire our endeavour.'

George blew his whistle for the second half. Angrily he wondered what he was doing here beneath arc lamps and unjust eyes, trying hopelessly to enforce fair play; but I must stick to it, he thought, listening to the howling of the hostile hermaphrodites, since it is just possible that I may be able to exert some authority; for he realized dimly how terrible would be the consequences of defeat to the losing side.

The Pros kicked off and the ball was caught in a fumbling manner by one of the opposing forwards. George, recalling the known interests of the Cons, did not blow his whistle for a knock-on, and was deafened by the angry shouting of the crowd. Before the Con forwards had time to gather round the ball its holder was violently upset by a flying tackle of the Pro captain. The ball rolled loose, and the Pro forwards were carrying it down the field at their feet at a great pace, while the heavier Cons were still standing still, facing in the opposite direction. A lucky bounce transferred the ball from feet to hands. It was magnificent to see the accuracy of the passing as the ball swung across the field from forwards to threequarters, each man of the defence being drawn until the final inside pass from a wing threequarter to a forward left the latter a clear run in. Even if they ring the bell for time, thought George, the match will be drawn, and he laughed as he ran after the forward, certain of a score. But as he ran it seemed to him that the goal posts were receding from him and, looking downwards to his feet, he observed that the rubber field was rapidly changing consistency, stretching out like elastic. Farther and farther retreated the goal posts as he, with the whole Pro team, ran on. The whole ground was expanding at a terrific pace, and looking over his shoulder George could not see the ends of the crowded stands. It is some damned mechanism, he thought, still running, and suddenly the lights went out and there arose a hullabaloo from the spectators above which, after a short interval, George could distinguish the rattle of a machine gun and groans, sounds of collapse all round him.

The lights went on again to the terrific cheering of the crowd. The ground had resumed its first area, and, standing by the corner flag of the Con goal line, George saw by his feet fourteen dead bodies, pierced horribly with bullets, distorted some of them with the pain of a broken spine or lead in the stomach, the team of Pros, while grinning from a large armoured car were the fifteen Cons, of whom one held the ball in his hand, showing it with stultish pride to vociferous sympathizers. The car moved forward and to the sound of cheering advanced to an undefended goal line, where the ball was grounded, and after that the Con captain approached George, saying 'We will not take the kick.'

George shouted: 'I have awarded two penalty tries to the Pros,' but his voice was lost in the roar of loud speakers and the frenzied cheering of the crowd. Men, women, and both rose from their seats and hurled into the playing-field the pink silk cushions on which they had sat. The Cons drove off in their armoured car and George, deafened with din, stood alone, struck every instant with a flying cushion. At first he hardly noticed the bombardment, but soon, so numerous had been the spectators, he found himself struggling towards the exits with soft feathers covered in pink silk about his knees. It was not long before the softness was waist high and George called for assistance, watching in angry despair the hordes dispersing. He was unnoticed and the cushions were about his throat, over his mouth, folding his eyes, and before the last throw he had become unconscious, softly inhumed, having wasted crying.

CHAPTER SIXTEEN

GEORGE was not killed. He survived to open his eyes, discovering a bare cell and his loneliness within it. On a stone floor, very clean, he lay, and in this apartment there was no furniture except a simple electric bulb suspended from the ceiling to illuminate white-washed walls.

George rose to his feet, cramped and tousled, recalling the events which had happened before he lost consciousness. His circumstances suggested that he was imprisoned and he wondered for what purpose he had been delivered from the load of cushions and brought here to answer what charge. He had offended the authorities, perhaps, by vainly trying to enforce the rules of a game and, having become more fully acquainted with the power of the Government, its inexplicable decisions arbitrarily carried out, he was ill at ease, remembering the Research Department, imagining the worst, but resolved to sell his life dearly. Now, not for the first time, he regretted his private adventure and cursed himself for having been equally a fool with his brothers, for disregarding the advice of the countryfolk and entering a city that could only be subdued by a regiment. His powerlessness in these surroundings had already been made evident to him, openly ridiculed as he had been by the police, incapable of instructing the students, having failed to stir anything but the outworks of Marqueta's body and mind, and now finally disgraced for having attempted to referee a match in which he had not been able to prevent the cruel slaughter of the likeliest team. And yet, he reflected, there is still some hope. I have been treated with ignominy, but my life is my own. For some reason or other the Government, while permitting, presumably, their subordinates to harass me, have not thought it advisable to put me entirely out of the way. And even now if I can only escape from this prison it is conceivable that by putting my case before them I may be treated with some justice.

Running his fingers through his hair, distraught while he concerted plans of escape, he was surprised by the opening of the door of his cell and the entrance of the Rev. Hamlet who was attended by Captain Cochran or one such another. Captain Cochran, if it was he, carried a chair and writing desk which he placed on the floor of the cell, keeping his face, which wore an unusually severe expression, turned all the time on George. The Rev. Hamlet seated himself and placed some papers on the desk in front of him. He had not yet looked at George, but he smiled broadly at the Captain saying: 'I say, Officer, would you do me a great favour and call the witnesses?' Then, when the policeman had left the room, he turned gravely to George. 'I'm afraid,' he said, 'that this is a terribly serious case.'

'What is?' said George, but the clergyman looked away from him, compressing his lips, murmuring 'There is no need now, I think, to dissemble'.

The door opened admitting Captain Cochran with David and Bob. George turned at once to David, saying: 'Look here, David, there seems to have been some mistake. You'll be able to get me out of this, won't you?' He pointed towards the bare walls of his cell, but David, who had evidently been summoned hurriedly and had only rouged his upper lip, was trembling, pale-faced, and looked away from his brother, affecting not to have heard or not to have understood his words. So surprising was his agitation that George cried out: 'What's wrong, David?' but David turned quickly to the Rev. Hamlet, and in a nervous piping voice said, clipping his syllables: 'Honestly I don't know how the man came to find out my name. I can assure you that I have never seen him before.'

While George was speechless with surprise the Rev. Hamlet rose from his chair and clasped David's hand, smiling into his eyes from face laid close to David's face. 'My dear fellow,' he said, 'we were quite sure of it. Don't please imagine for one moment that we were suspicious of you. What a ghastly thing suspicion is, isn't it? Go along now and have just as jolly a time as you possible can.' He kissed David on the lips, and David, evidently relieved, made to go out of the room after he had thanked the clergyman for all that he had done for him.

'Don't mention it,' said the Rev. Hamlet, and added in more significant tones 'You don't like playing with fire, do you?'

'Certainly not,' said David rapidly, and 'Good boy!' said the clergyman smiling abstractedly at the door after David had closed it behind him.

George stood stock still, amazed at his brother's treachery, speculating on the reasons for his cowardice and concluding himself to be in no small danger. 'You must know perfectly well,' he said, 'that that is my brother.'

The Rev. Hamlet looked at him sadly. He spoke slowly. 'Lying, dissembling, prevarication can do you no good now, my boy. No forged passports, no bogus credentials can save you from the consequences of your own actions. It would be in your own interests to make a full confession.' He turned to the police officer. 'But first of all, call the second witness.'

Bob stepped forward. George did not trouble to look at him, knowing what to expect. Indeed he hardly listened while Bob spoke briskly: 'Yes sir, I know the prisoner well. Dogged him from the first. Soon observed dangerous tendencies. Showed signs of disaffection. Full report, with dates, is on the table in front of you.'

'You have done very well,' said the Rev. Hamlet. 'We shall have to see what we can do about promotion eh! captain?' and he extended his hand for Bob to kiss before he left the room. Then, turning to George, 'Have you anything to say?'

'I should like to know,' said George, 'what I am being charged with.'

The Rev. Hamlet looked at him sternly, his compressed lips giving to his sentimental face almost an expression of idiocy. 'You,' he said, 'must know as well as I do that there is no reason for going into that. You will do yourself most good by making a full and prompt confession.'

'I don't know what you mean,' said George. 'I haven't the least idea why I am being tried, if you call this a trial, and I have nothing to confess.'

The clergyman suddenly smiled, effecting a change of expression so quick as to be almost startling. 'Look here, George old man,' he said in a thicker voice, 'I want to be friends with you. Don't think I'm your enemy. I want everyone to be friends. Let's be perfectly frank with each other. I think perfect frankness is a wonderful thing. And I'm going to start by being frank with you. Be a good chap. Own up. Honestly it's your only chance.'

At first George had been near to laughing at the abrupt change in the clergyman's manner, but soon he began to suspect that he must really be in a stronger position than he had thought at first. This is a plot, he thought to himself. They want to get something out of me, what exactly I don't know, but I'm not going to play their game. So he spoke coolly to the clergyman:

'After the political meeting at which you were a spy I told you my opinion of you. I have not changed it.'

'Obduracy,' said the Rev. Hamlet to himself, frowning at the floor, 'obduracy'; but he seemed somewhat at a loss, and George followed up what seemed to him to have been an advantage by saying: 'I demand first of all to know with what I am charged, and then I demand a fair trial.'

213

The Rev. Hamlet sat up stiff. He was looking at George male-volently. 'What trial could be fairer than this?' he said. 'Your own attitude has made it impossible for me to take any course but one. As soon as the doctor's certificate has been made out, you will enter the Research Department (you know what I mean) as a specimen, a very interesting specimen, of criminal lunacy.'

George, staggered by the sudden sentence which he had hoped to escape, cried out 'This is not justice', but Captain Cochran blew his whistle and soon the room was filled with policemen who joined in the laughter of their officer while George was being handcuffed. Already on the way from the room George shouted: 'I appeal to the King,' and the effect of his plea was instantaneous.

The Rev. Hamlet, who had been standing up with finger out-stretched towards the door, sat down heavily, staring in front of him, as though nonplussed. Captain Cochran fell back a pace and the constables removed their hands from George's shoulders and arms. For a moment there was heavy silence, and then 'I should advise you not to do that', said the clergyman, and Captain Cochran too, in tones of remonstrance, said: 'Oh no. I shouldn't if I were you.'

'I appeal to the King,' said George again, fancying that the evident embarrassment of his persecutors showed that he had taken a wise step, and, after another silence, the Rev. Hamlet nodded gloomily towards the Captain. 'Do your duty, Officer,' he said, and went slowly out of the room, without looking at George.

Captain Cochran loosed the handcuffs and led George from the cell down a staircase and into the street where a police car was drawn up by the pavement. As though to witness some notable execution crowds of people were waiting outside the prison and amongst them George particularly remarked a squad of white-aproned surgeons. As he followed Captain Cochran into the street there rose from the crowd a din of hand-clapping, hissing,

214

and cat calls, so bestial a performance that George, looking at the crowd of students (for it appeared that he was still in some quarter of the town near the Convent) was taken aback by the ferocity in their rouged faces, and instead of pitying them as he had done hitherto for their vacancy, he began to hate them with their dissembling trousers, their unwarranted shirts, their general malice. Happy he felt himself to have escaped their attentions and he smiled as he entered the police car and heard from the crowd a murmur of disappointment as Captain Cochran announced through a megaphone: 'The prisoner has appealed to the King.' And from the wide grumble George could distinguish some comments—'Impossible!'—'Effrontery!'—'We shall see, we shall see.'

The car moved forward slowly through the crowd and soon was travelling faster along empty streets where George had never been before, the industrial quarter of the town, he supposed, peering through the small barred window at the back of the van, for he could hear the din of machinery, metallic noise, and he saw a troop of workmen, big fellows in grey uniform, trudging in order through a gateway escorted by a number of diminutive laughing constables. The lights in this part of the town were dimmer so that it appeared to be night, and the streets, unlike those in the more fashionable quarters, were dusty and stained with oil. The poverty and the squalor in which the workmen lived was evident from the few dwelling houses which were built between the factories, high grey structures, with holes for windows, out of which hung stained pieces of cloth or were suspended cages where ill nourished canaries did not sing. In some of these windows, the honeycomb juxtaposition of which indicated that the rooms must be extremely small, George could glimpse the peaked faces of women, the sallow complexions of young children, and he reflected on the inequity of a system under which these people who alone in the city, apparently, could breed were of all people the worst provided for. And he was saddened and enraged by the thought that these families of workers could never have seen the sun, never have walked beneath a sky that was not a roof of concrete.

To his surprise it was in one of these mean streets that the car pulled up. Captain Cochran led him across the pavement to the opening of a tunnel marked 'Subway' in dirty red paint, and rang an electric bell which was inlaid in the wall. While they were waiting George looked up and down the street, seeing that it was empty, while from all directions beat upon his ears the harsh hubbub of machines, clanking and metallic sharp percussion, outlet of steam with shouts.

Bewildered by the noise and by the difficulty of believing that it was in such surroundings that a king could reside, George was aware of steps coming down the subway and soon appeared the figure of a butler, somewhat stout, dressed immaculately, into whose care George was committed by the policeman. 'This way, sir,' said the butler, turning back along the subway, and Captain Cochran, before relinquishing his hold on George's arm, whispered: 'You are acting very foolishly'; then, laughing loudly, he jumped into the car and drove at a great pace away.

George shrugged his shoulders, and followed the butler along a badly lighted passage till they came to an electric sign with the letters 'Lift' and, entering the conveyance, began to ascend rapidly. Up and up they went to such a height that George became convinced that this lift was installed in one of those high towers which he had observed from the desert outside the town, but when he questioned the butler on this point, the butler would make no reply. At length they reached the terminus, and when the butler had slid back the iron lattice George stepped into a bright light and an apartment that seemed all the richer by contrast with the scenes

216

on the ground below. The floor was paved with a glittering mosaic and in the centre was a pool where alligators lay amongst water-lilies, beneath the light drenching of a fountain. The walls, painted blue, were hung with pictures in the modern manner, and on some of the steel armchairs, upholstered in rubber, which were drawn up near the central pool, lay copies of the periodical magazines of different countries. From the high ceiling, gleaming with gold paint, projected downwards rods of aluminium to which were fixed horizontal perches of some metal painted scarlet, and on these perches were birds of all kinds, owls, toucans, singing canaries, love birds and Java sparrows. Each bird, George could see, was tied to its perch and beneath it was a silver tray to receive droppings.

Through this reception hall George followed the butler to a glass door on which the butler tapped softly. 'Come in,' came the sound of a ringing voice, and, opening the door, 'A young gentleman to see you, sir,' said the butler and then retired leaving George with the King, a tall good-looking man, still young, wearing a fencing jacket.

George glanced round the room, a comfortable one, though small, taking note of the pictures by modern French painters, the bookshelves full of modern literature in all European languages, the commodious armchairs, the foils and mask thrown carelessly into the corner by the steel and aluminium writing desk.

'Sit down,' said the King, after they had shaken hands, 'and tell me what's the trouble.' His keen brown eyes looked intently into George's face, while with one hand he smoothed carefully his small moustache.

'I've come to appeal,' said George, 'against a sentence passed on me by the Rev. Hamlet.'

'The Rev. Hamlet?' said the King, 'The Rev. Hamlet? Who's he? Don't let that worry you, my boy. I patronize the Arts. I'm starting a New Party, a party of youth, vitality, and initiative. Do you fence?'

'No,' said George, 'I've never done any fencing.'

'That's a pity,' said the King briskly, rising to his feet and picking up a foil which he whipped up and down. 'There's nothing like it for keeping fit. But I can see that I'm going too fast. I know something about you already. My organization is reliable. Efficiency and initiative. I'm going to give you some information, and then you must make your decision.'

George nodded his head, surprised at the apparent change in his situation from a condemned prisoner to a man to be canvassed by a King, but he had made up his mind to act cautiously, keeping always in view the object of his journey, and so he listened sceptically while the young king, lowering his brows and folding his arms across his tight-fitting jacket, continued to speak.

'My policy,' he began, 'is a policy of Action, a policy of virility. I want young men, live men, aristocratic young men. I want to start a renaissance. As you must have noticed, I patronize modern art. I keep in the vanguard of modern thought. The time has come to do away with every idea which is not vital in the most vital sense of that word. We are going forward already, and we shall go forward more rapidly still. The time has come for the free reign of the unfettered spirit. Away with the old morality, I say! Away with outworn systems of political intrigue! Our aristocracy will be the first genuine aristocracy that has ever existed. Everyone who is capable of it will be able to live as I do. Art, literature, science, sport, everything vital will be pursued by us in a virile way. The drudgery of life will be no drudgery for us, because we shall see nothing of it. Already we are producing not quite a slave class, but a mechanical class. You saw them in their burrows below the tower. They will supply us with raw materials. Creation is our own. So long as we lead, so long as Action remains our watch-word, the rest will follow, and an enlightened aristocracy, a modern aristocracy of Action and of Genius will usher in the new age. What do you think?'

'The men in the factories,' said George, 'in spite of the misery in which they live, seem to me not only more essential to society but also much stronger than the inhabitants of the Convent. Your tower is magnificent, but I cannot see that it is either wisely or securely based on the subjection of the workers below. Turn them into machines, you say, and certainly the process has already been carried pretty far, but can that process ever be carried through? I doubt it, because there is more vitality even in a hungry worker than in a connoisseur, however well fed. But my particular busi-ness is with the grievances of the countrymen. You must know how they suffer from the requisitions of the Government. Can nothing be done?'

But the King was no longer listening. Before George had got half-way through his speech, he had rung a bell and on the entry of a stenographer had begun to prepare the dictation of a letter or a speech. He turned quickly to George, who had risen to his feet, 'Your business is with the King,' he said quickly. 'You're not the right material, or not yet, Think vitally.' And he rang another bell to summon the butler. The fencer who was not, it seemed, the King gave him some directions, and as George left the room he heard the beginning of the dictation, uttered by the leader of the New Party who stood stiff in an attitude of on guard: 'Let us do away with the old shibboleths. Let us start planning. Let us—' The door closed and George went once more through the luxurious entrance hall to interview this time, he hoped, a real King.

It was not necessary for him to descend in the lift. Instead he was conducted to a door which opened on to a platform overhanging the city roof, in the open air. With immense relief George stepped on to the platform, feeling in his face a cold breeze, looking up to a real sky which was unconfined though murky, as it had been when he first entered the town, lurid with streaked clouds, but still the sky. The platform projected, as he had guessed, from one of the high towers, and looking in all directions George could not see the limit of the concrete roof, slit here and there for ventilation, with other towers, more than he had seen from the desert, rising to great heights in front of him and at each side. It was a grand prospect, and as he surveyed the extensive view George realized how much there was of this city into which he had never penetrated, how many towers inhabited by people of whom he had not been informed. From below, through yellow streaming ventilators, rose the confused din of life even to the eminence where he stood, a hum as of a hive, a general hubbub which, heard from a distance, gave an impression of unanimity of organization which to George's knowledge did not exist in the diverse world below the roof of concrete. In front of him, at the very cdge of the platform, was a large ring of iron, 4 feet or so in radius, which was the extremity of a green canvas hose pipe, like those appliances for the saving of life in case of fire. Towards this pipe George was conducted by the butler and, looking directly over the edge of the platform, he saw the green canvas stretching away in a gradual descent, but could not make out the point where it ended. 'You must get in here, sir,' said the butler, pointing to the opening, and 'Where does it lead to?' George asked, but the butler shrugged his shoulders, indicating that he did not know.

Somewhat fearful of a trap, but recollecting that so far the higher authorities had not threatened his life and that this conveyance was the only one possible for him, George entered the aperture, feet first, having looked with regret at the dull sky, and in a sitting posture began to slip downwards with a growing acceleration in the dark. For a long time, or so it seemed, he descended and had begun to take stock of the canvas walls into which he dug his knees and elbows to hinder the violence of his descent, had begun to gasp for breath when suddenly, almost before he was aware that he had seen light, he was shot out at the other end of the tube and landed breathless on a pile of cotton wool.

Blinking in the bright light he looked round him while he was assisted to his feet by two young men in white aprons who dusted his clothes gravely and with patience, restraining him from movement till they had made sure that no speck of dust or strand of cotton was upon him.

He was standing in a high room the floor, walls, and ceiling of which were cased in shiny white tiles. Where the walls joined ceiling and floor the angles were obliterated by curvature, and, though the room was full of the eddy of electric fans, there was a distinct and, to George, an unpleasant smell of disinfectant chemicals. Through this room George was led to a laboratory bigger and better equipped than any which he had seen. Along the white tiled walls, on glass shelves, were ranged innumerable bottles of varying size, and below them projected a wider shelf where flasks, phials, retorts, vascules, test tubes, some empty, some filled with brightly coloured liquids, scintillated bewilderingly in the strong electric light. Near the shelves, at a little distance from the walls, were fixed steel tables, twenty or more of them at each side of the room, and on these tables were Bunsen burners, electrical apparatus, and on the table nearest to the door the half-dissected body of a large black-bearded man, a peasant, to judge from what was left of him. Looking down the room, which was perhaps 20 yards long, George could see at the farther end two doors, with large lettering above them, REFERENCE LIBRARY and MACHINE ROOM. And in the centre of the wide space between the tables was a small writing desk at which was sitting a little spectacled man

221

wearing a white apron, who, at George's entry, rose to his feet and stepping to a stand near the wall surveyed George through a telescope.

George walked down the room towards him, and the King, for it appeared from the reverence paid him by the two attendants who now withdrew that this scientist was he, stepping away from the telescope said: 'Excuse me. I am a little short-sighted' and half-extended a small dry hand for George to shake. Then, thrusting his hands in his pocket, he puckered his wizened face, looking perhaps as pleasant as he could, though his spectacled eyes enlarged by the thick glass showed no humanity, and rocking backwards and forwards on his heels he said: 'What do you think of the lab?'

'It seems very well equipped' said George, 'but probably I can't appreciate it as I should, because I'm not a scientist.'

'No,' said the king, 'of course you're not. You're a natural historian. I've heard about you of course. Well, now, let's get down to business.'

He grinned rapidly, revealing beneath his thin lips rows of black teeth, and the snarl did not favourably impress George, who was beginning 'The Rev. Hamlet—' when the King with an impatient gesture cut him short, saying: 'Don't start telling me about the Rev. Hamlet. I want to talk about the oil beetle. Perhaps you can help us in our work on its metamorphosis.'

George, surprised to find that neither of the kings was interested in the sentence under which he had been condemned by one of their subordinates, wondered how to account for this apparent lack of cohesion in the Government, and was at a loss while the King continued to speak, showing by his quick nodding grimaces and the nervous movements of his hands a great enthusiasm for his subject.

222

'You know the problem,' he was saying. 'It has long been a set-back for science. Forgive me for going over old ground, but we had better have the main facts before us. The oil beetle deposits its eggs inside certain flowers and these eggs, we have excellent reasons for believing, are picked up by the visiting bee and carried to the hive. What happens then? Alas, we do not know. The eggs of course must become larvæ, and the larvæ must develop into oil beetles, but how the larvæ live, whether they destroy the bee grubs, or whether they receive some other nourishment, we have been unable to this day to discover. The difficulties of observation are, as you can imagine, immense, but I am solving the problem, slowly, perhaps, but surely.'

He paused, wreathing his hands, smiling for approbation. 'How are you setting about it?' George asked, and the King replied: 'By extermination of the race. I am collecting oil beetles from all their known habitats. They die without issue, and in course of time the problem of their reproduction will cease to be a problem. There will be no oil beetles left to reproduce themselves.'

Rubbing his hands together he grinned triumphantly into George's face, offending with his rank breath, but George was too surprised at the recital of this vindication of science to make any comment, and the King soon went on speaking. 'Not a bad achievement, is it? But I fear I am being selfish. You, I understand, are interested in wild geese. Now that is a subject which I have investigated myself. We must certainly exchange views.'

At last George began to see some hope, finding for the first time since he had been in the town someone who voluntarily had opened this subject which of all others was uppermost in his mind. Some useful information at last, he hoped, might be forthcoming, perhaps some assistance, and excitedly he spoke: 'For anything which you can tell me about the wild geese I shall be grateful. Alas, I know little enough about them myself, having heard them only once since I began my travels; but I imagine that their habitat is far from here.'

'I don't know so much about that,' said the King slowly. 'It's a very interesing subject, and we must proceed cautiously. But what species are you looking for in particular? The Grey Lag, I suppose?'

'No,' said George, surprised, 'not the Grey Lag.'

'Ah,' said the King, 'not the Grey Lag. That's important. The Brent, perhaps, the Bean, the Snow, or the Barnacle. There are some very interesting old legends about the Barnacle. But I'll tell you what. We're quite prepared to finance an expedition to explore the breeding grounds of the Lesser White-fronted. What do you say?'

Despondently George shook his head. 'We are talking about two quite different things', he said slowly.

The King peered at him over the rim of his spectacles. 'Sorry,' he said in a somewhat offended voice, 'sorry, I'm sure.' And then in harsher tomes: 'Well, is there anything else you'd like to know?'

'Yes,' said George. 'I'd like to know whether something cannot be done for the countrymen,' but before he could continue the King interrupted him with a sudden laugh. 'Come this way,' he said. 'Come this way and I'll show you. We've got the situation well in hand.'

He led George into the Machine Room, which was, to George's surprise, quite silent and contained no machines, but only a long table, studded with buttons and lights of various colours, shining through small circles of glass inlaid in the table. On one of the walls was a large sheet of glass, apparently a mirror.

'I see you're surprised,' said the King, 'not to see any machines, but here are all the controls and here (pointing to the mirror) is our observation screen. By manipulating the appropriate controls I can throw on that screen a picture, something like a cinematograph picture, of events taking place in any part of our territories. It is a question, as you will imagine, of being able to control the light waves. We have a similar installation which enables us to hear any conversation which we wish to hear, but the two apparatuses have not so far been connected together. That is a problem with which we are busy at the moment. But what shall I show you? Did you ever visit the vaults of the Anserium?'

George shook his head and watched the screen while the King bent over the buttons on the table, pressing down some, and sliding others to the right or to the left. The screen was becoming dimmed by what seemed a grey smoke and through this smoke black outlines began to appear with a growing distinctness, and soon George was looking at lifelike figures of men, bearded, and women of all ages, huddled together, packed tight, lying on a floor or standing against a wall of rough stone. That they were alive could be seen from the occasional twitching of an eyebrow, or writhing of a lip, but their wide eyes stared expressionless and their emaciated bodies suggested starvation. But apart from the suspended animation of these ghost-like figures what made the scene appear unreal was the fact that from the throat of each man and women projected a glass tube, one end of which seemed to be let into the flesh while the other end could not be distinguished for all the tubes penetrated the wall at one corner of this prison and there were lost.

'Peasants,' said the King, rubbing his hands, 'recruited from all the villages and fulfilling a very useful function. Would you like to see where the tubes end?'

George nodded and watched fade away the grim faces that were unconscious of observation, ghastly faces, and in their place succeeded the picture of couches laid in rows, shining with jewels, and on the couches were recumbent figures, wearing crowns, asleep but breathing heavily. Through the thick gleaming material in which these figures were clothed, in the region of their breasts, passed the thin ends of glass tubes, and 'Those are some of our dead kings' explained the scientist. 'A transference of blood is taking place.'

Wide-eyed George watched here and there a figure shift or turn over in his sleep. The faces were indistinct, and all the eyes closed. That thick breathing crowd of sleepers, dressed majestically, kept animate through a tube of glass, was a strange sight, and 'Do they never wake?' George asked in a whisper, fearful almost of disturbing their slumber.

'No,' said the King, 'they never exactly wake,' and he pressed a button causing to fade away the scene, while George's heart froze with pity and anger as he saw how terribly the living were penalized in order to preserve the uneasy repose of death. Should he seize the King, he wondered, with his two hands and strangle him? But he restrained himself, knowing that now was not the time.

He was shown the performance of other machines. There was one magnetic instrument capable of controlling all the ploughs, harrows, tractors, and other agricultural implements used on the farms. In glee the King showed him on the screen a team ploughing and then, when the appropriate button was pressed, George saw the plough tugged violently away from the horses to the terror of the ploughman and whisked out of sight. 'It is useful occasionally,' said the King, 'to demonstrate our power,' and he offered to show George the working of an instrument which, so he said, could kill noiselessly at a distance simply by the concentration of sound waves in an ear. But George asked instead to be shown the farm house and it was with relief that he saw the screen filled with the picture of the parlour with Joe sitting by the fire, looking somewhat older than he had seemed when George left him. Where is Joan, George wondered, and expected to see her as the door in the picture opened; but it admitted only the emaciated figure of Pushkov, who, covering his face with one arm, was shouting eager words to Joe while he peered, as though hunted, into every corner of the room.

The King pressed the button, dissipating the picture, 'Evidently,' he said,' an arrest is about to be made,' and he looked at George steadily as though to note the effect of his words.

'I can see,' said George, 'that the Government will never do anything valuable for the countrymen. If the King—'

But he was interrupted. 'I'll tell you what. You ought to see the King,' said the scientist amiably, and George realized that again he had failed to reach the highest authority. Still it seemed that each member of the governing class to whom he was introduced was more powerful than the last, and though he did not imagine that much was to be gained from an interview with a monarch who employed such officers and whose forbears were so grimly interred, he determined partly from despair and partly from curiosity to go forward until it was in his power either to retrieve or by some sudden action partly to atone for his past mistakes.

The scientist was saying: 'Let me see. Let me see. I don't know quite where His Majesty will be at present,' and he consulted a board on the wall where coloured lights were constantly succeeding one another, then 'Lucky coincidence', he said, 'His Majesty has been all the time in an adjoining room.' He led George out of the Machine Room into the Library, a large hall whose high roof was supported by massive marble pillars between which were bookcases filled with volumes on all kinds of subjects. Going over the thickly carpeted floor, the scientist conducted George behind one of the bookcases near the wall, where a small green baize door was discovered. Towards this door George was gently pushed, 'His Majesty is inside,' said the scientist.

George entered a small room and a stifling atmosphere. The heavy carpet, the big chairs upholstered in red velvet, seemed to contribute to the fierce heat emanating from the huge wood fire burning on the hearth. On the walls were bad reproductions of religious pictures and in one of the chairs, his legs stretched out in front of him, while on his lap lay purring a tabby cat, reclined the corpulent figure of a clergyman, apparently asleep. George was in doubt whether or not to waken him, and fixed his eyes again on the pictures, the colouring of which seemed to him strangely heavy, almost metallic. He then began to examine the furniture, which consisted of a writing desk and a revolving bookcase filled with bound copies of the Journal of the Society of Anglers, but he was startled by a sharp cough from the chair and turned to see the King wide awake, looking at him with twinkling eyes while he stroked the cat, pinching its ears between the heavy passes of his hand. Having received George's attention he yawned, stretching out a fat hand, unpleasantly moist, for George to take, and retaining George's hand, he beamed into his face, forcing him into a chair.

'You want to speak to me about the countrymen,' he said. 'Quite right. Quite right. Let me hear what you have to say.' And George, determined to make the best of what might even now be an opportunity for redress, gave as full an account as he could of the grievances of the agricultural workers. While he was speaking the King's eyes never left his face, and when he paused the King would nod his head and interject, 'Terrible,' 'I had no idea,' or 'It cannot be allowed to continue.' The heat of the room, the apparent concurrence of the King with George's pleas, something somnolent in His Majesty's voice and more than all this the strange glow of his big eyes above the cat's eyes fixed continually, unwinking, on George's face, combined to make George feel very sleepy, and long before he had reached the end of his list of complaints he began to wonder whether he was not repeating himself, began in irritation with himself to bite his lip in an effort to concentrate his attention to what he was saying. Yet, in spite of the exertion of his will, his

228

mind was becoming invaded with strange images quite inappropriate to the subject with which he was dealing, an apathy was overlaying his limbs, and almost in a dream he heard himself interrupted by the King, who was saying: 'And you, what is the object of your travels?'

George pinched himself, though he could not feel his hands or arms. He could not remember. Something, certainly of importance had impelled him to leave his home, something too which was very near the surface of his mind, but as he looked into the kind watery eyes in front of him he could not for the life of him recall what it was till he dimly perceived for a moment that the King had turned his eyes away, and he was quick to notice a change in their expression. Their mistiness, their twinkling irrelevancy, had been replaced by a glint of steel, a hard animal glow, and George jumping to his feet, threw off his apathy, realizing for the first time his danger. Into his mind flooded clear and distinct the memory of what he had seen and heard at the farm house and he shouted: 'The Wild Goose. That is the object of my travels,' then with a cry sprang towards the door, for he had noticed the King's peremptory gesture, and had seen from the picture frames, metallic indeed, the nozzles of guns advancing.

As he reached the door, not too soon, he heard the rattle and, without waiting to imagine the air of that study thick with flying lead, he ran through the library, through the laboratory and the vestibule seeking an exit. Turning back he saw behind him a patrol of police, swinging their truncheons and laughing, marching after him through the laboratory, but a door, which on his entry he had not observed, was open, and through this he ran, leaping down steps, throwing away his field-glasses, and at length found himself in the street. In front of him stood Captain Cochran at the head of a file of police. George dashed his fist in the Captain's face, and on falling he overset the man behind him who in turn caused the collapse of another till the whole patrol, like ninepins, lay flat on their backs. George did not wait to laugh. He noticed that fresh patrols of police, with some surgeons, were approaching from all sides and he sprang on to a passing tram car which bore in front of it the notice COUNTRY GATE. He had knocked the driver into the street, and pressing down the brass lever to Full Speed he was glad to find that the car was capable of considerable acceleration. Ringing the bell like mad he sped through the streets while all the traffic hurriedly made way for him and faces were upturned in consternation towards the flying tram. Already he was passing fast cars and in front he could see an open gate when from behind he heard the patter of bullets on the back of the tram and leaning out at the side could see two armoured cars gradually drawing abreast of him. He pressed the lever still farther down and with a grinding shock the tram stopped dead. He had inadvertently applied the emergency brake. The two cars passed him like flashes and collided in front of him. George leapt to the ground and ran towards the gate. Behind him he could hear voices raised imperatively, and in horror he could see the two iron valves of the gate beginning slowly to close. With bursting lungs he exerted every muscle in his body. He had reached the almost solid wall of iron. Sobbing, with strained mouth, he hurled himself at the chink of light. The iron grazed his clothing. He was through.

PART TWO

THE MANY CHANGE

CHAPTER ONE

WHEN George had run for perhaps a quarter of a mile beyond the city boundary and was again in the open plain, over which extended for as far as his eye could see a sea of stems swinging and heads rolling full of corn, an inundation, he looked back and found no trace of a pursuit, but only in the distance a policeman laughing at him. Stiff stood the blank walls of concrete, forbidding, and from within George could still hear the confused hubbub of a strange life, but except for the single constable outside the walls he was alone and, as he looked back on that enclosure and that laughing face, sights which were horrible to him, he felt free, at least for the time being, standing in acres of corn in a bright light that was surely of day. He sat down on a stone, letting relax his eyes upon the live earth, glad to be off asphalt, and while at the back of his mind was still the awareness of that laughing policeman, he reflected that they might well laugh at him, though the machine guns so narrowly avoided were no laughing matter, for certainly he had made a fool of himself from start to finish.

He said to himself: I entered this country, leaving my friends, if friends they were, with a view to chasing the Wild Goose. What have I accomplished? At the beginning I was full of confidence, intending to act painstakingly, and that was why I was too proud to do as my brothers did, to make a display, to buy a new bicycle or to have repainted an old one. I carried no revolver and no works of reference, only my field-glasses, which I have lost, and all this was because I was confident in my own ability to bring my inquiry to a successful conclusion.

Later I was not averse from taking responsibility for Bob, and perhaps I was pleased by the flattery of his empty geniality. Though we had no single aim in common I yet permitted him to accompany me on a journey of such importance, and for sure I have no reason to complain of his recent conduct in handing me over to the police. And later I might also have been diverted from my purpose by listening too long to the representations of the chef, Don Antonio's brother, who urged me to join his settlement where indeed I should sheepishly have fed my selfish pride, self-righteously alleviating misfortunes whose occurrence I would do nothing to prevent.

No wonder that not till I reached the farm house across the frontier did I hear rumour or see sign of what I was after. There I fell in love with Joan, and that was the best thing I have done so far. She is a good girl and I am longing to see her, though I doubt whether she has been any more faithful to me in my absence than I have been to her, and once when I was with her I actually heard the wild geese, witnessed speed and strength, a thing which seemed to me at the time a promise of further fortune. Why have I never heard that bird since then?

Perhaps because I have been too busy with other things, though I had every reason in so busying myself, because it was obvious that, arrived so far, I had to have a base for my operations, had to enlist sympathy from somewhere, have something for my fingers to lay hold on, for the toes of my feet to grip; but certain it is that I have busied myself to no purpose, that I have rejected the best advice that was offered to me, and in individual assurance gone to look for help in quarters from which no help will ever be forthcoming.

232

How clearly do I see now that the city and its kings can never be subdued, never even be seriously disturbed by adventurers! Only an army, only the organized movement of masses can shake that Government, and my place is on no pedestal of my own, but shoulder to shoulder with the peasants and with what portion of the town populace may be ready for revolt. Certainly I found the countrymen to be unlikely material for revolution. Apart from their livestock, every instrument of agriculture which they possess has been bought from and can be controlled by the people in the town, and yet they are impatient of organization; they simply go about muttering, cheating the townsfolk when they can, which is not often, otherwise idiotically resigned, though there have been occasions, I have heard, when some intolerable act of injustice has caused them to go mad, to devastate the countryside for miles, sporadic and ill-judged insurrections to be quashed eventually in blood. At the causeway, watching the loading of lorries, I had received this impression and it was confirmed by the events which took place at the political meeting. Pushkov, the agitator, is genuine. So is the young man, Alfred. So too, no doubt, is that puzzling character, Joe. But their fellow countrymen! They were mere appendages to their pipes as they stood with their hands in their pockets, shuffling, or leaning against the wall. How easily were they bamboozled by the spying priest! How they were laughed out of countenance by the constables! How they were pathetic instead of formidable!

Yet indubitably my place was with them. It was a selfish pride which kept me from acceding to Pushkov's appeal to stay and help, which led me on an inane and an individual adventure. I have been less formidable than anybody and more ridiculous even than my two brothers. Rudolph at least believes that in a day or two he has done the work of a lifetime. David, adept in suspending his judgment, is at least enjoying himself. Whereas I, having lived for I do not know how long in an environment with which I could never make contact except at the expense of renouncing wholly my aims, have achieved absolutely nothing, have by the skin of my teeth escaped, a right object for the laughter of policemen.

My quarrel with Joan was of a piece with the rest of my fool-hardiness. She gave me excellent advice and it was in her company that I first received an indication that I was on the right track. Yet I have behaved to her worse than my brothers behaved. I took her confidence, but never returned it. I never gave her fully to understand the urgency of my purpose, but instead I treated her as a person suited to love-making, and otherwise of no account. When she spat in my face I was nettled, not realizing that on her I was inflicting far deeper wounds. When my place was with her and with her people I chose rather to agree with the irresponsible Bob; when there was need for patience, I chose to be as egotistically daring as Rudolph. I rejected those who had proved themselves to be my friends, and fancied myself as an explorer, entering a city before I had consolidated my position in the countryside. Almost I paid attention to the stupid letter which David sent me, and was almost willing to believe that the Government might not be so black as it had been painted.

I was soon to discover that the people in the town were infinitely worse than anything I could have imagined. I would rather mutter in honest oppression about the crops than be so clever as not to know my own sex. And that fiendish operation which I was lucky enough to escape is, no doubt, a fitting preliminary to entering the Convent where my brother lives self-satisfied in a subordinate post. Their stuffed goose may be very pretty, but I could see at a glance that it was not the thing. Why did I not then return at once to the country, for I had seen enough? It was my curiosity and my conceit which impelled me to go on to the Convent, running for no good

234

purpose unnecessary risks. I might have known that there could be no possibility of compromise.

And as for the Convent, I found that to be the most depraved institution that I have ever seen or heard of. This was evident from the respect paid to Professor Pothimere, from the appalling immodesty of the statistician's wife, and from the massacre of the better football team of the two.

Those policemen who roar with laughter, and use that for a weapon, they are disgusting creatures, as wicked a force as there is in existence, able, too, to pull a trigger, dangerous when one remembers that they are backed up by whole arsenals of steel. And the kings, from whom I have so narrowly escaped, wield (there is no doubt of it) enormous power. Even if I may assume that I have been interviewed by the final authority (and who knows whether or not there may be other powers behind that seductive and ferocious person disguised as a clergyman) the clergyman very nearly finished me off.

I have learnt what I might have known already, that it is hopeless to imagine that the countrymen will ever receive the slightest consideration from the Government. I have learnt that the Government can dispose of powers greater than any I could have imagined. But I have learnt too that their measures sometimes miscarry. If this had not been so, I should not be here now. And I have detected, I think, some weaknesses in their organization.

Their power, or so it seems to me, rests more on the great prestige which they enjoy and on the submission of most people to this prestige than on either the devotion of the governed or on a really strong military force.

The students at the Convent are obviously unfitted for any kind of action. The police are formidable at close range, but I do not think they would be much good in open country. It is the possibility of remote control from a laboratory which is the most disquieting of all the powers which the Government claims to possess. Yet what evidence have I to prove that this power is half so efficacious as it is supposed to be. I saw a few experiments, but they may have been arranged for my benefit, since it is certain that for some time at least the policy of the Government was rather to induce me, by a parade of power, to become subaltern or slave, than to exterminate me out of hand. They are more willing to bribe than to destroy, and this is an argument of weakness.

Rested in his body and, as a result of having taken stock of the elements of his failure, with his mind more at ease, he rose to his feet and, without looking back, began to walk slowly along a path that led through the corn away from the city; and as he walked he planned his future conduct, how, when he had reached the farm, he would at once put his services at the disposal of Pushkov, would work for an insurrection which soon or late was bound to come, would marry Joan, supposing her not to have lost interest in him, would, in fine, by taking his place in the inevitable movement of the mass, by completely changing his method of approach, gain, he hoped, in the long run power to achieve what, he now saw, could never be achieved by the individual method of freethinkers, military adventurers, gymnosophists, aeronauts, gigolos, or members of a royal family. And so ardently was he longing for the time of his arrival in the village, so pleasantly excited was he when he envisaged his meeting with Joan, his interview with Pushkov, that in the confident current of his thought (for even now he did not stop to suppose that events might occur differently from his anticipation), he was carried away and took no account of distance traversed till he found himself, having left the field-path, on a broad motor road, which might lead to the village he sought, and certainly led away from the enclosed town.

So for what seemed to him many hours he walked down this road, hoping to meet someone from whom he could inquire whether he was in the right way. It was monotonous country, orchards interminable of apple and pear, but at last, when George was beginning to feel too tired to proceed farther, he noticed through the trees a glint of water, and, looking closer, saw a lake surrounding an island on which stood a large building of hetero-geneous architecture, domes and minarets above pediments that were raised on rococo columns, a fantastic sight. Here, certainly, will be people who can put me on my way, thought George, and turned from the road down a hill which was set above the lake. He stopped in front of a huge notice board on which was written: FREE STATE OF LAGONDA, wondering amongst what people he was coming, whether friendly or foes.

Arrived at the margin of the lake, he saw it to be bigger than he had thought at first. The level water stretched farther than he could see, and the palace on the island, behind which hung a sinking sun, was perhaps a mile away. But between him and the island was one small boat, furnished with what seemed to be a brass cannon, and on the deck stood several men looking into the distance through telescopes and field-glasses.

George saw them become suddenly excited. In response to a loud order from the smallest of the men on deck, the brass cannon was let off with a pop, and at the same time George could hear the quickly increasing roaring of an engine. He looked to his left, in which direction the field-glasses were turned, and through a cloud of spray could soon detect the nose of a speedboat, travelling at a terrific speed. In a flash the boat had passed the spectators, and the roar of its engines died away. Now in the distance George imagined it to have turned, for the engines could again be heard, and again it was commanded that the cannon should pop. But this time there seemed to be something wrong. The engines were labouring and it was only at a very moderate pace that the speed-boat was travelling, when it came for the second time fully into view. More and more slowly it advanced to the consternation of watchers on the deck of the pinnace, until just opposite to George, close to the margin of the lake, it stopped dead, and George looking at the driver and hearing him pronounce, 'Engine trouble, by God,' was amazed to recognize his brother Rudolph.

But before he had time to attract his attention, the pinnace steamed close into the shore and the little man, who had previously given orders for firing the little gun, had begun to address himself to Rudolph through a megaphone. 'Tamer of waves,' he was saying, 'accept this Ode!' And he began to read from a sheet of paper which he held at arm's length in front of him. He was thin, short, tense in bearing. His pale face was decorated by a soft hat, from which protruded the tail feather of a pheasant, and by a pointed beard. He wore knee breeches, and, over a black shirt, a jacket of soft purple velvet. From his neck fluttered a large yellow bow tie, and at his side hung a silver gleaming sword. His voice was rich, sonorous, and full of energy. George listened to the Ode.

> 'Speed! the flung mane of horses, the battling hooves!
> Boat! the sheer line of, the throbbing, the dash!
> Man! O mover! O triumph! O shooter towards the goal!
>
> Man first. Not for a silver cup, but for the mastery.
> Not for food, or for the cohabitation, but for the Ideal.
> To beat the record, this man holds his guerdon, his everlasting.
>
> Speed next. What is this? What disturbs this lake?
> Fly and flutter of foam. What of the lightning?
> The falling of a star? O rush! O onrush!
>
> Now boat. Built for a purpose, man's mistress, his loveliest.
> No flesh, but wood, but metal, but petroleum.
> O glorious sustained orgasm of the multi-engined!
>
> Man last. He started it. He clove to his course.
> Now in triumph returning he shall lie upon silk,
> Shall drink in the evening and shall be accounted fortunate.'

'I had the record in my pocket,' said Rudolph. 'If it hadn't

238

been for the blasted engine.' He bowed towards the pinnace. 'Thank you very much for the Ode, all the same. It's a bit above my head, I'm afraid. I can tell you I did my darnedest.'

After the brass gun had been let off once more, the pinnace approached nearer to the stationary speedboat.

'You'll have to tow her in,' Rudolph shouted, throwing a line. 'I can't tell you, sir, how sorry I am that this has happened.'

The little captain raised his megaphone. 'Courage!' he shouted, 'Youth! Victory!'

'Hullo, Rudolph,' George said, since so far no one had noticed him.

Rudolph turned round and, after looking George over quickly waved his hands excitedly in the direction of the pinnace. 'Here's my brother,' he shouted, 'and by God, I thought he was dead.'

The captain and crew of the pinnace turned towards George. Reunion!' shouted the captain through his megaphone, 'Hope! Futurity!' And then, addressing himself more particularly to George, he pronounced the words: 'Brother of the King of Speed, famous, no doubt, yourself, a welcome to the Free State of Lagonda is extended to you by me, First President of the Republic, a poet.'

George bowed, and, at Rudolph's invitation, waded through the shallow water at the edge of the lake, and took his place in the speedboat beside his brother. They were then towed backwards in the direction of the castle on the island. It was a gentle evening, with the sun, which at this distance from the town shone normally, just declining, and George saw with pleasure the lighted surface of the lake and from the farther shore the woods descending. Behind his back pounded the motor with which the President's pinnace was equipped, and, turning round, George remarked the President himself, standing stiff and solitary at the prow, staring ahead, his hand upon his sword. Beyond rose the curious castle, tinted pink and washed purple, a tall pile. Gnats were thick over the water and lazily, for he was tired from walking, George watched the fish rising and the widening circles that their efforts left as a trace. His late interview with the kings, his desperate escape, seemed long ago and far away. Settling himself in the stern of the speedboat, he listened to Rudolph who was speaking.

CHAPTER TWO

RUDOLPH said: "By God! George, I'd given you up for lost. How did you manage to cross the tundra, and on foot?'

'I've just escaped from the town,' George said, 'and I'm on my way back to the farmhouse.'

'You'll never make it,' Rudolph said, shaking his round head. 'But, first of all, I'll tell you what I've been doing,' and he recited some of the events of which George had already been informed from the diary. 'So you see,' Rudolph, who had insisted on going through the story again, concluded, 'I've done about as much as could be expected of me, I think.'

'I saw you in the red aeroplane,' George said, 'though you didn't see me. I thought you were going to settle down.'

Rudolph interrupted him quickly. 'Settle down!' he tossed back the hair from his handsome red face. 'Settle down! I wish I could, but I've got to be doing something. It seems that I'm not quite the same as other chaps. I just can't stop still.'

'Yes,' said George, 'but what did you do after you wrote your memoirs?'

'Well,' Rudolph replied, 'it's rather an awkward story. I thought first of all of going back to our town. You know little Minnie, the daughter of the town clerk. I knew she'd be waiting for me. But I couldn't make the distance. I hadn't got enough juice, and after all, I thought, what's the good? I wouldn't fit in any longer. Somehow I didn't like the idea of living amongst chaps who'd never been abroad, and I decided to go on sticking it. I knew there was a little girl, the daughter of the chief of the first tribe I had met, who had been heartbroken when I left.'

'You mean Joan?' George interrupted, and Rudolph nodded his head, 'Yes. The tribe speaks English. I thought it would be a decent thing to do if I were to marry that girl. Later, of course, I would become chief of the tribe. It would be a quiet life, certainly, but I made the decision almost more for the girl's sake than for my own. Well, to cut a long story short, I made a forced landing and then trekked in what I imagined to be the direction of the village. It was pretty stiff work crossing the mountains, but I won through. The inhabitants did not give me as good a reception as I had expected, and at first I thought that some of my enemies, revolutionaries perhaps exiled by Colonel Moose or some of my rivals in Ginkistan, had been before me; but it appeared that really the whole village was terrified of the Indian town from which we have both escaped. The medicine man had already been arrested and, by the way, I heard a certain amount of talk about you. They seemed to think that you had let them down in some way. I went straight to the chief's house and asked for the hand of his daughter. The old fellow, who seems a little daft, just laughed at me, and told me that she was married already.'

'What!' George exclaimed. 'Married already?'

'Yes,' said Rudolph. 'Why, what's up?'

'Only that I wanted to marry her myself,' said George.

Rudolph shook his hand. 'Bad luck, old chap,' he said. 'I know just what it feels like. Awfully rotten luck.'

There was a slight pause while they listened to the pounding engine behind them, drawing them nearer to the castle. After a decent interval Rudolph continued: 'As a matter of fact I saw her husband, a great hulking savage, a thoroughly nasty looking customer. As jealous as they make them too, because one night when I was hanging round his hut, hoping that I might get a peep at my little girl, he came out and threatened me with a great club. I didn't want any bloodshed in the village, so I let him off and came away. But before I left I had several chin-wags with the old chief. He was very anxious to hear about you, but of course I couldn't give him any news.

'Well I needn't tell you everything that happened after I left the village. I was damned sorry about the girl, and I expect you are, old man; but one's got to keep a stiff upper lip, hasn't one? Still it certainly upset me. I began to think that I wasn't much use to anyone and I decided that anyway I'd have my fling before I snuffed out.

'At one of the Indian villages I made a lot of money by riding in steeplechases. I spent it all on girls and drink. But, you know, I think that sort of thing's really jolly beastly, though at first it helped me to forget. Anyway I began to sink lower and lower. Before long I'd given up shaving and stopped wearing a tie-pin. It's pretty awful when a man's self respect begins to go. It got worse and worse. I spent all my cash and I was thrown out of the Racing Club, so that I couldn't ride in any more steeplechases. I had to live in a cellar with a woman, who was very decent to me considering everything. I don't know what would have happened if it hadn't been for the President. One day he came into the village, looking for someone to drive his speedboat. Half in fun someone pointed me out to him, and he offered me the job. At first I refused. I said that I'd come there to forget, but he clapped his hand on my shoulder and said "Cheer up! All is not lost," and honestly, old chap, it was like a breath of new life. I had a shave and a wash. I got rid of my woman, and the next day I came here with Koresipoulos. He's a great fellow, and certainly I owe him a lot. A bit eccentric of course. I don't pretend to understand his poetry, and he keeps a home for lost cats. Still he's a genius, and they all have a kink somewhere. He says he's a revolutionary, and that he conquered this Free State of Lagonda from the Indians. Certainly he's got guts, but I don't believe that anyone lives in the Free State except himself and his servants. But of course I've been busy with the speedboat and, by God, I'd have beaten the record to-day if it hadn't been for the blasted engine.'

George had many questions to ask. How, for instance, he wondered, had President Koresipoulos been able to wrest any concession, however small, from a government so strong as that in the town? Was it not possible that the town might have abetted an escapade of freedom? And most of all George wished for a further account of Joan's marriage and of Pushkov's imprisonment. He began to see that everything was not shaping exactly in accordance with his anticipations and desires; but before he had time to question Rudolph they had arrived at the island.

In a cove, the water of which was so clear that in 12 feet of it George could distinguish white pebbles at the bottom, stood a jetty. The pinnace drew alongside and, when the speedboat had been pulled close to it, George and Rudolph clambered to its deck where the President was standing. George looked past him and saw a flight of marble steps leading up to the main entrance of the castle. The domes glowed with a suffused rose and the minarets were tipped with gold. Twisted pillars by the door upheld a pediment which bore a group of sculpture, and underneath was an inscription 'FREEDOM EMBRACES HOPE'. Alongside the flight of steps were enclosures of wire netting where hundreds of cats were to be seen, some plump, some scraggy. Their mewing was intermittent, but loud.

'Oppressed creatures' came the voice of Koresipoulos, and George drew his eyes away from the strange sights on the island. The President was standing in front of him, with hand extended. 'Welcome once again,' he was saying, 'to Lagonda. Tell me, what path of glory do you pursue?'

George shook hands and explained that, having been driven

out of the town, he was on his way to a farmhouse in the country where he hoped to be able to get into touch with others who shared his detestation of the Government.

Koresipoulos smiled. 'Notable I see you are for freedom, as is your brother for speed,' he said. 'Let this be the end of your journey. Here all is freedom.' He turned to the crew of the pinnace. 'Brave boys, fire a salute!'

Until the gun had popped the group stood motionless on deck. Koresipoulos then led the way down the gang plank, along the jetty and up the steps. While they were passing the cats, he turned to George. 'Your brother may have told you,' he said, 'that I make it my business to succour, in what degree I can, the oppressed. Here are specimens of my beneficence.'

They ascended the long flight of steps, between the mewing of cats, and at the door were received by a blast upon a trumpet. Having entered a hall, in the furniture of which was displayed the same bizarre taste as that which distinguished the exterior decoration, the President paused.

'You two will have much to talk of,' he said gravely. 'And while you compare your adventures, I shall retire to compose an Ode which will make, I expect, this reunion for ever memorable. I shall read it to you later, after our democratic meal.'

He bowed and, attended by a single trumpeter, walked up a stone stairway to an upper floor. George stood at Rudolph's side on the thick carpet, and for a moment or two surveyed the retiring President and the furniture of his palace. Although Koresipoulos's legs are far too short, George reflected, he scales the stairway with admirable dignity; and next he noticed the painting on the ceiling, scenes of rustic merriment and the piping of goatherds. In one corner of the hall stood a piece of sculpture, a body not cut clear from the stone, and beneath was written: THE SPIRIT OF MAN. On the walls were hung paintings of nineteenth-century French painters, and portraits of Napoleon and of Garibaldi. Facing the door blazed a huge wood fire and at the corner of the mantelpiece were mummy cases and Chinese weapons.

Rudolph and George sat down in heavy armchairs and drew near to the fire. First George gave his brother a brief account of his adventures, and at the end of his narration Rudolph gripped him by the hand, saying, 'By God! George, I never thought you had it in you. You've been working slowly, certainly, but I reckon you've done your bit. And old David, he hasn't done so badly for himself, has he? Though it was a rotten trick to let you down like he did. Come to think of it, I never liked David. He's damned clever though.'

George interrupted him. 'Why not come back to the farm with me?' he said. 'I don't see what good you can do by staying here.'

Rudolph took out a cigarette case and, having lit a cigarette, stiffened his powerful jaw. 'I'm out to lower that record,' he said.

'What about the Wild Goose?' George asked.

Rudolph shifted his feet nervously. There was a long pause. Finally he said in a boisterous voice: 'There's no such thing!' and then looked rather shamefacedly into his brother's eyes.

'What do you mean?' said George. 'I tell you I've heard those birds. And our way is through the town.'

Rudolph was looking grave. 'It's a jolly awkward subject,' he said, 'for a man to speak about.'

'There's no need to speak about it,' George replied, 'or not just yet. First we must clear the way. Help the revolution.'

Shifting his feet nervously and with one hand massaging his chin, Rudolph, ill at ease, spoke. 'You may be quite right, old boy, for all I know. Perhaps the way is through that Indian town.

246

But how are we going to get through? That's the question. Danger's my element, but there's no point in chucking one's life away. Revolution, say you, but, after all, old fellow, one can hardly join forces with a lot of scallywags. Besides there's this record. And I owe Koresipoulos a lot.'

George would have continued, though he had noticed already with dismay that Rudolph no longer held constantly in view the object of their journey, to attempt to persuade him to join the countrymen instead of wasting his time in a defective speedboat, but at this moment they heard again the blast of the trumpet ushering Michael Koresipoulos downstairs.

The poet wore a dinner jacket and trousers of black velvet. At his side was still the silver sword. 'Greetings!' he proclaimed, pausing at the foot of the stairs. 'Shall we drink the health of the democracy in goat's milk?'

He led the way to a dining room lit by gigantic candelabra. On the table were bowls of fruit, with dishes of cheese, hard-boiled eggs, and nuts. George, who could not remember when he had eaten last, who indeed was disposed to believe that in all the time during which he had lived in the artificial atmosphere of the town he had eaten nothing, looked eagerly at this meagre repast.

'It is Arcadian diet,' the President was saying. 'Farm produce washed down by good goat's milk. I encourage the industries of the Free State.'

They sat down to the table and it was not until he had taken the edge off his hunger that George noticed in front of him the photos of young aviators and racing motorists with which the hall was profusely hung. Koresipoulos observed his attention. 'Young friends of mine,' he said. 'Followers of fame, like your brother,' and he went the round of the photographs, indicating one who had first flown across the lake in a glider, another who held the 100 kilometer record for 10·5 h.p. cars, and others with similar titles to notoriety. 'Next to Freedom and Glory,' said the President, 'I revere Speed.'

'I'm jolly sorry about that record,' Rudolph interrupted. 'If it hadn't been for the blasted engine.'

Koresipoulos made no reply but, rising to his feet, he walked slowly to Rudolph and kissed him on both cheeks, after he had pinned to the lapel of his coat a small silver medal. Rudolph, blushing, waited until the President had sat down before he too rose, and with an ambient smile, in a somewhat nervous manner, began to speak:

'Honestly, Mr. President, you do me too much honour. I did what I could, certainly. Which of us would not? But, owing to the blasted engine, I didn't quite pull it off. I don't want to make a long speech. I'm really not much good at that sort of thing. All I want to say is that she's the finest boat that was ever built and that I'm jolly well going to make sure of the record next time. Thank you, Mr. President. I'm jolly grateful to you, and I wish I had the gift of the gab, like some people, so that I could make my meaning a bit plainer. But I always feel rather an ass when I get on my hind legs and start spouting.'

He sat down again, while George and Koresipoulos clapped their hands. Rudolph whispered to his brother 'That was all right, wasn't it? Your turn now', and George wondered at the curious disposition of the President who apparently desired his dining table to be a Parliament.

The food and goat's milk was now cleared away by the serving man who had previously appeared in the capacity of trumpeter. When everything had been removed from the table, he was invited to sit down by Koresipoulos, who, turning to George, remarked: 'This is a Free State.'

The trumpeter, or butler, or citizen sat down, rather awkwardly, next to George. He was a young man of gigantic stature, with a sulky indeterminate face and slow eyes. Indicating him by a movement of the head, Koresipoulos explained: 'He pursues the path of service. There is glory in service. His name is Andria.'

Andria blinked and, after a short pause, the President called upon George to speak. Though he was very tired after his journey, George complied with the rules of the Free State and, rising to his feet, gave a brief account of his adventures in the town. He concluded his speech by saying: 'And so, you see, I have every reason to fight against that government to the limit of my ability. My way is towards the farmhouse where I can get into touch with the revolutionary movement among the peasants. You, Mr. President, must be sympathetic to that movement. You, Rudolph, I can't help saying, would win more glory by fighting against your enemies than by going very fast in a motor boat. And you, Andria, perhaps are a peasant yourself. Your place is in the ranks of your own class.' Turning towards his neighbour, he noticed a glint of interest in his large deep eyes, and sat down, while Koresipoulos and Rudolph applauded his speech.

The President sprang to his feet and in his rich vibrant voice began speaking: 'Votary of Liberty, hail! Protoganist of the glorious enfranchisement of the human spirit, receive this Ode!' And having produced a piece of paper from the pocket of his dinner jacket, Koresipoulos began to read:

'Winds of the sky!
Lightning! Thunder! Cloud!
Mother of corn, good earth!
Milky, meaty, and fleecy flocks!
All breakers of chains!

Unfettered O wind!
By the free sea walking,
I, Koresipoulos,
Became enamoured of Liberty,
A breaker of chains.

249

My home for cats,
My draughts of goat's milk,
My pinnace on the lake,
Voice my unalterable ideal,
A democratic regime.

And now to George,
A democrat himself,
With cordial delight, I,
First President of the Republic,
Extend a welcome.

Freedom! God! Joy!
Enthusiasm! Speed!
Beauty, Goodness, and Truth!
To these brothers diversely glorious
Extend a welcome.'

Rudolph and George clapped their hands, and during the applause George whispered to Andria, who was slowly stamping his feet on the floor, 'Where does his money come from?' but before Andria had time to reply to a question which had evidently surprised him, the President had begun speaking. He proposed, he said, to relate the story of the foundation of the Free State of Lagonda.

THE STORY OF MICHAEL KORESIPOULOS

'My mother was related with one of the Royal Families in the city from which you, my friend, have recently escaped, and in which my childhood and adolescence were passed. Very few children, as you may have observed, are born in the more fashionable quarters of the city, and I have heard that my mother's pregnancy excited amongst her friends a good deal of unfavourable comment. Some would have it that my father must have been a member of the labouring population, though how he could have had access to the quarters in which my mother passed her life was a thing which no one pretended to explain. And yet it remains true that of all my mother's accredited acquaintance there were few or none who could be supposed capable of begetting a child.

'So my paternity has always been mysterious. Devotee of Liberty as I am, I need not tell you that I pay no attention to the rank, or to the established paternity of anyone. I owe no allegiance save to the free human spirit of the individual. My mother, however, was, as I think I have said, related with one of the Royal Families.

'From my earliest years I was noted for the protection which I was willing to afford to the abject and the unfortunate. There are, as you know, no animals in the town, so I was limited to the championing of the interests of the oppressed classes. It was at my instigation that a bowling green was provided for the use of some of the foremen at one of the largest factories, and I can also claim the credit for a scheme, never put into execution, of providing for tuberculous children a dose of cod-liver oil twice in every quarter. This proposal of mine was, of course, one of extraordinary daring, and for some time I went about the city in terror for my life. But I am anticipating.

'My education was in the Convent, and from the first I was disgusted by the immorality prevalent amongst both professors and scholars. I could do little, however, to prevent its occurrence except by my own example and by the Odes which I wrote for every suitable occasion.

'My zeal for Liberty was kindled, I think, by the perusal of ancient books. In that fake and vicious atmosphere I longed for a simpler and more virile state. In athletics I gloried, and though I have never personally competed in the arena, I have paid the expenses of several champions. My mother, fortunately for the cause of Liberty, had died intestate, and her considerable fortune passed into my hands.

'I regarded that fortune, not as my own, but as a trust. My

dream was to emancipate the toiling masses, no less. Once I made a speech. On several occasions I composed Odes to Liberty, and I became suspect to the Government. My relations did all they could to bring me into line with the corrupt institutions against which I was in revolt. They argued with me that, as none of the measures which I had so far proposed was a of really revolutionary nature, little would be gained either by adopting or by rejecting them. I replied that even in small things I would never betray the cause of Freedom.

'So for a time the Government pretended to take no notice of me. Meanwhile I had put myself at the head of a small band of revolutionaries from the factory quarters of the town. I never actually met these men, but I corresponded with them secretly and sent them copies of my Odes.

'Partly in order to satisfy these followers of mine, who, lacking as they did a really democratic culture, were inclined to proceed too early to extremes, and partly in order to show the Government that they had to deal with one who could not safely be ignored, I promulgated my manifesto. In this I proclaimed not only my personal devotion to the cause of Freedom, but I also made certain specific demands, among which was a demand that the workers should be granted in the year at least one day's holiday.

'For some time the Government affected to take no notice. The suspense was terrible. I had no one in whom I could confide, since persons of my own rank were inclined to mock at my ideals. It seemed almost that I was forgotten, and in the streets people affected to regard me in the same way as they regarded others.

'I took my resolution. I ordered my loyal followers from the factories, some two hundred in all, to meet me at a specified time outside the city walls. Their enthusiasm and their devotion to me, their general, enabled them to escape their police escorts, and, riding on a white horse, I was able to review outside the walls the first Republican army.

'I caused a proclamation to be made of the main principles of Democracy. We then marched to this locality and from this castle, which was built for me by the Revolutionary army, I promulgated the constitution of the Free State of Lagonda. So far the Government had made no move against us and I had begun to dream of widening the borders of the Free State when I was apprised of the approach of the whole of the Air Force of the town. At the same time therewas disaffection amongst my troops. Alas! I had relied upon the support of poor material.

'These men, whom I had led to Freedom, began to claim credit themselves for what had been achieved. They demanded seats in the legislature, seats which I proposed to keep vacant until I had attracted to the Free State persons of my own culture. Some of them even questioned my title to the Presidency. They said that since the Free State had come into existence their hours of labour had been as long and as unremunerative as ever, and, though I spoke to them of the dignity of labour and of their place in history, their limited intelligences seemed unable to attach any meaning to the words which I pronounced.

'On the approach of the hostile Air Force many of them were for deserting me, and it was almost with relief that I received an embassy from the town, who came to treat for peace. Evidently the Government, though their advantages in men and material were enormous, were cowed by the daring coup which I had made; for this ambassador offered at once a full recognition of my position of President of the Free State of Lagonda. They offered also a crew to man my pinnace and one attendant for myself. In return for this I was to assemble my army in a plain beyond the boundaries of the Free State, and there they were to be bombed to death.

'Liberty, I felt, had demanded a terrible sacrifice from her votary. It is true that my army had, by mutinies and disaffection, forfeited all just claim to my regard, but I am reluctant to assent to the suffering of any living creature. Yet, I reflected, these men will be laying down their lives in the noblest of all causes, the cause of Freedom, and how should I rob them of the Glory with which, it seems, they are to be crowned by Fate? By their death they will give birth to a Free State. Could I be in two minds? Proudly I accepted the terms of peace, and from the top of a mountain I witnessed the massacre of my troops. In the plain where they died I caused a stone to be set, and on the event I composed an Ode.

'From that time to this day I have met with no obstruction from the Government, and I like to think that it was not in vain that my army perished. My home for lost cats was designed by a Government architect. My speedboat was a present from the police. And into this Free State I am able to welcome all victims of oppression.'

He sat down, while George stared at the table in front of him, abashed by what he had heard. So this was the end, he reflected, of an individual escapade. He spoke angrily: 'You and your cats be damned, you traitor. I shall leave here at once, and, as for you, Rudolph, I advise you to come with me.' He turned to the peasant. 'You, Andria, if you've never heard this story before, must make up your mind now. This man has murdered your brothers.' He looked again towards the President, 'You rat!' he said; 'I've a mind to strangle you myself.'

'Please, please, gentlemen,' Rudolph was heard to exclaim; but Koresipoulos, who had no lack of confidence, had risen to his feet. 'Secure him!' he said in his rich voice, his hand resting upon his sword. 'He has spoken ill of the Republic.'

But Andria was looking at the President through narrow eyes, with an odd puzzled expression on his face. Gradually, as though dragged from deep, words came to his lips: 'You killed my neighbours,' and now Koresipoulos grew pale as he saw shifting round the table the giant bulk of the peasant whose hands were stretched before him as though in supplication. He attempted to retrieve his authority. 'Sit down, my brave lad!' he cried, and then, as the peasant still advanced, he nervously hit him across the face with repeated blows, screaming. Andria had his hands about the President's throat and with an expressionless face he lifted the body easily from the floor, shaking it in a still silence, for the President had no air in his lungs. The sword broke loose from the velvet trousers and fell. Rudolph, with trembling fingers, was loading a revolver. George stood still and saw at last the bundled body of Koresipoulos huddle lifeless, dropped from Andria's hands upon the carpet. Andria, whose eyes were now shining like coals, wiped the sweat from his forehead. 'Come on,' George said, and the two of them went out of the room.

They passed through the open door into brilliant moonlight and, descending to the jetty, climbed into a dinghy which was moored there. George took the oars and rowed towards the farther shore of the lake. When they were half-way across they heard from the island Rudolph shouting 'Hi! man the pinnace! They shall die for this,' but they were out of danger.

CHAPTER THREE

THEY landed, tall figures, on a reach of sand silvered now by moon, and looking back saw twinkling the lights of the castle. George, though he hardly took seriously the danger of a pursuit, was nevertheless willing to follow Andria inland, and, as they climbed steeply through woods in starry darkness or over the laminated sheen of glades, he regarded with admiration the slowly swinging hips and broad back of the peasant who moved silently in front of him. After a time they heard from the shore below them shouting and the crack of a revolver shot. They halted and Andria, turning to George, grinned. 'We're safe enough now, neighbour,' he said. But for some hours more they continued to climb until they were high among the mountains, and then, clear of the trees, Andria pointed to a sheep shelter, lightly roofed, indicating that there they might sleep.

It was very cold and they were glad to find inside the shelter high piles of brushwood for beds, and cut heather and hay for coverlets. Andria stretched his arms smiling and to George it seemed that the slaying had given to the slayer his own strength, had roused within his loins a sleeping confidence and put an alertness into his eyes. So they smiled at each other and lay down, soon to be asleep.

At dawn George woke, stiff and cold. He stretched his arms, rubbed his eyes and glanced at Andria who was lying easily upon his back, smiling in his sleep, a giant whose dreams seemed innocent. George went out through the gap in the wall and saw in front of him the sky dabbed flame colour with the rising sun. Nearer to him cutting upwards were the misty slopes of mountains whose peaks half-hidden were still, he could discern, under coats of snow. Looking back he saw only a huddle of boulders and, far below him, the first fringe of the woods through which they had ascended from the lake. He had no idea of where the town was or in what direction he must go to reach the farm and when Andria came from the shelter to greet him he asked first where they were and whither they were going.

Andria pointed through the mist high among the peaks, explaining that there was the pass over the mountains, and below in the plains was his own village and not far away from it the village which George was seeking. So they set off, climbing rapidly through the rapidly clearing mist and on the way talked of what had happened overnight.

Andria's face set grave as rock when the name of the President was mentioned. 'I never knew it,' he said. 'I never knew that it was my neighbours that he had killed.' His eyes flashed while the rest of his face was stockstill as he felt again in imagination the pulpy neck of Koresipoulos wrung by his two hands.

He had been taken from his village, so he informed George, when a youth. Shortly afterwards his mother had attracted the attention of a Commissioner of Police, and Andria wept as he related this part of the story which he had heard a year or two later from a youth who had been transported to the town from his own village. His mother had been killed, and of his father and sister he had heard no news.

It was not long after this that Koresipoulos had made his escapade from the town. Andria had wished to join the factory workers who had participated in this revolt, but, as it was indeed a desperate undertaking to win clear, only 200 picked men had attempted it and he had been adjudged too inexperienced (for he was still bewildered in the town) to go with them. The workers who had been left anxious behind had been informed by the Government that their comrades had all died from starvation. It was pointed out that difficulties of transport and economic reasons which were not specified had made it quite impossible for any separate state authority to be set up; but that the Government had been able to attempt on a small scale an experiment in autonomy and had permitted the well-known revolutionary leader, Michael Koresipoulos, to found a Free State the government of which was at present chiefly occupied with the care of lost cats and dogs, but which might in a not too remote future be able to bring human beings also within its sphere of influence. The Government deeply regretted the loss of Koresipoulos's followers, but pointed out that this unfortunate event was due to their own precipitation in not laying before the Government in a constitutional manner complaints and suggestions which would certainly have received the fullest attention.

Many of the workers were impressed by the Government's announcement. Koresipoulos, whom they had never seen, was regarded as a leader whose integrity and loyalty were beyond reproach, and the fact that he had been allowed to found an autonomous state, however limited in its authority, seemed to many a proof that the Government, in spite of appearances, was genuinely interested in reform. At the same time police escorts were doubled, some workers who had been particularly friendly with men who had been in the army of refugees unaccountably disappeared, and wages were cut by twenty per cent. This last measure, it was explained, was a temporary one in order to secure sufficient funds to equip adequately the new Free State of Lagonda. Also, as wages had never been high enough for the recipients to purchase anything except food, it was observed that the cuts would make little or no difference; and soon wages were abolished entirely and the workers were supplied by the Government with food in tabloid form twice a day to be eaten on the way to and from the factories.

And so Andria had been pleased when he was informed that he need work no more in the factory since he had been appointed personal attendant to the President of the Free State. He carried from his fellow workers messages of greeting and petitions to the President and these messages Koresipoulos caused to be engraved in stone, after he had made a speech of which Andria and a young designer of gliders were the only auditors. But from the moment of his entry into Lagonda Andria had been puzzled, and, as the years went by he had become totally bewildered. He had been surprised when Koresipoulos had handed over to the police two revolutionaries who had taken refuge in the Free State, and it was his lack of culture, he had supposed, which had made him unable to understand the President's speech about the inevitability of gradualness. Indeed the President frequently took pains to emphasize the gulf that was fixed between himself, a man of enlightenment, and the members of the class which, he said, it was his mission to serve. He would often exclaim against the ingratitude of those whom he had striven to make worthy of democracy and, as time went on, though he spoke frequently of Liberty, he spent most of his time on his pinnace, enjoying the performances of aeronauts, racing motorists, and drivers of speed boats.

Andria had often to blow a trumpet, sometimes to carry a sword, but his main occupation was the feeding and care of the lost cats and dogs over which Koresipoulos exercised authority. And so, busied with these arduous and, to his mind, unnecessary tasks, he had ceased altogether to think about his comrades in the town, though still at the back of his mind lingered the determination some day to avenge his mother's death and degradation. He had hoped in time to absorb sufficient of the President's culture to be able to appreciate the constitution of the Free State, but latterly had begun to despair of what he had become accustomed to regard as his own stupidity and he had even thought of making his escape to his own village. Still slowly smiling, still uncertain of his mind, though his will was clear, he explained to George that he had been cheated all along and that in his village he would tell them that.

Now they had reached the pass and the mist had cleared. Looking backward from a great height they could survey a vast expanse of country. Below them, now a speck, was the shelter where they had slept and beyond, over the wooded ridge which they had climbed, far away gleamed the lake where Koresipoulos had ruled, and then the distant plain, the confused green of orchards and gold of corn cut clearly, even at this distance, by the wide straight avenues of parched concrete roads. The town was nowhere to be traced and with satisfaction George reflected that already he had come farther than he had thought possible. Yet over that way, he resolved, he would pass once more. Now, having filled his eyes, he turned, conscious of his elevation and of the strong presence of Andria beside him, to look forward on the descent which they were to make to the plain.

Their faces were burnt by the icy wind which whipped through the pass and the sun was running fire over the snow. Higher than eagles they looked down the precipitous way where soon the snow ended and black rocks, jagged eminences, rose above sheer ravines where birds of prey were circling. It was to be a difficult descent to what they saw miles away, the liquid green of fields, dots for trees, and shining bands of rivers. Villages could be distinguished through the frosty air and which of them, George wondered, was Andria's, and which the village which he most longed to revisit.

They began to descend, a slow business. There were icy tracks in which they had to cut themselves footholds with stones, giddy edges skirting the ravines and, lower down, crumbling rock, precarious for climbing. Here George took the lead, for Andria, though not clumsy, was so heavy and so little skilled in precaution that he would doubtless have slipped and been pulped at the foot of some precipice if George had not reconnoitred his steps for him. Very slowly they descended for a thousand feet or so, treading dangerously, but laughing to one another at every unexpected event, a loose stone rolling or the flurry of some startled bird, and then for the first time they noticed that the sky was becoming overcast and that mist or drifting rain was rolling up to them from the valleys. Soon a crack of thunder and then quickly the storm. The mist and rain was like a wall so that they would not have known they were among the mountains but for the burly reverberations of the thunder which burst from above to be buffetted backwards and forwards, banged, bashed, and angrily, a balloon of sound, swung from rock to rock, an unearthly bombardment. And as the lightning divulsed the air and the wind took the mist and shook hither and thither strands and billowing curtains, George laughed and eagerly grasped the hand of his friend, who stared at him for a moment and then laughed too. Now at last George felt washed clean and buffetted clear of the town, as he stood with Andria in the enormous storm, soaked with rain, in some danger of the lightning.

Suddenly he dropped Andria's hand and stood still in expectation. He had heard something through the thunder, and then again quite clear through the mist rang out that musical note, as of a bell, which once before he had heard. They looked up and like an arrow pierced the mist and was gone, flying towards the pass, the white figure of a bird, its neck outstretched, its huge wings easily riding the hurricane. For a moment they stared at the wall of grey vapour so quickly cleft, then, looking with shining eyes in each other's faces, began again to pursue their course.

The thunder was less boisterous than before, but the wind was higher, and now Andria led, for he knew the country. There was a rough track here, made by adventurous shepherds, perhaps, or by mountain goats, and to this track they kept though they were half-blinded by the driving sleet and had often to step cautiously for fear of being overset by the wind. So they went on, shouting to each other when occasion arose, downwards with difficulty for another thousand feet till the wind ceased and heavy and perpendicular fell the warmer rain.

The track let them along a swollen watercourse, whose grey frothy tumble made such a din among the stones set in its bed that they still had to shout if they wished to be heard. But soon the going was easier. The stream widened and they began to notice tufts of grass and flowers prostrated by the snow. It was not long before trees appeared. The rain gradually ceased to fall, the clouds separated and vanished; the sun shone and they found themselves on a hill above a forest, and not so far away the grassy meadows and distant dwellings of the plain. It was late afternoon and since they had crossed the pass they had not spoken to each other, except when now and again was a shouted warning of loose rock or slippery edge.

Now, walking more easily over a smelling mat of pine needles, between the steaming trees, George began to question Andria more closely. What, he inquired, were the conditions of life and what were the feelings of the factory workers, whose hovels only had been seen by him on his way to the first king. He learnt that previously to Michael Koresipoulos's evasion there had existed a strong revolutionary movement among the workers in the town, so strong indeed that Andria had heard it said that the Government had been seriously embarrassed. Then, interjected George, that rat Koresipoulos was doubtless their agent, and Andria nodded his head. But now, Andria continued, after the extermination of two hundred revolutionary leaders, after the specious assurances of the Government, which were at first believed, the mass movement had lost its impetus. Moreover, the police supervision was now so intense, and the rations allowed to the workers and their families so barely adequate for subsistence that it now required much more energy, much more vitality, much more skill than ever before even to talk of revolution, let alone make plans, hold meetings, organize demonstrations. Previously, said Andria, there had been some hope among the workers in the town; now there was the blankest despair. If they only knew, he said, the true record of Koresipoulos, they might still take courage, but, as it was, faced with the slender achievement of one whom they had regarded as their devoted leader, they were inclined to believe that no change in their lot was possible, so enormous was the power pitted against them. They were too weak to originate, but many would welcome a revolution, provided that it was organized in the first place from the outside by others. 'Always we have been cheated,' Andria concluded, 'by the Government, by priests, by our own leaders.'

'And what do you expect,' said George, 'if you take a leader who has been educated at the Convent? What do you expect from the Government and its priests? Are their interests at all compatible with your interests? If we were to rule ourselves, what would be left for the Government to rule?' And he went on speaking eagerly to his friend, telling him of what he had seen in the town, explaining his belief that the Government's power rested not so much on the ability to act but on the ability to persuade people to allow them to act. He told Andria, however, how he had been mistaken in supposing that anything but the revolutionary movement of masses could finally expunge that regime and win through to future territory. How clearly disastrous had been his own individual attempt and how miserable the lot of the self-regarding President Koresipoulos! He spoke of Pushkov, and of the meeting he had attended on his first arrival in the country. It was unpromising material, he admitted, but only by using that material was there any possibility of success. And then, somehow or other, the factories must be brought into the struggle. To penetrate into the town, so long as the Government remained there, was difficult, perhaps impossible; but much could be done by visiting the mines which were situated outside the town walls, and by calling for volunteers to offer their services to the Government in the town where they could work as agitators.

George spoke with enthusiasm and Andria listened carefully to his words, nodding his big head that was poised so lightly on enormous shoulders. Now, warmed with quicker walking, they had passed through the woods, and there, not an hour's walk away, stood Andria's village in the yellow light suffusing the shadowy plain. With delight Andria pointed out the familiar cottages, barns, and cattle, though his lip stiffened and his eyes, like levelled guns, were arrested when he spoke of the cottage where his mother and father had lived.

To their right, leading away from the village, was a winding cart track, and farther off a hill at the foot of which was visible a section of concrete road. With intake of breath George recognized the place for which he was making, and sought eagerly, fancying chimneys and the angle of a roof, among the trees at the top of the hill for the farm. And he asked his friend to come with him, assuring him that Joe would receive him well, whereas in his own village there might still be trouble to be feared from the police. But Andria shook his head, only asking that George would stay with him for a night or two at his mother's house. 'Be with us, neighbour,' he said, 'and take my sister, if you like her.'

But George refused, so eager was he to be back at the place from which he should never have departed as he did. So at the junction of the path to the village with the cart track that wound over the plain, they shook hands, glad of each other, and went each to his own place.

CHAPTER FOUR

Whistling to himself, lightly treading in spite of his fatigue, George went quickly along the cart track, hedged with wet gold, and as the sun set there rose a brilliant moon for light, whitening the fields, causing the swimming shadows far flung to run along the way. But between the hedgerows or over gleaming fields George noticed little, was not startled by scream of vixen from bracken or the close gliding of owl wings, for with every step he was drawing nearer to what he desired, a foolishly abandoned starting place.

Even Andria's late presence had faded from his mind, though every now and then, with leap of heart, he recalled the bird seen to soar between the mountains, and altogether his brisk thoughts were joyful till, with a stiffening of the eye he remembered (for it had been shut from his mind) that he had heard that Joan was married, that he had seen in the city a simulacrum of Pushkov's arrest. Still he smiled. Of Pushkov he had no certain news. As for Joan, he had other things to do, though it was bitter to think of that girl.

How long had he been away, he wondered, knowing that in the town he had had no means of tracing time. A year, he wondered, or two or three? And he cursed himself for futile delay in that timeless, sleepless, foodless, skyless city.

With a start he saw the moon high over him and below the moon the hill, and to his right the white river of concrete, the empty high road. A hundred yards, and he would be in the village. His heart beat quicker as he stepped on, wondering whether everyone would be asleep. Black-faced, but with surfaces a-swim

266

in the moonlight, stood the causeway where first he had insulted the police. Loops of the path, thick scented, were scaling the hill, and soon George beheld the still white walls of cottages in the village street. Tears of joy were in his eyes as he saw, lolling even at this late hour in the doorless entrance of one of these poor houses, the bulk of a man and glow of pipe and smoke escaping through the clear air.

He approached and in the moonlight recognized one of the peasants whom he had seen at the political meeting. 'Hullo, Dick,' he said, holding out his hand. 'I've got back. I was a fool to have gone.'

Dick, showing no surprise, turned his head away and slouched back into the house. Some indistinct words were shouted, and then other peasants with their wives and children came into the street. Soon the street was full of them, standing almost silent, except for muttered words and short laughter, pointing with thumbs at George, who stood alone, surprised at this reception.

He turned again to Dick, who had come out again with his family. 'Aren't you going to shake hands, Dick?' But Dick thrust his hands deeper into his pockets, staring sulkily with face made ghastly by the moon downwards to the ground. From the back of the crowd came the thin voice of a thin woman: 'Thought you were clever, didn't you?' and there was heard laughter with hoots, strange beneath the still sky in the white light. Indistinctly came the thick voice of a bearded old man: 'He was too good for us, eh? Too good!' And a young girl shrieked: 'He tried to hit the policeman, but he hurt his poor hand.' There was a scurry of laughter.

'I didn't think I was clever,' George cried. 'I only thought that you were stupid. And I was a bigger fool than anyone. But I meant well. Won't you have me back? I want to work with you.'

267

There was a long silence and then a young man spoke.

'We don't want you. Get back to the town.' There was a murmur of approval, and jeering, cackling, winking, and morosely silent the peasants went back to their houses leaving George stockstill in the rough street sluiced silver, his eyes fixed upon a swaying frond of creeper, a writhing funicle, which seemed by moonlight cut clean off from the eaves of Dick's house to be distorted by wind, an irrational growth in air.

So George stared at the unearthly branch for a moment, then turned and plodded up the street, sharp footsteps ringing in the abandoned place. He reached the farmhouse which lay low-silvered, its drab walls shining, and past the outbuildings where animals uneasily shuffled he trod, having seen one light. Knocking at the door, he opened it and stood blinking in the soft glow of the lamp, different illumination.

Joan sat sewing by the fire. As the door opened she looked up, seeking George's face as for recognition. In a second she knew him and had jumped to her feet, tumbling to the floor her sewing basket. She stepped back a pace, her mouth opened, expressing no certain feeling. George saw her a little different from what he had known. Her frank face was sterner and her eyes glowed larger in features that were less girlish than before. Her brown hair was dirty and carelessly twisted behind her head in a knot. Her clothes were drab, grey, and voluminous, stained with grease and soot. They did not disguise the mounting protuberance of her body from which soon must issue a child. Lovely her eyes, George thought, gazing at her while she stood, her movement arrested, with one hand supporting herself, leaning backwards towards the table, lovely still her body not by me increased; and from the scullery came a thick voice: 'Who the hell's there?'

George's eyes were still on Joan, who from gaping came to life. She twisted her head nervously towards the scullery, then turned to George, taking a step towards him, her face creased, her eyes narrowed. Before she could speak, George stretched out his hand. 'Take me in, Joan,' he said, 'I've come back. I wish I'd never gone. You were right after all.' Joan's too loud laughter scattered over the room. 'That's good,' she cried, between gasps of laughter. 'That's good. Take him in, the pretty little town boy.' Silently she looked at him long, her laughter broken off, her face twisted. Then with jerk of head, still keeping her eyes on him, she shouted: 'Here, Bill, you drunken swine, come and see what we've got here.'

Slouched from the scullery a giant, larger than Andria, yet not so well made, loose-jointed, red-headed, puffy beneath the eyes. He walked straight up to George, smiling good-humouredly, smelling of beer, and Joan said, though she had shrunk away as he had entered the room: 'That's my husband. So don't come hanging round this house like your brother did.'

Bill thrust his huge red face close up to George. 'See?' he said, 'Or it'll be the worse for you.' He stretched out one clenched fist from an arm and wrist covered with thick red hair, and shook it in George's face, narrowing his small red eyes. George hated the man. His eyes summed up his enormous stature, span of chest, and reach of arms. Moreover, though he was now drunk, his work had kept him in good condition. There was no loose flesh on those shoulders. Yet his head was cocky above his neck, not a glorious growth, like Andria's, and his feet seemed slow. As he looked into the broad red face, seeing the pinched eyes, short nose, handsome full mouth, and undistinguished chin of Joan's husband, George was thinking that if it came to a fight, he could settle his account, and the hatred within him, icy inside his chest, froze out the despair with which he had been filled a moment before.

'I may see you again,' George said.

Joan's eyes were like needles going from one to the other of the pair. 'Give it him now,' she said quickly, in a low voice. But Bill was not a fool. He knew that he was in no condition to fight, so taking Joan by the hair he flung her down on the hard wooden bench where she had been sitting. 'Sit down, wife,' he shouted, 'and don't chatter.' Joan stayed still on the bench, laughing to herself, her face stained with tears.

Bill opened the door unsteadily, jerking his thumb. 'Now you can get out,' he said, 'George or Jack or Jim or whatever your name is; and don't let me catch you round here in the morning.'

'Where's Joe?' George said.

'Where's my bottom?' said the peasant.

George went out again into the moonlight, heard the door slam, and walked, not noticing where he was going. He had forgotten the village street. Only burned inside him the desire to fight that man, to have away with, not to leave off while one of them could stand. Then suddenly he remembered his situation, outcast, and at the entrance to the farm paused, for he had heard slow steps. A bulk loomed between him and the moon. It was Joe. George stood silent.

From the broad mass before him came a chuckle. A thick voice said: 'It's the young squire.' Still George did not speak. Joe took him by the arm. 'Come this way, lad.' Then peering into his face, 'though you are not so much of a lad now.'

'How long have I been away?' George asked, and Joe said: 'Five years, as we reckon in these parts.'

They skirted the farm building, and stopped before a small shed on the floor of which was some hay. In the moonlight George could distinguish Joe's face, grim through the fat, as he inclined his head towards the house. 'They won't have you there,' he said, 'but you can get your sleep here just as well.' And, leaving George on the hay, he waddled off towards the house, from which he soon returned, carrying a plate with bread and cheese upon it.

George ate avidly, while Joe, leaning against the hut, blotting out the moon, watched him. Slowly he began to speak.

'Pushkov's in prison,' he said. 'They got him soon after you left, and the police said that he had been convicted on evidence supplied by you. Of course, I never believed that, and nor did Pushkov, but a lot of the men in the village believed it and young Joan pretended that she believed it.'

'What am I to do now?' said George, looking up from his bread and cheese. 'I wanted to join up with the rest of you.'

Joe nodded his head. His laugh was bitter. 'It'll come all right, lad,' he said. 'Only you'll have to lie low for a bit. To-morrow I'll give you work to do on the farm. Joan won't mind for the time being, if the work's unpleasant. But you must keep out of the way of that husband of hers.'

George remained silent. Yes, he would keep away from Bill, but not for ever. Perhaps Joe felt his thoughts, for he chuckled, saying: 'There's a time for everything, eh lad?'

George thanked him and gave him some account of his adventures in the town. His narrative was often interrupted by pertinent questioning in which Joe, speaking swiftly and incisively, spoke as one who knew what he was talking about. The precise equipment of the second king's laboratory, the appearance of the third king were points about which his most careful interrogations were made and, when the story was over, he spoke with a slow enthusiasm: 'You've done some good after all. To-morrow we'll discuss your information with Pushkov.'

'Can we visit the prison then?' George asked surprised.

Joe nodded. 'It gives the police a chance to insult us.'

'One more thing I would like to know,' said George. 'Who are you? You've been kind to me, when everyone else has refused me. Sometimes you speak like a peasant, ungrammatically, but your real voice is different. You are very cunning. No one knows what you are thinking about.'

Joe's great shoulders shook with laughter. 'For a long time I've been on the land,' he said, 'and I speak as I'm expected to speak. But it's surely time you knew more of Joan's family and you can listen to a story if you are not too tired. You've met my brothers already.'

'Your brothers!' said George. 'Where? In the town?'

Joe laughed again and painstakingly lowered his bulk into the hay by George's side. 'They never crossed the frontier,' he said, and there was contempt in his voice. 'Do you remember Don Antonio and his chef? Those were my brothers.' Astonished at first, George listened to the old man's story.

JOE'S STORY

'I was the youngest of the brothers. I loved my father, listening eagerly to the stories which he told of his impossible adventures, and pitying him for that mistrustfulness in his character which prevented him from crossing the frontier. When he killed himself, I was sorry.

'Whatever had happened, I think, I could not have stayed for long in my mother's house. The memory of my father, whose natural zest had been so damped by that evil woman, was too bitter. And then there was the insufferable Antonio, always my mother's favourite.

'I was only a lad when my father died, and the oppressive atmosphere of our house, where Antonio studied and my mother wept, drove me more and more to seek entertainment elsewhere. You would not think it, to look at me now, but at that time I was a famous athlete, a boxer and a runner. It was a grand time. I spent my days on the track or in the ring, and my evenings with friends who shared my tastes, young grooms, who boxed with me for half a crown, and sportsmen of all kinds. Those were merry nights, when with drink and our women friends we came together after some big sporting event, and we were a terror to the constabulary of our little town.

'Yet even at this time I was aware of some dissatisfaction, and at the back of my mind was always the determination to attempt what my father had never done. Events forced my hand. Antonio has told you of how meanly he acted when our brother, who is now of a religious turn of mind, wished to marry a girl. I did what I could to help them set up house, and for a year or two worked on a farm, so that I could assist them with a portion of my wages. Antonio, of course, kept a tight hold on our father's money. But when my brother began to preach, I decided that I would be off.

'Without saying a word to anyone I set out for the frontier, travelling across country, and arrived at this very village by much the same way as that by which you came. Nearly all of the men and women who worked here then are dead. One has to be strong to bear up against the work, when nine-tenths of what we get from the land goes to the Government. Things were much as they are now—the daily loading of lorries at dawn, the inquisitive police, the false news broadcast. In some ways the supervision was even more close than now; for now, I think, the Government believe that they are in a safer position than they were.

'Well, I got a job as a labourer in the village, and also spent some of my time working on this very farm, which was then owned by an old man who had himself come from beyond the frontier, who was always kind to me, and indeed finally left me the farmhouse in his will; for he had no wife or children.

'It was not long, as you may imagine, before I became interested in revolt. There was then, as there always is, a great mass of sleeping discontent among the peasantry, but we suffered then as we do now, from a lack of good leadership. I am no leader myself.

I prefer to leave the talking to others, but I think I, or any peasant, could have done better than the leaders whom we had at that time. Nearly all of them were men who had held posts of one sort or another in the town, who had been dismissed and harboured grievances which were personal. And what surprised me about these men was that instead of speaking plainly of their own grievances, they spoke to us of the abstract ideas of justice and of government, of parliamentary systems and general enfranchisement—words which conveyed very little meaning to us. These leaders, many of whom died bravely, though some were traitors, were out of touch with the life of us peasants, and their leadership was thus weaker than it should have been. Some, indeed, were for raising a statue to the Goddess Reason, and others exalted the life of a savage. And these silly sideshows occupied much of their attention which ought to have been given to our bread and butter.

'Still these men, however curiously they allowed their minds to work, were genuine in their desire to overthrow the government in the town, and so most of us gave them our support. For many years we worked in secret, reconnoitring the country, doing our best to escape the suspicion of the police. It was on one of these reconnoitring expeditions that I met my wife, the mother of Joan, our best leader, of whom you have heard something already.

'I had come one night close to the walls of the town, my job being to map out accurately the approaches to the aerodrome, when I met a woman running over the rough country away from the town. Her eyes were glazed, like two cobble stones in her white face. Her mouth was open as she ran, bumping into me, too frightened, I thought, to notice where she was going. I laid her across my horse and rode back to the village. After I had told her that I was no enemy of hers she was reassured and fainted, but before we had finished our journey she came to herself, turning

274

back to look at me, as she sat between my forearms on the horse's back.

'Her name was Freda Harrison and once she had been engaged to marry my brother Antonio, who deserted her at the frontier. She had gone her own way to the town after that. A girl inquisitive by nature, a great talker, good at tennis, she had been delighted at the prospect of entering the Convent, though she had refused to undergo the operation. Naturally she was soon disgusted. She had fancied that the inhabitants of the Convent were not maniacs. She had, just as you have, some craving for vitality, and so, with a skill and daring remarkable in a woman, she contrived to escape to the factory quarter of the town where she worked for some time at a machine.

'She threw herself into the work of the organization which at that time acknowledged Koresipoulos for leader, and she was by a long way the most successful speaker in the town. She it was who first clearly proclaimed that the struggle must be fought not on vague ideas, but on a class basis, and soon she was warning her audiences against the rotten method of Koresipoulos. No one, of course, had ever seen this gentleman, but, to her mind, his Odes were a sufficient condemnation. Her open advocacy of a more thoroughgoing revolt did not escape the notice of Koresipoulos or of the Government.

'She was seized by the police and it was decided, since she could not be bribed to act as a Government spy, to send her, as a specimen, into the Research Department of the Convent. She guessed something of what might happen to her there, and I could feel her stiffen against my arms as she told me of it.

'She was conveyed to the Convent again and would have ended her life there if she had not been able to play upon the sensitive character of Professor Pothimere. She persuaded this gentleman to allow her, before any experiments were made, to read to him some of his favourite poems by moonlight outside the city walls. The Professor agreed, and, accompanied by a strong force of police, they went out to a distance of about a mile from the city. On the way back the guard was dismissed, for Pothimere had actually imagined her to be interested in him. So, running hard, she had reached me, and, as my horse travelled faster over the uneven country than any policeman could go on foot, we were out of danger of the pursuit and I laughed at the receding searchlights of the town.

'Before we reached the first village she had fainted again from inanition and fatigue. It was long before she perfectly recovered her health, and I had long talks with her in which she explained to me all that she had seen and heard of the town.

'At about this time I came into possession of this farmhouse and here Freda Harrison came to live with me. Joan was our only child. She has never come under the attention of the officers of health, and she has retained some of her mother's remarkable spirit, being pig-headed to a degree. Well, for the time being she has got the husband she deserves.

'But I must get back to my story. Freda Harrison was the life and soul of our movement. She organized where our other leaders had only made speeches. And events began to move rapidly. It was not long before we were in a position to strike a blow. Here, however, Freda was opposed to the majority, who, pleasurably excited by their successes before crowded audiences, were for breaking with the town at once. Freda, on the other hand, insisted that we must have support from within. Until we were sure of the factories, she said, it was hopeless to think of revolt in the country. But she was outvoted, and, once the decision had been taken, she marched with the army.

'Joan was a baby then, and there are only one or two men left in the village who remember that attempt of ours. At first everything went satisfactorily. The villages refused to send food-stuffs to the town and the police were all recalled. We set up our own governments, meeting with no resistance whatever. And then our leaders called a halt. There were only a few of us who were convinced of the necessity of going farther, of de-molishing the town. The others fancied that they were already successful.

'But Freda Harrison did all she could to convince them, pointing out that we had won no victories, had simply walked into a trap. "So long as that town stands, shut in from the sky," she told them, "we are still as much slaves as ever." And she urged them in the names of their brothers inside the walls not to desist until they had either won a victory or suffered a defeat.

'Perhaps half of our total force was prepared to follow her. The rest were content with the land which they now held on so slender a tenure, and all our leaders, except one, Gobolov, whose name you have heard before, stayed behind.

'We marched on to the town and I was able to get inside the walls and inform the factory workers of what had been happening. Naturally, although their food had been more severely rationed, they had been allowed to hear nothing of the revolt. Arrangements were made for a general insurrection as soon as the firing next day was to be heard, and, proud of my success, I escaped again from the town and rode back to the army.

'It was a stormy night and those strange vividly illuminated clouds, which you must have noticed in the neighbourhood of the town, were scudding over the sky. I came to a great plain and saw some scattered figures running, and thousands of dead faces turned up from ground to the hurrying clouds. There were platoons of police in the centre of the plain. They marched away and I saw two black stakes on which the white bodies of Gobolov and Freda Harrison were impaled. I rode back to the town and warned our friends there. They looked at me and turned away. Then I came back to this village.

'From the few survivors I learned that to the leaders of both our armies, the army before the town, and the army which had stayed behind, information had been conveyed that a large enemy attack was impending. Government agents, pretending that they were deserters from the town, had assured our leaders that the hostile army had been, for the sake of secrecy, disguised in the clothes and with the weapons of our peasant militia. Each of our armies were, through these agents, supplied with arms more deadly that any we had possessed and at nightfall, according to the plan, they were brought into touch with each other.

'Even this trap might have been avoided if Freda's advice had been taken; she was for launching the attack on the town that very night. But the commanders, partly for the sake of our comrades who had been left behind, insisted first on keeping our lines of communication clear. And so in darkness our two armies, equally misled, opened fire upon each other, each thinking the other to be the enemy, and from the surrounding hills large forces of police shelled the plain. As you can imagine, very few escaped.

'Since then our villages have been underpopulated. The taxes have been increased and our work has been correspondingly heavier. But we nearly succeeded. Only the lack of unity within our ranks and the lack of policy among our leaders gave the Government their opportunity to divide and to destroy. The Government will only exert force when they can do so with overwhelming effect. Powerful as are its armaments, it is most powerful when it is least active. The laughter of the policemen is a formidable weapon; thanks to their Intelligence Department bribes, when offered, are usually accepted. And so, with much inferior numbers, but with the machines and with a propaganda that weakens those who are exposed to it, the Government are still

278

able to hold us, who might be infinitely stronger than they, in the hollow of their hands. And who is to say whether in our next rebellion we will not make the same mistakes as we did before? We will never find a better leader than Freda Harrison. Yet she and our armies were utterly destroyed.'

Joe ceased speaking and looked across the shed at George, who, in his excitement at hearing the story, hardly noticed the grief in the old man's voice. Soon, however, he was aware of Joe's individual loss, a splendid wife and his hopes from early youth.

'We'll get them,' George said, staring eagerly into his friend's enormous face, 'We'll get them next time,' and Joe heaving himself to his feet, looked steadily at the ground before he left George alone.

'Let's hope so,' he said.

CHAPTER FIVE

W<small>HEN</small> George woke the sun was broadly upon his face. He had slept well and late. Steps were approaching the shed and soon, blocking the doorway, stood Joe's body, precarious on its stumpy legs. The little eyes twinkled and the grim mouth, ringed with fat, smiled.

'It's late,' said George. 'Why didn't you wake me to help load the lorries?'

'Time enough for that to-morrow,' Joe said. 'The boys in the village won't mind you being here by then, not after we've met Pushkov and the others. Besides there's the police. They'll have forgotten about you by this evening, but one or two of them might remember you now. Of course at headquarters they have your whole record written down in a book, and they can refer to it if they are told to do so. But the ordinary constables never remember anything for more than a day; not in the country.'

George nodded his head and stepped into the farmyard to wash himself at the pump. Joe spoke again. 'I've been to the gaol already,' he said. 'Pushkov's in a bad way. They don't think he'll live beyond the morning. I saw some of the others too. We're to go round now.' And they rose to walk by a field path in the direction of the prison.

'What's wrong with Pushkov?' George asked and Joe replied: 'May have been poisoned. May have poisoned himself. There's no knowing. But he's clear in the head. He'll like to see us all.'

'Another leader gone,' George said. Joe nodded. 'He could talk well enough,' and George detected in his words a mistrust of those who had come aggrieved from the town. Joe, he reflected, has lived with Freda Harrison, and he thinks badly of other leaders. Yet, for want of anything better, he has continued to support Pushkov. And, though he shared Joe's opinions, he felt sorry for the lean schoolmaster now lying upon his deathbed. But still, he thought, this death will be no disaster. New methods and more direct ones than oratory, however impassioned, may now be attempted.

They reached the gaol, a tall building of concrete, windowless. At the entrance stood a patrol of police. Their officer took the finger prints of Joe and George, and then with a burst of laughter broke two bags of flour over their heads. 'Leave them to it,' Joe muttered as he wiped the flour out of his eyes, while one of the constables, screaming with laughter, stuck a pin into him from behind. George nodded, and they went into the prison. Here again they were discomforted by a variety of practical jokes. The boards of the floor on which they trod were continually, by some mechanism beneath them, being shuffled backwards and forwards. Over every doorway some booby trap was arranged and the police, who seemed to fill the building, held their sides with laughter as they saw now a basket of fish descending on Joe's head, now a doorhandle come off in George's hand. But at length they reached the cell, outside which stood Stanley, whom George had last seen at the political meeting, grave faced, beckoning them forwards. He whispered to them: 'Glad you've come. He can't last much longer now,' and they followed him into the cell.

Pushkov lay, propped up by books, on horizontal steel bars which projected from the wall and served prisoners for a bed. His body, more emaciated than ever, was clothed in a convict's garb, a long grey nightgown, variegated with the black heads of owls stamped on to the material. The pale flesh seemed to have sunk away from his face, ebbing from the bony promontories of cheekbones, nose, chin, forehead. His eyes were like monsters within their bony holes, glowing so dark. By his side was seated on the floor the young man Alfred, whose turn of the head, as visitors entered the door, seemed to indicate relief.

Pushkov, with his body and head motionless, was prodding the air with one thin finger, and speaking. George caught the words: 'United front. No compromise. Perhaps, mark you, it is already too late.'

'Look,' said Alfred, rising hurriedly to his feet. 'Here are some more of our friends,' and Pushkov wearily directed his eyes towards the door. George ran towards the bed. 'Pushkov,' he said, kneeling down beside the sick man, 'if its through any fault of mine that you're here, I beg you to forgive me.'

Alfred gripped George's arm. 'Don't you worry,' he said. 'We've been talking to Joe and we see you're all right. It wasn't your fault.'

Pushkov turned slowly his unnaturally blazing eyes.

'I forgive everyone,' he said, 'with one exception. The senior classical master I will not forgive.'

The others exchanged significant glances. Stanley was filling his pipe. He whispered to Joe. 'He's been like this for the last two or three hours.' They looked at the lean figure which lay with closed eyes, heavily breathing, and they were dismayed. The silence was broken by a muttering from the steel bars. Then, Pushkov, perhaps in uneasy sleep, began speaking, in a thin, piping voice. He might have been possessed. He was saying: 'I'll go to the town. I'll go some day. I'll play the piano. No one can say that I don't play the piano very well.'

'Thinking of when he was a kid,' Stanley said gravely, and with alarming suddenness Pushkov's voice changed to a slow guttural: 'Devils! Fiends! I cannot go into details.' His heavy breathing was renewed and his friends looked again into each other's faces, constricting their mouths. Pushkov spoke in a low voice. 'The signature was not mine. I am a victim of gross injustice.' For a long time after that his breathing was uninterrupted and the watchers whispered to each other. Alfred was putting proposals to Stanley, who listened despondently, sucking his pipe, staring at Pushkov's feet. Joe leant against the wall, stern-faced, impassive. 'He'll be gone soon,' he said to George, who was profoundly affected by the scene of Pushkov's collapse.

Suddenly Pushkov sat up on the steel bars, his hawklike head rising on thin neck erect from the grey nightdress. His eyes seemed live things secreted in a dead skull. 'I'm dying,' he shouted, while Stanley, alarmed, stepped back a pace, dropping his pipe to the floor. And Pushkov began cursing, rolling his body from side to side, shouting continually with distorted eyes. When he had wearied himself he said in a low voice: 'It's not fair,' and lay quiet. But soon he sat up much weaker, and with half-closed eyes began to speak in his normal voice. His face was like a death mask, and George was horrified at the present disintegration of one who had not yet died. Pushkov said: 'The best years of my life have been given for the cause of revolution. Other leaders have suffered, I am aware of it, but no sufferings have been comparable to mine. I have been mocked and insulted. I am dying like a rat in the county gaol. The revolution is no nearer. But I have done all that a man can do. My speeches have met with universal applause. But the town is too strong. They will always find men to be bribed. In bitter disillusion I leave life, and my advice to those who come after me is give it up. Live as best you can by yourselves. You will never disturb the town. I have failed to do so myself. I have failed, but perhaps I shall be remembered.'

He ceased speaking and afterwards his only words were delirious. Often would rise to his lips the name of the senior classical master and fragments of revolutionary slogans, and sometimes, clutching his belly, he would roll from side to side, cursing and slobbering from a mouth no longer tightened with will. But his transports became gradually feebler and from one interval he never wakened. Suddenly his breathing stopped, and going over to him Stanley nodded his head, indicating that the end had come.

So, cursing and making gestures, Pushkov was dragged from life, and George with the others round the bedside was despondent, having witnessed the revolutionary's miserable end. He had, it seemed, identified his own individual grievances with the cause of revolution, and still, as he died, were uppermost in his mind events long ago enacted, of no importance to any but himself. His pride had taken refuge in a glorification of his own sufferings. He had excused his failure, as Rudolph might have done, by the consolation of inevitability. And, defeated himself, he had prescribed defeat for others. Here, certainly was not a leader to new things.

George stared at the body, frightened by the tortured escape of life, and he looked long at the dead agitator's features, stone-rigid in death, remembering that, for whatever motives, he had constantly opposed the Government, that he had refused bribes, been subjected to insults, and now had lost his life in captivity. So with conflicting feelings he turned away to meet Joe's steady stare.

They were allowed to leave the prison unmolested by the laughing policemen, though at the door was thrust into each one's hand a photograph, which must have been taken from inside the cell by some hidden photographer, of Pushkov, his face distorted by pain, rolling from side to side, deliriously cursing. These photographs were presented to them by the officer in command who, politely smiling, begged them to take away with them a memento of this visit. But when they had left the prison enclosure they tore the photographs into small pieces, since they were terrible to look at. After they had walked some little distance, Stanley proposed to George that, in the evening, they should all meet again to hear his report of the things which had happened to him in the town, and George, seeing behind Stanley's spluttering pipe the trust in the man's eyes, knew that, thanks probably to Joe, he was accepted by the party leaders and his help still required. For the rest of the day, pleased with what had been lacking from the atmosphere of the town, both sun and air, he was happy, except when he thought of Pushkov's desperate end, of Joan, or of her husband.

In the night, beneath an enormous moon, they met near the shed where George had slept, and the account of adventure was interrupted frequently by Alfred's angry comments, less often by the slow shocked voice of Stanley. They went on to speak of the revolutionary organization then existing in the country, its weaknesses, and their plans for making it into an instrument capable of overturning their enemies; nor is it either necessary or possible here to describe the results of this discussion or of subsequent discussions. It will be enough to say that before many months had passed the organization had been transformed. George, warmly seconded by Alfred, had been able to persuade Stanley that the unity, which was, as had been all too clearly shown by the history of the last revolt, essential for their success, could be only attained by each member of the rank and file subscribing to a perfectly clear formulation of their aims. Not to rest until the town was destroyed, not to delegate power to any but the accredited representatives of the workers and peasants—these were the two points on which he was most insistent. And meanwhile, he recommended, let there be organized obstruction to the police in small matters. Only so could the members of the party gain the confidence and experience necessary for a revolutionary army. Only by a theoretical understanding of their aims, and by practical experience of the forces to which they were opposed could each man learn to be a leader himself. It was an army of leaders, not of followers, who would take the town, and was not this the object of every leader worth the name, to render his own position of ascendancy unnecessary?

To this last conclusion Alfred was inclined to make some reservations, but in everything else he gave George his whole-hearted support. And even Stanley came to be of the others' opinion when he saw how, after a slow start, new methods met with unprecedented success. The countrymen, no longer solicited to attend meetings, but invited to organize them, soon began to laugh at the thought of their own conduct in the past when it had been so easy for a Government agent, like the Rev. Hamlet, to mislead a packed auditorium. It was not abstract questions of religion or morality which they now discussed, but their own lives, and, as George had foreseen, their conclusions were the same as those which he had reached. The membership of the party doubled within a month; there were times when the lorries started late in the morning for the town; contact was made with the miners whose villages were close to the town walls, and even with some of the factory workers within the town itself.

And now George's days went quickly as he sped through time to a certain goal. It was not for many months that the peasants would speak to him, so deep-rooted was their mistrust of one who had returned unbroken from the town; but by degrees they got used to him, and soon those of their number who were most ardent in the cause of revolt began to be convinced of his good intentions, seeing how he was trusted by their leaders, how his advice was sought even by Stanley and Joe, and how willing he was to under-take difficult or laborious tasks within their organization. In this way, before the harvest was cut, George made many friends, though at the farm house he had still to sleep in the shed, for Joan would never speak to him, and her husband, proud of his authority among the labourers, would order him about, but otherwise treated him as one removed to a great distance.

But it was still with Andria that George was most at ease. One day, not long after his arrival at the village, Andria had come to visit him. He had walked up the village street towering a head above the tallest and had been mystified when his inquiries for his friend had met with grudging or sarcastic response. And it was the confidence which he showed in his companion which was largely responsible for the peasants' final acceptance of George as an ally and a friend. For a long time George and Andria had talked together and George had noticed the disappearance from Andria's eyes of that bewilderment, that baffled knowledge, which had marked his face when he was in the service of Koresipoulos. Now his slow sentences were forcible, for the weight of his will was behind them. He accepted without reservation the policy of the Party, for he saw clearly to what end it was directed, and he began to lead and organize groups in his own village and in its neighbourhood. They never spoke of that bird which they had seen together in the thunderstorm, but instead they spoke of the demolition of the town, of ways and means.

So time passed and three harvests had been garnered before their work drew near to its end.

Joan's child was born soon after George's arrival. At night he was awakened by her screams and as he stared from his shed towards the black house whose bulk seemed cleft as by the lightning of those sudden yells, he saw Joe open a door and come to fetch him. He followed the old man into the parlour where Bill sat, his head in his hands, staring into the fire. Bill looked angrily at him, and cursed him, but the big man was frightened by the woman in pain and made no move as Joe led George upstairs to the bedroom where Joan lay groaning (for that fit had passed), her red face damp with great clots of sweat, her legs doubled up. She turned up to them sick eyes, and grasped George's hand tightly, not looking at his face.

287

Soon the pains were upon her again. Among the odours of the childbed, watching her freely contorted body, her desperate effort, hearing first her curses, and then her cries and grunts, 'How like a beast she is!' George thought, and admired her for that. As if she had been a cow they tended her, pitying her agony, and towards morning she gave birth to a dead boy.

When they had made her calm, they descended to the parlour and 'Is it a boy?' asked Bill, smiling greedily, nervous, rubbing his hands.

'Dead,' said Joe, and Bill's face fell. He swore and went out with them to do the morning's work. By him Joan never conceived again, and they lived together unhappily.

Often George would hear curses and cries from the house. Then he shrugged his shoulders and thought of the future, for still Joan would not speak to him, nor pass him without looking the other way. So he was sad when he thought of her body, beautiful again, being marred by a stick or a piece of rope, and he was sad when he remembered the flight of birds, seen and heard so long ago.

But if Joan was unhappy, Bill was not at ease. It was only occasionally that his outraged temper drove him to violence against his wife. More often it was she who with her sharp tongue and her disdainful ways made his house unbearable to him, and he spent more and more of his time with the neighbours, though in working hours he was as arrogant as ever, as he shouted to his men, his cocky head standing up above their heads, or as he swung lightly his huge body into the saddle of a horse, whose jaw he held viciously with tightened rein. At such times George hated him, and now and again he saw that his enemy was looking him over curiously.

CHAPTER SIX

Iт was a year after the birth of Joan's dead child that there took place in secret a remarkable encounter. One summer's evening Andria arrived at the village and, when he had greeted and been greeted by his friend, he asked to see Joe, since he had a message for him.

'What is it, lad?' said Joe, as he looked over the two young men, one a giant, straightbacked, fairheaded, with jolly eyes, and the other a strong man too, browned by sun, hardened by wind and work, tightlipped now, a master; and Andria said: 'There is an old man who for long has lived in my father's house. He is dying and he asks to see you. He says you will remember the two stakes.'

Joe frowned and all three of them walked over the shadowy fields to Andria's village. As they went Andria told them about his family. Of his mother he could not yet speak without the tears rising to his eyes. She was dead, but he would avenge her. His father had long been crippled with age and with infirmity; and both he and the other old man, their guest, had to be tended hand and foot by Andria himself and by his younger sister, a girl who was nearly a woman. Of this old man, now on his deathbed, Andria knew little. All he could tell was that he had been in the house ever since he could remember anything and that he was held in great respect by his father. He seldom went out of doors and so was practically unknown to the other villagers. A thick beard covered his face; but that morning Andria had, at his request, shaved him, after he had promised to carry his message to Joe. Since then the old man had been impatient for the message to be delivered, for he was very weak, and could scarcely last more than a day or two more. Of who he was or of where he had come from Andria knew nothing; but he had been surprised at features, hard and resolute even in extreme age, which had been revealed by the shaving away of the beard.

Joe shook his head. 'I don't know who he is,' he said. 'I was the only living man who saw those stakes.'

They arrived at the village and the low hut thatched with long grasses where Andria and his family lived. Outside the hut, shading her eyes from the sun against whose setting disk the three men stood huge before their shadows, was a girl, Andria's sister, a young giantess. Red sunlight was caught and twisted in her wiry hair. Her honest mouth smiled welcome and her grave blue eyes were undisturbed by strangers. On straight legs she stood, and upraised her brown arms were powerful. She was deepchested, a generous being, and when she spoke to them her voice was low.

As the men smiled at her she bade good evening to Joe, and to George she said: 'My brother has spoken of you.' Her tranquil eyes took like pools his intent stare, as he smiled and held her by the hand. She stood still, receiving his eyes, and the blood rose like a rosy smoke beneath the skin of her neck and face and forehead. She turned and led them into the hut.

A candle lit feebly the interior where Andria's father, a very old man, sat in a wooden chair. He was asleep and his head nodded to his short uneasy breathing which puffed through his mouth disturbing the strands of a beard which reached almost to the floor. In his time he must have been a strong man, for his height was great and even now his hands looked powerful; but his face was sunken and in sleep he was like a ruin. Though they stepped quietly they wakened him and, as his deep blue eyes opened, they saw them to be filled with fear, for in that country a stranger was not always a friend. But the next instance he recognized his son and smiled as he rose with difficulty to greet the visitors. Standing he towered above the heads of Joe and George although age had stooped his back, and George wondered at the old man whose thin legs could hardly support that tall body, emaciated as it was. In a thin face great eyes shone with a strange intensity as the bearded man stooped towards Joe and smiling said: 'Can you not recognize me now, captain?'

Joe's mouth was hard. He gripped the old man's hand. 'Were you, too, one of the survivors, Jim Dennison?' he said, and he looked sadly at the ground, then laughed as he still held the hand of his old companion.

Jim Dennison, the father of Andria, laughed too and said: 'It's good to see you again before I die. I never dared to summon you before. For twenty years I've never been outside this hut, because I was afraid of the police. I was not so brave as you. Neither of us was.' And indicating another, he inclined his head towards a curtain which screened off one portion of the room.

George, too, looked with admiration at Joe who had never hidden himself since the death of his wife and the destruction of the army, but had gone about as before, defying the police, who had not seriously interfered with him. Yet other revolutionaries who were not, presumably, cowards had from day to day trembled for their lives.

'It's been all right, Jim,' Joe was saying. 'The police have never come near me. Perhaps the order was mislaid. But who else have you got here?'

Jim drew the curtain and they saw propped up by the pillows a small man whose unblinking eyes were turned upon them. His hair was white and there was little colour in the bony face, but the chin was still powerful below the thin lips which, for all their determination, curved exquisitely to a mouth which denoted not only strength but sensitiveness and, what one would not have expected in so old a man, a relict of charm. But, beautiful as was that small mouth, the eyes were still more beautiful. They were big in hollows of the skull, piercing and at the same time profound, live pools lit from deep. So the old man, holding up his sick head with dignity, stared at those whom he had summoned to him and, though his mouth curved to smile, his forehead and his eyes were full of melancholy.

Joe was looking at him as at a ghost. Andria's father took him by the arm. 'Yes,' he whispered, 'it is the general who is alive,' and then from his bed of cushions the old man began to speak slowly in a deep voice miserably, calm, and easily coming upon his words.

'Joe,' he said, 'it is true that I am alive, and you who were once my captain may recognize indeed the General thought dead and long inactive, Gobolov who worked with Freda Harrison, but not to the end. And you, Andria, the son of Jim, a foot soldier who survived the slaughter, may know now the name of the guest who for so long has lived in a peasant's hut, away from battle. You too, George, may learn from another leader, powerful in his time, but worsted and mistaken. For you will fight when I am dead; but I, though not a coward, forsook the war.'

He ceased speaking and his steady luminous eyes surveyed the group of men. Joe was nearest to him, eagerly, with his little slits of eyes, peering into the face of one whom he had believed dead. Jim had sat down at one end of the bed. Andria and George stood side by side and behind them, near the door of the hut, was Andria's sister, looking on.

Joe spoke: 'You are Gobolov,' he said, 'our leader. Yet I saw your body and Freda's body impaled on trees. How is it that you live, and why is it that you live here?'

Gobolov's beautiful voice filled the silence of the room. 'This is my story,' he said.

THE STORY OF GOBOLOV

'What is it, old comrades and new leaders, which makes a revolutionary? Not hunger, though hunger must be there to move the mass. There are districts, as you know well, where hunger has led not to revolt, but to starvation and the loss of life. Not envy, though each man tends to desire those things which he does not possess. Yet the envious man, as every leader has found, is a poor soldier, not capable of courage when the odds are against him. Not abstract thought, nor the consideration of barren principles. The thinker, who loves thought most of all, has always been the first to turn his back, the quickest to change his colours in time of crisis, the least resolute of fighting men; and yet without him we work to no end. Nor is it the desire for glory which is the first cause of a man's becoming a rebel in this country; for it is only the rich who can afford the luxury of fame.

'It is love which makes the revolutionary, but not the love of women, nor the love of men. He who loves another to distraction will certainly be torn in pieces, He who would lose himself in love, can have little to love. Few things are more satisfying than the clasp of naked bodies; and few courses of action are more miserable than the tampering with that happiness. Men tamper with it by shutting their eyes or by opening them too wide, by noses, inquisitive or blunt, by fingers, furtive or icy, and by talkative tongues.

'And so, in each other's arms, they are filled with disquiet, and fearful of the strong delight of their own passions they seek a subterfuge. They wash themselves; they worship; they attend the sick. They love their friends less and their enemies, out of fear, they do not hate.

'It is from the region of the belly that men and women are drawn each to each. But men have sought safety first, fearing the delightful blood, and so their bellies have fallen apart and they have knocked their heads together. They have loved not passionately, for happiness, but wildly, for distraction; and, as I say, that is a tearing in pieces.

'I know that love, as it was this which made me the leader of a revolution. But, as I shall tell you, it was a false star which I followed, and now I end my life, not greatly daring, though I know what is best to do, but skulking in a hut.

'In early youth, out of ambition, I crossed the frontier. You, Joe, must remember this part of my history. You will not have forgotten how in my first days in the village I met Freda Harrison and how I worshipped her. I had intended to go on to the town, for my intellectual abilities were considerable, but, having once met your wife, I desired to stay always at her side. At first I would talk to her for long hours on end, explaining my scheme for the abolition of all authority, and for the production of a new race of men; but as I talked it was of her body that I thought, and when she laughed at me, I was pleasantly excited.

'I tried to win her love but she, still laughing, refused me, telling me that, since she was content with her husband, I should do better by courting some other woman. It was excellent advice, but I did not take it.

'I gave up all designs upon her, and began to think of her as though she were a being not of flesh and blood, but of something heavenly. And at the same time I abandoned my intention of seeking wealth and fame in the town. Instead I took pleasure in performing the most menial tasks, and in my mind I congratulated myself on my choice of a peasant's life, thinking well of my resolution to forgo honours which I might have attained.

'I could not think of other women while Freda Harrison was in the world, and I had given up all hope of possessing her. Soon, however, my busy mind discovered that I was in love with the general public, with the distressed portion of the human race. With new indignation I watched the requisitions of the police, and, if I saw a peasant child crying for food, I would feel that hunger in my own body.

'And so with new enthusiasm I flung myself into the work of the revolution. I had a natural gift for oratory, but what made the people follow me was my unswerving attachment to Freda Harrison. I believed that I loved every man in the army as a brother, every woman as a sister, and every child as a child which I had begotten myself.

'I shall tell you now of that battle outside the town in which the work of twenty years was utterly destroyed. It was in the darkness that our two armies fell upon each other, ignorant that friend was killing friend, and the machine guns had done their work before the remnants of our forces met face to face and gradually in scattered portions of our lines men would recognize each other and astonished at what each side believed to be the treachery of the other would grimly renew the fight. I fought in the first line by the side of Freda Harrison, and, in that position, I fought well. I shot Georges Dupont and called him a traitor as he died. Fighting with a bayonet I maimed Samuel, the negro wrestler, who looked pitifully at me with cool eyes while his body was distorted. Cotler, Kaldas, MacDonald, and Abdulla all perished before the heavy artillery of the town began to bombard the plain and we few survivors realized that we had been misled. Now in the searchlights we saw the police descending from the hills and, fifty or a hundred men and women, we looked in one another's faces, and some smiled, knowing that the game was up.

'Then my courage forsook me and, falling on my knees before Freda Harrison, I said: 'For years I have worked for you. Kiss me once before we both die.' She looked at me in astonishment and continued to order the troops as best she could. And I was aware of a great emptiness and of fear. Men, whom I had loved as my brothers, gripped my hand, but I hardly noticed them. I was anxious only to escape from Freda Harrison who had condemned me.

'As the police cordon drew near I fled from the ranks, intending to meet death quickly; but they did not shoot. I was seized and brought before an officer. He shook my hand, smiling. "We have to carry out our orders," he said. "Freda Harrison we know. Which is Gobolov?"

'Hurriedly, not knowing what I was doing, I pointed out to them a man whom I saw dimly to be standing by Freda's side. How could I, having lost my nerve, avow myself to be the General? "That is Gobolov," I said. "Now kill me."

'They smiled and, keeping me under escort, continued their advance. Their fire was well directed. Two or three may have escaped, and Freda Harrison with the man whom I had told them was Gobolov were taken alive.

'When I saw the stakes set up and what they were about, when I saw Freda looking at me I cried out: "That is not Gobolov. I am Gobolov"; but they still smiled at me and whether they believed me or not I do not know. But I was indignant that I could not share the death of the woman whom I had loved.

'I saw their tortures. It was terrible to hear that man's howling; but Freda Harrison never opened her mouth, though she did not die soon. I must have fainted, for when I opened my eyes I was alone alive on that plain and the sun just rising. I looked around me at the two stakes and the upturned faces and the sight did not affect me in the least. I knew what had happened but I could not think of it and slowly I picked my way among the dead bodies, wandering back by the way in which the army had advanced. When, about midday, I drank in a pool of water I was not surprised to find that my hair had turned white, but I would not think of why this was so.

'Straying in the hills I met Jim and allowed him to lead me to this hut in which I have remained ever since. At first, out of fear of the police, Jim would not let me go outside; and soon I did not wish myself to go. Sitting quite still I reflected upon the past, being too tired to move hand or foot.

'Of you, Joe, I heard from time to time and dimly I admired the courage which kept you from going into hiding. I heard of Pushkov, the new agitator, and have no doubt that he did valuable work, though what his motives were I did not know. I watched these children, Andria and Felice, his sister, grow up. I was aware of the kidnapping of the boy and of the torture of his mother. And when I reflected on these things I would ask myself what I was doing, the famous general, to help the cause. Sometimes I was on the point of coming out into the open. I would attend one of the political meetings and well I knew the cheers with which I would be greeted, how the young men would look with trust into my eyes, how old men would grip my hand and feel the safer for my presence. Yet these imaginations were like ashes in my mouth. I did not want applause. I had not strength to fight.

'So from a fighting man I became a thinker, and my thoughts have brought me no comfort. I saw first how foolishly I had betrayed myself for loving. Lacking a woman, I had proposed to adore the human race, and had persuaded myself that I was successful in this. Yet through me a comrade had taken my place at the stake. And now I thought dispassionately of those dead men and women whom I had loved so much. They were dead. I was alive. What did it matter?

'By indiscriminate affection I had dissipated my soul and was left a husk; a philosopher. Freda Harrison was dead and my spirit had gone with her. Yet I never doubted that when I followed her I was following to a desirable goal. I never doubted the necessity of the revolution, though I was too weak to help it.

'And still I say to you, my friends, that it is love which makes the revolutionary. Not the love which I had, but the love with which Freda Harrison was ennobled. It is the love not of a man, not of a woman, not of a class or of a society. All these loves are bitter ashes, the crying of a sickly child. It is the love of life which makes the revolutionary. It is the love of living, of delicacy, and strength.

'It is the lively, it is the rich body and the candid mind, which are the lovable things. We love the country not because it is oppressed, but because it is alive. We hate the Government, not because it is wicked but because it is dead. I believe that it was a bird which Freda Harrison pursued.

'So I say, love life. Hate your enemies, powerful death. But keep yourselves whole. Never worship what you can touch. Help your comrades. Lead them, if you can; but do not love the mass, or you will betray it.

'O! young men, do not compromise with death. Do not take what they offer you. Do not rest till you have destroyed those kings. Love life. Help the revolution. These are good words from a broken General.'

After Gobolov had finished speaking he shook their hands and lay back upon the pillows, closing his eyes. His face seemed even paler than before. They were turning to go when Joe held them back, and walking to the bed gazed intently at the reclining figure. He felt the body with his hand, then turned back into the room, shaking his head. Gobolov had died. They looked again, with some affection, at his beautiful face, for, with all his failings, the General had made a noble end. Jim Dennison and Joe looked in each other's eyes and sat down beside the body, while the young people left the room.

But George was discouraged and perplexed, frowning as he gazed on the dusty earth outside the peasant's hut. True, he thought, oh very true that Freda Harrison had pursued a bird; but she had been impaled upon a stake; Gobolov had been for long inactive, and Pushkov had died ignobly. Men and women had thought accurately, had felt feelings of exaltation. Excellent advice had been given but nothing of any value had been achieved. And was he a better man than Gobolov to contest these kings? Were the peasantry now any the less likely to be tricked than they had been in the past?

George raised his head and saw the smiling face of Felice, Andria's sister. Andria had gone, and in the last glow of the sun the mud huts of the village shone pink and red, standing bigger to the sight. The girl stretched out her hand. 'This is where you may sleep,' she said, and led him to a hut in which was a pile of dried heather. 'You will have to start early,' she said, and as George looked into her steady eyes he began to feel happier, as though relieved of a burden, forgetting the dead General. 'Sit down by me,' he said, and she looked closely at him, taking her place at his side, as the blood again suffused her neck and face.

Feeling her to be near him George was conscious of a warmth, almost of security, and he gazed beneath his eyelashes at the splendid woman of ample strength and of gentle manner. But as his eyes fell on the shadows outside the hut he forgot her presence and in bitterness reflected 'Even if our movement is successful, what then? To what end are we leading the farmers? When the country has been devastated by war and the town walls laid in ruins, will some new thing arise? If men can be cajoled in defeat, how much more easily will they be seduced by victory. What is the purpose of this work?'

The girl had touched his hand. 'What is it?' she said. 'Are you sad because of the general?'

The eyebrows bent above mild eyes were an incentive to love.

Looking at her George felt the decline of his mood, a restfulness and the stirring of desire.

'Not for him,' he said. 'He is dead, but we are alive. I was thinking of myself.'

She still held his hand. 'You work hard,' she said, while he knew his mind to be darkening in peace and to be laying away those bitter thoughts, 'and you have been treated badly, so Andria says.'

George drew her to him and kissed her, anticipating bliss, and she folded her arms about his neck, offering a firm face. But as George touched her with his mouth, again there broke in upon him urgent misgivings. 'What hope is there? What hope is there? What hope when Freda Harrison has failed and Gobolov has disgraced himself.' And then he thought of the football match, of what he had seen of the Convent, and of Joe so long defying the police, and he thought 'The town must be destroyed. Time enough later to think of what does not concern us now. The wild geese must be in the marshes on the farther side whither few people at any time have been able to come, but latterly no one.'

And as he thought of those birds his heart grew light again and warm within his body. Gobolov, he reflected, had worshipped a woman and Pushkov an ideal, but as for him he was in pursuit of a bird. Gladly he turned towards the girl in his arms and pressed his lips upon her lips till their teeth met and they looked laughing at each other.

She drew away from him, smiling as she blushed. It seemed that there were tears in her eyes, and George covering her big hand with his brown thin hand, wondered at her delicacy, her beauty, and her strength. 'Andria has told me about you,' she said. 'I wanted to see you. Andria will be glad of this,' and she laughed.

George put his arms about her and she rested against his breast, saying 'You can marry me, George. Joan has treated you badly, but I shall love you.'

George's body stiffened as he thought of Joan with whom he had anticipated great joy, but she had never ceased to insult him since he had escaped from the town. He could do without her, but he could not forget her wiry body, so much his own, her quick gestures and the openness of her injured nature. He stroked Felice's hair. 'Why do you want to be married?' he said.

She looked up startled. 'I want children,' she said, 'and I want a man to be faithful to.'

'That is your nature,' said George, 'but I can't marry you.' He was sad again as he saw her withdraw from him, though in his mind were pictures of an army and of fighting before the town.

They looked at each other and George saw again and loved the surety of her wide eyes, but now he would not sink his own in their depth.

'You're right,' she said. 'You still love Joan.'

'I left her for a bird,' said George, and they smiled at each other, their thoughts far apart. Andria's body appeared at the door of the hut. Felice rose to go. 'Goodbye, George,' she said, while Andria looked perplexedly at his friend, and she left them.

George watched her feet passing through the door and then raised his eyes to Andria's face. 'Why don't you get married, Andria?' he said.

'When we've taken the town,' Andria said. 'There isn't time to be kind to women now, and many of our women can't understand that. The best of them want to live with one man and to have children, but the Government has made that a difficult thing for a good man to agree to.'

'We shall still be busy,' George said, 'even when we've taken the town; but we must certainly have our women. When we have taken the town we shall understand each other better.'

'Yes,' said Andria. 'When we get married here, we have to fill up

301

a Government form and our wives have to be tattooed by a medical officer, that is if they were not tattooed at birth.'

And so they talked for a while and then slept. Before dawn George rose and made his way with Joe to his own village in time to do the Government work. They did not speak of Gobolov, and to George it appeared that the general's death had affected Joe deeply. The old man did not smile as they walked back, and George began to notice that his friend was indeed old, whereas till then Joe has seemed to him, in spite of his fat and his slow gait, a man still active. But now George saw that his companion walked with difficulty, puffing for breath, and that his face was grim. He only spoke once. He said: 'You did right not to take that girl,' and George nodded, thinking of the day's work, though in his mind was still some regret for Andria's lovely and reliable sister.

CHAPTER SEVEN

IT was, as I have said, more than three years since George had returned to the farmhouse before the majority of leaders felt themselves ready to attempt the thing for which they had been working; so, on a certain evening, George listened impatiently to Stanley who was speaking to delegates from all the districts, urging at least a six months' delay. George knew the decision which would be taken, and he wished that the speaking would be done for he was anxious to return to the farm when the business was over, since there he had left Joe lying ill. Ever since Gobolov's death the old man had been ailing. He busied himself less about the farm, and sometimes a look of irritation, incongruous on his merry features, would pass across his face when he looked at Bill or heard Joan cursing at the man. He had spent much of his time with George, sitting by him when he worked, and discussing all the details of the revolutionary campaign. But that day he had fainted in the afternoon and had been put to bed. George had helped Joan to make him comfortable and, in this emergency, the girl had seemed glad of his help, and Joe had smiled when he came to and saw them together. Still George was impatient to be back, as he sat on the ground, scanning the faces of the delegates. The meeting was being held in one of the barns attached to Joe's farm. Lanterns had been placed on the floor, and in the dim light sixty or seventy men and women were gathered together. There were old peasants, still hale, who could remember the departure of Freda Harrison's army. There were young men, tall and deep-chested, whose eyes were resolute as they listened in disapproval to Stanley's speech. There were miners, with wry faces, glancing quickly from side to side, uneasy in the open air.

Stanley was concluding his speech. 'I speak,' he was saying 'not for the executive committee, but for myself.' He paused to light his pipe and some of the delegates looked at each other, smiling, for Stanley's honesty could not be questioned. His pipe was alight and he turned to them again, speaking slowly. He said: 'Look before you leap, comrades. We're better organized than we have ever been before, but is that saying much? Where are our arms? We haven't a single machine gun, not a single rifle. What about the Air Force of the town? What about their armoured cars? Wait a little longer, comrades. Don't throw away the work of our lives. Have I ever let you down so far? Trust me this time, then. Though whatever you decide, you can count on me to support it.'

He sat down among some half-hearted applause. He was loved as one who had given his life to building up the organization, but George, looking from face to face, saw that the temper of the meeting was resolute, not to be put off from the war.

Alfred had risen to speak. The young man stood stiff, his slight body quivering with feeling, his small mouth smiling as he looked confidently at the delegates. He pointed towards Stanley who had sat down again on the floor and was knocking out his pipe on the heel of his boot. 'There is no question,' Alfred said in his quick incisive voice, 'of trusting a single individual. We are here to debate the motion of the executive committee, that we should prepare immediately for war. As for that single individual, I can say now that he, with his go-easy programme, has stood in our way from start to finish. I am going to propose that he be expelled from the party.'

He paused and several of the delegates got to their feet, shouting. No one had dared to speak of Stanley like this before. One old peasant, his face twisted with rage, yelled: 'And who wants to step into his shoes? Tell us that, you bloody little whippersnapper!' Others shouted for order. George bit his lip and saw Alfred go pale. Still he continued his speech. 'Stanley is no better than a spy,' he shouted, and then he ceased suddenly, realizing that he had gone too far, for all over the floor men and women were scrambling to their feet, shouting, cursing, some on Alfred's side, most indignant that their veteran leader should be attacked.

George pushed Alfred down to the floor. 'Keep your mouth shut now, for God's sake,' he muttered, and jumping on to the raised platform from which Stanley had spoken, he raised his hand for silence. The miners' delegates who knew him better than the other leaders, grinned to each other and assisted him in restoring order. One by one, grumbling and with sour faces, the peasants sat down again. George kept his eyes on them and began to speak.

'When I first came to this village,' he said, 'everyone made a fool of himself by listening to the priest who was chief of the town Intelligence Department. Wasn't he adored, with his lovely ideas? We wouldn't think much of him now.' He paused, and saw that many of his audience were smiling, amused at the thought of the Rev. Hamlet. Speaking with greater insistence he continued: 'And wouldn't the Government laugh now if they could see us squabbling for sweets? We who were called together to discuss war. Haven't we anything better to do than to insult our leaders? Let me tell you this. If we fail to act together we haven't a dog's chance. Think of what happened last time.' There was some applause. They listened intently, as he continued. 'The executive committee controls our policy. You yourselves have elected the members of that committee. If you don't like them you can recall them at any time. As for Stanley, I have never agreed with him, but he has never refused to follow the decisions of the Party. It is ridiculous to call him names, when he has worked for us all his life. Let us have no talk of expelling anyone from the party who has not acted against the party. And let us get down to the business which has brought us here.

'The executive committee proposes that we prepare at once for war, and open the campaign in two weeks from now. This proposal is to be voted on by delegates from every village, every mine, and every factory with which we have been able to get in touch.

'Our organization is now as perfect as we can make it. At present the Party has the full support of the people. If we delay now our friends will wonder what we are waiting for and we, having nothing to do but drill, will ourselves be surprised at our inactivity. To strike too late is always the most dangerous course of all.

'The question of arms is irrelevant. We can never be better equipped than we are now. We shall never obtain arms from the town, so what is there to wait for? Our plans include a surprise attack on the aerodrome and the instant paralysing of all the war industries. We shall have to arm ourselves as best we can. If we are lucky, we may overpower a patrol of police at the beginning and capture a machine gun or two. It is all we can hope for, and for the rest we must trust to our numbers and our knowledge of the country.

'But this is not the time to discuss tactics. They have been worked out, as you know, to the minutest detail. The question you have to decide is this—will we ever be better prepared for war than we are now? I say we will not. Many of us will lose our lives. We have reckoned on that. We may fail. We have examined that possibility. But if each man trusts his commander, and if the decisions of the executive committee are unanimously supported, our force is, in the long run, overwhelming.

'I know which way you are going to vote. Here is one word of caution before we begin the war. Not till the last king of that town has been laid underground is our job finished. Long live the revolutionary army of peasants and workers!'

He sat down and, when the applause had subsided, men and

women whispered excitedly to each other in the still night, feeling in the air the tension of a great decision, the beginning of the war. The lanterns shone on faces, smiling and grim, all full of life. Eagerly, as though they did not know the result, the delegates watched the voting papers being counted. Stanley stood on the platform. In silence, trembling, he said: 'There is a unanimous vote in favour of the motion of the executive committee. Long live the revolution.'

Silently the delegates dispersed, shaking hands at the door, and returned to their houses in villages patrolled by police. George stopped to exchange hurried words with other members of the executive committee, arranging a meeting early next day. There was much to be done in the next fortnight. Then he left them talking, and as he nodded to Stanley he noticed that Alfred was standing by himself, biting his lips; but he had not time to attempt a reconciliation. For a moment he paused at the door of the barn, looking out into the night, at the familiar buildings, and the groups of delegates passing from one band of moonlight to another. On such a night he had returned to the village three years ago and had been rejected by everyone except the old man who this evening had been too ill to attend the meeting. And now the last days of submission were running out. In two weeks would be tested the strength of the organization which he, with others, had created. This time there could be no escape, for things were moving to a conclusion. His eyes were level as he looked into the night. He had maps. He had examined the estimates. He knew the spirit of the army.

Stepping lightly he approached the farm house and, passing at the door, heard from upstairs the stifled sound of someone crying. His eyes stiffened and his blood seemed arrested in his veins. He knew what he would find. Entering the house he passed quickly by Bill who stood as though to block his passage, and running upstairs opened the bedroom door. Slowly he went up to the bed beside which Joan was kneeling, her hair loose, her face buried in the bedclothes, sobbing. Joe's huge body was extended. The eyes were closed, the jaw set. He was dead.

George stood still and his throat seemed to rise against the roof of his mouth. There lay that colossus, what remained of his friend, of the man who had never shown fear. Outside the revolutionary army was preparing for war, but Freda Harrison's husband would never know of the measures which they took. In bewilderment George saw that he had parted for ever with this noble man, who had never forsaken a friend, never given in to an enemy. 'My father, my father,' he muttered as he surveyed the swollen body, and this, he thought, was the body of a young athlete, a jockey, the brother of Don Antonio, of a man who unassumingly preserved a brother's life, who crossed the frontier, calmly wrested a great leader from the hands of the Government, and by her had a child; later he was a captain in the army, was undismayed by defeat, was generous, was a friend. This man had never aimed at acquiring wealth, had never written a sonnet, standing by the verge of the sea; he had never exalted women, or despised them, never gone into a corner with a dog and a pipe, never perfumed himself.

Joan raised her head and her red eyes looked into George's face. 'I never did anything he wanted,' she said, and again, howling, she fell forward over the bed. George could not think of her. He stood without moving.

Bill came into the room. He touched Joan on the shoulder and she twisted round as though she had been burnt, staring at him with wide eyes, not breathing. 'Get out,' George said, and as Bill turned on him, he led the way downstairs. In the parlour Bill rolled back his sleeves from the red hair of his arms. 'You going to get out of my house?' he said. 'I'm boss now.'

'Yes,' George said, hardly seeing him. 'The war will start in a fortnight's time.'

Bill fell back a pace. 'What!' he said, bending his head forward, staring narrowly. 'You've not decided?'

George nodded and went to the door. 'Bloody fools!' Bill said after him. 'You'll never do it'; but George did not listen. He went to the shed, and throwing himself down, wept and slept.

CHAPTER EIGHT

In the morning, as soon as the Government work had been done, the executive committee met to complete their plans for the first stages of the campaign. On the floor of George's shed the maps were laid out and round them sat the six men, Stanley with Alfred and Andria, representing the peasants, two miners (their names were Arthur and Clarke), and George whose post had been one of liaison between all districts.

Stanley went through quickly, in a low voice, a summary of their plans which had long ago been decided upon. The first step in the campaign was to be the destruction of all the police stations in the country districts. The details were to be left to the committees in the districts concerned, but the attacks were to be delivered simultaneously. It was to be expected that many of the police, at least in those districts where there were armoured cars, would escape, but it was anticipated that the raid would ensure the capture of a certain amount of rifles and ammunition.

At the same time as, or slightly before, the attack on the police stations, George and Andria were to lead a squadron of cavalry to the hills overlooking the aerodrome. If they decided that there was even the slightest prospect of being able to surprise the guards, they were to descend into the plain and do what damage they could.

Meanwhile the army from the mines was to lay ambushes at fixed points along the main roads leading to the town. Here they were to harass the fugitive policemen and to assist the cavalry in making good their retreat in case they were pursued from the other direction.

Finally, in the afternoon of that day, all forces were to assemble at a fixed place in readiness for a general advance.

So Stanley summarized the plans, reading in a low voice from a piece of paper, calmly as though these were the minutes of some ordinary discussion.

George, clasping his knees as he sat on the ground, looked up at Arthur. 'If we could catch them in the rear,' he said.

Arthur nodded, bending his mouth to a wry smile. 'You're right,' he said. 'I'll take two hundred men up the road from the mine. It's not worth risking more. But if we can get through, we'll do some damage.'

He stared sombrely at the ground and the others murmured approval. They thought of the underground passage leading from the mines into the heart of the town. 'You'll have to ask for volunteers,' Stanley said quietly. 'There'll be plenty,' Arthur said.

And so they talked in even voices of what they had discussed long ago and it seemed to them now that their words meant little or nothing, lagging as they did still behind the action for which their minds and bodies were prepared. But painstakingly they examined the smallest details in the plan, lest they should in the end be outwitted, for they knew, and none better than George, that they were to be engaged with an enemy relentless as they were, stronger in armaments, holding the advantage in communications, but most dangerous because he was cunning, able to make them pay dearly for mistakes which in ordinary warfare would be unimportant but which a rebel army might never be able to retrieve.

So it drew to midday and suddenly they were alarmed by the sound of shouting and running feet.

They went to the door of the hut and, as they passed the threshold, they saw lounge away from them the huge figure of Bill, who, it seemed, had been standing against the wall. George and Andria looked at each other. Many times these two had expressed to the others their opinion that Bill was a dangerous man, as likely as not to support a Government which allowed him at least more independence than his fellows, but the others had been unconvinced, for Bill had grown up with them from boyhood, and his strength had made him important. Yet this was not the first time that he had been seen, apparently idle, but possible eavesdropping, near the places where they had discussed their plans. George thought, should he stop Bill now and question him? Should he bring matters to a head? But he could not, unless he had the support of the rest of the committee, or more evidence, and besides he must see what all the noise was about, and whither the people were running. So he shook his head in answer to Andria's glance, and with the others he followed a crowd of twenty or thirty peasants who were running past the farm to an open field.

Here they stood in a circle, gazing up into the air. George followed their eyes, and saw receding, in the direction of the town, at a great height, an aeroplane, and above their heads a figure, waving its arms, descending slowly through the air beneath the umbrella of a parachute. With reason the peasants were excited, for none of them had seen before a display of this kind.

The parachute came lower and lower; the man tumbled to the ground, and was dragged some yards over the field before he was able to get to his feet. The peasants ran shouting towards him, but he stood still looking not at them, but obliquely, fidgeting on his feet, as one who did not know what to expect. Only when the men from the village were close to him did he turn his eyes towards them and let it be seen, from lack of understanding in his face and from the uneasy gestures of his hands, that he was blind. A thick beard covered his face, but in spite of his age he stood erect and from beneath his great eyebrows his blind eyes shone like stones. His mouth smiled as he held out his hands in a motion of supplication.

312

George stared, bewildered. Through the thick beard he could envisage the features with which he had been familiar. In spite of the age and the blindness he knew his brother Rudolph. Quickly he elbowed his way through the crowd and took the blind man's hands, while the peasants looked at him in surprise, in silence. 'Rudolph,' he said. 'This is George. What has happened to you?'

Rudolph turned his unseeing eyes to George's shoulder. His words were slow and calm; his aspect was noble. He said: 'It's good to meet you. You are still young, and I have news for you; but first give me something to eat.'

They led him to the village and George spoke to the peasants, begging them to disperse, for they would hear the news later. Laughing they went back to their work, while George, with Andria and Stanley, brought food and set it before Rudolph. He ate clumsily with a grave face, and George, looking at him, was amazed at the change which had come over the motor cyclist, the racer, the man who had imagined scenes of distinction.

When his meal was over, George told him of the men who were listening, and as he mentioned the name of Andria, Rudolph smiled and stretched out his hand to shake Andria's hand. 'You are a man,' said Rudolph, 'and still young. Good luck to you.' He waited silent, while Andria looked in perplexity at George, for this bearded figure was unlike the young officer who in the house of Koresipoulos had found his revolver unloaded.

Rudolph turned towards George's voice and began to speak. 'What you must think of me, my brother, I can imagine; for of all of us you have been the only one to attempt the things of which our mother told us. When you have heard my story, perhaps you will think more kindly of me. But first of all, let me tell you this. The Government is informed of all your movements. Either you have failed to escape the supervision of the police, or else you have been betrayed by some spy. They know the date which you have

313

fixed for the beginning of the war. Probably they know your plans. My advice is that you should revolt at the earliest possible moment, for they do not take your movement very seriously, and at present they are only prepared to destroy your cavalry, hoping that this will be sufficient to deter you from the campaign. So, if you are, as I believe, in earnest, you have no time to lose.'

He paused and his hearers looked, in disquiet, in each other's faces. Andria said: 'I'll have the horses guarded to-night.' George nodded, anxious to hear what else Rudolph had to say. The blind man sighed, and, leaning back against the wall of the hut, began to speak.

RUDOLPH'S STORY

'Since last I saw you (and I must imagine you now to be different from what you were then) I have done my best to retrieve some of my earlier mistakes. I would, if I could, go beyond the town and seriously endeavour to pursue the bird of which we have been told, but now, perhaps owing to my own folly, I cannot see to walk, though I can tell the right from the wrong, the beautiful from the ungainly. With my mind's eye I can see still what I can never really encounter. I am a poet, of some value to others, but it is you who must clear the track, and your work is the nobler.

'After Koresipoulos had been justly slain I attempted without success to capture you and Andria. At that time I was impressed by all kinds of grandeur, and the state with which Koresipoulos lived had led me to identify my own aims with his fortunes. All feeling was wine to me and I swung with ease from one emotion to another, from loyalty to ferocity, from fear to audacity, from a kind of love to a kind of hatred. Till then my range of feeling comprised only those states appropriate to situations of which I had been informed in our High School. Thus I knew well the lives of the explorer, the officer, the devoted friend, the implacable foe, and the lover despised. You, being a naturalist, would call my emotion unreal; but I can assure you it was none the less intense for that.

'And so I, having no interest in politics, would support always with favour what was nearest to the surface of my life. I had, or so I believed, attempted to break a record in the service of Koresipoulos, and so I pursued his enemies. But by the time I got to the shore of the lake you had escaped, and in any case I could not have been dangerous to you as I had no ammunition in my revolver.

'I returned to the island and dispatched the captain of the pinnace to the town, for still something in me bade me pursue you. Your visit had impressed me, and that night I lay awake, turning over new thoughts in my mind.

'I had, as you know, in some sense or other, already travelled far and seen strange sights, but none had been so vivid to my mind as that scene of Andria's revenge. Uneasily I wondered what distinguished that event from the many scenes of bloodshed, of love, of degradation, of danger and of delight of which I had believed myself to have been previously a witness. Those adventures had stirred my feelings, but they seemed to lack some quality not perhaps of intensity, but rather of solidity when compared with what I remembered of the death of Koresipoulos.

'And as I thought of you two escaping over the mountains I was profoundly discouraged. I recollected occasions when I had been helpless in the face of strange tricks of circumstance, occasions when I had left my revolver behind, when I had been unable to start the engine of a machine, when I had been afraid to make love. I wondered whether all my achievements had not been achievements in a quite individual sense, and whether another person, if his opinion were to be invited, might not say that there was no evidence that they had ever taken place.

Bewildered by these thoughts I fell asleep, and as I slept I

315

dreamed that the birds which we pursue had flown in the night over that castle. They flew silently, like ghosts, and I was standing at the window watching their enormous bodies glide between the clouds. Each one, as he passed me, turned his head and it was, as he turned it, a human head. I saw carried on wings the faces of all those whom I had known, the face of our Prebendary, of Colonel Moose, of David, of a guru, of chieftains, kings and aeronauts; and all these faces looked at me with still eyes, being dead, though they were set on magnificent bodies of flying white. But amongst those faces would recur your face, George, and the face of Andria, and your faces were different from the other faces. There was life in your eyes and in the eyes of Andria, life, and a variety of expression. Sometimes your vivid eyes would look at me with contempt, sometimes with anger, with pity or with friendliness, and then they would turn away as from an object of small importance and, bent to what was before, be carried through the clouds on wings. But most dreadful to me were the times when your face, happy or resolute, would glide past me and be undisturbed by any recognition of my presence. Then I saw that you were concerned with matters of which I had taken no account at all, and was for the first time oppressed with a sense of loneliness. But I took some courage when I thought of those birds, unnatural as their appearance to me had been.

'I awoke before dawn, still perplexed, still oddly discouraged. I felt no desire to issue orders; indeed I could think of no orders to give; and the crew of the pinnace returned from Lagonda to the town. I sat in my bedroom, thinking over the events of my past life, in a fever of anxiety, for I could not determine in what sense these events could be said really to have occurred. I was struck by the thought, that, do what I might do, it was impossible for me to find any eye witness who could corroborate my own account of my travels. I then attempted to recollect some one thing which I had acquired as a result of these adventures, a wound, perhaps, or dexterity in some employment. I could produce no visible evidence of suffering or of learning, and I was overwhelmed by a new feeling, a sense of inadequacy, of weakness, of inability either to do anything or to know what I had done. There were many passages in my life which I was now able to remember only very indistinctly, and my memory of other events was incongruous. I could recall with equal clarity different endings to the same stories, and was unable to decide between them, which was true and which false. It was a failure of nerve, but it taught me that I had been on the wrong track.

'Angrily I determined to give up what I could now only dimly remember as my career of a racing motorist and to attempt at last a serious pursuit of our object. I resolved that I would travel slowly, with a note book, and would write down what I saw; in order that I might know exactly what I was about; but when I considered further what my first step should be, in what direction I should set out, and with what equipment, I was quite unable to decide any of these points. So for some days I lived on at the castle, writing down in a note book descriptions of the scenery and of other scenery which I hoped, when I had summoned up my resolution, one day to visit. During this time I was profoundly unhappy, for I had begun to doubt whether I should ever be able to leave that place, whether I should ever regain my courage, which had so strangely forsaken me.

'What would have happened to me if I had been left undisturbed I do not know. Perhaps I should have gone mad, for in the midst of the careful work which I did in describing on paper my present surroundings, I was in a perpetual state of disquiet, and at night, though I sometimes imagined that people would come to visit me, I was not sure of their presence and began to be startled at my own isolation.

317

'But within a few weeks I was arrested by a force of policemen and taken to the town on a charge of complicity in the murder of Koresipoulos.

'As you can imagine my trial was a parody of justice, and I should no doubt have been condemned to death, or, worse than death, to the Research Department, if it had not been for a lucky accident. It appeared that David, who holds a subordinate post on the teaching staff of the Convent, had, out of curiosity, decided to examine the luggage which had been brought with me from the island. He discovered my note-books and at once took them to a higher authority.

'I was released from prison and taken to a laboratory where various tests were carried out on my blood and on my muscular reactions. The tests were, from my point of view, satisfactory, and I was informed that I possessed a rare ability for the writing of poetry.

'At first I was grateful to David for my release, though later I began to think that he had simply been carrying out his professional duties, for, though I saw him every day, his behaviour to me was always distant and he would never tire of putting obstacles in my way when I demanded to be allowed to leave the town. I never left the town until I had lost the use of my eyes; and I spent most of my long life there in one room.

'It was in a library that I was confined. For most of the time, which was continuous, for there were no days or nights, I was left alone, but at regular intervals a librarian would come to take away what I had written and sometimes I would be visited by students, neither male nor female, who professed to admire my work. I was informed that I was held in great honour, but I was not allowed to leave my room.

'With great care, adhering to my original resolution, I wrote descriptions of the furniture of my apartment. I then described the covers of the books and wrote something on the title of each one of them. It was uninteresting work but preferable to death. Though I could keep no account of time, I observed that I was growing old in captivity and I begged to be allowed, even if I might not go outside the walls, at least to see the streets.

'My request was granted, and a window, overlooking one of the principal thoroughfares, was made in one of the walls of my room. I now began to describe the people whom I saw passing to and fro. They interested me profoundly, though I could not help remarking that many of them were only just alive and that most of them were in some way deformed. Gradually I began to notice a change in the bearing of the librarian. He no longer smiled and bowed when he took away my manuscripts and he began to suggest to me subjects for composition with which I was unable to cope, for I could only describe those things which I had seen or things like them.

David called on me. He too has grown elderly, though he has not aged so rapidly as I. He told me that the Government were seriously embarrassed by some of my work, and that he himself was distressed that I could no longer produce poetry of the same quality as that which had dealt with furniture and the covers of books. He hinted that I might be running into danger.

'My captivity had not yet reduced me to a slave, and I quarrelled with David. I told him that if I was, as I had been told, a great poet, I should know best what I was about. I blamed him, somewhat unreasonably perhaps, for all the disasters which had overtaken me, and I demanded to be allowed at last, though with a poor hope, to continue the pursuit of those birds of which, during this time, I had never ceased to think. I upbraided him with his own cowardice, and handed him a description of himself which I had just written.

It was soon afterwards, I think, that a Government oculist

deprived me of the use of my eyes. I began to see more clearly into what hands I had fallen and often I thought of you and Andria, still young in the country, and I remembered that you had spoken of destroying this town and I was glad.

'Now, though I could see nothing, I could still write descriptions of events which passed before my mind's eye and I was, to my delight, no longer perplexed by questions concerning their reality or unreality. I described the life in the town, even the life of those quarters beyond the street into which I had looked. I described the country which I could not see, and the life which would follow a change of Government. I was happy at what I could now see, though I was constantly being interrupted by the angry voice of the librarian or by the cruel voice of David. But I had suffered enough and would give in no more. When they told me to write a National Anthem, I laughed. When they asked me to compose a proclamation, I spat on the floor.

'And so they decided to get rid of me. I was to be carried over the frontier in an aeroplane and here I was to be left in some spot where I would be likely to die of hunger. I wondered why I was being treated so well. Inside the town are many means of death and in the Research Department are refined instruments of torture. But I think that the order for my extradition came from a high authority. Perhaps they feared I might influence my executioners. Perhaps I was now an object of such loathing to them, that they would not even dispose of my body in their territory. I do not know. Possibly they were ashamed at having at one time honoured me.

'Be that as it may, I am glad to have escaped.

'While travelling in the aeroplane, unwilling to die, I felt by me a parachute and with infinite care I managed to get the apparatus over my shoulders without being noticed by the pilot. It took me a long time and, even when it was in position, and I held the cord between my fingers, I hesitated, not knowing where I should come to earth, not knowing whether the parachute was in working order, whether even it might not be something which was not a parachute at all.

'Gingerly I freed my legs from the controls and felt for space into which to throw my body. Only sound could tell me if I was observed and so, when my mind was made up, I leapt quickly. It was indeed a lucky chance which brought me here.'

He ceased speaking and smiled. The men looked at him and at each other, astonished at his easy bearing and his calm. Stanley said: 'Why didn't the aeroplane land to pick you up?'

Rudolph leant forward towards the voice: 'Because the pilot was afraid,' he said. 'They know what you are doing here. Look out for them. Look out for your cavalry.'

George grasped his brother's hand. 'Well done, Rudolph,' he said quietly, for he had been deeply moved by the story which he had heard. 'Now you must stay with us until we have taken the town.'

Andria spoke. 'Let him come with me. It's no place for a tired man, this hut. Felice will look after him when we're away.'

So they talked, and Rudolph, with his gay smile on that furrowed face, had fallen asleep, leaning back against the wall, with the sun shining on his legs.

CHAPTER NINE

A<small>ND</small> now events were to move more quickly than any of the leaders had anticipated. It was in the afternoon that they had agreed to meet again, and meanwhile Andria had taken Rudolph to his house, where George had promised to visit him next day. Andria was to make arrangements before he returned for trebling the number of men who were guarding the sixty or seventy horses which were to be used in the attack on the aerodrome. These horses had been put to graze in fields near Andria's village. They were the only horses capable of being used in an attack, and the other ones, old and deformed, which had been reserved for transport, had been undernourished in order to keep the cavalry arm in as good a condition as possible.

In the afternoon Andria hurried to the meeting. From his pale face and angry eyes the others saw that some calamity had occurred. They looked at him, waiting for him to speak. He spoke slowly, holding his head down. 'I've just ordered the horses to be destroyed,' he said.

Early that morning, while Andria was away, several policemen had visited the field. The men on guard had at first decided to resist them, but the police had given them a note, signed apparently by Andria, authorizing them to inspect the property. Still the men had hesitated, for they knew the value of the horses. They had consulted Bill, who happened to be passing by, since one of them said that Bill was a leading man in the next village and had lived in Joe's house while the old man was alive. Bill cursed them and sent them away, saying that he would deal with the policemen himself. So from a distance they watched the horses being driven into the stables and barns at the far end of the fields. Though they were still uneasy, they did not realize what was happening till they heard the animals' screams. Running over the fields they arrived in time to see the police depart. The horses were hamstrung. Bill grinned at them before he too went away. He said he did not know how Andria had come to permit this, and he had swaggered off while they, bewildered at what they had allowed to be done, did not dare to attack him. That was the whole story, except that already the news was going round the villages, and that the peasants, perplexed by conflicting reports (for some would support Andria, while others feared to speak badly of Bill) were not receiving the news well.

Stanley looked glumly in the faces of his companions. 'I'm sorry,' he said, turning to Andria, 'that I never believed you and George when you warned us against Bill. Still, bear up, lad, you couldn't have prevented it. And now, what next?'

Alfred spoke quickly. 'There's no time for delay. We must open the campaign to-morrow. And to wipe out what we can of the bad impression which this piece of carelessness will make, we'd better court-martial the men who were supposed to be guarding the horses. As for Bill we'll have to wait till to-morrow. Then it'll be easy to put him out of the way.'

'I'll see to him,' said Andria in a low voice, as in a dream; but Stanley put his hand on his arm. 'Leave him alone for to-day,' he said. 'He's strong and you won't get the others to help you until the campaign has started. Out of the army they're afraid of him. But to-morrow it'll be easy.'

Andria looked at him as though he had not heard his words. Clarke, the miners' deputy, spoke. His little eyes were shining with anger. 'We'll fix that fellow,' he said: 'but leave the lads alone who let the police in. They're fools, but they'll get another chance.'

323

George and Arthur nodded their heads to this and George said: 'The only thing we have to do now is to make our arrangements for mobilization, as we decided previously. It ought to be possible to assemble at dawn to-morrow if every contingent gets its orders by sunset to-night. We'll have to drop the attack on the aerodrome, and I suggest we should leave the police stations alone too, as the police evidently know our plans. As for Arthur's attack through the mines I suggest that it should be delivered a day later. It would be suicide to attempt it to-morrow, whereas if the workers in that mine pretend that they're not going to join the revolt and turn up for the morning shift, probably some of the police will be withdrawn and sent to the front. Clarke and the others can bring their men, according to our original plan. If there's only one mine working, you can be pretty sure that the Government will treat you well there. Then, if you can attack the day after to-morrow, it seems to me you'll have a better chance than you would have had if we had kept to our first plan.'

They debated his proposals quickly. No one, not even Stanley, questioned the necessity for opening the campaign on the next day, though they all knew the dangers of attacking insufficiently armed a Government which could dispose of every kind of armament. Yet in daring was their only hope. George's proposals were agreed to and arrangements were made to issue final orders that night to every contingent of the army. Nothing more was said about the cavalry. The loss was irretrievable and they accepted it as such. But Andria sat silent, frowning, ashamed that it was in a department under his authority that the first mistake had been made.

After the meeting was over and they were separating, each to do his own work, George took Andria by the arm as they walked together towards the village. The others were saying good-bye quickly, with bright eyes, thinking of to-morrow. In the fever of the moment Alfred pressed Stanley's hand. Arthur and Clarke talked together in low voices. They were starting for their districts, to which some of them would not return again. But first they were to witness the settlement of an account.

Round the corner of the farmhouse came Bill with a number of peasants with whom he had been working. Some carried felling axes and others pushed on a trolley great logs of wood. Bill was unconcerned at the meeting. He leant his axe against the wall of the house and then turned to them, grinning, one hand held behind his back. In the triangle of his open shirt the red hair shone in the sun. His belted body was like a rock and his legs were firm as he swung his insolent head backwards and laughed.

'Seems there's been some mistake about the horses,' he said. 'You'll have to put off your fireworks'; and he turned to the peasants behind him, who fell back from him, frightened, though some looked at him with malignant eyes.

Andria, brushing Stanley's hand aside, stepped forward. The two men stood face to face. Bill was the taller, and he did not yield, though George could see his small eyes flicker as they lit on Andria's great arms and chin thrust forward over his breast. So they stood, poised, one serious and the other affecting jauntiness.

Andria said: 'You led the police into my field,' and they saw that he was only waiting for a word before he took Bill in his hands. But he did not see that Bill had a knife behind his back. George saw, and cried out to his friend. But Bill had struck as Andria's last word was uttered. His arm moved with a speed that could not have been expected from so big a man, and Andria fell back, clutching his shoulder, into which the knife still stuck, thrust by such strength.

Stanley seized Andria by the other arm and attempted to draw him away, but Andria shook him off. His eyes were blazing and his breath came through his lips in a roar as he looked at Bill who stood now on one foot, laughing, though he watched narrowly his disabled enemy. No doubt that Andria would have renewed the unequal fight if Arthur and Clark had not held him, muttering words into his ear, and forced him back to the ground where they examined his wound.

The peasants who had accompanied Bill, and others who, having heard somehow of what was happening, had arrived from the village, stood in a sullen group, not loving Bill, but not daring to affront him. But they drew their breath when they saw Bill turn quickly to another quarter, but not quickly enough to avoid the blows which George delivered.

On seeing Andria fall George's heart had swelled inside his body. His friend, he could see, was wounded, but not dangerously, and now it was for him to satisfy the honour of the army and his long hatred. Often in his mind he had measured himself with that giant, that jaunty tyrant, and he knew that though he would be outweighted, he would be quicker on his feet.

Bill had turned to meet his first blow and it had sent him to his knees. Pausing there, resting on one hand, he had looked up to see George standing above him, and the arrogance on his face had given way to bitter hatred. 'This time you'll get it,' he said, rising to his feet, and he scowled at George, who stood still, his face set, reckoning where next he should strike.

Stanley was calling to the peasants to come between the two. Some of them, with Arthur and Alfred, stepped forward, but George angrily waved them back. 'Leave him,' he said in a low voice which they could only just hear. 'Just see that he doesn't get a knife.'

So the two men fought, and from the village came the peasants to watch the fighting, but those two took no heed of them, for each had determined that his enemy should not escape.

As Bill rose to his feet, blinking and shaking his head, George stepped in again, landing in quick succession his left and his right on Bill's face, and darted back before Bill could get in a counter blow. From the peasants came a low gasp, of surprise and of satisfaction, as they saw blood stream from a cut above Bill's eye, but George knew that light blows would not embarrass his opponent. Still so great was the joy inside him, as with calm eyes he watched the body of his enemy, that he hit now as he could, only waiting till he could see the opening for his right with the body behind it which he knew could overset the bigger man.

Bill brushed the blood from his forehead; his eyes were red with anger and he shouted indistinguishable words. Whirling his arms he rushed at George and George stepped backwards or sideways, avoiding the blows, hitting Bill as he pleased on the neck, the nose, or the forehead, but, as he knew, not hitting him hard enough. The peasants smiled as they saw how easily George fought, but the fighting was not easy.

Bill, sobered by repeated blows, changed his tactics. Now he advanced slowly, guarding himself with his thick forearms, stepping toe to toe, and aiming at forcing George into a corner where he could come to grips; and George would retreat, landing his blows where he could, till, already almost penned in a corner, he would dart forward—for a second of two they would exchange equal blows, till Bill, falling back ever so little, would give George the opportunity to slip past him to the centre of the ring.

And George looked for his moment. He was sore about the ribs, and knew that Bill was still fresh. He saw his chance. He had landed a blow on the eye which stung his enemy. Bill's eyes left his for a second, as he fell back. George rushed in and swung his right into the stomach. He knew that blow would take effect. Bill fell forward, his arms apart, and, as he fell, George uppercut him with his left. It was like hitting a rock. Bill's body straightened out, the arms flung wide. He crashed backwards and lay huddled on the ground.

Some of the peasants cheered. The rest waited. George was dimly conscious of Andria's eager face and of Arthur grinning, but he saw these things as things very far away. Now he stood above the fallen body. He did not smile, for the fight was not over.

Slowly, cursing, Bill rose to his feet and George, swinging his left to his chin, sent him down again. Next time Bill was more wary. He waited, knowing that George would leave him till he was upright. Then as he rose and George came at him again too carelessly, he ducked to the ground and George stumbled. Bill's fist caught him behind the ear and he fell. Before he could get to his feet Bill's arms were round him and the two men rolled side by side, each trying to get on top of the other.

George slipped free and struggled to his feet; but he could not escape the wrestling. Breathing thickly, Bill locked his arms round him and they swayed together, with foot and pressure of the back struggling each for the advantage. Looking into Bill's eyes, George saw in them a glint of triumph. Here with weight and height to help him, with his gigantic arms, he knew himself the better man. For long they struggled before Bill, breathing like a furnace, heaved George off his feet, and they fell together to the ground with Bill on top. His knee was in George's stomach and with both fists he battered George's sides; but George, in falling, had got his hands about his enemy's throat and there he clung, for he could do nothing else.

The blows and the intermittent keen pressure sickened him. His face was bleeding and his whole body seemed on fire as he tightened the grip of his fingers, knowing that if he were not first beaten to insensibility, his enemy would have to break loose. He heard, as from a great distance, cries from the crowd. His mind was conscious of nothing vivid, as still his fingers drove into flesh and muscle, and heavy blows fell more slowly upon his body.

Then, gasping for air, Bill flung his head backwards and George rolled from beneath him and scrambled to his feet. Both men were covered with blood, and Bill with one hand was feeling his throat. His little eyes were like the eyes of a ferret. His broken lips twisted as he renewed his anger.

George, but dimly conscious of his surroundings, felt still the strength of his hands. He began the attack, but, as he moved, he felt a thrill of pain in his left shoulder and knew that it was with his right hand that he must give the blow. He feinted with his left and the pain ran shivering through his body; then, with all his strength he drove his right into Bill's face and Bill went down as a stone falls.

George stood above him. His mind was a-swim. He had no thought of what next was to happen. He saw Bill slowly contract an arm and open his eyes. The eyes of the two men met. Their hatred was not dead.

Unsteady on his feet George watched Bill turn to look at the crowd, slow to rise. George waited till he could give the next blow.

Suddenly Bill sprang sideways and staggered away from him. Was he running away George wondered as he staggered in pursuit and heard a sharp cry from the crowd. Bill had snatched a felling axe from one of the peasants and now, holding it in his two hands, he advanced slowly, his back bent, looking at George sternly from beneath his eyebrows. George sprang past him. His danger made his limbs light. He took another axe and turned to face his enemy. This time there was to be no escape.

So they looked at each other for the last time. Then, shouting, Bill raised his axe and sprang forward. George kept his axe poised. He side-stepped the blow, and all but avoided it. The heavy blade missed his body but glanced on his little finger as the blow came downwards to the earth. As in a dream, he saw his finger on the ground. Now he could strike and, as he was striking this last blow, as the axe was raised and its fatal descent was beginning, a thought came into his head. Should he spare this man? Should he strike with the flat, stunning him only? For his enemy looked glum, standing there for this least part of a second, powerless to avert his own death. But behind him stood the farmhouse where Joe had died and where Joan had been beaten. George thought of nothing. The axe fell, splitting the skull.

George dropped it from his hands and looked around him. In a window of the farmhouse was Joan's face looking at him as at a ghost. The peasants were cheering. George turned to Andria and, as he turned, his knees gave way. Faces were round him and arms.

When soon he recovered consciousness his brain was clear. He lay in his shed, looking out towards the setting sun. Someone was sponging his face and, as he turned his neck to look backwards, pain shot through his shoulder and he remembered the fighting. His body, as he lay motionless, felt as light as thistledown and his mind was serene, as though bathed in light. From behind him came the voice of Clarke: 'How are you feeling now?'

The sponge was laid down and Clarke stepped in front of him. The young miner's face glistened with joy as he looked at the recumbent man.

'You've done a good day's work,' he said. 'The whole village is mad with joy. There won't be a man who stays behind to-morrow.'

George smiled, knowing that an obstacle had been removed. He interrupted Clarke. 'How's Andria?' he said, and his question was answered by the arrival of Andria himself with Stanley and a group of peasants, who shook George's hand, looking at him proudly, for he had killed their enemy.

Andria's eyes were grave. He was still thinking of the axe so narrowly escaped and of how his friend had taken his place in the fighting. Then he laughed and eagerly grasped George's hand. The two men were glad of each other's safety. 'A day or two will put us right,' they said, for both of them could still use their right arms.

Soon, as both Andria and Stanley had work to do in their districts, they took their leave, bidding George rest well, and be ready for to-morrow. 'Look after Rudolph,' George said as they were going, and Andria turned back. 'You should have seen him when I told him of the fight,' he said. 'He moved his fists as though he were fighting himself. And now he's writing a description of it. All day he's been talking to Felice, and she's never tired of listening to him. He's all right, poor chap.'

So they went away through the dusk, and George lay down again, feeling his limbs, excited, but not thinking much of the war. Dreamily he watched the full moon rising above the trees and the regressing shadow of the farmhouse. Hearing a small noise he focused his eyes to a nearer point and saw standing in the doorway a slim figure outlined against the white light. It was Joan. George did not move.

For some moments she stood looking at him. He could not see her shadowed face, but his eyes dwelt upon the shadows as he thought of her hard life and of her unbending will.

She stepped forward, and diffidently, as though she feared what she was about to touch, she took his hand. He drew her towards him, and she lay down at his side. In dim light they sought each others' eyes, calmly gazing, as animals, not as nervous men.

George knew her to be his woman and it was sweet to find her close to him, not arguing, not making reservations. Not till she was in his arms did she begin to weep, relieved that she had come to rest, and not till much later did either of them speak a word.

They slept well and in the morning Joan woke him early, for the time had come. And now she did not attempt to stay him, but passionately kissed him, wishing him well, as with the other villagers, an hour before dawn, he set out to join the army.

Smiling, intoxicated with the sweetness of that night, he went away and his heart was soft for her and confident in her love. But soon, in the press of men, among the dark figures and stumbling feet, his mouth stiffened as he thought of the day to come and the forces against which they must fight before there was any peace.

The sky was growing grey and in the east glimmering to dawn. The first glow of roses glinted on rude steel weapons and they came to a plain and saw the assembly of their army.

CHAPTER TEN

Now, as the sun rose over the level plain, where yesterday only horses and cattle had pastured so that it had seemed a scene of peace, a shouting and a din of feet and arms rose from the dense masses of men, and soon their whole array was illumined. With their men stood the Generals and let their eyes dwell upon the battalions. Behind them were the woods and fields, in front the mountains, to be reached by rocky ways, and to left and right stretched the inflowing ranks of men, rudely armed, with banners or without, clamorous or silent, awaiting the command.

They were in four detachments, from the mountains, from the woods, from the plain, and from the mines; and one small detachment, perhaps the bravest men of all, had been left behind with Arthur, the miner's leader. They were to work in the mines for that day, and on the next to attempt to deliver that underground and dangerous attack of which they had spoken.

So, soon after dawn, with a fresh breeze behind them, the dense masses rolled into the plain, and till about midday they followed the roads and their scouts brought in no information of any activity on the part of the Government. The signposts which they passed bore misleading inscriptions, which had been freshly painted, and the men laughed as they went by. They wondered how it could have been thought that they would be imposed upon by such childish deceptions. But the leaders were disturbed, anxiously wondering what they were to expect, conscious of the weakness of their army if attacked from the air, especially in this open country over which they must march for more hours yet until they reached the foot of the mountains.

333

At midday those in the rear heard shouting in front of them. They looked upwards and saw in the distance a single aeroplane. Orders were given quickly. The men scattered for cover. Carts were drawn off the road and hidden beneath branches. The fields, alive with an army, seemed tranquil, waving with corn which sheltered outstretched bodies.

George was in a ditch at the roadside, screened by a bush. He held his rifle ready, expecting that the plane would fly low, though he was puzzled that only one aeroplane, out of the whole air force, was here. As it drew nearer he smiled with relief, for it was not a bomber. What was the purpose, he wondered, of this visit.

Above the fields, four or five hundred feet up, the aeroplane circled for some time. Of course, thought George, the columns must have been seen from a distance, but now the pilot is uncertain of the exact position of the army.

The plane made as though to fly back to the town, then turned, and descending to within 20 or 30 feet of the road began to fly towards them. A rain of paper leaflets was falling from the machine as it flew up the road. George smiled. It was going to be an easy shot.

The plane roared towards him. George looked along the sights. He saw the top of the pilot's helmet and fired into the fuselage below, aiming to hit the body; then snatched another rifle from one of his men, so that he could fire again if his first shot missed its mark. But there was no need for another shot. The machine tilted over and slipped downwards. The engine had been shut off. It seemed as if the pilot were about to land perfectly on the cemented road. But the tilt had been too great. The tip of one wing hit the ground and with a sudden rending noise the machine swung round, somersaulted, and crashed upside down in the fields to the right, from which now soldiers sprang shouting.

George ran towards them and arrived just as the first flames were to be seen. The pale face of a small man protruded from beneath the shattered body. He was pinioned and screamed for help as he saw the flames. George ran forward and, with two or three others, pulled him clear, though some of the men shouted that he should be left where he deserved to be. They dragged him back just as the whole plane burst into a ribbon of fire.

The little pilot was clutching his shoulder where the bullet had hit him. His frightened eyes surveyed the threatening crowd. George looked more closely at him. He recognized Humberto, the chief statistician, Marqueta's husband.

'He's not a policeman,' he shouted to the men who, gripping their clubs, were stepping forward to do the airman to death. 'Let him be. He may be useful.' But it was reluctantly that the men obeyed him, and, while George was talking to them, Humberto crouched on the ground, shivering with terror, jerking his leg backwards and forwards.

George summoned the other leaders, and after Humberto's wound had been examined and found to be only a slight one, they proceeded to question the prisoner. Alfred had at first been in favour of putting him immediately to death, but he was overruled by the others who agreed that he was, unlike a policeman, the type of man who might be able to give them useful information.

The leaflets which had been dropped from the aeroplane had been collected. They were all copies of the same pamphlet. On the outer pages were photographs, one of George lecturing to the students in the Convent and one of Andria cleaning the boots of Koresipoulos. Above the photographs was printed the statement 'These are your leaders.' On the inside of the pamphlet was written:

'To the People

'People, you are being misled by a small number of reckless fanatics of Jewish origin. These men, who have no stake in the community, are simply seeking to stir up disaffection. They represent the Spirit of Evil in the modern world. Their specious profession of having your interests at heart masks a determination to destroy all existing institutions. Only the other day they were very properly characterized by the Dean of Cog as "furious vagabonds, the Thersites of our day."

'To meet this menace the Government has taken very necessary and very proper steps. For the first time in the history of this country a General Election has been held and a truly national Government, representative of all classes in the community, has been formed. The urgency of the occasion has rendered it impossible and, in our view, unnecessary for candidates to visit their constituencies or indeed for any polling, in the ordinary sense of the word, to take place. But every man, and every woman, in this vast country may rest assured that he, or she, is represented by just those men of light and leading whom he, or she, would have elected had it been possible for the facts and (more than the facts) the urgencies of the situation to have been placed frankly and freely before him, or her. Men and women of good will will co-operate in the tasks which now face the Government.

'Of these tasks the first must be the arrest and the punishment, too long delayed, of that little band of splenetic and disgruntled agitators who are attempting to stir up trouble where there need be none. The working man of this country is, if left to himself, a very good fellow, but he is, unfortunately, only too ready to listen to the wild words of unscrupulous demagogues, many of whom are men of education. It is the duty of the Government to stamp out, and without any delay, this nest of hornets and to restore our farmers and our workmen to the arms of their wives and to the amenities of their homes.

'Let there be no mistake. Recent events have given us furiously to think. It is the duty of every man, whether he be a bricklayer or a man of standing, to co-operate in the capture of the ring-leaders. For those who, even if they have up to now listened to the deceitful promises of their self-styled leaders, are yet willing to return to their homes, and, in the words of the psalmist, to "seek peace and ensue it", a full pardon is promised by the Government. Let these men reflect, before it is too late.'

While George, once or twice interrupted by laughter, was reading this document to the Generals, Humberto had been staring into his face, with large frightened eyes. At the conclusion of the reading he stretched his hands out and spoke rapidly.

'Perhaps it won't do much harm,' he said. 'I have just thought that perhaps your men cannot read.'

Clarke laughed. 'Those who can'll enjoy it,' he said. 'Why don't you go on the stage?'

George turned to Humberto. 'Did you write this stuff?' he asked.

'Yes,' Humberto said. 'I was promoted. I was made editor of the chief newspaper. That is part of one of my leaders.' Even his terror did not suppress his pride.

'Someone ought to put him in a frame,' Clarke said.

Stanley turned to George. 'You know him,' he said. 'You do the questioning.'

George stared at the frightened statistician, the pompous journalist. He reflected that if he had not shut off his engine he might have escaped, but probably he had misread some instructions in a flying manual. George knew he would speak if he was frightened. He frowned and said: 'If you want to save your life you'd better tell us all you know. Where is the rest of the Air Force? What preparations are the Government making? Who is your Commander-in-Chief?'

Now that he was faced with definite questions, Humberto seemed more at ease. 'I'll tell you everything. I'll tell you everything,' he said, and then, as he went on talking he began to warm

337

to his subject, slapping his leg, frowning when he dealt with difficult points.

'It's very hard,' he said, 'it's very hard to give you accurate answers. As a matter of fact we can hardly be said to have an Air Force at all. The machines are at the aerodrome, all in excellent condition, bombers and fighters, but the pilots have been dead for many years. I could fly because I had read a book about it, and I was told to distribute pamphlets; but the book has now been lost, so it seems to me really our air force is not going to be of much use to us. As for our Commander-in-Chief really I don't know at all. We get our orders on small slips of typewritten paper, but whether they come from the Headmaster or the King or from someone else no one knows, though we talk about it a great deal. And, as I have only received my own orders, I can't tell you what the disposition of our forces is. Of course we have the police and the territorials, and lately some of the students have been drilling. But no one knows what it all means.'

He paused and the Generals looked at each other with astonishment in their faces. 'Can he be believed?' Stanley asked.

George questioned Humberto more closely. 'Surely new pilots were trained to replace the old ones?' he asked.

Humberto shook his head. 'Not for many years now,' he said. 'Some mistake must have been made. The order may never have been given or it may have been mislaid.'

'What about the machinery of remote control?' Stanley asked.

Humberto rubbed his hands together. 'Ah!' he said, 'on that point I can speak with some authority. The invention is still in its experimental stage. With the right atmospheric conditions and with a suitable receptivity at the other end we have had some marvellous results already. At present, of course, the invention is of no use to us in practical warfare. Indeed much of our knowledge of the electro-magnetic forces to be employed is still

338

theoretical. But Rome was not built in a day, eh? Rome was not built in a day.' He slapped his leg and they laughed at the scholar's enthusiasm.

George, however, was not at ease. He continued to question Humberto, but the little man had already revealed all that he knew. They ordered him to be placed under a guard, having assured him that his life would be spared.

As he was led away he seemed to remember something and, fumbling in the pockets of his jacket, produced at length an envelope which he handed to George. 'Marqueta gave me this,' he said, 'before I left. She said that there was a chance I might meet you.'

George nodded, and put the envelope in his pocket. Then he turned to the Generals. 'It's too good,' he said. 'There must be something wrong. We must be on our guard.'

They nodded their heads, for it seemed that he had spoken sense, and all that afternoon and evening the army marched on and the scouts brought in no news. At dusk they left the main roads, since they were approaching the tunnels in the hills. Alfred had been in favour of forcing these tunnels, but the others knew that it would be a difficult, if not a hopeless, undertaking. And, though it might be hard to guide an army over the high passes, there at least, as George had pointed out, they were not likely to be obstructed by the enemy, whose police had never been seen above the foothills. Often George had endeavoured to find again the route by which he and Bob had first reached the town, but all his efforts had been in vain. The peasants knew of no other approaches except the main roads and the passes, and they smiled when George attempted to describe his own journey which had seemed to him an easy one, for, as far as he could remember, he had crossed no high mountains and certainly had not been through a tunnel. After his return, he had explored the country himself, but he found no scenery which could recall the way by which he had gone before, and at length he came to the conclusion either that he had made a very long detour and had not noticed the distance, or else that since he had been in the town the character of some parts of the country must have been altered, by a landslide, perhaps, which would have made it necessary for a tunnel to be built where there was none before, or by some deliberate obstruction which may have been ordered by the Government and would have been accompanied by the destruction or camouflaging of prominent landmarks. But all this he had now put from his mind, for, although it was a thing which needed explanation, the route over the passes would in any case be the best one for the army, and he had little enough time to think of any of the mystifications of that country which did not immediately concern him.

So, towards nightfall, the army camped below the hills which they were to ascend next day. They were in a dusty place, though there was water, and some trees still to be seen a good way off. In front of them rose a sheer wall of rock, and, far to their right was the beginning of the ascent. It was a safe camping ground. Nothing, it seemed, could pass the hills in front of them; but sentries watched the roads to their left and the passes to their right, since it was not inconceivable that the enemy might choose to attack even on such unpromising ground.

The army was at ease and around the fires men sang far into the night, eager for the next day, not worrying yet about wives and children so lately left behind. It was a fine sight, mile after mile the glowing fires of their enormous force, with here and there a shadow crossing a fire.

Before going to sleep George remembered the letter which Humberto had given him from Marqueta. He held the envelope between his fingers and recalled to mind her face, the gentle face of a delicate and intelligent woman. She had been unaffected by the

340

operation and yet she was unaware of the motions of her soft responsive body. What did she want of him now? he wondered; for it was surprising that she should remember him, being, as she was, so forgetful of herself. He opened the letter and read:

'Dear George, you remember the room in which I am sitting, and I curse the walls which hold me back from you. Since you came to the town and I spoke to you after the lecture, my whole life has been changed. I can't bear any longer to go with Pothimere, and I don't like Victor Hugo. Last night I dreamed of you. You were sitting on a white donkey and were dressed in a blue cloak. It was in a mountain valley and crowds of people, dressed like Arabs, stood listening to you as you spoke to them. Then you threw off your cloak and were quite naked. The people began to go away and I saw that you were covered with terrible wounds. I was alone with you in the valley and I came to dress your wounds. But you did not smile at me and I went away too. Wasn't it a curious dream? When I woke up I was crying.

'But I am not saying what I mean to say. I don't want you to think badly of me. Remember that I gave myself to you. Don't remember that I denied it afterwards. You, who are so strong, can understand how difficult it is for a girl to live in the town, even though she wants with all her heart to be good and natural, like you are. What can I do? I can only read poetry, and I hate it. Or I can let people make love to me, and then afterwards I feel rather small, because the men and women here are not real men and women. There is something very odd about us all, which I can't explain. And I don't agree with people being tortured. I want everyone to be happy, but how can one be? I don't think anyone here is happy at all, except perhaps the very high officials.

'Dear George, still I am not saying what I want to say. I love you. That is it, but it looks silly, doesn't it? three words put down in black ink on white paper. And they don't express anything at all. My heart is like a saucepan full of boiling water, and these three silly words are like three white eggs which I see, when I look into the hot liquid, rolling from side to side and sometimes swinging up to the surface. The silly oval things! What do they know except the heat? And they are no part of my hot heart. They must have been dropped in with a spoon. So when I say "I love you" I tell you nothing. For women will always be ready with their bodies, and when I speak of how my heart, like the tide of the sea, moves dimly towards you and suffers when it is only beating against sand, what will you think? Will you think "here is a woman who is fond of refined feeling"? Well, and why not? Must all women be monkeys? It is true that I love beautiful things, that I am not a peasant. Does that mean that my feelings are worth nothing? I know it does not and you would know it too if you could see beyond these words and read the truth which love always writes between the lines.

'Have you read as far as this? Will you visit Marqueta when your armies enter the city and you are a great man? Good-bye ,George. All the time I am thinking of you and almost praying (for love is superstitious) that you will avoid danger and the treachery with which our armies fight. Good-bye, George, and don't hurt with your thoughts.

'Marqueta.'

Frowning, George read twice through this letter. Then he put it in his pocket and, since he was tired, went to sleep.

CHAPTER ELEVEN

HE was awakened some time before dawn by what had seemed to him, startled from sleep, the sound of a gun. Hurriedly he got to his feet and looked round him. It was the darkest hour of the night, no moon and the stars obscured. Only gleamed here and there in intervals of darkness the camp fires, and near at hand could be seen the huddled bodies of men, some of whom were still sleeping while others, surprised too by the noise, were scrambling to their feet. There was scarcely a sound from all the miles over which the army was extended.

Alfred's voice came from behind him: 'Did you hear anything?' George nodded. 'What about the patrols?'

'They've just been relieved,' Alfred said. 'All's well. There's been no sign of the enemy.'

So they stood, looking into the night, listening; but except for the sights and sounds of the camp there was nothing to see or hear.

After a few minutes Alfred laughed. 'Nerves,' he said. 'They can't be going to attack. Our position is too strong,' and, though they were puzzled, they were about to sleep again when the first rocket went up.

Apparently from the sheer cliff in front of them the sound came and a green light writhed into the sky. Now there could be no doubt that the enemy, wherever they might be, were contemplating some move. The call was given to stand to arms, and large detachments of men were sent to reinforce the patrols; but it was not from the flanks that the attack was to come.

The army of the Plain who were in the centre of the encampment

343

stood in their ranks, straining their eyes as they looked to right and left, expecting the sound of firing. Meanwhile from in front of them, from the face of the rock, where there seemed no foot-hold for a goat, rocket after rocket plunged into the air.

For about an hour they waited, watching the fireworks, ready every minute to meet forces which never appeared. Reports had come in from the patrols. There was no sign of any activity on the part of the enemy. Scouts had gone high up into the passes and for some distance along the roads without meeting a living soul. So, in bewilderment, the Generals wondered what was the meaning of this show of rockets on the strongest part of their front, and the men, standing in the cold air ready with their arms, began to grumble in disquiet, for there was something in this irrational display which, hours before dawn, might well make an ordinary man uneasy.

A light went up and broke in the air with a deafening explosion. For three or four seconds the whole landscape was lit up. In brilliant green light the thickly crowded faces, with their staring eyes, looked livid and unreal and the cliffs in front seemed to weigh over their heads with tons of rock. A cry broke from the army and men fell back, stumbling on those behind them. They had seen the cliff move and then, as darkness was renewed, came a terrific sustained roar of shell fire or of a breaking mountain. 'A landslide,' men shrieked, or 'they have dynamited the hills', and in panic they began to turn backwards. Some men were crushed beneath the stumbling feet as, in that enormous noise, the soldiers listened to no orders. There succeeded an interval of silence so complete that it might have been believed that the rockets and the bombardment had been no more than a dream and that this was a calm summer night. George, Alfred, and the leaders of the various companies ran along the ranks, staying the retreat. 'It's some trick,' they assured the men. 'How could they disturb the

344

mountains?' But they too were bewildered, for they could not guess what was the plan of their enemies.

Another light went up and now it was clear for all to see that the face of the mountain was moving. But it was not a landslide. Rather it seemed as though the rock was being drawn apart in the middle as a curtain is drawn, for slowly in that solid wall of stone a gap yawned through which could be seen stars that had been hidden before. Every instant now the scene was being illumined by the green lights which burst in the air like shells. But the army was standing its ground. Men gripped their arms as they stared at the gaping mountain. Here and there a soldier, unnerved by the long waiting and now by the sight of what seemed incredible, would scream and turn to run, but his comrades held him back, cursing him, for they too, like all men, were apt to fear what they could not understand. The leaders, uneasy themselves, were going from man to man. 'However they've broken down the hill,' they said, 'they can only bring policemen or tanks through the gap. We can manage policemen and you know what to do if it's tanks.'

But no one was prepared for the attack which was now delivered. In the cliff face was a gap of 30 or 40 feet. The green lights were still momentarily lighting up the wavering army and the enormous rocks. There was a continuous roar of artillery, and soon searchlights, from the summit of the hill, began to play over the plain. Someone screamed, looking in front of him, and when the next green light rose, they saw standing in the gap between the hills the figure of a man, 30 feet high, stepping towards them through the storm of sound.

The sight was so incredible that for a moment the army stood silent. The searchlights were focused upon the figure. The face, proportionate in size to the body, was that of a young man. The black hair was brushed back from a high narrow brow, pale in the light. His eyes were open and stared in front of him above a thin nose and thin beautiful body. There was no expression in the face. Below the neck the body was like a tower, clothed in the uniform of a policeman. The arms swung mechanically at his sides and in each hand he grasped tightly some rounded object. Fascinated they watched him take a step forward into the plain. One hand was flung forward and a missile thrown. As it fell to earth it exploded, sending up a shower of broken stones into the air. They saw the figure jerkily, like an automaton, put his hand into his pocket for another bomb.

And now, behind him, other giants were coming through the pass. The searchlights shone strongly on their faces, the faces of old men, of young women, all of the same height, all armed with bombs.

No wonder that the army wavered, faced with these monsters in the night, in the glow of searchlights and terrific din of explosives. As this army of giants, twenty or thirty stiff figures, all carrying high their expressionless faces, advanced, the men in the front ranks began to turn and fight their way backwards, though still there were many who listened to their leaders and stood their ground.

George stood in front of his men with a rifle. 'If these things are alive they can be killed,' he said, and took careful aim, while his men watched him, not willing to desert.

The target was too big to be missed, yet, when he fired and, in the bright light, it seemed to him that his bullet had pierced the forehead of the giant who had first come through the mountains, his bullet took no effect. Still the figure paced slowly forwards, and now the bombs were breaking among the army. As George took another rifle a severed leg was hurled past him like a twig in a storm. Conscious of the cries and the breaking ranks he fired again.

This time he saw clearly the wound he had made in the giant's

346

chin. The teeth were shattered but there had been no change of expression in the face, and still the troop advanced and the bombs burst among men who had not left their leaders alone.

Stanley appeared, since his men on the left wing were not in action. 'We must order a retreat,' he said calmly, unaffected apparently by the unnatural invasion.

George swore softly and lowered his rifle, aiming at the giant's knees. He fired and the figure tottered. He shouted for another rifle and quickly, for the figure was not 15 yards away, put a bullet into the other knee. The thing collapsed and fell huddled to the ground.

George turned quickly, smiling. 'Get the archers at once,' he shouted. 'Order them to shoot at the knees. It's easy, if we're not fools.' He wiped his forehead, for he too had been affected by what had seemed to him impossibilities.

'What is it?' said Stanley, while the order was being carried out.

'They're machines of some kind,' George said. 'I was frightened into believing in them and fired at the heads. Of course they must be worked from below. Send an order to Andria and see if he can't occupy the pass. It'll save time.'

Still the bombs were breaking as the other figures advanced; but soon the archers had arrived. After one of the giants had fallen the army had regained its courage and as the archers, under George's direction, shot their arrows into the legs of one after another of these colossi, and the huge bodies toppled over, as in the east the beginning of dawn was made, the rout was stopped and men ran, gripping their arms, to examine the fallen figures. They found beneath the clothes a complicated mechanism of steel and padding to give an illusion of life. In each of the legs, beneath the trousers, was a car which had been steered by a policeman. The two cars were connected together in such a way that first one would move the distance of a giant's stride and then stop still until the other had advanced the same distance beyond it. In the region of the navel another policeman had been stationed who had co-ordinated the movements of the two cars and had attended to the throwing of the bombs. But what was remarakble was that the heads and necks of these machines were covered with real flesh and hair. It would be difficult to say how many men and women must have died to supply such material for scientific surgery. Flesh had been grafted on to flesh. Many eyes had been blended together. Even the teeth had been formed from the union of many human teeth, and the hair, carefully woven, had been glued or pinned to the scalps.

Within some of the figures policemen were still alive, slightly wounded or not at all. They were killed by the men who first found them, except for two who were saved to be questioned. Eighty or ninety of the police must have been killed, but in the army the casualties had been heavy, several hundred men having been destroyed by the bombs. Had it not been for the fact that George had realized that they were being deceived by apparitions, it was clear that so insignificant a force of police might have made havoc of the army. Yet now they were victorious and had learnt something of the methods of their enemies.

Dawn was breaking when a message came from Andria that his mountaineers had occupied the gap in the cliff through which the giants had come. It had been held by a small force of police with machine guns and some heavy artillery. Andria had attacked in a roar of gun fire and had destroyed the police without losing a single man. The guns had been firing blanks.

George went into the pass to summon his friend to the morning council. As he looked up at the high rocks, cleft by the gap, he knew them to be familiar. This was the road by which he had first travelled to the town when Bob had been with him. Again he was to admire the engineers who in earlier days (for the work had not

348

been done recently) had built the defences of the town. The cliff face, apparently a mass of stone, was in reality a curtain of steel sheathed in rock, and this steel curtain, by the aid of powerful mechanism at the other side of the pass, could be withdrawn like a sliding panel into the high mountains at either side. Now he could recognize the very spot, where, years before, he had sat down to read Rudolph's diary. Since then the road had been closed and no wonder that he had not been able to trace it.

He soon came upon some of Andria's men returning from the gates which they had gained. 'How many policemen?' he asked them and they shouted 'Fifty' as they waved to him and went on.

He found Andria in the centre of the pass. He had sent scouts through the gates and posted sentries by the controls of the mechanism. Now he was standing among his men, laughing. His left arm was still in a sling, but at his feet were the bodies of two men whom he, leading the charge, had killed with his club.

George told them the names of some of those who had died from the army of the Plain. He described the fantastic attack in which they had perished and of which Andria's men had only heard the noise, though on both wings of the army there had been rumours that the centre had been destroyed. Now in the daylight it was difficult to imagine the perturbation into which they had been thrown by the terrific din and those figures of giants. 'We were scared by story-books,' George said and he could afford to laugh now at his bad shooting. Yet he knew that had he not recovered his wits in time the army would have been utterly routed, and he was vexed with himself for having once more underestimated the enemy by having forgotten that it was precisely the strongest position that they were always most likely to attack.

With Andria he returned to his troops and found the other Generals assembled sitting on stones. The prisoners were brought before them to be questioned, two startled policemen, each indistinguishable in dress and features from the other. As they stood close together, puny creatures in their isolation among the big peasants who formed the army of the Plain, it was difficult to believe that such men as these had terrorized the countryside for a generation, helping themselves to what they wanted of women or cattle, mocking those of whose angry strength they were now so utterly afraid. They began speaking rapidly, begging for mercy, before they had been threatened. One of them was, according to his own account, the greatest living authority on the cuckoo, and the other had a recipe for removing fur from the tongue. They had not yet realized among what people they were and imagined that these qualifications would, as might happen in the town, be regarded as titles to privilege.

Stanley stopped their talking. 'Listen,' he said, drawing the pipe from his lips. 'We're not going to hurt anyone who helps us. Answer my questions then.'

The two policemen stood, nodding their heads. Alfred looked angrily at Stanley. For his part, he would have put an end to every prisoner who came into their hands. George watched the men closely. He did not mind what happened to them.

Stanley asked: 'First of all, who is your Commander-in-Chief?'

Startled, the two policemen spoke together: 'We don't know. No one has seen him for a long time now.' And one of them fumbled in his pocket to produce a sheet of typewritten paper which he handed to Stanley, saying: 'Those were our orders. That is all we know, sir.'

They examined the paper and read:

'To the officers in charge of tunnels and passes. E/P YLT 368498 Dup. ex Plan 3001art. 40 α.

'Proceed immediately to the old road with every man at your disposal. Operations as in section 3 (c) of schedule M. Machines being forwarded from the town. Regret unable to send ammunition, but bombs should suffice. Take no prisoners.'

The order was initialled, signed, and countersigned in handwriting which was illegible.

'What's the reason for the shortage of ammunition?' Stanley asked. 'How can you expect to hold a pass if you can only fire blanks?'

'Indeed it's very inconsiderate of the Government,' said one of the policemen, pouting.

'You'll remember won't you,' said the other, 'that if we had had ammunition things would have been much worse.' And he began to smile, as though he had earned gratitude.

'What exactly do you know about the supply of ammunition in town?' Stanley asked again, but it was soon evident that the policemen knew nothing except that, for some reason or other, no ammunition had reached them. Perhaps the Government had anticipated that none would be necessary, that the display of giants would be enough to rout the army (indeed, such a thing had nearly happened); or, perhaps there was really a shortage of ammunition in the town, in which case, thought the Generals, it would be to their interests to advance with the least possible delay.

The policemen, still attempting to explain their good intentions, were taken away and Humberto, now rather more at ease, was summoned. He could give them no definite information. It was impossible, he said, to be sure of what the Government had intended by the attack. It was safe, perhaps, to assume that they had hoped to destroy the army then and there. Though he had been in the Government service for a long time, he had never heard of the plan for that kind of night attack or of the type of machines which had been used. But then, he added, he was not in the psychology department, though he had known several of the

351

professors who had been engaged in that work. It might, of course, have been part of the original plan that the artillery was to be used simply for sound effects. Or the Government may have decided that, in the event of the mechanical and psychological attack failing, nothing was to be gained by holding the line of the mountains which could be crossed in so many other places. Or, finally, said Humberto, who was enjoying his argument, it might be possible that there was actually no ammunition available except the bombs, which, he had noticed, were of a very antiquated pattern. It might be that owing to some flaw in the organization, such as must have been responsible for the lack of pilots in the air force, no orders had been given to the munition works for many years. Indeed he had heard that one, at least, of the old munition factories had, since the last revolt, been scrapped in order to provide a site for a factory which was to make cheap ash-trays. It might be that, though the shells had been made in sufficient numbers, the fabrication of some important part, such as the detonator, had been overlooked. It might be that the transport services were temporarily disorganized. It might be that the revolt in the mines had led to a shortage of fuel. It might be—and it seemed that Humberto would gleefully have gone on for ever advancing theories. But Clarke cut him short.

'Put him back in his case,' he said. 'We know all that. We haven't time to waste. Arthur will be attacking to-day.' He was eager to advance, for his men had not yet been in action; but his face saddened when he thought of Arthur and his picked men, miles beneath the earth.

Humberto was sent away. The Generals had little to delay them. However well or badly the Government might be munitioned they must still advance, trusting to their numbers and their unity, in order to be at hand should Arthur's attack not end in his destruction. That day they would reach the walls of the town, since much time had been gained by the capture of the pass. Of what opposition they would meet there they had, and could have, no knowledge; and now it was not only Stanley who realized the desperate nature of their adventure. Yet they knew that, with things as they were, they could hope for no more security than they had now. They had beaten off one attack and in future would not be scared by hobgoblins. Though they had lost many of their friends, they had utterly annihilated all the forces which had come against them and in hand-to-hand fighting their strength was still overwhelming.

Not long after dawn the order was given to advance and the army, laughing and singing, streamed through the narrow gates of steel. The miners led the way. Then came the army of the Plain, and Andria's men brought up the rear. Already, as was usual in the vicinity of the town, the sky was overcast, but the black shadows of the high cliffs and the close air did not repress the lightheartedness of the soldiers who, forgetful of their panic in the night, now laughed at the inventions by which they had nearly been destroyed.

George, marching with his men, could now recognize the country through which he had come eight years ago, alone except for the timid musician. Now he was in different company. They passed the gates and reached a sandy plain, broken by huge rocks, a desert.

CHAPTER TWELVE

So they marched all day and perhaps longer (for the sky was uncertain) when in the van of the army someone, standing on a rock, shouted that on the horizon were lights. All day they had come on no trace of the enemy, but now, as they advanced more quickly, and began to distinguish clearly the circling searchlights and soon the high walls of the town, new sights to most of them, their confidence was replaced by wariness, muscles in leg and arm were tightened, eyes, turning to right and left, strained through the murky air, for all had made up their minds that here they must fight for their lives against an enemy deemed invincible, of whose strategy they had little or no knowledge, but whose character they knew to be pitiless. Men looked up at the black ribbons of cloud that scudded across a moon or sun. Far away to their right was cultivated ground, the orchards which had surrounded the Free State of Lagonda, and was this the plain, men wondered, where Freda Harrison's army had been destroyed, as they took note of the few silent hills from which in the past had burst the destructive shell fire.

As they drew nearer and nearer to the enormous walls, and their scouts brought in no news, it seemed to many of them that their objective had been almost too easily attained, for here they were, after a single engagement, at the avaricious heart and brain of the country and still no enemy to be encountered. In low voices (for they were awed by the strange lights and the stupendous walls) men questioned each other, would the enemy stand a siege, could they carry those gates by storm?

With their men the generals marched, perplexed themselves at the absence of enemy forces. How far could they rely, each of them wondered, on there being a shortage of munitions in the town. Should the shell fire break out they would still have to advance, but in the open plain they could lose, if the fire was heavy and well directed, the half of their army. So their faces were grim as they marched on quickly, knowing that they could not retreat, with a mile between them and the walls.

There was shouting from in front where Clarke's men were. One of the gates had been seen to open and through it was streaming a crowd of people dressed in white, whether men or women it was impossible at that distance to say. The army, which for the sake of speed had been marching in columns, changed its formation to an extended line with the miners on the right wing, the army of the Plain in the centre, and Andria's mountaineers on the left. While the manœuvre was being carried out George, with the other generals, had hurried to the miner's army towards which was approaching a procession of perhaps two hundred from the town.

When they found Clarke standing in front of his men they were surprised to observe that they were being approached by a procession of clerics, old men with white beards, portly, some of whom carried banners on which were depicted scenes from the lives of the saints or mottoes of a religious character.

Clarke stood frowning as this procession of patriarchs, singing a psalm, advanced to within twenty yards of his army. 'What's to be done?' he said, as the other Generals came up to him.

'Charge them and club them down,' said George quickly. 'You ought to have done so already. We can't take chances at this distance from the town.'

Stanley spoke in an authoritative voice. 'For God's sake, George. How can we kill a lot of defenceless old men? I'll never agree to plain butchery. Besides they may have come to offer terms.'

'They can't offer terms which we can accept,' said Alfred angrily. 'George is right. What's a priest more or less?'

355

Clarke looked doubtful. 'It'd make a bad impression,' he said, and Andria nodded in agreement. 'Wait a bit anyhow,' he said. 'We can see they're not armed.'

George would have urged them further, but now the procession of ecclesiastics had come within speaking distance. They seemed a venerable body of men as they stood with their heads inclined slightly backwards, their beards blown sideways by the wind, and sang the concluding verses of their psalm.

They ceased and their leader stepped forward, raising his hand as if in blessing. 'Enter the town in peace,' he said, 'and do with us what you will. The King has fled, and we, who serve another Master, are left behind. We will work with you for the good of the country and of every soul.'

He was continuing to speak, but his voice was drowned by the cheers which rolled along the lines. 'The King has fled,' men shouted, throwing their caps in the air, cheering, embracing each other. And from one end of the army to the other rose a roar of voices.

Stanley took George's hand, smiling. George shook it away from him angrily, muttering something in a whisper. He saw the priests altering their positions so as to form an extended line on the right and on part of the front of the army, who in the flush of their exhilaration took no more notice of them. He saw an old man fumbling with his cassock.

He sprang forward and took hold of the leader of the procession by his beard and, as he sprang, he saw the malevolence in the old man's eye. The beard was easily ripped off. 'Hamlet,' George shouted, as he recognized the old chief of police, and he tore aside the surplice and cassock, beneath which he saw a metal cylinder accounting for the bulk of these clergymen.

He turned with straining eyes to the army. 'Club them down,' he shouted, 'quickly, if you want to live. It's gas.' And, before the Rev. Hamlet could get his hands to the nozzle of his cylinder, his brains had been dashed out and George had leapt at the man behind him.

Of the army, put out of countenance by the reversal of their hopes, Andria was the first to move. The others followed him. The priests, cut off from escape and surprised by the discovery of their real identity, did their best to get their cylinders open in time. Only one succeeded. With a quick turn of the wrist he unscrewed the nozzle and there spread into the air rapidly a thin green spray of mist. Then he was struck down by Clarke, but as he struck the young miner felt the gas on his face. He shrieked. His resolute bright eyes twisted in their sockets. His legs gave way and over his face spread a thick chocolate coloured rash. Writhing on the ground he was soon still, and no one could reach him, for the gas, escaping from the cylinder, drifted down wind along the army, and some hundred men, all whose feet, clothing, or skin had come in contact with the least particle of it, died as Clarke had done, and more too would have died, if, all along the line the order had not been given to advance at a double out of the danger zone.

Had another second of time been given to this disguised police force, enough for all the two hundred of them to loose the gas they carried, there can be little doubt that the whole army would have been destroyed. As it was they left Clarke and some hundreds of his men, horribly discoloured by the gas, lying on the plain, and had no time to think with regret of the death of the young miners or of how narrowly they themselves had escaped, for now they were to attack the very gates of the town.

As the army, at a run, stumbled clear of the gas-infected zone, points of flame needled out from the grey walls, the air was convulsed with roar of guns, and behind them rose up columns of flung earth from the bursting shells. No doubt some general of the

357

town had followed the movements of the priests and now, having seen the failure of their last stratagem, was bringing into action the final defences of the Government, the big guns for so long unused.

The revolutionary army knew what to do. This bombardment was what they had expected, what they had discussed over and over again in past years, reckoning the dangers. They knew that many of them must fall before they covered the mile between them and the walls, but they knew that to attack was their only hope and not a man hesitated to obey the order. So silently, keeping their formation, they advanced through the shrieking of flying steel and the heavy repercussions of shells bursting. At first the firing was ill-directed, and it was only in their rear that the earth rose in jets to the sky. Many of the shells, too, were duds and buried themselves foolishly in the earth where they fell. It seemed that both the gunnery and the supply of munitions in the town were not what they had been in earlier days when dominion was lately acquired. Long ease had encouraged false security and now the powerful ordinance would not serve to wipe out an army whose weapons were sticks and stones and knives.

Yet the shell fire was destructive enough. Before long many of the gunners had got the range and, though there were still spurts of earth going up miles in the rear of the army or hundreds of yards in front, those shells which broke among the extended ranks did damage. There was no time to stop to succour the wounded, and all knew it. The safety of them all depended on the speed with which they could reach the gates; so you might see men with their hands shot away or scarcely able to put one foot on the ground still struggling forward supported by their friends, and left behind were only the dead and the hopelessly wounded, many of whom, in great pain, watching the army roll past them, would put knives to their hearts, for they knew they could not live. It was a dismal sight, the marks of all this flying steel, severed limbs and corded entrails lying separate from the body, while for an instant perhaps, a man who had had a part of himself ripped away would gaze, white faced, in front of him, as if he had seen a ghost, before he died from loss of blood or in hopeless pain killed himself. You might see an old man who had promised himself the sight of the captured town, sitting on the ground, his leg ripped off from the thigh, smiling for a moment sadly as he saw the army move past him, and then he would become aware of his situation and of the pain, and die rolling on the ground with twisted lips. Young boys screamed when they felt the steel inside them and some wandered blind till a friend would take them by the elbow and lead. A few fell cursing the revolution which had led them from the slavery of their homes to violent death in front of a town to which they would get no nearer. But still, stark faced, unable yet to strike a blow, the army moved on and reckoned the mutilation of friends against the Government which they were determined to destroy. They had survived treachery, and now, wading through steel, they were not to be stopped. They did not look back on the swathes of dead which covered the plain behind them, but kept on, hoping for the time when they would have covered the distance and be inside the range of the big guns.

Nearer and nearer they came and now could see clearly the gun emplacements in the walls and the long guns leap and shiver as they shook steel into the air. Soon the first flood of the army was safe from them and paused to reform ranks, now within reach of the gates. They had left thousands on the plain, but they were still an immense army, in naked anger, longing for fighting hand to hand.

There was no long delay. In front of the barbed wire which netted the gates were the machine gunners and now their rattling fire took the place of the furious din of the big guns. These men, if their posts were captured, could not hope to escape, and now they handled their guns neatly and the bullets were like a flying scythe mowing men.

Behind the few sandbags which had been brought through the shell fire, George, with those of his men whom he had taught to shoot, replied to the machine guns with rifles which had been captured from the police. These inferior weapons were still effective. The authorities of the town, not having taken into account the possibility of the rebels being armed with fire arms, had supplied inadequate protection to the gunners, and soon George and his men had silenced two of the nearest guns. Even the archers and slingers were brought into the unequal fight and disabled with their missiles two or three of the gunners.

But still the men went down like corn. Half of the men with George had dropped their rifles from dead hands, and though along the unprotected front of the army men took what cover they could behind rocks and in depressions of the ground there was still a huge target for the spray of bullets, and so close to the walls as many men were dying in agony as had died through shell fire in the plain.

It was on the left wing that Andria attacked and saved the army. With twenty men, stealing along a hollow, he contrived to get to the rear of the extreme post. Then, from twenty yards, he charged. They got the gun round. Their lives depended on it, but Andria himself with three men reached the gunners and clubbed them down.

He turned the gun to the left, enfilading the other posts. The nearest one, surprised, was soon silenced. Others turned their guns on him, but, by doing so, exposed themselves to attack from the front; for, once the rain of bullets ceased, the army would roll forward and, leaving their dead, strike down their enemies like flies. It was soon over and no gunner left alive. The move of Andria and his twenty men had paralysed the system of machine gun posts which had evidently been arranged carelessly, no note having been taken of the possibility of such a manœuvre. But of the men who had done this Andria alone survived, and he had miraculously escaped, for his face and arms were scarred with the grazing of bullets. Men looked at him as at a hero and had no time to speak. Now they must attack the gates.

The barbed wire cutters were brought forward. As the first of them touched the wire with his shears his arms contracted, his body seemed to wither as his face twisted in sudden pain. This he had not expected. He fell soft to the ground. He had been electrocuted. Men in the army looked in one another's faces. They could not retreat. They could not reach the gate.

Stanley came up to George. His face was white with anxiety. Had they led the army to a dead end, to certain destruction? Andria stood at a distance, leaning on his club. He did not move. Alfred ran from man to man, encouraging them, but they did not hear. They looked sternly at the walls.

Certainly the speed of the attack had embarrassed the Government at first. The Air Force was out of action. By the mountains the guns had fired blanks. Even here the shell fire had not been perfectly directed and many of the shells had been duds. The machine gun posts had been hastily arranged. All this was evidence of neglect and an underestimation of their forces. Yet the shell fire had strewn the plain with bodies; the machine guns had had plenty of ammunition; and here in front of the gate in which they had hoped to make a breach was a barrier which they could not pass.

George looked quickly along the walls. Impossible with battering rams to break up that concrete and, no doubt, it was for this reason that only the gates had been protected with wire. This was the gate through which long ago he had been led. The turnstile had been removed to make room for the barbed wire entanglement.

361

Inside, he knew, was a ball room. The details of his first entry came back to his mind. He remembered that in two steps from the gate, he had been upon the polished floor. He remembered, too, that from outside he had been able to hear the confused noise of the dancers. Looking at the gate he saw the heavy iron set in a plane with the outer surface of the wall. Then the gates were for show, not for defence. Though in the periphery of the town a great weight of concrete must have been used to support the enormous structure, just here, it seemed, by the gates, the walls must be thin, capable of being demolished. That it was only the gate itself which was protected by wire was of a piece with the rest of the Government strategy. They had had little time to put their defences in order and, in all probability, had not expected the army to force them to fight so near home. And, if a weak place was protected, who would expect that a still weaker would be left undefended?

He quickly explained his theory to Stanley. The battering rams were brought up and set to work against the walls. At the same moment a cry rose from the army behind. From the plain to their left and right tanks, which must have issued from the other gates, were crawling towards them. Between the tanks, the electric wire, and the barrage which, in the event of their retreat, could be raised in the plain they were trapped, unless in these last moments they could break down the wall. Never had their adventure appeared so desperate as now when men watched the strongest of them working at the rams and nearer and nearer approaching the big grey grubs of steel, with their long guns, the tanks. From the nearest of these, shells had already begun to fall among the army before the rams could make any impression upon the walls.

George supervised the work anxiously. The sweat ran off the big men as they swung the heavy ram back and brought it with dead shock against the unyielding wall. They shouted, for a crack had appeared. A few more swings and a shower of loose stones and rubble descended. A breach was being made, and men turned their heads anxiously now to the wall, now back to the plain where volunteers were feebly resisting the advance of the tanks with the captured machine guns. No lucky chance enabled their bullets to find a weak spot in the grey armour, and they were retreating fast as the shells fell more thickly among the men about the walls.

But the breach grew wider. Now daylight was let into the town and from within could be heard the sharp orders and cries of the defenders. Through the gap George could see a second wall of sandbags being hastily constructed. He caught a glimpse of an old man, grey in the face, shouting through a telephone. The army moved nearer, holding their weapons, ready, if they were not first destroyed, to make havoc of the town; and still the shells fell among them, and the tanks advanced, and inside the breach the wall of sandbags was being built apace.

One of the companies of men with a ram had been wiped out by a bursting shell. The other worked on. Their breasts heaved and their eyes were sightless with the strain of labour. Their teeth were clenched, and around them their friends went down.

And suddenly from within the town sounded the noise of a terrific explosion. Those farthest back from the wall saw one of the towers topple over and from its base a sheet of flame flung into the air. There was a cry from within as the battering ram widened the breach and defenders ran back from the sandbags. Along the wall where the tower had fallen red fire pointed to the sky.

A roar of joy went up from the army. They knew that Arthur and his men had got through. They turned back to the tanks. The shell fire had stopped and from the turret of each grey fort a white flag was flying. The breach grew wider. Shouting to each other, stern faced or grinning like wolves the men went in waves through

363

the opening. On the plain half of the army were dead or dying, but in two or three days they had done what they had planned, and the town had fallen into their hands.

George stood still at the breach. He thought of the marshes beyond the town. He thought of Clarke's dead face. He was joined by Andria whose face was covered with blood, and together they looked back at the plain and, in dim light, the piles of dead and the motionless tanks. They turned to follow the men into the town. Even had they wished it they knew that they could do nothing to stop the slaughter of policemen which was now taking place. After some time, when the army had sated its long hate, they would have much to do. Now they wiped blood and sweat from their faces.

CHAPTER THIRTEEN

W<small>HEN</small>, some hours later, the Generals assembled in the Convent, a central building which had been selected as their headquarters, they and their army ruled in a city very different from that which George had entered in his early youth. Now, in many places, owing to fire or to explosion, the roof had been rent, and warm sunlight was spread over the streets, making inconspicuous the glow of those electric lights which had not been smashed in the fighting. Looking up, men who had spent their lives beneath concrete beheld with surprise a sky and George too was surprised to see so pure above their heads the blue, for always in the vicinity of the town the sky had been overcast before now. Was there, he wondered, some connection between the bulk of concrete with its projecting towers and the weather outside? Had the fall of these towers and the ripping open of the roof destroyed laboratories, perhaps, for the production of clouds? Had there been instruments known to the Government by which the very atmosphere could be controlled, or else the senses of those who were surrounded by it? Whatever the cause, the effect was evident. Sunlight lay along the shattered streets and students shielded their eyes from the sun.

It was in the centre of the town that most of the devastation had been done. Here Arthur and his men had met with final resistance and here, in the neighbourhood of the barracks, the last regiment of police had been surrounded and destroyed. So now the men were busy clearing the roads of heavy furniture which had been thrown from windows, broken glass, bodies, helmets, and truncheons.

Arthur sat with the Generals. He was unwounded and his

shrewd eyes twinkled with the joy of achievement as he told them how he had led his men from the mine. On the first day of the revolt they had turned up for the first shift at the usual hour and had, each man of them, been decorated with medals by order of the Government. It appeared that the Government, adept in deceiving others, was capable of being deceived itself. But at first, by their lavish promises and by the unusual consideration which was shown to the miners that day, the authorities had made it clear that their position was far from being a strong one. Later the miners were informed that the whole revolutionary army had been destroyed. They knew that it was probable that this story had been invented, yet many of them, lacking certain news, were disposed to be uneasy. Still they were ready to strike next day, and when they arrived in the morning they were heartened to find that many of the guards had been withdrawn, a fact which seemed to indicate that every available man was wanted to defend the town from the rebel army. Without difficulty they overpowered the guards who remained and then began their hazardous advance up the road leading underground to the town. Naturally they had not been able to prevent the escape of the officials at the pit head and sooner or later they expected some move to be made against them. And soon, as they had anticipated, water began to flow towards them from the higher reservoirs of which they had heard. The Government was flooding the mine.

Arthur had ordered his men to bring with them heavy rivets and these were now driven into the roof. Ropes were drawn through them and the men slung themselves up, seven or eight feet from the ground, as though in hammocks, and watched the growing flood beneath them, since this was all they could do and their only hope was that they had climbed already to a level which would not be wholly submerged. The black water tumbled below them and fell in cascades to the ground at the bottom of the shaft. It began to

366

fill the tunnel to the roof of which they clung like bats. Breathing became difficult and for a long time they pressed their faces to the rock, with backs and sides wet from the stream, expecting drowning, silent. But they were saved by inches; gradually the water began to subside and, after hours of cramp, they could wade on to the town, hoping only that they would not arrive too late to be of any service to the army. The narrowness of their escape led them to believe that the Government would not expect to hear more from them.

So, after a long march, they reached the empty reservoirs, underground, from which the mines had been flooded. Advancing further they came to an undefended gateway and issued into lighted streets. They were in the factory quarter of the town. Entering the first factory to which they came, they destroyed the small guard of police, and told the men at the machines the news, that an army was, they hoped, outside the gates and that they had come to annihilate the Government. In glad bewilderment the workers welcomed them, and, here and there, one would recognize among the miners a father or a friend left behind at the time of the deportation.

But there was no leisure for remembering the past. They marched into the streets, and, as the news of the revolt spread, men threw down their tools, overwhelmed their guards, and rushed to join in the advance on the centre of the town. For some moments they were checked by a regiment which, from Arthur's account, George conjectured to be the bodyguard of the First King who long ago in his sitting-room had eulogized Action. Arthur described a figure, now rather elderly, in a fencing jacket, who led into action a number of young men in sports clothes. He had desired to make a speech, but had been knocked on the head by a brick. His followers soon fled and it was not until Arthur and his men had reached the centre of the town that they encountered any serious resistance. At this time they could hear the heavy gunfire and knew that now their friends were outside the walls, that now was the moment when they could be of the utmost service to the revolution. They saw in front of them forces of police marching away, being concentrated, no doubt, on the defence of the walls, and they expected to go forward as easily as they had come.

But from the houses along the way broke out a withering machine gun fire and they came to a stretch of road where the paving had been removed, leaving bare a strip of glass-like material, electrified so that those who trod on it fell dead. On the further margin of this strip stood a man, wearing an apron, black-toothed, rubbing his hands. This was, so George conjectured, and verified his conjecture later, the second king, the scientist who once had spoken to him of the oil beetle.

Arthur spoke with emotion when he described how his men had stood in a spray of bullets, powerless to advance, while they heard the roar of guns whose fire, they guessed, was destroying their friends. But here, as in the flooded mine, his forethought had saved his men. While some stormed the houses which were nests for machine guns, he ordered others to bring forward the high explosives which earlier he had taken from the mines and kept dry above the water. And these explosives which the miners carried proved the decisive factor of the war. They blasted their route. The tower fell and outside, though they did not know it, the tanks surrendered.

Over the body of the second king they advanced and soon were met by a horde fleeing from the breach. At their heels came their own men, miners, mountaineers, and the army of the plain. Terrified now, for they knew that they could expect no mercy, the police and their generals dived down alleys, doubled like hares, were cornered and done to death, or in the open road fell like grass mown.

For hours the slaughter had continued. Fires had started in some parts of the town, while the greater part of the civil population had fled into the Convent where they were discovered organizing deputations.

But, once the police had been destroyed, the army was contented. Discipline had soon been restored. The fires had been put out and the refugees in the Convent driven into the streets to make room for the troops. Detachments had been posted at all the gates and reliable men had been ordered to search for and arrest all civil authorities who could be found. Meanwhile the Generals having listened to Arthur's story, were debating their future conduct.

Alfred had risen to speak. His eyes flashed with pride as he glanced round the room in which they were sitting, a high hall in the Convent, at the centre of the town against which he had worked all his life, and into which he with others had just led an army victorious. Now he spoke eagerly, with frequent gestures, not paying much attention to the other generals, although still, when his eyes encountered Stanley's eyes, he would look narrowly for an instant at the older man, despising him but envying him his position. Alfred said: 'Comrades, having encountered fairly all the deceit and all the power of our enemies, we hold at last the town in our hands. For ever will be remembered Andria's courage, the sharp-shooting of George, and Arthur's skill and determination. Stanley too, no doubt, will have his place in history. And for myself, I am ambitious to be remembered as one who faithfully interpreted the wishes of the rank and file, refusing to compromise. I believe I shall be interpreting these wishes correctly if I make this proposal, that we make a clean sweep, that in this town we leave no one stone standing on another, and that then we return to our own country. Was not this the aim which we set before ourselves so many years ago? Shall we go back on it now, tempted perhaps by the riches we see around us or unsettled by our travels? If we do, we shall be betraying the army; for what do our men want with motor buses and libraries and factories for cigarettes? They want only to return to their homes and possess their farms in peace.

'Let us then, as soon as the army is rested, set fire to the town. Let us not be withheld by any misplaced sentiments of pity. What harm will it do us if the students and lawyers and shopkeepers burn with their libraries and their art-galleries, their ledgers and their wigs? And let us bring nothing away with us from here. What do we want with their trinkets and patent foods? Let the town be ruined, never to be inhabited again.'

He sat down, having spoken with assurance. But now they listened to Stanley, who had risen to his feet, rather red in the face, and began to speak with some exasperation.

'Comrade Alfred,' he said, 'you amaze me. When you speak of destroying the public servants of the late Government I have some sympathy with you, but let us, in the name of all that is holy, spare the Art Galleries. It may be that a deep sense of our wrongs has distorted your view of this affair. I ask you, what is to be gained by destroying stocks and stones? And the pictures! The priceless treasures of art and literature which are stored within these walls! Are we to deprive our fellow countrymen of them? Surely, Alfred, no. I have always, as you are aware, been keenly interested in education. Now is our opportunity to do away with illiteracy and to prepare the minds of our people so that they may be able to enjoy those beautiful creations which you propose to destroy. No, Alfred, I can never be a party to the destruction of works of art.

'Let us reorganize this Convent. I suggest that George, who has had some experience of its inmates, should take the matter in hand. Let him provide us with qualified teachers, first for reading and writing, later for more advanced work. Let us organize a great exhibition of painting before we leave the town, and let us establish here a new university and in our villages primary and secondary schools. I should be happy if I knew that I had been instrumental in furthering the cause of culture among our people.'

He sat down, looking gravely at the floor. Alfred jumped up again and began speaking angrily. 'This is reactionary nonsense,' he said. 'The town must be wiped out. Already, in the affair of the priests, Comrade Stanley has revealed his inadequacy as a leader. Why listen to him now?'

Andria and Arthur sat silent, looking from one to the other of the disputants. They were bored. George, angry at this fresh outbreak of quarrelling, interrupted Alfred. 'By the way you are talking,' he said, 'one might imagine that we had won the war. Let me remind you of this, the king is still alive. True, that his forces have been wiped out, but I say he is still dangerous, and it is foolish to think of art galleries and new constitutions till we have caught him. Have we lost all our senses to be letting our minds leap so far ahead? Have you forgotten that in addition to our own army we have the factory workers and a large civil population to feed? Then why talk about art treasures?

'Our first job, obviously, is to reorganize the transport services and ensure a regular supply of food. Arthur is the best man for that job and there is no reason why half the army should not be withdrawn at once so as to get in the harvest. These two problems, of transport and of food supply, must be the first to be tackled.

'Now, as to our policy in the town. At another time I might share Stanley's enthusiasm for art, though from what I have seen of it I should say that the culture of the Convent is absolutely without value to us, and I can assure you that very few of the students in the Convent are capable of becoming good school-masters. Once we have improved our own standard of life we will find our own culture. It is not an expensive education, but a little leisure and a great taste for life which makes a man of culture. Already we have in my brother Rudolph a poet who associated himself with our cause at a time when it seemed that we had no prospect of success. It would be a good thing to get his advice about our future programme of education. For the present, if you like, I will undertake to do what I can with the Convent. The system certainly needs overhauling. But all this is, at the moment, quite unimportant. I would destroy all the pictures and all the works of reference in the town if, by so doing, I could lay my hands on the king. Indeed, the only merit I can see in Alfred's proposal to burn down the town is that possibly the king might perish in the conflagration. But, of course, it is an impossible plan. Can you not see, Alfred, that the factories in the town are of the utmost importance to us? It is true that at present many of them are used for the fabrication of worthless articles such as artificial grass and wigs, but we cannot afford to lose any machines or any technicians.

'How are we going to raise the standard of living in the country if our doors remain off their hinges and the wind continues to blow through our broken windows? How are we going to get the best from the land without steel ploughs and artificial manures? But with the aid of the machines here and of the technicians who served the Government but must now serve us our life can be transformed. We will rebuild our villages and have high houses for the light and air, with lavatories and reading rooms. We will have swimming baths and race tracks, nurseries for children.

'Did we take the town in order to go back again to our old life? Of course not; and if anyone wants to go back to his cow and his acre and his drudgery because he is too tired to think of new life, we must speak kindly to him and say to him that, much as we admire his fidelity to misfortune, we are going to do our best to make him happy. But without the machines in this town we shall be able to do none of all this, and it is sentimentality or madness to talk of destroying them. Let us, then, enrol the technicians and reorganize industry as quickly as possible. And let a thorough search be made for the king. I say again that we have not won this war until he is dead and underground.'

He sat down, and Andria and Arthur spoke in support of what he had said. Stanley too, though he had been nettled by George's references to the art galleries, came to agree with the majority. Only Alfred remained intransigeant. Angry at finding himself in the minority, he threatened to leave the meeting and resign his command, but at last they succeeded in restraining his anger by putting him in charge of the search parties which were to scour the town for the hiding king. Still, as they went away from the meeting, he approached George and took him aside.

'Listen to me, George,' he whispered, when the others were out of hearing. 'You know as well as I do the incompetence of Stanley. Andria and Arthur are good at fighting, but they're slow on the uptake. Yet the army must be kept in hand now. We want, as you pointed out, careful organization and no nonsense about art. Well what do you say?'

'What are you getting at?' George said, looking narrowly at him.

Alfred took his arm. 'Proclaim a dictatorship,' he whispered. 'You and I can put things through. I can canvass the army. You can easily talk round Andria and Arthur. It would be the best thing for us all.'

'You can put your proposal before the committee,' George said sternly. 'Meanwhile don't be a fool. I shouldn't hesitate to get rid of anyone who seemed to me likely to split the army. Get the king. That's your job.'

He walked away and Alfred looked after him angrily. George determined to keep his eyes open for any trouble which might come from this young man's ambition. He did not believe that Alfred would openly revolt from the rest of them, but mistrusted the nervous face, reckless, of the young revolutionary and reflected that if, as they had planned, Arthur and Andria left the town to organize the food supply and the transport services, he would have his work cut out in reconciling the opposition between Alfred and Stanley.

But his immediate business was with the Convent. It had been arranged that the troops that were at present quartered there were to be withdrawn and billeted in various districts of the town, and George, with one regiment of his own men, was to be left to do what he thought fit with the large number of students and professors, some of whom were still hiding in attics, while others wandered about the streets.

George went to his room in one of the first quadrangles, a room whose walls were hung with curtains of mauve silk. The floor was soft with thick carpets. On the floor were armchairs and sofas upholstered in scarlet and a small writing desk.

Sitting down at this writing desk, he had issued the orders for the evacuation of the troops and the summoning of students and professors to the Convent, and was beginning to compose some plan for dealing with these people when he heard a knock at the door. 'Come in!' he shouted, and two soldiers, grinning, entered the room, carrying between them a large box, which they deposited in the centre of the carpet. They straightened their backs.

'A present for you from some of the students,' one of them said.

George laughed. 'Looks as though they think they've got stuff to bribe us with,' he said. 'It's probably artificial pearls. Either of you want it?'

The soldiers shook their heads. They told him that they were men from Andria's army and were going home to get in the harvest and tell their wives about the war. 'Then we'll come back again,'

374

they said, 'and help set the town going. Good luck, General. Shall we leave the box?'

'Yes, leave it,' George said. 'It'll be useful to sit on,' and he saluted them as they went away. Then, for a second or two, he stared at the box, wondering what it contained and what section of the students had first thought of offering him a bribe. Thinking of them, his face grew harder and he dispatched an order for the arrest of Professor Pothimere and for the close guarding of the Research Department. His mind was busy with plans for the reform of this institution and he began to walk to and fro in the small room.

His thoughts were interrupted by a noise of tapping, and it was not until he had looked outside the door and examined the walls that he realized that the sound proceeded from the box which he had imagined to be full of pearls or money or other articles deemed valuable by the students. Interested, he unbound the cord with which the lid was held down and, lifting it up on its hinges, saw inside the box something moving beneath a black silk cloth. He pulled the cloth away and there, sitting down, breathless, and slightly redder than usual in the face, looking up at him with grave eyes and the beginning of a smile, was Marqueta. Her black hair, a little dishevelled, lay low over her dusky forehead and beneath the brow were the full eyes, innocent, the small nose, soft mouth, and curious chin which George remembered. But the expression in her face, as he stared down at her, was not so confident as it had been when she, a favoured student, had welcomed in her own room the bewildered traveller who now controlled an army. Now, sitting in a box, her eyes and mouth showed diffidence, modesty, but not fear. She looked like some gentle beast. He remembered her letter and read in her expression the shame of love ready, with encouragement, to be flaunted and puffed to passion. He bent down and lifted her from the box,

375

while her eyes ran over his face, and he set her down on a sofa. Then he laughed, for indeed this was an interesting meeting.

She began to speak and George, if he had expected her to speak now the words which she had written, was disappointed. With one hand she tidied her hair. She spoke calmly: 'I heard that you had Humberto with you as a prisoner.' George nodded, feeling as he looked into her eyes that his laughter had perhaps been a trifle impolite. She smiled as she pointed to the box. 'That seemed to me the best way of getting here.'

So assured was her behaviour and so obviously unwilling was she to introduce into her speech the sentiments of her letter that George, unable perfectly to understand her, was put somewhat out of countenance, and yet he was afflicted by her beauty, by the delicacy of her face, and the certain low inflexions of her voice. Something in her eyes and mouth distracted his attention from her body. He began to feel, whether as a result of her letter or of the manner of her present entry, that he was in some way uniquely interested in her, that some sweetness in her was exposed only to him, and that she, for her part, perhaps from a fundamental likeness to him which underlay the obvious discrepancies between their characters, was really, as once she had claimed, able to understand his aims and in her own way to sympathize with them. And yet the effect of this novel feeling was to make him embarrassed. There was tension in the room as if the two of them, leaning away from each other, were still attached each to each by a band of elastic, certain to draw them together, were they to lose their uneasy balance.

Flustered, George went to the door. 'I'll see about Humberto at once,' he said, and he shouted downstairs: 'Set the prisoner Humberto free and bring him up here as quickly as possible.'

'Right, General,' shouted the man on guard, and there was some laughter, for the soldiers had heard the sound of a woman's voice upstairs.

George came back into the room and met Marqueta's large eyes, waiting for him. He looked above her head and saw his face reflected from a mirror in the wall. He was unshaved, dirty, with bright eyes, and had not remembered that he must look like that. The slim figure of Marqueta seemed to him, after the fighting, a thing out of place, and was it his fatigue, he wondered, or what that made him so uneasy as he looked into her comprehending eyes?

'I received your letter,' he said in a dull voice that was not his own, for, though his heart beat quickly, he seemed to himself to be speaking of some matter that was not within the range of his experience, an algebraical formula, or a recipe for cooking. He listened intently for her reply.

Her wide eyes were upon his face. 'Did you?' she said. 'And is Humberto well?'

'I don't know,' George replied. 'I haven't had time to inquire about his health.'

She looked at him sadly. It seemed to them both that the conversation should have taken another turn. They felt in the air the twining hot fingers of their minds, intimate, that like spiders were shackling their bodies and tying up their tongues.

George heard the trampling feet downstairs. 'They have brought Humberto,' he said. 'Go with him now and come back in the morning. You will notice the proclamations in the streets.'

He led her to the door and, without waiting to witness her meeting with her husband, in great agitation returned to his bedroom where, for the sun was setting, he soon fell asleep.

CHAPTER FOURTEEN

GEORGE had caused it to be proclaimed that each student should, within twenty-four hours, decide upon his or her sex. The decision, once taken, was to be irrevocable. Meanwhile they were to assist soldiers from the army in the work of demolishing the roofs of their quadrangles. George was very anxious that the students' eyes should grow used to the light, but long before he was ready for the day's work he could hear from the quadrangle below his room the high sound of their voices raised in remonstrance, dismay, or mockery, and when he looked out of his window he saw a crowd of them, who showed in their faces the most varied feelings while they stood in front of his lodging and debated what they should do. Many of them, it seemed, were, a day after the battle, unwilling to believe that their state had really been changed. These, still dressed bisexually, looked with contempt at the soldiers, and spoke in loud voices sentences in which the word 'liberty' would often recur. Others were speaking of a deputation, and a few, in despair, stared with dissatisfaction at their clothes.

There was a short silence among them and then a renewed hubbub. George looked towards the gate and saw the uneasy figure of Professor Pothimere escorted by two soldiers. In one hand he carried his cornet; in the other his red beard. His thin lips were twitched into a smile. The students surged towards him. Their faces were white; their lips were red; their gestures were short, hesitating, ineffective. They could not help themselves. 'Save us, Pothimere!' they cried. 'Save civilization!'

The Professor nodded to them. He was a little unsteady on his legs. He did not appear very interested in the students, but

378

frightened for his own skin. Being led to George's window, he began to speak. 'I was the first,' he began, 'to acclaim your brother as a poet,' and it would have been better for him if he had had something else to say.

The soldiers looked up at George inquiringly. George nodded to them, remembering Freda Harrison, Rudolph, and the words which long ago he had heard spoken by the Professor of Love.

'Yes,' he said, 'he blinded my brother. Get rid of him quickly,' and they took him away screaming.

The students fell back in terror, but now the soldiers whom George had sent for, men who had skill in building, arrived with their tools and long ladders. Each of them, grave-faced, took as many students as he wanted for his share in the work of demolishing the roof, and, with little or no protest, the students did as they were told. Soon the ladders were set up and everyone was busy. It was a strange sight, the oddly dressed graduates and undergraduates climbing on ladders or wheeling barrows. But it was unskilled work, and they were able to do it.

George watched them for a while, and then, taking twenty men with him, marched through the other quadrangles, where similar work was in progress, in the direction of the Research Department, for he had determined to visit this innermost recess of the academy quarters which had not been occupied by troops, and indeed he was not without hope that a thorough search might give him some clue to the whereabouts of the king who had escaped. But, whether he was on the track of the king or not, it was his business to investigate the educational system of the Convent, and this Research Department, of so evil a reputation, was, he knew, a place which, perhaps before all others, was in need of reformation. He thought of the cry he had once heard near the head master's lodge, of Pothimere's experiments, Freda Harrison's escape, and of the hopeless game played by the Pros, and thinking of these things he advanced with his men to the confines of the department. In the house where, years ago, he had had an interview with the head master he ordered a search to be made. The rubber curtain and the typewriter were still to be seen, but no living person was in the building. This was the furthest quadrangle of the Convent which up to now had been occupied by the army, and just beyond the head master's house was a blank wall with no passage through it, but only an iron gate ornamented with sculpture and an inscription '*Ars conscia Artis*'.

The men under George's command had little difficulty in forcing this gate and, going through it, they found themselves once more in a covered space, dimly lighted, for, of course, there was no sun to see and many of the electric lights had been extinguished as a result of the fighting far away. The roof was in the form of a dome and over the floor space were erected innumerable partitions, of about six feet in height, enclosing rooms, some large, some mere cells, which were connected with each other either directly by communicating doors or by winding passages, some of which were so devious that the soldiers, making their way into the department, might have thought themselves to be wandering in a maze.

In the first chamber which they entered they found a middle-aged man, sitting at a comfortable writing desk which was covered with papers. All over the whitewashed walls of the room were scrawled numbers, and letters from the Roman, Greek, and Arabic alphabets, but it was the appearance of the man at the desk which at first held their attention. His eyes were bulging out of his pale face and his wasted body was like a cloth thrown over a chair. In front of him was a tray on which food and drink were set, but he had left them untouched, and was, it seemed, in the last stages of exhaustion. He did not appear to notice the irruption of the soldiers into his study, but when George touched him on the arm he looked up, and said in a weak voice: 'God must be a great mathematician.'

George smiled at his simplicity and pointed to the untasted food, but he had to shake the mathematician by the shoulders before he could induce him to keep body and soul together. After he had eaten and drunk George informed him that the town Government had been overthrown, but the scholar could attach no meaning to these words. George questioned him about the papers on his desk and the curious signs, neither letters nor numerals, with which the surface of the paper was covered. These were, said the mathematician, his experiments in the discovery of a new system of notation, but when asked to what objects or ideas his system was designed to apply, he could make no answer. He could not remember, he said, and neither could he remember how long he had been in that room, nor what he had done before he entered it.

'Would you not like to see the country?' George asked him. 'Would you not like to be married?' But the fanatic shook his head, not having understood the meaning of the words.

It was difficult to know what to do with this puzzling character. George put him into the keeping of two of his men and directed them to escort him out of the town into the country. He hoped that a change of air might restore the mathematician's sanity and perhaps enable him to turn his knowledge of figures to some worthy purpose.

In the neighbouring cells were discovered other men and women, all equally obsessed with some science or art which they exercised in its purity, all equally unable to give any account of their activities. There was a poet who had invented a new language, but could neither pronounce a syllable of it nor attach any meaning to any of its words. There was an artist who spent his time rapidly arranging fir cones on the floor of his cell, and sweeping them

381

together again with his hand when he was for an instant satisfied with their arrangement. A critic had discovered what literature ought to be; but he was unable to write. A philosopher had explained the world of sense; but he was blind and deaf, had lost his sense of touch, and had been, he informed them, since childhood unable to distinguish one odour from another.

All these harmless enthusiasts were, by George's orders, conducted into the country. He hoped that the fresh air would do them good; and, even if they never recovered an interest in sights, sounds, and emotions, he was sure that the country people would pity them and give them something to eat.

But now, beneath the centre of the dome, they came to a great curtain of glass beads, each lit from within by electric light. Picked out in red letters on the shimmering surface were the words, 'Department of Ethics. Know thyself. *Mens conscia mentis.*' And George knew that he had reached that portion of the Research Department of which Professor Pothimere had once spoken so wickedly. From beyond the curtain could be heard shrieks and low sobbing and the sound of blows and of laughter. George raised the curtain and saw inside a man lying on his face, grinning, while another lashed him with a whip. At the same time he heard the sound of running feet and saw speeding towards him along a passage which ran obliquely from the entrance the figure of a man, his head held low. The man ran to the curtain and stopped there, covering his face with his hands. 'All wasted,' he whispered. 'Terribly mutilated.'

He took his hands from his face and looked, frightened, into George's eyes. It was David, older than he had been. He no longer wore a skirt and his face twitched with fear or with nervousness as his handsome eyes surveyed the soldiers. His usually alert body seemed crumpled. Lines by his mouth and beneath his eyes showed his fatigue.

He made a quick gesture with his hand. 'Destroy them,' he said. 'You have enough explosive.' His voice pleaded.

George said: 'Are there no prisoners there to be rescued?'

David shook his head. 'One or two, but it's too late. The rest like it.' He shuddered, and again, as though warding off a blow, put his hands before his face. George, remembering how David had deserted him and had betrayed Rudolph, was still affected by the sight of his brother's distress. 'Look after him,' he said to two of the soldiers, and stepped through the curtain alone.

Before long he returned. His eyes were wide open and his mouth was tightly shut. He ordered up the explosives and set the train himself. They stood round silent while the gunpowder was being lighted, and David stared at his brother, clasping and unclasping his hands. They retired to the iron door at the entrance to the Research Department and soon the roar of the explosion and the mass of masonry flung into the air told them that their work was done.

George sent three or four men back to inspect; then he turned to David, eyeing him grimly. David said: 'I know what you're thinking, and I don't blame you. Kill me. You'll be quite right.'

His nervous eyes could rest nowhere while he was speaking and George pitied him who had been so confident in his own success. 'Come back with me,' he said, 'and tell me what has happened since I left.'

David followed him into the next quadrangle where the students were still working on the roof, but as he came into the sunlight he collapsed, and George with another soldier carried him to his room. After he had been given food and drink he sat up on the sofa and looked excitedly at George.

'I'll tell you what,' he said. 'I'll tell you what I've found after this long stay abroad. I've found Nothing. I mean it. You don't know what it is to find that.'

George got to his feet, wishing to keep David quiet, for he was speaking wildly. David smiled. 'It's all right,' he said. 'I'll come to that later. I can still talk sensibly.'

George sat down again. He was sorry for his brother's distress and he half forgot his anger as he listened. David spoke.

DAVID'S STORY

'Believe me, George, I am not angry with you for making a name for yourself. And when I think of Rudolph I lose confidence, and I am horrified to remember old maxims of morality learnt by heart long ago. Words recur to my memory, such words as "traitor", "coward", "receiver of bribes", and in amazement I wonder "Is this I? Am I this traitor? Am I this coward? Am I this receiver of bribes?" And I think, "I never knew this. I never meant this. All this has happened behind my back." I greatly dread the thought of my own smiling face.

'But I am speaking incoherently. It is the result of illness, not of a desire to deceive. Indeed, why should I want to deceive you with sophistries? I cannot even deceive myself. And I don't want to excuse myself for deserting you and for blinding Rudolph. You can do what you like with me. You have overthrown the Government. You are a great man, at least for the time being. Why should I, in spite of my excellent examination results, claim any consanguinity with you?

'No, it is not for that reason that I am speaking. But I want to explain to you how I have failed. I should like you to know precisely how hopeless my position is, I should like to be sure of precisely what measure of success you can claim.

'Let us start from the beginning. I was not exactly malicious, but certainly when the three of us set out, I despised you both. And I carried away with me from our town a memory of applause, not a clear image of our object. I knew that Rudolph would be

384

scared by his own thoughts. I thought that you would never arrive at all. I thought that you would settle somewhere in the country, marrying the first good-looking girl you met, and would pass your life peaceably on a farm. That was because I knew you were not ambitious as Rudolph and I were; and, indeed, even now I am surprised at your resolute face and your presence in the town at the head of an army. You, the natural historian, the plough-boy whom I despised so much. It seems that nowadays fairy stories are coming true, and the youngest brother is destined at least to achieve something.

'I lied to you about the goose. At least, that is what it amounts to, though it was not exactly a lie that I told. I did not really believe that the thing in the Anserium was what we wanted, but neither was I willing to admit that it was a quite worthless object. And yet I had heard the birds and I would have seen them if I had gone to the window. Up to this moment I have scrupulously concealed this fact. It was interested policy; for, if those had been the birds, then the stuffed effigy was not the thing and I was wasting my time in the town. So, since I was anxious to keep my job and fancied that I was enjoying myself, I did my best to forget what I had seen at the farmhouse, and in this I succeeded for a time.

'Sometimes, certainly, I would remember that girl and how in her room I heard the birds go past the house away from me like a storm. I had not been able to bring myself to associate with that girl. She was beautiful, but only the daughter of a farmer. Her beauty attracted me; but my belief in my superiority to her held me back, and at the same time I was repelled, almost frightened, by her rude health. I thought of my own body, almost insignificant in contrast with hers, and I felt a chill come over me. And yet I wanted her. Although it was the first day of travel, I was curiously unhappy, curiously in need of some sympathy. As you know, in our town I had no time for friendship, being surrounded always by admirers, but now, in my isolation, I was ready, though I pretended indifference, to beg for some comfort from a girl.

'Then I heard the birds and I cursed her. If I had been outside the house, I reflected, I should have seen them plainly. I might have taken a photograph, but even to have seen them in flight would have been a rare distinction. I cursed my weakness and remembered her ignoble birth. Next day I made haste to the town.

'But now, looking back on that episode, I see clearly that I then threw away the last chance that was offered to me of completing my education. If I had stayed at the farmhouse even for a little time I should have learnt something about the town. As it was I entered it as though it was Paradise. The system of Government, the courses of study, the conventions of morality seemed to me just those ones which I had imagined to be ideal. It was like visiting a house and finding it to be a house of which one has dreamed; and it is only recently that I have discovered that my dream was not a dream, or was too much so, that reality is not and can never be made of dreams. There is always included in the real some indefinable substance that cannot be pictured in the mind. Yet if this element, so difficult to distinguish, escapes one's notice, one is often in great danger. Say that there is a glass of water and it contains poison. It can be studied accurately with the eye, and with the eye closed one can imagine it occupying space. One can place a mirror behind it and see it doubled identically. One can place other mirrors at the sides and obtain all kinds of different views. Then perhaps a doubt will strike you. You will think, "I have so multiplied this image that I begin to doubt its existence." You may not be thirsty, but to reassure yourself you will stretch out your hand and be delighted when your fingers close over glass. You will drink the water and now will enter into your experience a thing which you had never considered. All your close study of images, of the refraction of light, and of perspective will not have taught you what is the effect of poison in the body. This was something about which you never bothered to think. You had accurately envisaged your object, but until you stretched out your hand you had never contemplated the possibility of its being incorporated with yourself. It was a stupid oversight, you may reflect, as you die painfully, and yet how were you to know? It was in the contemplation of light and of various shapes that you were chiefly interested, and as for the substance, you had heard that it was drinkable. Were you not almost justified in believing that you knew everything about this particular glass? Such consolation may, or may not, sweeten your death. But we have, you and I, George, before we crossed the frontier, dreamed of drinking. Now in this country we are in constant danger of poison, and the more we were attached to our dreams the more likely we are to overlook, as I say, just that difficult element, often of poison, which distinguishes what we think we know from what is. Nor will chemical analysis help us unless we know the meanings of formulae and how they are to be applied to ourselves.

'So I, entering the town, entered into my dreams and lived luxuriantly there. Only lately I have discovered that a reality which one has overlooked is much more terrible than a nightmare. One thinks, perhaps correctly, that one makes one's own dreams. What happens when they make the dreamer, when they carry him away, luring him on ever further and further from friends who might hold him back, from safe houses or familiar fields, till at last he fancies that he opens his eyes and, if he can, he closes them again, quickly, for he has seen that he is not in his bed, but somewhere quite different, and a shadow of himself?

'That is what has happened to me and how incredulous some of our old friends would be, if they knew it. "David!" they would say. "He, of all people, is the least likely to lose his head. He, noted for his accurate scholarship, for his complete absence of sentimentality, how can he be called a dreamer?" And I am not now conceited enough to excuse myself by pointing out that it has been just this conscious accuracy of the brain which has destroyed me. I was never confused, like a poet. I never mistranslated. I was fascinated by a million aspects, each of which I could set coolly before my eyes; and just that negligible thing, that element, that infusion which distinguishes the real from the ideal, escaped my notice and ruined me. Late in the day I perceive that I am the plaything of tremendous forces, and I never suspected that they existed until they had knocked me flat. It is not a nice feeling, George. All day you have been at a party. Your hosts have been scrupulously attentive to your wishes. They have been almost embarrassing in their expressions of good will, have shown you round the garden, and entertained you with the best food and drink. Towards the end of the day you realize that you have been completely mistaken in your judgment of the situation. These people have carried out a plot with perfect success. You notice them laughing behind their hands. You have afforded them amusement, and now you find that you have made some terrible mistake, having perhaps given away your friends, or made some admission which is certain to be used against you.

'I beg you to keep all this in mind while I continue my story. I am not excusing myself. What good would that do? But I want you to hear an accurate and a precise account of my failure. I want to speak as clearly as possible.

'You, no doubt, who have led a revolution must think of me as the servant of a monstrous Government, and, of course, you are right. But this was not how it appeared to me at all. I hardly gave the Government a thought. I almost imagined, from the absence of restraint put on me, that the Government meant little or nothing to me. Of course, I held a Government post, but I

388

had very little work to do, and when orders came from my superiors I carried them out, but I never identified myself with their purposes, never even bothered to attempt to understand them. No; I was too busy with myself, too delighted with what I imagined to be my liberty.

'I was very pleased with the result of the operation, and for a long time I thought of nothing else but the varied pleasures I could procure for myself from my body. I estimated the degrees of emotion which, so I thought, were felt both by a man and by a woman. Under the guidance of Professor Pothimere I drew up a calculus, and it never occurred to me that I was myself neither a man nor a woman. I never stopped to think that, though my blood pressure had been registered, I had never felt anything but curiosity and that, so far from acquiring the knowledge of Tiresias, I had not gone so far into reality as a dog. And if anyone had pointed this out to me then, I should have laughed at him. I should have told him proudly that I had my own ways of experimenting with reality. I should have asked him what he meant by asserting that his way of looking at things was better than mine. Did he dispute my conclusions? I could set figures before him. Yes, that is what I should have said, like a fool. Poisoned water. That was my dream.

'But I was conscious of some moments' uneasiness after I had told the Commissioners of Police that I never knew you. Of course, I knew that nothing I could have said would have affected your fate and I argued with myself that, this being so, I might as well take advantage of the occasion of your arrest by increasing my own popularity with the authorities. Why be Quixotic? I asked myself, and I could find no reason for being so.

'Yet from that time I found that the Government made more demands on me. My pay was increased, however, and I never took my work very seriously. I would pass my time either in talk about love and philosophy or in the deliberate attempt to procure pleasurable sensations. I was very popular both with the students and with the professors, and I thought that I was having a fine time.

'When Rudolph was arrested, Pothimere and I decided that we would draw the attention of the authorities to his ability as a poet. We were the most original literary critics in the Convent and we desired to show the catholicity of our taste. Orders came to us from above that Rudolph was to be confined in one room. I thought this hard on him, but I did not remonstrate. Again I reflected that I could do nothing, and why should I risk losing my own job? But Rudolph was allowed to look out of the window and after that the poems that he wrote were branded as seditious. His work had been widely read in the Convent and his great reputation naturally doubled the effect of his new poems, many of which were frankly revolutionary in their trend. I became frightened and when I read his poems I was more frightened still, for I found that I could almost understand them, and I began dimly to suspect that all was not well. Lately, in my bitter shame, I have reflected that if it had not been for this, if I had not been moved to uneasiness by his words, I might have protested against his cruel blinding. As it was I fell back, in my own defence, on the authority of the Government. I said to myself that this Government, of which I knew next to nothing, which I had never really imagined as controlling my own actions, must know best. Yes; this was the limit of my stupidity. I actually identified myself with the Government, and I did this unconsciously. I never dreamed that I was not free while in this way I was preserving my job and my peace of mind.

'I informed Rudolph of the sentence. I said I was very sorry and I would have been very sorry if I had realized that I, having sold myself in a dream, was blinder far than he was to become.

'But after that event I never quite recovered my confidence. I spoke of the Government as carelessly as before, but I began to find that my work was increased and I began to be curious about the people who were giving me orders. At the same time I became vaguely dissatisfied with my complicated pleasures. I began almost to feel the need of fresh air, and one day I remembered (and it was something of a shock to me) that, of course, I would never be allowed to leave the Convent.

'I became depressed, and at Pothimere's request I was transferred to the Research Department. It was the reward for a mind considered emancipated.

'You have seen that place. I wish I had never seen it. One is there encouraged to gratify every wish, however absurd, however repulsive to the ordinary mind. They had told me it would be a tonic to me; but they must have known.

'For some time I played with mathematics. Then I began to attempt some of those cruel and disgusting actions which you have seen. Of course, to me they were not cruel or disgusting. I had learnt to forget the meaning of those words. I was, they said, learning to know myself.

'It was with startling suddenness that I realized that I had lost my sanity. Oh George, you would pity me if you knew. Never to be able to leave that place! To be condemned to excesses of the mind and body, and to find these actions which I was forced to perform not pleasant, not even exciting, but merely meaningless! I had learnt to free my mind from every restraint, and I found that my mind had gone. I had no single desire left; and now, behind iron doors, I woke up to the fact that I was a prisoner of this Government to which in the past I had paid so little attention. This was the dreadful eye-opener of a sleeper who discovers that he is not in his own bed.

'Even the clothes I wore were unfamiliar to me. I searched in vain for some clue to my identity. I tried to think of just one thing which I desired, of just one object in which I was interested. I found myself a bare shadow, not a self, and confronting this shadow I saw enormous walls of iron, the trap of a roof, terrific powers, the reality which I had overlooked.

'Elaborate systems of torture, unheard of experiments, were put before my eyes, and I, who now could not distinguish myself from other living beings, found that it was I myself who was being tortured, I myself who was the torturer. How previously I had been enraptured by the intellectual consideration of such a union of subject and object! How terrible was the reality! My self, which I had considered inviolate, was dissipated over the walls and floor of my room, and a reflection, a puppet, something that would show in a mirror was the mere toy of a system of Government which, late in the day, I found that I had never understood.

'I heard the falling of the towers and guessed that your rebel army was entering the town. What hope was there for me? I had betrayed my brothers, and hardly given that matter a thought. Even if you were to forgive me, could you give me back my self? You may travel farther and draw nearer to the object which we set out to seek. I do not want even to think about the Wild Goose. How should I have strength for the journey? I have known myself to be a shell, not a master, but a subordinate, a brilliant linguist, good at figures, a smiler. I cannot hold a gun. I would not know what to shoot at. It would be better if I had not been born.

'And now let me ask you something. Are you going to succeed? Believe me, I should like you to do so. My emptiness is too spacious for envy, and, unable now to imagine myself in action, I feel for the first time generous towards rivals, wishing frantically that they should do well. And you, George, have overthrown the Government, a great thing to have done. But this is what I want to know. Are you any nearer to the Wild Goose? Will these peasants of yours put up with your absence? They have not the vices of the previous Government, but have they not their own methods of obstruction? Or are not you yourself in some danger of settling down? After all, you have led a strenuous life. No one would blame you now if you started to enjoy power, or rested with women. What are your intentions, George? You have achieved much and I less than nothing, but have you got half-way, do you think?'

David ceased speaking and looked across the room at George.

CHAPTER FIFTEEN

AND George, looking at his brother, pitied the nervous twitching of his face, the romantic intensity of his weak eyes, evidence of his complete collapse.

'I'll tell you, David,' he said. 'I've hardly started to think yet of what my next step will be. We haven't caught the king yet, and until we have done that we have not really won the war. It's something, certainly, to have destroyed the police. They were a constant danger to foreigners. It's something to be in control of the Convent and to have blown up the Research Department. But these things, important as they are, are not of fundamental importance. The police obeyed orders; the Research Department was merely a symptom of the disease. And now, though the king's government is very much weakened, though our party is certain to inaugurate a new and a better system, yet we are not out of the wood.

'So my first job is to catch the king and to help in the reorganization of the country. The route will then be clear, at least up to this point, and I shall go forward, and perhaps my wife Joan will come with me.

'As for knowing whether I have got half-way, how can I know? There may be other obstructions as formidable as was the government of this town; or the birds may, as has sometimes happened, change their nesting places, may even migrate to another country. One can't tell; but I can say this, that I can see no reason for supposing that I am now much nearer to our object than when I first crossed the frontier. I have, with great difficulty, retrieved a mistake, and that is all.'

David nodded. 'Yes,' he said, 'but still you are in the race, not out of it altogether, like Rudolph and I.'

'That's true,' George said, 'but no guarantee of success. I feel uneasy when I think that better men than I have fallen before the town. Joe, for instance, that great man; and Freda Harrison, the courageous woman. But perhaps you, David, will be able to come when you have recovered your health.'

'Are you laughing at me?' David said. 'Isn't it quite clear? I shall never be strong enough to take a single step by myself. Conquer your cities, and I will be a capable secretary for any Governor, will study his tastes and send in accurate reports. But do I look like a General? Haven't I made it plain that I can initiate nothing?'

George looked at his brother and knew that his estimate was correct. 'Do you know anything about botany?' he said.

'I've read all the textbooks,' David replied.

'Well then,' said George, 'I'll tell you what you can do for the time being. Go on staying in the Convent, but get out into the open as much as you can. You'd better begin by making a catalogue of the flowers and trees which are to be found in the country. Then I'll put you in touch with the people who'll be in charge of forestry and horticulture and you'll be able to help them. You'll have a lot of open-air work, which will be good for you.'

George was not sure how his brother would take this proposal, and he was pleased to see David's eyes grow bright and to hear him laugh.

'Thank you, George,' he said. 'Don't think that the literary critic feels insulted at being turned into a gardener. It's not so. I'd like to do that work. I believe that the planting of conifers was neglected by the Government.'

He began to talk, almost with enthusiasm, of this new subject which had been put before him, and George was glad as he listened, and saw hope for his brother's recovery.

There was a knock at the door. The door opened and David, with twisting lips, shrank back in his chair as he saw entering the room the tall bearded figure of Rudolph, whose empty eyes rested nowhere, but whose mouth wore its gay smile.

'Well done, George,' he shouted. 'I met the messengers half-way. I shall write a description of the battles. You have fought like tigers.' And he stretched out his hand for George to take.

George gripped his brother's hand warmly. His eyes were upon David's wide-eyed face. 'Rudolph,' he said, 'David is here.'

Rudolph's body stiffened as though to meet a blow.

'He's had a bad time,' George added.

'He deserved it,' Rudolph said, blindly looking at the floor.

George watched David's terrified face. He spoke again, telling Rudolph something of David's story and describing his present state. Before he had got to the end of what he was saying, Rudolph stretched out his hand. 'Where is he?' he asked, and George led him to the chair in which David still cowered.

Rudolph took David's hand and David's eyes were like an animal's eyes as he looked up to Rudolph's full smiling lips.

'Both of us are lucky to be alive,' Rudolph said, 'and both of us are crippled. So why should we hate each other? We've still much to do. I shall write descriptions of battles which I never fought. What will you do?'

David, whose sensitive mouth showed his gratitude to his brother, said timidly: 'I am going to make a catalogue of flowers.'

'That's very good work,' said Rudolph. 'My wife and I will often come with you into the country.'

'Your wife?' said George, incredulous.

Rudolph's boisterous laughter filled the room. 'Yes,' he said, 'Felice, Andria's sister.'

George laughed too, and shook his brother's hand. He remembered that excellent girl and knew that Rudolph would be happy. He remembered, too, how Andria had told him that the girl would listen spellbound to Rudolph as he talked, describing to her what he had seen and what he had not seen.

So the three brothers for the first time since they had left their homes were together in friendship. Rudolph told how, impatient for news, he had left Andria's house before any messenger arrived from the army, how in the country the women were divided between fear and hope, how anxious they had been when they had heard the sound of firing and seen above the hills flame rising and long cords of smoke across the sky. He thought that Felice and Joan, with many others, would come to the town as soon as they heard the good news of its capture, and he, he said, when he had spoken to those whom he knew in the army, proposed to go back and meet them.

George smiled and said that Rudolph and his 'description', as he called it, would be certain to exaggerate all the events of the war, but Rudolph would not speak of this in a playful tone. 'You do not see everything with your eyes,' he said. 'If you did, you would not talk so easily of "events of the war". I tell you that my descriptions are more accurate than news. Events are scratches on the skin; but those who describe them properly must know the hand that pulled the trigger and movements underneath the skin. No. You have fought like tigers fight.'

George nodded his head, for he knew that Rudolph could see things which escaped the notice of one such as himself, a pioneer and, by accident, a General. He reflected on the great change which had taken place in his brother, now that he had learnt to look, although with blind eyes, steadily at an object, and he was glad to think that, in their work of reorganization, they would have the advantage of his judgment.

David, too, followed Rudolph's words closely and, out of nervousness, seemed reluctant to speak himself until, hearing Rudolph mention the fact that the man who had guided him to the town was busy with his friends, he rose to his feet and, crossing the room to the chair in which Rudolph was sitting, said: 'Let me go back with you, Rudolph. I can guide you, and you can protect me, because the peasants know you.' And he looked earnestly at the face which he had helped to mar.

Rudolph, sensitive to the sound of his brother's voice, looked up quickly. 'You are standing there,' he said, 'with pale lips and a lack of resolution. You are conscious of your heartbeats, so shadowy is your body; and all because you can't forget what you did to me, and to others and to yourself. Give it up, David. I was as mad as you were till I began to take stock of my surroundings. And now I am married, and happy because the Government has been destroyed. Come over to our side. Catalogue the flowers. Get some fresh air. You'll be all right.'

David's lip quivered, so deeply was he moved now by an offer of friendship, and Rudolph smiled as though his eyes could see.

Soon the two of them left George alone, for he had much to do. They would start next day, Rudolph said, and asked whether George would write a letter to Joan. George said that he would not, but that he would be glad to see her.

Left by himself he began to think of what steps he should take next in his reorganization of the Convent. He decided that he would talk the matter over with Humberto and Marqueta, and would ask them whether he would have to expect any opposition from the students or whether, as he thought would most probably be the case, he would find that the students were quite willing to do what was required of them. So he sent for Marqueta and her husband, and, while he was waiting for them to come, he thought again of the letter which Marqueta had addressed to him and of how self-possessed her behaviour had been after he had helped her out of the box. She, he felt, would understand his plans for the future of the Convent and indeed, he went on to think, she might even sympathize with him in his further object, the pursuit of the bird to which he attached such importance that, in comparison with that aim, all his fighting and the years of preparation seemed as nothing.

She entered the room, stepping quickly, her cheeks flushed. Behind her came Humberto at a more sober pace. They sat down, and George asked them how they had enjoyed their work.

Marqueta's childishly remote face broke into a smile that seemed to bring her miles nearer to those in her company, like the confident stretching out of a hand, and George felt what he had felt before, an uneasy delight that it was to him that she drew most near, a thrilling of the brain, not blood. She said, 'I've enjoyed it, George,' and looked into his eyes.

George turned quickly to Humberto. 'What about you?' he asked.

Humberto grinned and rubbed his back. 'Not so young as I was,' he muttered.

George laughed and began to ask them the questions which he had prepared. He endeavoured to address them both, but he found that it was to Marqueta that he spoke and it was an effort for him to turn his eyes to the enthusiastic red face of Humberto, who was listening to him intently, slapping his knee and grinning when, in his opinion, George made a point with particular clarity.

George explained to them that the Revolutionary Army, although it had never had any reason to think well of the Convent, was not going to suppress the place, but instead wished to reorganize it on different lines. His private opinion, he said, was that one of the most important prerequisites of education was that a man or woman should know his or her own sex, and he asked first of all what was the opinion of the students on this subject.

Humberto frowned and said, with a great show of enthusiasm, that it was impossible to say what they thought. And he was continuing to speak when Marqueta interrupted him.

'Humberto is still speaking like we used to speak,' she said, 'when it was not considered respectable to have a definite opinion about anything. But I'll tell you what I think. I think that they are all very thrilled at this new opportunity. The only thing is that many of them find it rather difficult to decide what to be. Of course, one can understand their difficulties, though I'm quite at ease personally, because I've nearly always been a woman. No, I don't think you need worry about that, George. But there are a lot of other questions I'd like to ask, if you've got the time to listen to me.'

George nodded and she went on to speak. 'Do you think that in all the years before the revolution we in the Convent achieved absolutely nothing that was valuable? I'll agree with you that our life was very empty and that we wasted a lot of our time; but aren't some things worth preserving?'

'What things?' George asked.

She smiled and George realized that, owing to the agitation which was caused in him by her mere presence in the room, he had spoken with undue ferocity. More gently, he said: 'Some of you may have done good work. I don't know. Certainly many of you have great abilities; but you were all servants of the Government and not less so because some of you were unaware of it. And don't you realize that your Government existed by oppressing the peasants and used its power to block the way of travellers who in the past were in search of what I too am seeking? How can a servant of such a Government do anything either useful or disinterested?'

Marqueta was listening to him eagerly and George had become unaware of Humberto's presence in the room, for he felt that his words were falling naturally like rain on to the ground of the girl's heart and were there drunk in. His thoughts were meeting her thoughts as hand meets hand, and no gloves on the hands.

She spoke again. 'And yet you too have set up a Government of your own. It may be a better one, but it isn't exactly of our own accord that we students are tearing down the roof. We still take orders. Some say that they have lost their freedom. They say that whatever the Government may have been like before the Revolution they, at least, were hardly aware of it; whereas now they know that there is a Government and they call it a tyranny. What do you think about freedom, George? Does it mean nothing?'

'Yes,' said George, 'it usually does, though sometimes it means the ability to hurt others. No one is free, and no one has any right to expect to be free. What valuable thing can a man do by himself? Nothing. I thought I was free when I entered this town alone, but I was driven back in disgrace, and now I am an officer in the army. Just as a woman, who will not submit to a man, just as a soul that stands off from its body is a blighted weak thing, so is a man who will not lead others or serve others. The students cannot lead. Let them follow, then, and they will be happier than they are.'

Marqueta said, 'Yet they thought that they were in the front of civilization. They lived for the highest culture they knew. Poetry and art were in the chief places of their minds.'

'Poetry and art were on the tips of their tongues,' George said. 'And they were loyal servants of a villainous king. Let them get ahead with their poetry and art, if they can, once they have learnt to earn their own keep. If they have any ability, let them show it. We will put no obstacles in their way. There is only one thing that we will not allow them to do, and that is to recall the king. Perhaps you, with your sophistical training, will say, "Why shouldn't they recall the king, if they want to?" I say, because we know best. You will say, "How do you know best? Is not one point of view, one taste, as good as another?" And I say no; our point of view is better than theirs because we have been starved and beaten, but more important than that is this: the king's Government has way-laid adventurers; it has not permitted us to chase the bird. So, leaving aside all criticism of your senseless morality, your inane studies, your lunatic police, your oppression, your deliberate cruelty, your stupidity, your jigging, it is sufficient reason for me utterly to condemn your Government because it adored something stuffed, and killed those who chased the real thing. And if one is not free to do that, what freedom is worth a halfpenny?'

Marqueta's eyes were tender. 'Will your peasants chase that?' she asked.

George shrugged his shoulders. 'Some will. Some won't. Naturally food is the first thing.'

Marqueta spoke slowly. She had leant forward and was staring at the ground. So George had first seen her and he was conscious of a quickening of the brain, a readiness of words to come to the tongue as he watched her and was delighted to speak with her. She said: 'Yes, I suppose food is the first thing, but aren't you going to forget some of the other things? Now that you are reorganizing the factories and the transport system; now that you are instituting classes in engineering; now that you have wiped out those irresponsible policemen; will you have time to think of anything else but efficiency? No doubt housing conditions will be improved and the fertility of the land increased, but what then? Is that everything? Listen, George, I can make myself clearer in this way. I have read poems and sometimes been struck with the extraordinary daring of words. These words are capable of running like tigers, of rising massively like mountains, of melodious cascades, of unearthly freshness, lark flights and the breaking of mould by green grass tips; a short phrase may burst like an explosion, taking one's breath away, or may load the air with perfume; and these living words, so disparate in their nature, so sharp often in their outline, are at the same time fluid in more directions than we know. Each casts light or shadow on his neighbour and seems to share voice with all his fellows; as most unlike things seem to commingle or to stand indifferent side by side, as if it were tigers joining hands with lambs, grass gorgeous with cherries, machinery in a tree, or ice burning. And these, are they not, George? are haunting worlds. I have read poems and so admired their strange truth, the close dancing of thought with sound and more than that, for there is colour too, softness and hardness, perfume, all passions, that I have said to myself that these poems are better than anything. What does anything else matter, I have asked myself. Why need I care for food or for houses, for changes of government? Let me love this disinterested work of the spirit and not bother about politics.

You are smiling, and, of course, I see that that attitude is wrong. But wait a bit. It's true that these worlds, these poems, were created out of hard stuff, being beaten to form by troubled brains. They are not at all the same thing as sugar candy, and their authors were men, some of whom were blinded, like Rudolph, and all of them alive. Yet this is what I want you to understand. Were not these men more important than loaves of bread? Would you not rather have one of them than many factories? I know you would. Yet now, while you are feeding the peasants, building club houses and lavatories, what are you doing to encourage the disinterested work of the spirit? You won't even allow the students to dispute your orders. Is not this to stamp minds in a mould? And is that a good thing to do?'

George began to speak at once, looking earnestly at her. 'These thoughts of yours, Marqueta, are as familiar to me as my own. First I'll give you the answers I have given myself and then I'll make a confession. First, about food. It is as necessary to us as air and I think we are right in organizing its production and distribution as efficiently as possible. For the most disinterested work food is raw material. But you think that when we have our food and our swimming baths and our lavatories that we will think of nothing else except more food and bigger swimming baths and more commodious lavatories. Why should we? Don't forget this, that the peasants and workers are a new race of men, unlike the students and the policemen and the hangers-on of the late government. You have been students and amateurs. They, when they have filled their stomachs, will want to create for themselves worlds just like those which you so much admire. Words are dug from mines and grow in fields. Critics, but not poets, are at tea tables. I have studied the past history of this town and it is a long time, I think, since a disinterested or an independent man was honoured there. Such men have been visited by police during the night, and exiled unless they were willing to take a government post.

'But our army is full of men who are very different from your professors of literature or of love. Our men are ignorant and know it. They are also capable of exerting themselves. They will honour those who tell them what they never knew. Why should you think so badly of us, who govern ourselves, as to suppose that we will have less ambition than you, who were slaves?

'We are only tyrannous in one respect. We will allow no one to have any dealings with the king. And we are right in this. Are we going to risk losing what we have fought for? But when the king is dead, there will be no Government. We want to live, not to govern. Now our tyranny is self-defence.

'And this is my confession. From it you can gauge the real temper of the army, for I am trusted by them. I am not interested in food or in fighting. I am uniquely interested in chasing the wild goose. This revolution, these ambitious schemes of re-organization, I have worked hard for them, as I work for my bread, because they have been necessary things. But like bread they are only means to an end, and, important as they are, they are no more important to me than a crust of bread when I compare them with my ultimate object. Do you understand, Marqueta, exactly what I mean?'

Marqueta looked up at his agitated face. She nodded her head slowly. 'Very well, George,' she said, 'and when you have caught the king—'

But here she was interrupted. Heavy steps sounded on the stair-case. The door was flung open to admit Stanley who grinned at George, as though he had some good news to impart. All three looked at him, waiting for his words. He said: 'Alfred has been in communication with the king.'

'In communication?' George repeated. 'What do you mean?'

Stanley's grin widened. 'It's all right,' he said. 'It's arranged that a deputation, that's you and Alfred and me, wait upon him this afternoon,' and he looked proudly at George.

'A deputation!' George shouted angrily. 'What do we want with a deputation? Why hasn't Alfred had him shot?'

Stanley's face fell. 'Come, come,' he said; 'we must do things in order.'

George looked at the sturdy figure in surprise. 'Let's hear more of this,' he said, and taking Stanley by the arm led him out of the room.

CHAPTER SIXTEEN

'A DEPUTATION! A deputation!' George continued to say to himself, as they were going downstairs, and, when he reached the quadrangle, he turned impatiently to Stanley, who seemed to have been put somewhat out of countenance by the way in which his news had been received.

They walked out into the streets towards Stanley's quarters and, as they went, Stanley told how Alfred, while he and his men were searching the houses in the vicinity of the Anserium, had received a typewritten message, purporting to come from the king's secretary, giving him an appointment. Alfred had not consulted Stanley before keeping this appointment, and for this Stanley was evidently displeased with him. However, it seemed, according to Stanley, that Alfred had done his work well, for he had arranged that all three of the Generals should visit the king later in the day in order to discuss the articles of abdication which the king had professed himself willing to sign. 'And so,' Stanley concluded, 'everything will be done in order.'

George, when he had heard this recital, could not contain his indignation. 'Articles of abdication! Appointments!' he said. 'Are we a lot of children? What on earth is the good of these nursery games? Why did that fool Alfred allow the king out of his sight? Why didn't he take half the army and burn him out? And you, Stanley, you're not taking this talk seriously, are you? He's probably escaped already; but if he does intend to keep this appointment, as you call it, let us at least visit him with machine guns.'

'That would be a gross breach of trust,' said Stanley gravely, and George looked at him in amazement. 'When has there been any trust between us and them?' he said. 'For heaven's sake, Stanley, don't fall for it. Alfred's ambitious and the king has probably been flattering him, but what reason have you for losing your head?'

'It seems to me,' said Stanley stiffly, 'that it is you who are talking somewhat wildly. No one disputes your great services to us, but you might remember that on this point Alfred and I are in a majority and it is your duty to support us, as I have often supported you in the past, even when I did not agree with you.'

'But this is different,' said George. 'This is sheer stupidity. A child could see that you're wrong. If Andria and Arthur were here they would laugh at you.'

He was pursuing the wrong tactics. Stanley began to speak reproachfully. 'Andria and Arthur are not here,' he said, 'and while they are away we have a right to expect your loyal support.'

And so they talked, George remonstrating and pleading, Stanley standing more and more on his dignity, till they arrived at Stanley's quarters and found Alfred waiting for them. The young man's eyes were bright. Evidently he was pleased with himself. 'Glad you've come,' he said, smiling at Stanley, and nodding to George. 'It's time we were starting.'

George looked at him sternly. 'Why are you acting in this way?' he said. 'You have always been for more extreme measures than any of us, and now you want to negotiate with our greatest enemy. What has he been saying to you?'

'There's no reason why we shouldn't negotiate,' said Alfred angrily as he looked at George with a kind of suspicion in his face. 'You've always told us frightening stories about the king. I find him quite a pleasant old man and he has explained to me that for a long time he has had very little direct contact with the work of the Government.'

407

George interrupted, 'Is this just because he has been flattering you, or do you think you're going to get anything out of it?'

'Please, please,' said Stanley, hoping to prevent a quarrel, but Alfred had turned on George in a rage. 'Listen to me,' he said. 'You may think you're very clever because you're popular in the army and happen to know how to shoot. But let me tell you this. It is Stanley and I who have worked longest for the revolution. We stayed with the peasants while you were wasting your time in the town. And we are not going to be browbeaten by a person like you, who seems always to be after something else. We are in the majority here. There's not time to ask the opinion of Andria and Arthur. Your duty, as a member of the Party, is to support the majority decision. Are you going to do it?'

George shrugged his shoulders. He saw it was useless for him to attempt to break down this unnatural alliance between Stanley and Alfred. But why, he wondered, were they proposing to act in a way so contrary to common sense and their past professions? He remembered the proposal which Alfred had made to him the day before and he suspected him. Stanley, he assumed, was merely standing upon form, and also, perhaps, he was unwilling that the whole credit for a treaty should go to Alfred.

'All right,' he said at last. 'I'll go with you, but I'll take a gun and have a guard of soldiers outside. And I won't sign any agreement with the king until Andria and Arthur have been consulted.'

Alfred looked at him scornfully, Stanley with reproach. 'If you're afraid,' Alfred began, but Stanley put his hand on the young man's arm, restraining him. George took no more notice of them. He put a pistol in his pocket and, as they walked out together into the streets, he thought incessantly of what the king's plan could be, and whether Alfred had been won over by flattery or by something worse.

They reached the Anserium and passed through the carved doors into the open space, still filled with empty chairs, as it had been when George had first visited it. They let their eyes wander over the tremendous dome and George observed still swinging the golden basket from which no one had yet troubled to remove the effigy. Alfred led the way to a small door half-hidden by one of those ribs of steel which supported the high roofing. He tapped on the door and it was opened to them by an elderly man, very thin, in evening dress, who bowed to Alfred and to Stanley, and looked coolly at George's eyes. 'What's the idea?' said George, grinning, though he was in a very bad temper; but the butler, for this, it seemed was the man's profession, appeared not to have noticed him. 'This way, sir,' he said to Alfred, and to Stanley, 'Kindly follow me, sir.' Alfred, after having flicked a speck of dust from his collar, went in through the door, and Stanley, clearing his throat, followed him. George was amazed at their demeanour. He kept his hand in his pocket where the gun was, and went in after them into a cold corridor which led to a flight of steps. Having mounted the steps they reached a door of green baize which admitted them to a small comfortably furnished room. There were large armchairs with small tables by each of them and flowers and ash-trays on the tables. The walls, painted sunlight yellow, were decorated with sporting prints, and there was a faint aroma of lobster in the air. At the far end of the room was a row of four pillars, supporting the roof, and between the pillars hung curtains.

The butler bowed again to Stanley and to Alfred. 'His Majesty will be with you in one or two minutes,' he said.

'Certainly, certainly,' said Stanley, shuffling a little in his thick boots, and Alfred slipped a coin into the man's hand. The butler bowed once more and retired behind the curtains, from which he soon emerged again carrying a pile of illustrated papers which he put down on the table in front of Alfred.

George was closely examining the walls of the room, tapping

them with his knuckles, and the pictures, for he remembered how other pictures had almost killed him; but he found nothing suspicious. He had reached the curtain and was about to peer behind it when he heard Stanley's voice: 'Really, really, George! Is this quite the thing? Let us show the king that we know how to behave.'

He looked round angrily at Stanley's grave face and stiff figure supported on the padded chair. Next to him was Alfred, nervously rubbing his hands together. George laughed bitterly. 'So this war was a lesson in table manners, was it?' he said. 'You two fools! I'd advise you to keep your eyes open and not bother about touching your caps. I'd have had the machine guns up here by this time.'

He saw Alfred and Stanley rise suddenly to their feet bowing and smiling, and at the same instant heard at his elbow a voice: 'Now would you have done that? I am sure that would have been most awkward for me, most awkward indeed.'

He turned aside and saw that the king had come through the curtains. He was wearing a dressing-gown of pale blue silk and, as he spoke, he prodded the air with a thick forefinger. He had not yet put on his collar, and so George could not tell whether he was still disposed to impersonate a clergyman, nor indeed was he quite sure that he would have recognized him if he had met him in different surroundings. The fleshy face still wore such a benevolent smile as George had seen in the hot room by the library, but the mouth appeared to be now more flabby, the eyelids heavier: though, gazing fixedly at the eyes, George saw their strength and guessed that by that feature the king, however disguised, could always be recognized. Now the king had turned away from him and George stared at the large figure swathed in the silk dressing-gown, the heavy head with scant hair oiled and brushed back, the fat cheeks, delicate nose and slightly pendulous upper lip.

Round his neck the king wore a white silk scarf and in one hand he carried a table napkin. The fingers of the hand with which he poked the air, emphasizing his words, were bright with thick rings of gold set with precious stones.

After his few mocking words he had taken no more notice of George, but had made two or three short steps across the room when he appeared to notice the table napkin which he carried in his left hand. He smiled at Stanley. 'Really, General,' he said— 'General Stanley, I believe—you must forgive me,' and he pressed an electric bell which was concealed at the back of one of the chairs. The butler entered the room and the king handed him the table napkin. 'You should have reminded me,' he said. 'You should have reminded me, Carter. Most remiss of us both.'

Then he turned to Alfred. 'I have just been taking my midday meal,' he said. 'Something quite light: lobster and two glasses of Chablis. Delicious. Perfectly delicious.' His eyes rested on Stanley. 'You agree with me, General?'

Stanley blushed. 'Never had it, I'm afraid, sir,' he said.

The king chuckled. 'Well now,' he said, 'you must be a very exceptional man, most exceptional. But I can assure you that there is a pleasure in store for you. Perhaps one of these days you will honour me by taking lunch in my apartment, that is, of course, if I can get the lobsters.' He indicated Alfred with a smile. 'As our young friend, General, or, may I be allowed to say, Comrade Alfred, was telling me only this morning, there has been a lot of trouble in the country lately, and I expect we shall all have to put up with some hardships. Well, well, there are a lot of things which I would rather give up than my lobster at lunch.'

George noticed with disgust that both Alfred and Stanley were hanging on the king's words. Stanley, supporting most of his weight on one leg, was smiling more than he was used to do and, in his nervousness, was twisting his cap between his fingers. The

411

king stretched out his hand and took it from him, smiling. 'I can't allow you to spoil your cap,' he said. 'A trick of nerves, is it not? I have suffered from it myself when I was young, a long time ago now, I'm afraid.'

George walked across the room and stood between Alfred and Stanley. He looked straight into the king's eyes. 'Here,' he said, 'suppose we cut all this out. What can you offer if we let you escape with your life?'

For a second George saw in the king's eyes that look of malevolence which had warned him once before. He kept his finger on the trigger of his pistol. The king's eyes looked at him coldly for another second, and then turned away. Stanley nudged his arm, whispering: 'Remember where you are, George.' Alfred addressed the king. 'Don't take any notice of him, your Majesty. He's never been noted for his politeness, and, since the battle, his nerves have been rather out of order. I can assure you that you will find my friend Stanley and myself only too willing to consider your point of view when you are ready to negotiate with us.'

The king inclined his head and, after glancing at George, smiled. 'Something of a rough diamond, I can see,' he said. 'I've had some experience of them myself, these rather too outspoken men. They're very honest. Oh yes, perfectly honest, most reliable fellows for the most part: but they do make things so difficult. Still, in this instance, I've no doubt that your young friend's quite right. There is no need for us to waste time. So let us consider the articles of abdication, since it seems that you gentlemen have the better of me.'

He sat down in one of the chairs, after having made a gesture of invitation to the others also to be seated. Then he clapped his hands and the butler reappeared carrying three cups of coffee on a tray.

'You must excuse me for not joining you,' he said. 'I shall have

412

my cup a little bit later on. One hour after a meal is my time for coffee. If I take it earlier it invariably disagrees with me.'

Stanley and Alfred took the small cups and balanced them gingerly on their knees. George shook his head when the butler approached him. The king looked up at him. 'Can I not prevail upon you?' he said. 'No,' said George, who was now beside himself with anger.

The king leant back in his chair, pressing his finger tips together, frowning as though in thought, while Alfred and Stanley sipped their coffee. When they had set down their cups empty upon the table, he began to speak.

'Let us look quite broadmindedly at this question of my abdication, and I think we shall be able to reach an agreement without much difficulty. As I informed this young man whom, I say again, I hope I may be allowed to call Comrade Alfred, for a long time now I have had little direct contact with the Government of the town. I am a man of simple tastes and, though in my youth I was keenly interested in politics, I have in recent years left most of the work to subordinates. I was very sorry to hear this morning that these subordinates have betrayed their trust, and I should not like any one of you gentlemen to imagine for a moment that I entertain the slightest feeling of enmity towards you who have made efforts, and I think I might almost say successful efforts, to overthrow my Government. In every state there comes a time when the subject has a perfect right to revolt, and, from what I have heard, my Government has in recent years been so oppressive, so irresponsible, that it would have required a great deal more inside knowledge than any of you gentlemen possess to convince you of the ultimate futility of any drastic change in the organization of the state.

'But, though this is true, as I hope to convince you, you have nevertheless a perfect right to demand a thorough change in the

413

personnel of the various ministries. On that issue I shall be in complete agreement with you.'

He paused, and looked closely at Stanley who was rubbing his forehead with his hand. 'I trust you are not feeling unwell, General,' he said.

Stanley shivered, and looked up. He pressed his finger tips against the veins at the side of his head. 'I'm not feeling very grand, sir,' he said. 'A bit of a headache.'

The king rose to his feet. 'How I sympathize with you!' he said. 'I suffer a great deal from headaches myself. Let me fetch you one of the tabloids which I have had prepared for me. They afford instant relief.'

He patted Stanley on the back and went quickly through the curtain; but he had hardly disappeared from their view when Stanley's condition began to get very much worse. He felt pains in his stomach, he said, then in all his limbs. His face grew very pale and he bit his lips to keep himself from crying aloud.

George took the pistol out of his pocket. 'You've been poisoned,' he said.

Stanley struggled with his words. 'No, George, it can't be that. The king has been very kind. Besides Alfred took the coffee too.'

George looked at Alfred whose thin lips were pressed tightly together. 'Why doesn't he come back then?' he said, and then jumped to his feet to support Stanley who was slipping off the chair on to the floor, shaking his head between his hands. But when he gripped his arm he felt the body to be a dead weight. The limbs flicked out, then were still. Stanley was dead.

George picked up his revolver and ran towards the curtain, but before he reached it he turned back and looked grimly at Alfred who was still sitting, pale-faced, by Stanley's side. George's

414

eyes rested fiercely on him. 'This was a put up job between the king and you, you traitor,' he said, and then, as he saw Alfred's hand move towards his pocket, he shouted: 'Keep your hands up, or I'll shoot now.'

Alfred, scowling at him, began to raise his hands, but when they were half-way to his head, he gave a sharp cry, of pain or of surprise, and clasped his head as Stanley had done. His face became paler than it had been before. He held his breath and then, looking at George as though for pity, he attempted to smile, saying: 'I deserved it. I've got it, too.'

George ran to him, questioning him, but Alfred was now in great pain, and could speak only in short disconnected sentences. 'He talked me round,' he said. 'I was to be Prime Minister. I've deserved this.' And then he tightened his lips, as Stanley had done, stifling cries. He was on the point of death, but before he died he looked up quickly, as though he had remembered something. He forced himself to speak. 'Look out for yourself, George. Safety catch. Picture.' Trying to say more, he fell forward.

George grasping his pistol, ran towards the curtain behind which the king had disappeared, but before he had taken two steps the lights went out. He hurled himself against the curtain in the darkness and felt a wall of stone or steel. At the same moment he heard the king's voice and fired quickly in the direction from which it seemed to come. He heard laughter, and the voice continuing. 'It is no use wasting your bullets. In fact I should advise you to keep at least one for yourself, my friend. But if you insist on shooting it's just possible that you may hit the speaking tube through which I am speaking to you. I am quite safe behind steel.'

George had kicked off his shoes and was groping along the walls. He had remembered what Alfred had said about a safety catch. 'What are you going to do to me?' he said.

415

He could hear the king chuckling. 'I am going to crush you to death.'

George laughed. His hands were busily going over the walls and behind the pictures. 'You've been very clever,' he said. 'But why did you kill Alfred? He might have been useful to you.'

The king spoke again. 'I haven't got much time to spare in gratifying your curiosity, but I'll tell you this much. Comrade Alfred was an ambitious young man and resented the authority which you and Stanley had with the soldiers. I don't think, to do him justice, that he really supposed I was going to put you both permanently out of the way. We spoke only of a term of imprisonment. Comrade Alfred's mistake lay in supposing that once he had brought you here, I could have any further use for him. And now, are you ready to die?'

'Not for a minute or two,' said George. He had examined two of the walls and had found no means of escape. 'What exactly do you mean by "crushing to death"?'

'Why,' came the king's voice, 'I should have thought that the meaning of those words was plain. If you had taken the trouble to examine rather more thoroughly the walls of the room in which you are now, you might have discovered that beneath the panelling is steel. A simple mechanism will draw two of these walls together, and between them you are now going to be, as I said, crushed to death.'

'One moment,' George said, in as unconcerned a voice as he could produce. 'Do you really imagine that by killing three of us you will destroy the revolution?'

'I shall at least succeed in weakening it,' said the king. 'And now I must say good-bye to you.'

George heard behind the wall the sound of some piece of mechanism being set in motion. He smiled. Behind the last picture which he had examined he had discovered a button and had pressed it. He squeezed his body through the opening which was made in the wall and, as he heard behind him the increasing noise of machinery he groped his way down a passage, having seen in front of him a dim light. When he reached this light he found that it came from another passage, well lighted, which at this point joined the tunnel by which he had escaped and, after wandering for some time, he reached a door which admitted him to the interior of the Anserium at the opposite side of the building to that by which three of them had entered the king's apartment.

CHAPTER SEVENTEEN

H<small>E</small> crossed the hall of the Anserium and, as he stepped into the street, he stumbled over a man kneeling. He was for hurrying on but he felt a hand on his leg, and looking back saw the bowed head of the man and heard his voice: 'Don't be hard on me, your Highness.'

The man raised his head and George, in spite of the haste that he was in, laughed as he recognized Bob, his cowardly companion. Bob's face, now screwed into an expression of supplication, was unchanged by the years, but the grey hair on his head showed that he, like David, had grown older than George had done in an equal time.

'For old time's sake,' Bob said solemnly, and looked at George with evident terror in his eyes.

George frowned at him. 'The last time I saw you you were giving evidence against me to the police,' he said.

Bob's limbs, fatter than they had been, trembled. 'Things look black, sir,' he said. 'Very black. I admit it. But I was never really attached to the band.'

'You were never really attached to anything, were you?' George said. 'Don't you think you deserve to be court-martialled?'

'Oh no, sir,' Bob said, his lips trembling. 'No, I don't think so.'

George smiled. 'No one's going to hurt you,' he said. 'Only find a job for yourself, and don't come worrying me.'

Bob's eyes opened wide in relief and gratification. He clung to George's hand. 'Oh sir, I'd do anything for you.'

George pulled his hand away. 'You can't do anything,' he said, 'so don't bother,' and he was going on his way when he heard

418

Bob's voice: 'Aren't you looking for the king? I could tell you something about that.'

George swung round quickly. 'Out with it,' he said. 'What is it you know?'

Bob had now recovered his confidence. He rose to his feet and winked mysteriously. 'It's a long story,' he said.

George shook his arm. 'Cut it short then,' he said, but Bob, seeing George's impatience, was disposed to bargain. 'How much will you give me if I tell you?' he asked.

George beckoned to two soldiers who were passing in the street. He had no time to waste in being amused. 'I'll have you shot in two minutes unless you tell me all you know,' he said, but his ruse missed its effect on Bob, who, when he saw the soldiers approaching, fell to the ground in a faint. It took them some minutes to bring him round and then he began whimpering: 'I don't know anything, I'm afraid. I don't know anything.'

George cursed him and was turning his eyes away when Bob seemed to remember something. He spoke eagerly. 'I know who might know.'

'Who?' said George, and the earnestness in his voice made Bob feel important again.

He winked. 'There's a lady,' he said. 'The king was a bit sweet on her.'

'What's her name, you idiot?' George shouted, beside himself with impatience.

Bob raised one hand as though to calm him. 'Why,' he said, 'it's Miss Marqueta.'

'Marqueta!' George exclaimed. He turned again to Bob. 'Are you sure of this?'

'Yes,' said Bob gravely, drawing nearer to George as though he were a partner in some discussion of importance. 'It was the talk of the town. Would you like me to give you my advice?'

'No,' George said and hurried away, disregarding Bob's pained outcry. He would go to the Convent and see Marqueta himself, and, as he hurried through the streets, his thoughts were busy with her. Could she, he asked himself, with her delicacy, have had any intimate relations with that fat eater of lobsters, that powerful evading king? The thought of it disgusted him. And if there was anything in Bob's story, he reflected, could he trust Marqueta now? Occupied with these thoughts he hardly noticed a hand being laid on his arm. He looked up. It was Andria.

George grasped his hand, sighing with relief. Now he could give all his attention to the pursuit of the king, who must still be, he supposed, in some underground retreat. He led Andria to his room in the Convent and told him of the events which had just taken place. Andria listened to him gravely and at the end of the story said: 'They should have listened to you, George. But I'm sorry for Stanley.'

Rapidly they discussed what next to do. Andria had returned to the town in order to ask for more men to help with the harvest. Both Arthur and he had experienced great difficulty in their work, and they suspected that among the men under them were agents of the old government. Some of the motor lorries, essential for transport, had unaccountably broken down. Such reaping machines as there were in the country were found to be useless, as important pieces of their mechanism had been removed. And knowing that unless they could organize the supplies quickly there was likely to be a serious shortage of food, they had decided to ask for contingents of reliable men from the main revolutionary army, and to dismiss all those who had joined up since the fall of the town, since it was certainly among these men that the wreckers were hidden. Just before Andria had set out, they had intercepted a typewritten message containing a systematic plan of sabotage, and so, Andria said, they had determined to ask the Generals in

420

the town to prosecute the search for the king with the utmost possible energy.

George nodded. The king's plan was clear. He had aimed first at destroying the Generals and then at weakening the army by ensuring a shortage of food. Though his entire police force had been destroyed, though there could be no question of the loyalty of the factory workers to the new regime, it seemed that there were still some people ready to take orders from him. 'We must keep an eye on the technicians,' George said. 'It'll take them some time to get out of their old habits.'

Andria agreed with him. For some minutes they discussed the situation in the town and George gave his friend details of the arrangements which had been made there. It was understood that Andria would remain in the town while George devoted all his time to the pursuit of the king.

George rose to go. 'I'll get the girl,' he said, 'and take with me four or five men who are good shots.' He took Andria's hand. They knew that it was a dangerous job, but they smiled as though it were child's play.

'Look after yourself,' Andria said, as George went out of the room. Hurrying downstairs, George held in his mind for a moment a picture of his friend before he dispatched messengers, one to summon Marqueta and one to fetch those soldiers whom he trusted most.

Marqueta was the first to arrive and it was no particular aspect of her that quickened the beating of his heart and sharpened his eyes as she approached. In a green dress, delicately walking, when she paused and raised her small shadowed face with eyes and mouth expectant, she was like a flower, in such suspense, swaying on a stalk; and yet it was not that beauty and airiness, it seemed, which charmed him most, but rather some quality of the spirit vibrating, some hint of intimacy, the mutual knowledge of a secret code. And so he asked her no questions about her relations with the king. He said: 'I want your help. Do you know the underground passages beneath the Anserium? It's the king I'm after.'

He saw her quick glance, as though for pity, and understood that there was something in Bob's story, but that she would help him.

'Yes,' she said. 'I know. If he's escaping, he'll be far underground.'

George took her arm, reassuring her, and, as he touched her, she turned her face towards him with such love in her eyes that he would have kissed her had he not had a more weighty task to accomplish. Now the soldiers for whom he had sent arrived, and together they went to the Anserium. They entered the secret passages at the door by which George with the two Generals, now dead, had been admitted earlier in the day; but from the entrance they turned in the opposite direction to that of the room from which George had escaped, and pursued a path, well lighted, which descended gradually. Marqueta and George were in front, and behind them tramped the soldiers. No one spoke a word till they had gone far, deeper and deeper into the foundations of the town.

Gradually the passage in which they walked grew wider and there was more space above their heads. They could hear the squeaking of bats and were sometimes fanned by skinny wings. In crannies of the rocks, high above their heads, out of reach of the electric light, these creatures lived and were now disturbed by the tapping of boots.

Marqueta touched George on the arm. 'Perhaps near here,' she said, and George turned to his men, showing that he held his revolver ready cocked.

The passage made a turn to the right and, sure enough, as they rounded the corner, they saw a hundred yards ahead of them, walking rapidly away, a figure clothed in a blue dressing-gown, indistinct among the conflicting lights. George fired and, thrusting Marqueta back against the wall, made way for his men to fire. He had missed, as was likely with a revolver at that range, but a volley would fill the passage with steel. The men in front fell to the ground, while those behind took up their positions kneeling or standing. Now it seemed that their enemy could not escape, yet as the first finger pressed the trigger he vanished from their eyes, having found some way, it seemed, through the side wall to his left. They did not stop to curse, but, with George and Marqueta still ahead, ran down the passage to the place where the king had been, and here they found a chink in the wall, just large enough for a body to pass. George pressed through first and Marqueta followed him. 'Steady,' George shouted to the others. 'Don't come through too fast. There's no room here.' And, indeed, they were standing on a narrow ledge, the brink of a precipice. The roof was so high that they could distinguish nothing above their heads, and far below glittered lights in a gulf of which they could not see the bottom. At their feet was an iron ladder, clamped to the rock, descending the precipice to those distant lights. George began to lower himself over the edge. 'Now,' he shouted, 'you can come through one at a time.'

He heard a startled cry from Marqueta and, with his feet on the ladder, looked up. The chink through which they had entered was there no longer. Silently the rock had closed and now they were alone. George smiled at Marqueta. He was not so simple as to suppose that he would be able to help the men on the other side to pierce through the rock. 'You'll have to come with me,' he said, and began the descent, having first fired repeatedly his revolver down the ladder into the darkness below.

Marqueta stepped on to the ladder above him and for a long time they went down, feeling for the rungs with their feet, sometimes stopping to listen, for George fancied that he could hear the sound of feet below them. At last they came to the lights which they had seen from the top of the chasm, and, in an increasingly brilliant illumination, descended more rapidly. The walls of the gulf began to incline and soon the ladder was replaced by steps. Here George turned and, though he was dazzled by the lights, was able to make out running down the steps below a figure in flowing robe of blue. He took careful aim, fired, and shouted with joy as he saw his enemy stumble and fall. It was the last bullet which had had effect and, leaping down the stairs, he soon came to the spot where he found a body, dead, lying on its face. He turned it over. It was the king's butler whom he had shot.

But he had no time to lament his mistake. He heard Marqueta's voice from above. 'There George! By the lake,' and, shading his eyes, he looked downwards to see that he had nearly reached the bottom of the flight of steps. He saw indistinctly chairs, tables, cases full of books, and other objects over which his eye passed rapidly, and all these at the brim of a large lake which reflected dazzlingly the thousand lights with which the great vault was marvellously festooned. But these beauties he did not stop to admire. For there, pacing backwards and forwards by the lake, was the king himself, looking upwards, in evident terror, to the stairway where they stood. So they confronted each other, not 50 yards apart, and George saw the king's hand go to his pocket. A bullet went past his head and thudded into the wall behind him. He raised his own revolver. The king could not know that it was not loaded. As he raised it he stepped sideways into the cover of a balustrade which accompanied the last flight of steps to the lake. The king did not wait to fire again. Throwing off his coat and waistcoat he plunged into the lake and began swimming in an accomplished manner towards the farther wall where George could see an opening in the rock.

424

He sprang down the remaining stairs, kicked off his boots, and plunged in, thinking that now at last had come the reckoning; but the king had got a good start and it was only gradually that George, excellent swimmer as he was, could gain upon him. It was a distance of about 100 yards to the opening in the rock through which, no doubt, the king was aiming to escape, and by the time that he had covered the distance George's hand was almost upon his heel. As the king's head passed into the tunnel George grasped his ankle and received a blow in the mouth from the other foot. He relinquished his hold, being sure to have his enemy in the next two strokes he took; but, as the king's legs passed through the tunnel he heard a noise above his head and, looking up, saw descending rapidly from the roof a curtain of steel, like a guillotine. He twisted round in the water, and the weight of the steel fell an inch from his shoulder, blocking the tunnel by which in nick of time the king had escaped.

George turned, glad at all events that he had not been cut in two by that knife, and swam slowly back to where, on the farther side of the lake, Marqueta was waiting for him, and as he swam he could not but admire what in his haste he had not noticed before, the water as clear as glass, atmosphere for coloured fishes which whisked by him with wriggles of long blue bodies or hung, golden red, spike-finned, gazing at him with goggle eyes, in suspense above the white pebbles, earth of their heaven. And above, still under the ground, was another heaven, hardly seen by fish, where glowed ropes of variously coloured lights hung high up from juts of rock, as above a well from crevice to crevice might be creeping plants all bursting with flowers. Three parts of the circumference of the lake were bounded by rock, but the third part towards which he was swimming was bordered with a rim of lapis lazuli, and there Marqueta stood, watching him. At her back were the flights of steps and the balustrade behind which he had taken shelter, and all around her were arranged tables and chairs, small bookcases, rugs gorgeously patterned, sofas, and divans. It was an apartment excellently furnished, without any visible roof, a good place for the eyes, where there were so many shapes, so confusing an array of lights so variously refracted.

George reached the brim and climbed out of the cold water. He stood, dripping wet, shivering, but there was an electric fire by one of the sofas, and Marqueta had switched this on so that George could warm himself while she searched for something for him to wear. In a cupboard by the stairs she discovered towels and a dressing-gown. George stripped and dried himself while Marqueta watched him closely, a thing which rather surprised him. Then they sat down in front of the fire and Marqueta said: 'What are we going to do now?'

'Do you know anything about this place?' George asked her, looking round still in amazement at the high lights, the fine furniture, and the smooth clear water.

'I've heard of it,' she said, and paused, 'though I've never been here.' She went on speaking rapidly and George saw that she was distressed to think that she had known some of the king's secrets. She said: 'I've heard that there was a retreat which he had made ready in case at any time he should be in danger, and this must be it. We should never have found it if it had not been for the butler.'

'And where does the tunnel go?' George asked her, pointing to the rock through which he had chased the king.

Marqueta's eyes rested proudly on him. 'This time,' she said, 'you've chased him out of the town. The tunnel goes right outside the walls in the direction away from the country districts from which you came. He may drown there, or, if the water is shallow and he escapes he may be caught by the army.'

George shook his head, though he was glad that now the king had been, if not captured, at any rate driven into exile. 'He'll be too clever,' he said. 'They won't get him. But anyway we've done something,' and he smiled at her, for now he knew that the army in the town was safe, at least for the time being.

'Yes,' said Marqueta, 'but what are we going to do?'

'Pass the time as happily as we can,' said George, who, warmed by the fire and delighted even with the partial success of his chase, was in no mood to take a serious view of the situation. 'They'll send out search parties; and meanwhile we're very comfortable here,' and he lay back in his chair, warming his feet, smiling at Marqueta's disturbed face,

For a few moments they said nothing, and then Marqueta, looking down at the floor, said in a low voice: 'I don't think you can think much of me now, George.'

George sat up, and, though in his present frame of mind he had not wished to talk seriously, he looked at her intently and said: 'You mean about the king.'

She looked at him quickly and there was such distress in her face that George forgot his carefree mood and was brought thrillingly in touch with her agitation. She said: 'Yes, and you heard about it just when I was trying to be like you, trying to let you see that I was on your side.'

Seeing how grieved she was, George took her hand and said: 'Don't be so silly. What does it matter? You're free now.'

'Yes,' she said, now holding aloof from him, 'I know that, and it isn't that at all. I want you to have a good opinion of me, and how can you now? This is what I want to say. It's not having to do with the king that matters so much, but I enjoyed it.'

George looked at her delicate face, her gracious body, in surprise. Could this beautiful woman have enjoyed the embraces of a fat man, a bald one? He said: 'I suppose he was more of a man than the other creatures in the town.'

Marqueta's eyes rested gratefully upon him. 'Yes,' she said, 'that was just it. He was powerful and I liked that. I knew that he didn't love me. I felt that I was treating my husband rather badly. Sometimes I hated him when he let me see what his mind was like, cunning, cynical, sensual, and, what is most surprising, stupid, yes, terribly stupid. He it was, who, through his ministers, controlled the Convent, yet he was unable to read. He kept books for show and only looked at picture-papers. If I mentioned the name of a poet, even if I admired a piece of furniture, he would look at me so cruelly, with such contempt that I was terrified. And yet Humberto, with all his knowledge, was a baby compared with him, and I was like a live thing held in hands of brass. Need I say any more? I don't want to think about it.'

'Would you enjoy it now?' George asked, and she started to her feet.

'No, no, no!' she cried. 'How can you think it?' and then in a quieter voice, 'Haven't I told you, George, that it was you who changed my life? I saw in you one who in the end would drive the king out, and I could understand you. While you were away I had to submit, and, as I say, a part of me enjoyed making a sacrifice of what was real in me, but starved. But more and more often I would think "this is brass or iron, some base tough metal". I could be crushed by it, but I could never love it. And it did me good to read poems in my spare time. I thought constantly of your rousing the peasants to revolt and I knew that your determination and the comradeship of your army could overthrow any idol. I knew, too, that your mind was set on something much more difficult even than this, and I thought that this is what men ought to be, tough in their bodies, resolute in their characters, and all but crazy in the pursuit of something out of the common. I tell you I hated the king. I hated him. And yet, so weak was I that I enjoyed it.'

George had been thrown into a violent perturbation by her words. Now he took both her hands and, looking into her eyes,

428

said: 'Forget it, Marqueta. Others have suffered as much or more than you by doing violence to themselves. Think of David, who has lost the determination which he had, and Rudolph who was blinded. But you are still young and beautiful. The king has left the town. Now is the time for you to be happy.'

Now that she had spoken Marqueta's face was sadder than it had been while she was telling her story. She leant forward in her chair and turned her eyes timidly to George's eyes. George put his arms round her and she relaxed her body, falling on her knees, with her head on his breast, sobbing, but in contentment, and George looking over her head at the dangling ropes of light, the level gleam of water broken by darting of fishes, thought of other things till he felt her body brace itself in his arms, and, inclining his head, saw her muscular neck twist backwards, her eager face bent on his and the lips half-open urging the words: 'I love you, I love you.' He lifted her to her feet, embracing her tightly while she covered his face with fierce kisses like a flood released by the breaking of a dam.

They spoke few more words then, but a look of misgiving came into her eyes. 'I'm thinking of Humberto,' she said. 'He's been very good to me,' and George, surprised and shocked, drew back from her, but she, with a little cry, pulled him closer, frantic in her desire, between sobbing and laughing, and soon they were at ease, lying on a divan miles beneath the surface of the earth, yet in a space that appeared limitless, a vault, hung with the most carefully contrived illumination, and not far from them a shining lake that might have been one of the properties of a fairy land.

CHAPTER EIGHTEEN

So for a time which they did not count they lived in that agreeable grotto, love-making, talking, reading, angling for bright fish which they afterwards ate; and in their seclusion they were drawn together by an affinity of heart or some congruity of their nervous systems. Their expressions of face and gestures were known to each other and one would seem to voice the other's thought. They spoke hardly at all of what was shut from their view, the town, the country, and their friends, though George would sometimes sit silent, gazing into the water, thinking of these things, and Marqueta, watching him, would frown, as though this were a trespass. But she, alone of all those whom he had met, would talk to him about his ultimate aim, and on this subject he was glad to speak with her, although he knew that no words could advance him. He found still in talking to her a pleasure very difficult to describe. The words which they exchanged were like needles which seemed actually to probe the matter of their minds, so sure were they of inlet, but what was extraordinary was that this accurate reception of words, gestures, and the intonation of words would set up in the mind a titillation, a pleasant anxiety, something like an invitation to, and a suspension of, action. Even now, when they were free with their bodies, the first touch was like touching spider's web or hot metal, so curiously were they restrained each from each, so ethereal was even the heat of their passion.

Once, they did not know how long since they had been first buried underground, they were talking in some such a way as this. They had woken from a sleep and Marqueta had asked George if he was happy. 'Of course I'm happy,' George said, rubbing his eyes.

430

'But I mean *really* happy,' she said.

'And I don't know what you mean by that,' he replied. 'I remember meeting an old man, the brother of my great friend Joe, and he talked of happiness. He was scared out of his skin. His was the kind of character which was quite unfit for anything notable, and although he assured me that he was the happiest man alive, in despair he killed himself. No, Marqueta. What does one want with "real happiness" as you call it? It is the bird which I am after. I can imagine worlds where "real happiness" might be possible and desirable; but I know that this is not one of those worlds.'

Marqueta said: 'So you could not bear to live here for ever among these fish, in this comfort, with my love?'

'What an idea!' George laughed. 'Think of all the things we've got to do in the town, not to speak of what is more important.'

'But you've enjoyed it,' she asked, 'haven't you?'

'Of course I have,' he said. 'I've never known anything like this before. I've never talked to anyone, not even to Andria, as I can talk to you. I wouldn't even be able to talk to myself so clearly, and yet all the time there you are, not me, but someone else, touchable, lovable.'

Turning towards him, she put her hand over his mouth while her fingers dented the flesh of his cheeks. She spoke slowly, looking down on him as she supported herself on her elbow. 'You love me, don't you?' And then, not waiting for an answer, 'this is real love, this understanding, and the trust which we have in each other. I used to find even my body dull, but now it is sensitive even to the touch of feathers. I could stay here for ever and forget politics.'

George said: 'Other kinds of love are real too. This is just different. It is another world.'

'The world where happiness might be possible?' she asked, and he said: 'May be; but we are underneath a real roof and our thoughts must go up through it. How can I forget the army? We have rarely time enough to bother about being understood or to ask ourselves whether we are trusted or not.'

'I hope they never find us,' she said, with some bitterness in her voice.

He raised himself on his elbow and she threw her arms round his neck. Then, calmer, she said: 'If we are found, I shall see nothing of you. But tell me this. You do love me more than you have ever loved anyone else, don't you? You do love me more than Joan?'

George looked at her, half in pity, half in exasperation. 'What do you mean?' he said. 'Why need we talk like this? I've never thought about it, and love isn't like arithmetic. Why must people talk about love.'

She looked away from him. 'All right,' she said, and he wished he had not spoken so harshly. There was a silence, and then she said, 'I suppose I am thinking of impossible worlds.'

'I have thought of them, too,' George said.

'But is it so impossible?' she went on. 'Is our love nothing but our food and no difference between two loves other than the difference between bread and caviare? There have been people for whom love was everything.'

'You are thinking of some poets,' said George, 'but for them their poetry was everything.'

Her eyes turned on him angrily. 'You are stupid,' she said. 'Have you ever met anyone who could understand you and sympathize with you as I can? And am I not both beautiful and intelligent? Well then, ought you to discuss my love so easily?'

'What should we do with each other's love if we thought of nothing else?' George said. 'No, Marqueta. Those are the impossible worlds. Love is rocky here.'

'I can tell you what we should do,' she said. 'We should be bold enough to put all our happiness in each other's hands. We would be constantly delighted as we watched each other living. Our pleasures would be the mating of our bodies and the comprehension of our minds. We could do our jobs as usual, but they would not be the important thing. Each to each would be important. Those ordinary things which need doing would be done by us and could be done well, like actions of a dream, and our reality would be our love. Cannot that be worth while, George? —to grow so confident in each other that each one of us would have the strength of two, to have always the certainty of our bodies and the intimacy of our minds. Could we not conquer space and time that way and grow ecstatic, knowing more than others?'

'In some other life, perhaps,' George said. 'But now it is not to be done. Can't you see, Marqueta, that it was not you or I who made the grass grow? Is the town a figment of our imagination? Are my friends dreams? Listen, Marqueta. Would you dare to say that a man didn't love you unless he would betray his friends? And it is betrayal to treat a man as a ghost. Love is all the better with no ecstasies except what the body affords.'

'You are cruel,' she said, and looked away from him, while George, his eyes fixed upon her declining neck, felt for the first time the great difference between them. 'We are the victims of some tremendous misunderstanding,' he thought, and he was reluctant to touch her.

She turned to him again with such sadness in her eyes that he took her in his arms, and now it seemed to him that, though her body was yielding, there was in all her softness something hard, unoccupied with the flesh, hostile to him and of this she herself was unconscious.

For some moments she kept her head hidden from him. Then she tilted her neck and he saw that she was smiling and that there were tears on her face. 'I'm sorry,' she said. 'We've been so happy and now it is I who am making things difficult. You've done so much for me, George. You brought me to life and I'm grateful to you. It's only my love that makes me exacting. It is because I look on you as more than a man. I adore you. Will you promise never to leave me?'

The sight of her strained face, the sound of her husky voice were affecting, but George felt ill at ease as he listened to her, confused in his mind, angry with her for saying such things, though he pitied her distress. He spoke gently, though he was at his wit's end. 'How can you ask me that, Marqueta?'

She thrust her face into his, kissing him feverishly while her breath came in sobs and he drew back, ashamed of such loving. She rested her hands on his shoulders. 'Then I hope and pray God,' she said, 'that they will never find us.'

Hardly has she spoken when they heard from the gulf far above their heads a shout. George sprang to his feet and ran to the bottom of the stairs, shouting himself. A great voice, trembling with excitement, came again from the darkness:

'George! Is that you, George? Are you all right?'

'Yes,' George shouted back. 'We're both all right.'

Through the echoes the voice came back: 'Thank God, George! It's me. It's Andria. We've been trying to get to you for days. Joan and Humberto are here. We're coming down.'

George turned to Marqueta and saw her lying face down upon the bed, as though she were a lifeless thing. He touched her on the shoulder and it was not at once that she seemed to feel the touch, but only after some seconds had passed she sat up and looked at him as though she was looking at him for the first time.

'They are coming down the ladder,' George said, and she nodded her head, glanced rapidly round the scene of their seclusion, and followed him to the foot of the stairs.

434

Soon, below the highest lights, they could see dim shapes like bats against the face of the rock, and then footsteps could be heard and bodies plainly seen at the top of the steps, and then their friends were running to meet them. George smiled as he saw Andria, in spite of his great body, leap lightly from step to step, outstripping the others, and his heart swelled as he saw behind him the eager running of Joan who had far out-distanced Humberto.

Andria, laughing, jumped down the last steps and clasped George in his arms. 'We thought we'd never find you,' he said, and George returned the pressure of his arms, glad of his friend. Andria turned to Marqueta, and now Joan had reached them, and without speaking a word had flung herself into George's embrace, half-crying, half-laughing. George, holding her eager body, was inexpressibly delighted at the touch of her and the sight of her face which seemed to him like water for quenching thirst or the refreshment of the wind. So they stood, looking at each other, sure of each other, and when they had had enough of this George led Joan to Marqueta, who was standing silent with Andria at her side. And now Humberto arrived, smiling, red in the face, but he did not embrace his wife for something in her bearing repelled him. He stood in front of her, grinning, rubbing his hands, an amiable fellow.

Soon they sat down and the newcomers admired the strange retreat. George and Andria talked while the others were silent and Joan would look intently at Marqueta who looked at nothing, and then she would look at George, but there was no room now for jealously in her and, when her eyes met his, they would dance in joy, as George too was delighted with her perfect and her unhesitating eyes. He told Andria of how he had chased the king through the rock and Andria gave him the latest news. It was as Marqueta had predicted. The king had reached the country outside the walls and from there, in a fast car, had escaped towards the farther mountains on this side of the marshes. For a day a squad of soldiers had pursued him, but they had lost track of him at last, and had returned, confident at least that he would trouble them no more for the time being; and indeed the effect of his departure was soon evident. Arthur was now able to ensure a regular food supply, being no longer hampered by inexplicable breakdowns or secret destruction of crops. Meanwhile Andria had led the search parties to find George and Marqueta and had experienced great difficulty not only in cutting through a wall of rock and a sheet of steel, but also in locating the exact place where the rock had closed, for the soldiers who had been with George at the time, despairing of his safety, had not marked the spot where they had last seen him.

'And now,' Andria concluded, 'we must be going. It is late in the morning, and this afternoon we are holding a great demonstration in the Anserium to celebrate the end of the war. It was Rudolph's idea, and the soldiers have taken to it. I sent a message when I found the sheet of steel, as I reckoned I'd get through to you soon, and I hoped you'd be alive.'

They rose to go, and George turned to Marqueta. 'Now,' he said, 'the new life is beginning for us all,' but she seemed not to hear him.

They ascended the steps and began to climb the ladder, Humberto and Andria in front, then Joan, then Marqueta, and then George. When they reached the lip of the precipice they passed through quickly into the passage, for on the ledge there was only room for two to stand. Marqueta stood there, as George clambered up last and, though his heart was full of Joan and of his plans for reorganizing the country, he looked at her lovingly, hoping that she would not take this change too much to heart. Her pale face smiled, as though reading his thoughts. 'In some other world perhaps,' she said, and jumped. It seemed ages before he heard the fall of her body on rocks below.

The others must have heard his sharp cry. They looked back and saw him standing, his face covered with his hands. Joan led him into the passage. They knew what had happened. She whispered into his ear and in her face was as much sorrow as appeared in his. Soon he held his head up and went forward. Only then did they notice Humberto, who was standing on one leg, scratching his head. He did not know what to think.

They went on silently and George's heart was numbed by that throwing away of life. Sometimes he looked at Joan beside him and her grave eyes looked up at him.

But wholly dispirited he reached the Anserium and, before the door was opened, was amazed at the sound of music. He remembered the demonstration and, as he passed through the door, wondered at the sight which met his eyes. The whole floor space of the vast building was packed with men and women. Around the circuit of the dome in galleries more people were crowded together, and all these, as they saw him enter safely among them, cheered and cheered until it seemed that the whole massive dome was a paper hat balanced on a tempest of sound. In the middle of the floor, beneath the apex of the dome was a dais on which stood Arthur and Rudolph, whom David led by the hand, and other leaders of their Party. In a gallery opposite George saw a band, and among the bandsmen he noticed, and began to be amused, the enthusiastic face of Bob crossed by the long silver of a trumpet. But in the great throng it was difficult for him to recognize the faces that he knew, so unanimous was the expression of joy, so impersonal the strength of the assembly. There were the distinct faces of peasants, each of its own nature, the face of one who loved women or of another who could tame horses; there were little men, humorous, and the lanky ones who had been the most discontented; there were the pale faces of those who had worked in the town and the stern faces of the miners. Women were there too, girls with bright

437

necklaces, staring, not ready for men; young wives, sweating with joy; some bedraggled ones, surprised at the scene; peasant women, strong in the limb, as resolute as their men; and amongst all these were scattered students with their nervous faces, now dressed decently, carried away with the others.

So rich was the detail of the crowd in which every man was himself, and yet it was not by the detail that the mind of a spectator would have been most moved, but rather by the mass, the embodiment of so much unreflecting joy, It could not have been of yesterday or of to-morrow that the men and women were thinking, although their fears and their humilations had passed with yesterday and it was on to-morrow that their hopes, still ill-defined, were set; but now, poised between the past and the future which were the springs of their being, their momentary joy was clean, and George, as he made his way to the dais, walked erect, thinking of the great conquest which had been made and of nothing else, for the sight and the sound of so much liberated life had, like a hot iron or a flood, cauterized and douched quite clear his mind from every second thought which dwells upon a tragic event past or a doubtful future.

In the tremendous cheering he and Andria and Joan climbed the dais. Arthur, than whom no one had rendered better service to the revolution, grinned at them, and Rudolph, led by David, embraced his brother.

Gradually the noise of cheering subsided and George stepped in advance of the others and began to speak. This was what he said.

'Comrades, what does this mean? We have overthrown the government, have we not? We have driven the king out of the town. We have utterly destroyed the police. Very good. But what does it all mean?

'Does it not seem to you a little surprising that we who in the past were regarded as the lowest elements of the population should now have no superiors, real or imagined? We are workers and we have been compared to the body of a state, as if the body were a drudge, while the government of scientists and of policemen has been compared, even by great philosophers and wonderful stylists, to the mind, as though the mind were a master. Very well, then. Let us accept the comparison and say that the body triumphs and that in future we shall expect philosophers entirely to change their tune.

'Let us consider for a moment this wonderful government, which was as an intellect directing our stupid flesh. We have had excellent opportunities of studying it in operation, for have we not for generations been starved, deprived of what our hands have made, cut off from our wives? Have not all our best men been exiled if they would not take the bribe? Have not all our movements to better our conditions been crushed mercilessly? Has the government, this bright mind, this spirit ruling by right, ever made the slightest effort to understand us, ever treated us with anything but contempt?

'But, perhaps, we, poor bodies, were supporting something reputable. I tell you that we were not. We were supporting critics and jugglers all the time, men capable of devising philosophies of love, incapable of begetting children, men who took pleasure in arranging fir cones, men who were proud of the police, men, finally, who, so far from doing anything notable themselves, made it their chief business to serve the king in his work of blocking all the roads, of making sure that every adventurer would be thrown into prison. They separated their minds, scrubbed them very clean, folded them away like clothes; and there was no one to wear those clothes. They thought they were clever, but they had no guts. Whom we have overthrown was not a brilliant charioteer, but a dangerous and oppressive ghost.

'Well then, this government, this intellect, has been overthrown.

The masses, the despised body, have taken its place. Do you not see what this means? It means a new life, something which has not been heard of before, something even imagined only by a few, and certainly not by the philosophers. We shall choose our own way of living and it will not be the way of kings or scientists. We shall keep the routes clear and welcome travellers. We shall make use once more of time and space and shall be particularly attached to the earth and to the sun. The government which we destroyed was of air and water. Ours will be of earth and fire.

'Comrades, let us think no more of our dead friends, or of the wasted portions of our lives, since we are on the way to create a new civilization, something which has not existed for a long time, if ever.

'What our old leaders most respected we chiefly despise—the frantic assertion of an ego, do-nothings, the over-cleanly, deliberate love making, literary critics, moral philosophers, ball-room dancing, pictures of sunsets, money, the police; and to what they used to despise we attach great value—to comradeship, and to profane love, to hard work, honesty, the sight of the sun, reverence for those who have helped us, animals, flesh and blood.

'Let us live, comrades. Long live the Revolution!'

And hardly had he spoken the last words when the bands played and the choirs began to sing the song which Rudolph had composed for the occasion. Nothing could adequately describe the effect of that singing, the volume of sound, the words swung from choir to choir, the sea of faces, the joy.

But when the singing was over and the crowd and the generals were standing for a short moment still, before dispersing, there occurred an event so amazing that it may perhaps seem to some too big to be believed; for we know, all of us, the nature of steel and concrete, how stiff and intractable is their material, and how little apt for volatility or dispersal; yet, if this story is to be believed, in the short pause that followed the conclusion of the song, the whole massy structure of the Anserium, blocks fitted each to each and long ribs of metal, framework, surface and matter of the stupendous dome, was suddenly whirled away, winnowed and dissipated in the upper air like grain or stalks of straw; and what is perhaps even more remarkable than the event itself is the fact that this convulsion of nature was no hurricane, but happened in complete silence and a dead calm.

Now, looking upwards, they saw the whole blue sky and the sun, and across the sky streaming the white shapes of flying birds, a horde, from horizon to horizon; nor was their number more to be wondered at than the size and splendour of each one of them; for these creatures were altogether uncommon, with wings wider than playing-fields, bodies like boats, and straight extended necks like a flying forest. From close down and brilliant pinions the light shone in a dazzling whiteness or was refracted in every rainbow colour, with a glint of gold behind the stern black of each powerful advancing bill. Very slowly and in complete silence the birds passed, going like galleons, huge ships with sails set and filled majestically by some wind that blows beautifully on the sea, though the watcher on the shore stands in admiration with not the smallest breeze to fan his cheek. And so for mile after mile and for a time that no one could reckon the enormous wild shapes of beauty and of strength went over the army, and George looked reverently at the white flying and at the men beneath it.

Now to him all the future, and the adventures that were waiting for him there, could be represented only dimly in his imagination of the children he would have, of the great public buildings to be erected, of his next journey, after the government of the people had been firmly established, of how he would set out either alone, or accompanied by his wife, or with friends. Never for long had he

441

lost sight of a purpose that had been always powerful and some-times distinct. But now, at the top of the temporary avenue up which his present triumph had led him, he could only envisage vaguely the shapes of difficulty, success and danger that were to come. The crossing of the marshes, the final battle with the king, birth in the desert and the strange customs of some remote tribes — of all this he thought then, and of all this we too have received strange and often self-contradictory information. Yet at this moment the light was clear and it was dead calm. Be the future as it might be, and no doubt that complete success was distant still, he knew that something not unworthy had been achieved already as he stood with the men and women, holding Joan's hand in his hand, and observed some of the Generals looking at him with an odd expression in their eyes, and their mouths smiling.

FINIS

442